KEBABS AND KISSES

DESTINATION WEDDING TRILOGY BOOK 3

THE WAY TO A WOMAN'S HEART SERIES
BOOK SIX

SHERI TYLER

For Christy, Lauren, and Chris Anna
*Writing, like life, is a mix of **leaps of faith, unexpected plot twists, and just the right amount of chaos.** Through it all, you've been my steady ground, my sounding board, and my source of endless encouragement.*

Your wisdom, humor, and generosity overwhelm me in the best possible way. I'm endlessly grateful for your friendship, for always showing up, and for making this journey a little spicier, a little sweeter, and a whole lot more fun.
This one's for you.

BIBLIOGRAPHY

Contemporary Romances
By Sheri Tyler
The Way to a Woman's Heart series - the **Coming Home** trilogy
Slow Simmer
Here's the Scoop
From Bitter to Sweet

The Way to a Woman's Heart series - the **Destination Wedding** trilogy
One Cup of Chemistry
Say Cheese
Kebabs and Kisses

Historical romances
By Sheridan Jeane

Gambling On a Scoundrel

Secrets and Seduction series:
* *Lady Cecilia Is Cordially Disinvited for Christmas*
*(only available via Sheridan's VIP club)
It Takes a Spy…
Lady Catherine's Secret
Once Upon a Spy
My Lady, My Spy
Along Came a Spy

Duke By Dawn (Novella, part of the anthology *Dukes All Night Long*)
August 2025

The Rose and the Spy - a Victorian-era Romantic Suspense trilogy
2026
Whispers and Spies
The Spy In Disguise
Protect the Prince

1

OPULENCE AND OVERWHELM

KENDRA

I'd left New Jersey at six that morning, my stomach twisting the entire drive. I needed to get here early enough to head to the airport for Sonya's destination wedding. By the time I pulled up in front of my sister's new house on this picture-perfect, tree-lined street in Sewickley, I was running on caffeine and nerves.

Was this really happening? Moving in with my sister and her new family felt like a step backward, not forward. Yet here I was, at noon, staring at the life she'd built while I still felt like I was playing catch-up.

I knew Sonya had moved in with her fiancé, Max, and young Emma, his niece who he was now guardian to, but this house? This was something else entirely. My gaze climbed the brick façade, past the grand columns and wide porch, up to the elegant second-story balcony that practically screamed *old money*. Max had mentioned coming from wealth, but Sonya had failed to mention *this* level of wealth.

The place was out of a movie—the kind where people had trust funds and summered in the Hamptons, not the kind where you learned to stretch a box of mac and cheese across three meals.

It made my scrappy New Jersey upbringing feel even more out of place.

What was I even doing here?

A part of me was already bracing for the moment I'd misstep, and this whole charade would come crashing down.

I grabbed two moving boxes from my car, stacking them high enough that I could barely see over the top, and made my way to the front door. If this was the wrong house, I'd apologize, make a run for it, and call Sonya to tell her she'd given me the wrong address. We'd have a laugh, and she'd direct me to some *reasonable* house down the street—one that didn't look like it required an intercom and security clearance.

Balancing my load, I poked at the doorbell. The chime that echoed inside was so elegant, I half expected someone to greet me with a tray of champagne.

Instead, Sonya yanked open the door, grinning. "Welcome home, Kendra!"

I peeked past her at the grand foyer. "Are you sure this isn't a five-star hotel?"

"I promise, it's home. And now it's yours too." She glanced around like the chandeliered foyer was no big deal, as if she hadn't just casually walked into a scene from *Downton Abbey*. "You belong here."

I raised an eyebrow. "Do I, though?"

Before she could answer, Max appeared, already reaching for the boxes in my arms.

"Let me take those upstairs for you."

I handed them over, grateful for the help. "Thanks, Max."

"Make yourself at home," he called over his shoulder as he disappeared up the sweeping staircase.

Before I could process *any* of this, a dark-haired blur skidded into the foyer.

Emma.

She came to a halt in front of me, her brown eyes wide with excitement. "Aunt Kendra! You made it!"

Sonya shot her a look. "She's not your aunt quite yet. Not until after the wedding."

Emma rolled her eyes. "You expect me to call her *Miss Gambit* for two days and then switch? That's just nuts."

I grinned. "She's got a point, Essie."

Sonya rolled her eyes. "Don't remind me. But no teasing, considering you're the one who came up with Essie."

"Es is for Sonya, right? So Essie makes sense."

Emma grabbed my hand. "Come see my room!"

She dragged me toward the stairs, pausing in her doorway to gesture proudly at a pink four-poster bed. A beautiful painting of a girl holding an umbrella under a colorful rainstorm hung above it.

"It's super safe here," she declared. "We have fire extinguishers on every floor and sprinklers in every room."

My heart ached for her. Emma had lost her parents in a house fire a year ago.

I gave her hand a gentle squeeze. "I'm really glad to hear that, Emma. That's smart."

She nodded solemnly. "Uncle Max made sure of it."

Sonya reappeared beside me, her voice softer. "Come on, I'll show you your space."

As we continued up the stairs, Max brushed past us, carrying the last of my things—including my dive bag. The well-worn duffel with "Dive" emblazoned on the side, and packed with my regulator, wetsuit, and fins, was a sharp contrast to the pristine luxury around me.

He grinned. "Figured I'd bring the rest of your things in, too. Can't have you missing out on any dives."

I exhaled, relieved to see something so familiar. "Thanks. This bag is the most *me* thing I own. It's good to see it here."

Sonya smirked. "And yet, you're still acting like we're about to kick you out."

Max arched a brow. "You do know this isn't a trial run, right? You belong here."

I let out a breath, nodding. Maybe, in time, I'd believe it too.

We continued upstairs, passing room after room, each one more luxurious than the last. Rich fabrics, elegant furniture, tasteful artwork—every single inch of this house whispered *money*. It was beautiful, but it was also overwhelming.

Sonya stopped outside a doorway and smiled. "Here we are. You have the whole third floor to yourself."

I blinked. "I—what?"

"You thought we'd stash you in a room under the stairs?" she teased. "We save that for the house elves."

I followed her up the last few steps. "Does the third floor come with a butler named Jeeves?"

"Sadly, no. You'll have to make do with Max, Emma, and me."

She pushed open the door, and I stepped inside—only to stop dead in my tracks.

This wasn't the storage space I'd been expecting. It was a *suite*. A massive bedroom in deep blues and warm grays with pops of chartreuse for vibrancy, sleek but inviting, with a modern, minimalist office across the hall. And the bathroom—*the bathroom*. The rainfall shower head gleamed under soft recessed lighting. The countertops stretched on for miles, topped with neatly rolled towels that looked like they belonged in a spa.

My old apartment had a shower so finicky you had to perform a ritual dance just to get hot water.

I turned slowly, taking it all in. "I… I don't know what to say."

Sonya leaned against the doorway, looking pleased. "Then don't say anything. Just get comfortable."

I pressed a hand to my forehead. "It's *so much*. I feel like I just won a contest I didn't enter."

She reached out and squeezed my arm. "You're my sister. This is your home, too."

I swallowed the lump in my throat, feeling the weight of everything all at once. The years of scraping by. The constant feeling of being an outsider looking in. The disbelief that someone had made room for me—not out of obligation, but because they *wanted* me there.

I forced a smile. "Thanks, Es. I'm just… adjusting."

Sonya didn't push. She just gave a knowing nod. "Speaking of adjusting, let's pack for the wedding. We leave for the airport in an hour."

That snapped me back to reality. "Wait. An *hour*?"

"I thought you knew!"

"I—Sonya, I haven't even picked out a dress for the rehearsal dinner!"

She shot me a look. "You just graduated with a civil engineering degree. I think you can handle choosing a dress."

"That's a completely unrelated skill set."

"You'll figure it out." She patted my shoulder, already heading for the door. "There's a book club brunch tomorrow morning, so make sure you have something cute to wear for that, too."

I groaned dramatically, worrying about my sketchy wardrobe. "Is this what having a rich sister means? Surprise dress codes?"

Sonya smirked. "Welcome to my world."

As she left, I stared at my suitcase, my heart still racing.

This was it. A fresh start.

And all I had to do was *fake it till I made it*.

2

___

LEAVING THE PAST BEHIND

SINAN

Mid-August heat rose in waves from the pool, the scent of chlorine thick in the air. I stood barefoot on the patio, overlooking Pittsburgh's skyline from my house on Mount Washington, but my attention wasn't on the view. Instead, I watched Riley, one of my interns, wrestle with the pool skimmer like it had personally wronged him.

"Check it daily," I instructed, crossing my arms as he scooped out a few leaves. "Last thing I need is a clogged filter while I'm gone."

Riley—blond, grinning, and looking like he belonged on a surfboard rather than in a neurosurgical lab—flashed me a thumbs-up. "Got it, Dr. B. But, uh... how strict is the no-hot-tub rule? Because it's calling my name."

I smirked. "Knock yourself out. Someone should get some use out of it."

He grinned and tossed the skimmer aside before diving cleanly into the pool, cutting through the water with the kind of ease I envied. No tension. No deadlines hanging over his head. Just movement.

I rolled my shoulders, forcing my thoughts away from the

work still waiting for me—surgeries, research, paperwork that refused to complete itself. The never-ending hum of responsibility I couldn't seem to silence. This wedding trip to Turks and Caicos was supposed to be a break, but instead of looking forward to the sun and sand, all I could think about was how much work I wouldn't be getting done.

I exhaled sharply and turned toward the house. Maybe if I focused on packing, I could trick my brain into believing I was actually ready to leave.

Inside, I climbed the stairs to my bedroom on the top floor. Each step brought me past windows showcasing the view of the city, but I barely noticed. My mind was already circling the mental list of tasks I had to complete before I could even think about enjoying the wedding. Pack for the trip. Submit the paper. Figure out how to pretend I wasn't working the whole time.

I stood in the middle of my bedroom—modern, sleek, every-thing in its place—and reached for my favorite suitcase, a Paravel Aviator. Every detail mattered, even something as simple as pack-ing. I carefully folded two Italian suits, crisp shirts, and tailored trousers, each piece chosen with precision. Everything had to be perfect—because if my clothes weren't flawless, then maybe I wasn't either.

As I packed, my mind drifted to Barry and Hailey. They would have been in the thick of the wedding chaos, laughing, making everything feel bigger and brighter—*if they were still here*. I reached for my sunglasses, my fingers brushing against an old watch buried in the drawer—a gift from my brother when I grad-uated from med school. The ache of their absence never fully faded, and seeing Hailey's family without them would only sharpen it. Max raising Emma as her official guardian kept us connected, but there was no filling the space they'd left behind.

Reaching past the watch, I grabbed casual beachwear and added it to the suitcase—a couple of linen shirts, tailored shorts, and custom leather sandals. Everything screamed understated luxury, just the way I liked it. But the truth was, even in this moment, I couldn't stop thinking about work. I grabbed my laptop and my notes for the paper I was submitting. Even on vacation, I couldn't turn it off. That paper about the minimally invasive surgical technique I'd developed—it needed to be flawless. My name was on the line. If I didn't check off every box, would anyone take me seriously?

I promised myself I'd finish it on the flight. Then, and only then, I'd relax. *Right. Just like every other time.* But that ticking clock —the one that told me control was slipping with every second I wasn't working—was impossible to ignore.

I zipped up my suitcase, feeling the tension settle into my shoulders, and headed downstairs. The Jaguar gleamed in the driveway, but I didn't feel any lighter. Just more weighed down by the constant need to get things right.

As I reached the door, my phone rang. Miranda's name flashed on the screen, and an old knot formed in my gut. I hesitated, but answered.

"Sin, it's me," her voice was thin, almost fragile, as though she was afraid I'd hang up. "Big news. I'm out of rehab. As of today."

"Miranda." My chest tightened with the flood of emotions— relief, anxiety, anger, and betrayal all colliding. But I couldn't let her hear that. I had to stay solid. For both of us. "That's good news. How are you feeling?"

"I've been better," she said, and I could hear the plea in her voice before she even asked. "Look, I'm in trouble. I'm facing charges, and I need help. My parents cut me off. You're the only one I can turn to."

Her desperation tugged at me, and I hated it. My grip tightened around the phone. How many times had I fallen for this before? "Miranda, I know things are tough, but…"

"Please, Sin. Just this once. If I can't pay my lawyers, I'm done. My hearings are coming up fast, and if I don't have legal representation, I'm finished. I've burned every other bridge."

I closed my eyes, inhaling deeply. The last time she'd asked for help, it had ended with her stealing from the hospital and nearly destroying both our careers. How could I even begin to trust her again? "You told me so many lies, Miranda. How do I know you're not lying now?"

Her voice cracked. "You don't. But I'm sorry. I don't know if I ever said that, but I am. I messed up everything between us, and I don't deserve your help. But I'm asking anyway."

The sincerity in her voice hit me like a sucker punch. Saying no would've been easier—cleaner—but that wasn't who I was. More than anything, I needed to make things right, even if it wasn't my job to fix her. "I'll help you. But this is the last time. Send me the info for your lawyers, and I'll wire the money directly to them. That's as far as I go."

Her sigh of relief was palpable. "Thank you, Sin. I won't forget this."

As I ended the call, the weight of it settled over me like a familiar burden. Miranda had been part of my life for so long, but every time I thought I'd closed that chapter, she found a way to reopen it. Trust wasn't something I gave easily anymore. Not after what she'd done.

But that didn't mean I could just walk away from someone in need, even if it made me feel like I was perpetuating the same cycle of lies and betrayal. *That's the problem with being a doctor—it bleeds into every part of my life. I'm always trying to fix things, even when they can't be fixed.*

I stepped outside, spotting Riley stretched out by the pool. "Don't forget to check the skimmer," I called, sliding on my sunglasses as I headed for the Jaguar. "I don't want to come back to a swamp."

Riley gave me a lazy salute. "Got it, Dr. B. Enjoy the wedding."

I waved, but my mind stayed stuck on Miranda and the wreckage she'd left behind. *How am I supposed to trust anyone when I've already been played so completely?*

The Jaguar roared to life, and I sped toward the private airfield, the city skyline shrinking behind me. But even as I drove, the weight of everything—Miranda, work, my brother's absence —clung to me like a shadow.

As I pulled up to the airfield, Ford and Mara stood by the private jet, chatting like they had all the time in the world. Their easy laughter cut through the last remnants of tension coiled in my chest—though not enough to loosen it completely.

Ford—Max's older brother and, by extension, my brother-in-law—spotted me first and shook his head with a smirk. "Look who's punctual."

Mara tipped down her sunglasses as I stepped out of the car, adjusting the cuffs of my linen shirt. "Damn, Sinan. You look like GQ's 'Billionaire Doctors Who've Earned a Vacation' cover model." She gave a slow once-over, taking in the crisp button-down, the tailored trousers, the custom leather loafers that had never seen sand. "Try not to overshadow Max when you stand next to him as his Best Man. And please, tell me you packed at least one wrinkled t-shirt."

I exhaled, slipping on my sunglasses. "Guess we're about to find out." I nudged Ford. "But if I start diagnosing patients on the beach, feel free to stage an intervention."

Ford chuckled, but his gaze flicked over me like he was assessing whether I could actually do vacation. "Noted. Though, looking like that, people are probably going to assume you own the resort."

I scoffed, rolling my shoulders as if that would shake off the weight of the past few weeks. Miranda. Work. Barry. This trip was supposed to be a break, but I wasn't sure I knew how to let go.

I scanned the tarmac. "Where are Max and Sonya?"

Ford checked his watch. "Still packing, probably. Or more likely, Sonya's packed and Max is trying to convince her they don't need five suitcases." His grin widened. "But don't worry, they wouldn't miss their own wedding."

As if on cue, a black SUV pulled onto the tarmac, kicking up dust that glinted in the sunlight. Max emerged first, looking relaxed in a way I envied, followed by Sonya and another woman

I didn't recognize—tall, with dark curls caught in the breeze. She hesitated at the car door, taking in the private jet with wide eyes that suggested she wasn't used to this world any more than I was used to vacations.

Mara nudged me. "That must be Sonya's sister. The civil engineer?"

I nodded, watching as the newcomer adjusted the strap of a well-worn bag slung over her shoulder with the word *Dive* emblazoned on it—the only thing about her that looked completely at ease. Something in her hesitation resonated with me, that feeling of being out-of-place even when you're exactly where you're supposed to be.

"Time to play nice with the wedding party," Ford murmured, already moving toward them.

I exhaled slowly, taking one last look at my phone before tucking it away. Whatever was waiting for me could wait a little longer. For once, I'd try to be present—even if every instinct screamed against it.

But as we walked toward the plane, I couldn't help but wonder if anyone else was as good at faking vacation mode as I was about to be.

3

DOCTOR SIN AND THE GRADUATION DRESS

KENDRA

The limo ride to the private airport felt surreal, like I'd stepped into someone else's life. Plush leather seats, champagne holders built into the armrests—so far removed from the cramped public buses I used to take in New Jersey. Beside me, Emma practically vibrated with excitement.

"We're flying to the wedding on a private jet! This is going to be the best trip ever!" Her brown eyes sparkled with anticipation.

I forced a smile, trying to ignore the knot in my stomach. "It sure is, Emma. I've never flown on a private jet before."

Max, seated across from us, smirked. "A friend loaned it to us for the day. Wedding gift."

I arched a brow. "A friend? Someone in the movie business?"

His smirk widened. "They prefer to remain anonymous."

Before I could press him, the limo pulled to a stop on the tarmac. Emma was out the door before the driver had fully opened it, her excitement pulling me along in her wake.

I stepped onto the blacktop, smoothing my sundress, and froze. The jet gleamed under the late afternoon sun, polished and perfect—but it wasn't the plane that made my stomach flip.

It was the man standing beside it.

Tall, dark hair, a quiet intensity in his gaze as he scanned the group—he looked like he belonged here. The effortless kind of wealth and sophistication that came with private jets and tailored suits.

"That's Sinan," Max said, following my gaze. "Emma's uncle. You'll be seeing a lot of him since he's my best man."

I nodded, suddenly self-conscious in my simple sundress. His presence stirred something I couldn't quite name—an awareness, a pull. Handsome, sure, but there was more to it. Something magnetic in the way he carried himself, like he was perfectly at ease in this world.

Shake it off, Kendra. Focus on getting on board that airplane.

I'd never been on a private plane before, and when I stepped aboard the Gulfstream, it didn't disappoint.

Resisting the urge to be impressed was a losing battle. The space, the plush leather seats, the kind of luxury that made regular air travel feel like being crammed into a flying tin can—it was all so ridiculously over the top. Instead of rows, the seating was arranged like a high-end lounge, passengers facing each other like we were about to sip cocktails at cruising altitude instead of choke down tiny bags of pretzels.

While I was still trying to figure out where to stash my carry-on—no overhead bins in sight—a smooth voice cut through the soft hum of the wedding party.

"I've got it."

I turned, my grip tightening on the bag's handle. Sinan.

Up close, he was even more annoyingly put together—dark hair neatly styled, shirt crisp. He took the handle, lifting my bag like it weighed nothing, his forearm brushing mine in the process.

I stepped back before I could notice too much—like how he smelled faintly of cedar and something deeper, richer.

"I can handle my own bag," I said, keeping my voice even.

"Clearly." He slid it into a sleek side storage cabinet I never would have noticed, then met my gaze. "But why waste the effort?"

I didn't have a good response to that, mostly because I wasn't sure if I was annoyed because he'd just saved me from an awkward situation, or thrown off by how effortlessly he fit into this world. He gave me a small nod, like we'd just concluded some unspoken agreement, and then moved to his seat next to Emma.

Emma, oblivious to whatever had just happened, leaned over with a conspiratorial grin. "Uncle Sinan's a doctor. Did you know that? On my dad's side."

I did now.

I studied him as subtly as I could. He was angled toward the window, fingers idly tapping against the armrest, his expression unreadable. I wasn't sure what I'd expected from Emma's uncle, but it wasn't… this.

The plane took off smoothly, and conversation drifted between Emma and the others. I mostly stayed quiet, stealing glances at Sinan without meaning to, catching him doing the same once or twice. It wasn't much, just a flicker of awareness, but it was enough to set something on edge inside me.

And I really, really didn't need that. Not with so many big changes going on in my life.

The wedding rehearsal was later that afternoon, and I was trying my best to blend into the background—difficult, considering I was standing next to Sinan and not wearing any shoes.

Poor planning on my part. Shoes plus sand equals chafed feet, so I was now barefoot and feeling not a little bit awkward.

A double wedding meant double the coordination—and double the potential for chaos. My sister Sonya was marrying Max, while his brother Ford was tying the knot with Mara, a woman with blue-tipped hair and a small dog in tow. I wasn't entirely sure what to expect from this event, but with this crowd, one thing was certain: it wouldn't be boring.

The wedding planner barked instructions with military precision, and I focused on my cues, hyper-aware of how close we were. Every time we shifted positions, I caught the faintest trace of Sinan's cologne, something warm and woodsy that made my pulse stutter against my better judgment.

Standing this close to him shouldn't have made me this tense. It was just a rehearsal—a practice run for a wedding that had nothing to do with me. We were placeholders, standing in position, existing in the same space. No big deal.

Except it felt like a big deal.

And just when I thought there was enough chaos, Mara announced her dog would be her ring bearer. Because that wasn't a disaster waiting to happen.

Grayson—Mara's brother and the other best man—broke the tension by holding up the wedding rings with a grin that suggested he was about to commit a minor catastrophe. "I plan to juggle these during the ceremony. Very dramatic. Big moment."

Mara shot him a flat look. "You'll catch them before they hit the ground, right?"

Grayson shrugged. "Maybe. Maybe not."

Ford sighed. "Good to know our wedding rings are in the hands of an amateur juggler."

When it was Sinan's turn, he executed the ring handoff so smoothly it looked choreographed—no hesitation, no theatrics. Just a quick, precise transfer, punctuated by a slight bow that made Grayson look like, well… an amateur.

Sinan shot him a grin. "That's how it's done."

I exhaled, tension easing from my shoulders. Between Grayson's antics and Sinan's effortless precision, my own awkwardness landed somewhere in the middle. And with that, the afternoon shifted—less stiff, more natural. Almost fun.

The wedding planner clapped her hands. "No stampedes for the exit. Let's have an orderly process. First Mara and Ford, then Sonya and Max."

She gestured toward Emma, who beamed. "Emma goes next, then Courtney and Grayson, and finally, Kendra and Sinan."

I nodded. "Quick and easy. Just how I like it."

"Now, that's a shame," Sinan murmured, just low enough for only me to hear.

Surprised to see this side of him, I arched an eyebrow. "Oh, don't worry—I make exceptions for special occasions."

His lips twitched, but he said nothing.

Which, for some reason, felt like a win.

***

The rehearsal wrapped, and the others made their way down the beach to the rehearsal dinner, but I lingered, letting the quiet settle around me. The sunset stretched across the ocean in streaks of gold and soft pink, the kind of view that made you pause, breathe, and maybe—just maybe—start to accept all the sudden changes life had thrown your way.

I watched the waves for a while, letting the rhythmic sound wash away the awkwardness of the rehearsal, before finally making my way toward the poolside event space. The path wound through lush tropical gardens, tiki torches casting warm light on the stone walkway. As I approached, the sounds of laughter and clinking glasses drifted out from the open-air pavilion.

By the time I arrived to join the others, the place was buzzing with residual energy from whatever disaster I'd just missed.

I barely had time to settle in before Mara leaned in, smirking. "So… you and my ridiculously polished new brother-in-law. That was quite the performance back at the rehearsal."

I reached for my drink, keeping my expression neutral. "It was a wedding rehearsal, not a performance."

Sonya arched a brow. "Oh? Because from where we were standing, it looked a lot like you two were… in sync."

I shot her a look. "It's called following instructions."

Sonya hummed, unconvinced. "Right. And that little exchange during the recessional I overheard? Totally standard best man and maid of honor banter?"

Mara grinned over the rim of her wineglass. "Looked more like flirting to me."

I exhaled, shaking my head. "You're both ridiculous."

Sonya gave a knowing hum. "We just have good instincts."

The conversation drifted, and I let myself relax, the warm ocean air mixing with the sound of laughter. Being with Sonya had always been easy, but even with Mara—who was technically a new member of my extended family—it felt natural. A rare kind of easy, like we'd been doing this for years instead of hours.

Later, after dinner, I found myself wandering toward the beach, drawn by the rhythmic pull of the waves. The resort lights cast a soft glow over the sand, but the farther I walked, the quieter it got, the noise from the party fading into the background.

I needed the space. The past few days had been a whirlwind of packing up my apartment, selling all the furniture, moving in with my sister, and now this unexpected tension that had settled in my chest.

"You thinking about making a run for it?"

The deep voice made me turn.

Sinan stood a few feet away, hands in his pockets, breeze teasing his hair, watching me like he'd been expecting me to be here.

I huffed a small laugh. "Tempting. But no."

He stepped closer, close enough that I could see the hint of exhaustion in his face—the kind that wasn't just physical.

"You don't like being the center of attention," he noted.

"Not really." I toed at the sand. "You seem to handle it just fine."

"I've had practice." He glanced toward the waves. "Though I think I prefer this."

I studied him, trying to figure him out. "You don't seem like the type who avoids things."

"I don't." His gaze flicked back to mine, sharp, assessing. "But I don't chase things that aren't worth the effort, either."

The weight of his words landed somewhere unexpected.

I swallowed, looking away. "Must be nice. Being that sure of everything."

He was quiet for a moment. Then, softer, "No one's sure of everything, Kendra."

Something in his voice made me glance up.

A breeze picked up, cool against my skin. I should've changed the subject, but instead, I let the quiet stretch between us until he finally asked, "So, what are your plans while you're here? Other than wedding duties."

"Scuba diving," I said, relieved for the easy topic. "There's a dive shop a few minutes from the resort. I booked a couple of morning excursions."

Sinan's brows pulled together slightly. "You know you shouldn't fly right after diving, right?"

A flicker of irritation sparked. "I'm an instructor. I've been diving for years."

His mouth twitched like he'd expected my reaction. "Good to know. I wasn't implying you didn't understand the basics."

"Sure felt like you were."

He exhaled, tilting his head slightly. "Fine. I apologize for assuming. I see a lot of people make bad choices, so I default to caution."

I folded my arms. "And why's that?"

"I'm a neurosurgeon," he said simply.

That gave me pause.

Huh. Okay, that was… something.

It didn't completely wipe away my annoyance, but it did make his concern slightly less condescending.

I let out a breath. "Well, thanks for the PSA, doctor. But I promise, I know what I'm doing."

His lips curved. "I'll hold you to that."

Something about the way he said it made my pulse skip. Before I could analyze it too much, I noticed something half-buried in the sand. I reached down, fingers brushing over the smooth surface of a deep green piece of sea glass.

I turned it over in my palm. "It's kind of funny. Something

broken gets tossed around, worn down, and then suddenly, it's… something else."

Sinan watched me carefully. "Yeah." His voice was quiet. "Funny how that works."

I looked at him, pulse thrumming, but before I could read too much into it, he exhaled, glancing toward the resort.

"We should head back," he said.

I nodded, slipping the sea glass into my pocket. But as we walked side by side, something lingered between us—something unspoken, uncertain.

And for the first time in a long time, I wasn't sure if I wanted to pull away from it.

4

PRE-WEDDING OUTING

SINAN

When I walked to the gathering spot the following morning, I found Emma already waiting for me, her sandals digging into the sand as she bounced on her heels. "Uncle Sinan, you're late," she declared, hands on her hips.

Adjusting the sunglasses on my face, I smirked as I checked my watch. "I'm early."

She grinned. "Nope. We have islands to explore, and everyone else is already here."

I had no doubt that she'd been up since dawn, eager to join us guys on the boat while the book club women did their brunch thing. Max had given her the choice, and she'd picked adventure without hesitation. I admired that about her—how she threw herself into new experiences with zero reservations.

"Are you ready for this?" I teased, nudging her shoulder as we walked toward the docks.

Emma scoffed. "Duh. The real question is—are you?"

The marina was already buzzing with activity as we approached. Max and Ford were deep in conversation with the captain, while Grayson, the other best man, stretched dramatically like he was preparing for an Olympic event.

"Did you stretch this morning?" Emma asked me, mimicking Grayson's pose.

"For sitting on a boat?" I asked dryly. "Not really."

Emma rolled her eyes and then bent over, touching her nose to her knees. "Amateur."

I chuckled, slinging my backpack over one shoulder and stepping onto the dock. The boat gleamed under the sun, but my attention drifted elsewhere—to the previous night, to Kendra, to the way I couldn't quite shake her from my thoughts.

Sure, I'd noticed her before the rehearsal. On the plane, watching me like she was trying to decide whether I was a puzzle worth solving. But something had shifted last night. The way she challenged me on diving safety, her confidence, the way she moved through a world that could have easily overwhelmed her.

Women who knew exactly who they were? Always my weakness. But Kendra wasn't just confident—she had gravity. The kind that pulled you in before you even realized you were drifting. And what made her even more intriguing? That flicker of doubt she snuffed out the second it sparked, like she refused to give it air.

That thought was still echoing when the boat roared to life, cutting through the turquoise water like a knife. The wind whipped against my skin, the salty spray cool against the heat of the sun. Emma whooped beside me, her hands gripping the railing, her excitement contagious.

For a little while, I let myself relax into the moment.

The afternoon passed in a blur of island hopping, wading through crystal-clear shallows, and watching Emma collect seashells like she was hunting treasure. The boat hadn't even finished anchoring at a quiet beach before people were wading ashore, dropping towels in the sand and letting the sun warm their salt-streaked skin.

Emma and I walked along the shoreline, her arms full of newly discovered shells. "I'm gonna bring these home and make a necklace," she announced. "Do you think Aunt Sonya would like one?"

"I think she'd love it," I said, scanning the beach. Up ahead, I spotted someone moving in a series of choppy, exaggerated steps.

Emma narrowed her eyes. "Is that… Uncle Grayson?"

We exchanged a glance before heading toward him. Grayson was mid-spin when Emma called out, "Are you breakdancing?"

Grayson stopped short, startled, then let out a laugh. "Not quite. I'm working on a dance for the reception. A little surprise from me, my sisters, and my mom."

Emma looked skeptical. "That was dancing?"

"Rude," Grayson muttered, ruffling her hair.

I crossed my arms. "How confident are you that no ankles will be broken in the process?"

Grayson smirked. "Let's say… I'd put the odds at sixty-forty."

Emma giggled. "I like those odds."

I shook my head. "Well, break a leg."

"Ha. Let's hope not." Grayson shot Emma a wink before turning back to his routine, earbuds going in.

Emma tugged my hand. "Come on, let's find more shells before we have to head back."

As we walked along the water's edge, the waves lapping gently at our feet, I found my thoughts drifting again. But this time, I wasn't thinking about work or responsibility or even Barry.

I was thinking about Kendra. And wondering how the hell I was supposed to stop.

5

A HAIR-RAISING MISHAP

Kendra

The late-afternoon sun bathed the beach in gold as I stepped out of the bridal suite, my gown shimmering with every movement. The fitted bodice hugged my frame, the flowing skirt catching the light like liquid gold. It was the most elegant thing I'd ever worn, but the confidence I projected was more practiced than natural.

I could feel the weight of the event pressing in—the picture-perfect setting, the polished crowd, the kind of wealth that made it easy to feel like an outsider. I wasn't insecure, not exactly, but there was a fleeting moment—just a fraction of a second—where I felt the difference.

Then I shook it off, lifted my chin, and did what I always did. Adjust. Adapt. Own it.

Stepping outside, I found Sinan waiting near the aisle, already dressed in his black tuxedo, looking effortlessly composed. Of course he did. He belonged in a place like this, moving through it like he'd been born to.

Our gazes locked, and a teasing smile curved my lips. "You clean up well, Dr. Bachar."

He leaned in slightly, his voice smooth. "You look absolutely stunning."

I hummed, letting my smile linger. "And you look sinfully gorgeous, but I'd expect nothing less from someone named Sin."

The music swelled, signaling the start of the processional. Emma floated down the aisle ahead of us, followed by Grayson and Courtney. I rested my hand lightly on Sinan's arm as we stepped forward, moving in sync.

For a fleeting second, the moment felt surreal. Like this wasn't just Max and Sonya's wedding, but something else. Something personal.

I shook the thought off as we reached the altar and took our places. Sonya's entrance stole the breath from the entire crowd. She walked alone—because that was her *choice*. She owned the moment. I saw it in the way she carried herself, in the unwavering connection between her and Max when their eyes met.

She handed me her bouquet with a small, grateful smile before stepping up beside him.

And just like that, the ceremony began.

The music softened. The air stilled. All eyes turned toward Zephyr.

The tiny papillon strutted forward in a miniature tuxedo, the wedding rings bouncing in a box tied to his collar.

Beside me, Sinan murmured, "A disaster waiting to happen."

I stifled a laugh, my lips barely moving. "He's got more poise than some of the guests."

Sinan smirked. "True, but we've still got time for things to go horribly wrong."

I tilted my head slightly, trying to get a better look at the dog as he approached. At the same time, Sinan raised his arm to brush back his hair.

A sharp tug stopped me mid-motion.

I frowned as my head pulled slightly to the side.

What the—I inhaled sharply at the unexpected tug at my scalp.

Sinan went rigid beside me.

Oh. No.

We turned our heads slowly, meeting each other's eyes with a dawning realization.

Somehow, part of his watch had hooked onto one of the delicate gold seashell hairpins woven into my updo.

My stomach dropped.

I tested a small movement—bad idea. The pull at my scalp confirmed that we were, in fact, stuck.

Sinan barely moved his lips. "What the hell just happened?"

I exhaled through my nose, my voice tight. "Your watch just proposed to my hair."

His expression remained unreadable, but I caught the twitch at the corner of his mouth. "I'd say we should take things slow, but apparently, we're skipping straight to the vows."

I hissed under my breath, fingers hovering near the tangled spot, trying to assess the damage. "If you rip my hair out, I will actually kill you. We still have wedding photos to get through."

"I'd rather not lose a hand tonight, so I'll be careful," he murmured, tilting his wrist to see where the pin had hooked.

Meanwhile, chaos erupted around us.

Zephyr spotted something—no, someone—a seagull perched on the floral arch. His tiny body stiffened, and then, in a blur of fur and determination, he launched himself toward it.

Mara shrieked. Someone dove. Zephyr dodged and bolted down the aisle, the rings bouncing in his collar.

I winced as Sinan tried to move again, yanking my head slightly forward.

"Sinan."

"I know."

"Fix this."

"Working on it," he muttered, trying to free my hair without making the situation worse.

I could see guests leaping to their feet in my peripheral vision. Mara ripped off her heels and sprinted after Zephyr like a woman with nothing left to lose. Her dad tried to help, only to trip on the aisle runner and go down like a felled tree.

And yet, not a single person noticed that Sinan and I were literally stuck together.

He exhaled, shifting the angle of his wrist. "I think I almost—"

A sharp tug.

"*Son of a*—" I sucked in a breath. "Be *gentle*."

His voice was dry. "That's not usually the feedback I get, but noted."

I swatted at his arm with my free hand. "Sinan."

"Relax," he murmured, his breath warm against my skin. "I promise not to scalp you in front of a hundred people."

I forced myself to still as he worked the pin loose. He was too close. His cologne—woodsy, clean, unfairly good—filled my senses, the warmth of his breath brushing my jaw. My pulse fluttered.

Oh, this was bad.

And not just because of the hair. He gave a soft exhale, and a shiver ran down my spine.

I held my breath as Sinan gave a final, careful twist of his wrist, his fingers brushing against my temple with surprising gentleness.

The pin slid free.

I jerked back instantly, my hands flying to my updo, checking for damage.

Sinan smirked. "Don't worry. You look perfect."

I narrowed my eyes. "If you messed up my hair—"

"Relax." He adjusted his cuff. "You're still gorgeous and furious, just how I like you."

Before I could retort, the thunderous applause of the guests erupted.

Zephyr, the pint-sized menace, was finally captured and now firmly held in Chris Pitt's arms. The dog wagged his tail like he'd just saved the world.

Mara, breathless and barefoot, trudged back toward the altar as Courtney calmly smoothed out her veil and brushed sand from her dress.

"Don't worry," Courtney assured her. "Thanks to Zephyr, no one will remember anything else going wrong today."

Mara groaned. "That dog better have the rings."

Still flustered, I turned back to Sinan, whispering, "Do you think they survived?"

He flexed his wrist. "Let's hope."

Grayson stepped forward and pulled a velvet box from his pocket, holding it up with a smirk.

"You really think I'd trust your rings to a dog?" he asked.

A collective sigh of relief swept through the crowd, followed by laughter.

I exhaled, the tension finally slipping away, but my cheeks still burned from the sheer mortification of the past few minutes.

Sinan leaned slightly closer, voice low. "Having fun?"

I tilted my head, side-eyeing him. "I suppose I should be thanking your surgical precision."

He exhaled a quiet laugh, shaking his head. "I'll add 'saving wedding up-dos' to my list of specializations."

I let out a breath, finally—finally—fully relaxing again.

And for just a second, as I smoothed down the last of my almost-ruined updo, I let myself acknowledge something unexpected.

Sinan had been on my mind all day.

And considering that the 'I do' Sonya had uttered moments ago made us relatives of sorts, that was a problem.

A big one.

6

PARDON ME, WAITER

Sinan

We posed for photos after the wedding, but I was dismissed from duty before Kendra. At the reception, I spotted Chris Pitt near the bar, effortlessly holding court with a cluster of guests. Ever since Ford and Max cast him as the lead in Ghost, he'd become a fixture in their world, his easy charm making him as popular off-screen as he was on it.

I wandered over, catching Chris mid-conversation. He flashed me a grin. "Sinan! They say never work with kids or dogs, right?"

I chuckled. "Not sure Zephyr got that memo."

Chris laughed, clapping me on the shoulder before a fan intercepted him for a photo. As I turned back, my gaze landed on Kendra across the reception, her gown catching the light. She met my eyes with a warm, teasing smile, and—just like that—the pull was back.

I closed the distance.

"Did I mention you look stunning?" I said, slipping into her orbit.

"Only once or twice," she replied, a light blush dusting her cheeks.

28

We stood there as the party buzzed around us, the music and chatter fading to a distant hum.

"And Zephyr," she added, eyes sparkling. "Absolutely stealing all the attention so no one noticed my hair mishap."

Her laughter was infectious, bright and unrestrained, and for a moment, everything felt… easy.

Just then, a man in a perfectly tailored black suit moved past us with a tray of champagne flutes. Kendra reached out. "Excuse me, could I have a glass of champagne?"

The man turned, a bemused smile tugging at his lips. *Chris Pitt.*

With an amused lift of his brow, he handed her a glass. "Here you go," he said, barely holding back a laugh.

Kendra's eyes widened as recognition dawned, her cheeks flushing deep scarlet. "Oh my *God*—I'm so sorry! I didn't realize…"

Chris chuckled, leaning in conspiratorially. "No offense taken. I used to wait tables. Guess I still remember the basics."

I grinned. "Kendra, meet Chris Pitt—*Ghost's* star and all-around decent guy. Chris, this is Kendra Gambit, Sonya's sister and Max's new sister-in-law."

Chris shook her hand warmly. "Great to meet you, Kendra. And you made a fantastic maid of honor."

"Thanks, and… sorry again!" she laughed, still a little pink.

Chris shrugged. "Honestly? Kinda nice to be treated like a regular guy."

As he disappeared into the crowd, Kendra turned to me with a quiet laugh. "Thanks for the save."

"Anytime. But to be fair, with him holding the tray like that, *anyone* could've made that mistake."

Her laughter softened, the lights flickering across her face, pulling me in. For just that moment, everything else faded into background noise.

Just then, the music shifted, and Grayson took the stage with his mom and twin sisters in tow. The opening chords of *My Girl* filled the air, sending a ripple of excitement through the crowd.

Grayson—never one to play it cool—embraced his role with wild enthusiasm. His long limbs flailed like a puppet in a windstorm, his face twisting into exaggerated expressions. His mom and sisters, on the other hand, moved with effortless grace, their synchronized movements making his chaos even funnier.

Beside me, Kendra stifled a laugh. "I think Grayson might be the human embodiment of a traffic accident. You can't look away."

"He's leaning into it," I said, watching as he spun wildly, narrowly missing one of his sisters. "This is a calculated disaster."

Sure enough, *Marry You* by Bruno Mars kicked in, and Grayson's movements somehow got even more unhinged. He flung himself into a dramatic twirl—one that had absolutely no business being attempted on a sandy dance floor. The moment his feet lost traction, his trajectory shifted straight toward me.

I barely had time to react before he crashed into my chest, arms flailing. Instinct kicked in, and I caught him mid-fall, bracing against the momentum to keep us both upright.

A collective gasp rippled through the crowd, followed by an explosion of laughter.

Grayson grinned up at me, still catching his breath. "Nice catch, Spider-Man."

"With great power comes great reflexes," I shot back, setting him upright.

Kendra laughed, tipping her head toward me. "You really are racking up the rescues this weekend."

"What can I say? I have a thing for saving damsels, up-dos, and disastrous dancers." I smirked, watching the way her lips twitched, fighting a bigger smile.

As Grayson returned to his family, striking a final ridiculous pose, the crowd erupted into applause. Kendra clapped along, her eyes still sparkling with amusement.

"That was fun," she said, turning back to me.

I didn't respond right away. Because in that moment—with the music fading, the laughter still lingering in the air, and the warmth of her standing so close—I realized something.

The wedding had already surpassed my expectations.

And it had absolutely nothing to do with the ceremony.

"Dance with me?" I asked, the question feeling as natural as breathing.

"Absolutely."

We found a spot on the dance floor, moving instinctively to a reprise of *Marry Me*, laughing when our steps didn't quite sync. The warm, fragrant air wrapped around us, the kind of night that made everything feel lighter, easier.

Then the music shifted. The first notes of *Can't Help Falling in Love* floated through the speakers, and couples instinctively moved closer. I pulled Kendra in, her arms slipping around my neck as we swayed to the slower tempo.

"Careful, Dr. Bachar," she teased, her voice low. "If you hold me any closer, people might think we're enjoying ourselves."

I smirked. "The scandal. A serious neurosurgeon? Having fun?"

She grinned, her eyes glinting. "Next thing you know, you'll be barefoot, doing the cha-cha."

"Let's not get carried away. Charlize Theron and Chris Pitt might be watching."

Her laughter bubbled out, warm and unguarded, and something about it made me hold her a little closer.

"The wedding's beautiful," she said, glancing around. "The lights, the ocean, the stars—literally and figuratively. It's like stepping into a dream."

"Ford and Max know how to put on a show," I agreed. "But even in all this, people still deal with the same things. Trust. Doubt. Wondering who really sees them."

Her smile softened, something flickering behind her eyes. "I guess it's easy to forget that when everything looks so perfect from the outside."

For a few beats, we swayed in silence, the sound of waves and distant laughter blending into the music. Being here with her felt like stepping outside of time, like I'd been waiting for this moment without even realizing it.

"What about you?" she asked. "Tell me something about yourself."

"Well, my parents are from Turkey," I said, my voice lighter at the memory. "They lived in Chicago when I was born, but moved back to Istanbul after I left for college."

"Do you visit often?"

"Not as much as I'd like," I admitted. "But I try to go at least once a year."

She hesitated, then said softly, "Sonya told me about your brother and sister-in-law. I'm sorry."

The familiar ache stirred, but this time, it felt like something I could share. "Thank you. Barry and Hailey were... incredible. Losing them was hard, but having Emma—and Max and the rest of the family—helped more than I can say."

Kendra squeezed my hand gently, grounding me. "Emma's lucky to have you."

Something tightened in my chest—something unexpected but not unwelcome. "Thanks. We're figuring it out."

A comfortable silence stretched between us, the kind that didn't need to be filled. Every hesitation I'd had earlier—the doubts, the age gap, the questions—faded into the background. None of it seemed to matter anymore.

"What about your family?" I asked. "Any other siblings?"

A shadow crossed her face as she shook her head. "Just me and Sonya. We lost our mom a few years ago. As for our dad... let's just say we're better off without him."

And suddenly, the empty space beside Sonya as she'd walked down the aisle made sense. I squeezed Kendra's hand in quiet understanding. "I'm sorry."

She exhaled, her smile tinged with something bittersweet. "It's been hard, but we have each other."

Before I could say more, a squeal of microphone feedback cut through the air. Dante, ever the showman, took the mic, grinning like he lived for these moments. "Ladies and gents, fasten your seatbelts—it's time for the main event. Let's unveil these wedding cakes!"

Excited murmurs rippled through the crowd. Dante, a close friend of Ford and Max's and the owner of one of my favorite restaurants, Not a Yacht Club, had created the wedding cakes as wedding gifts. He took his job as seriously as any director helming a blockbuster, and judging by the eager faces around us, he'd managed to turn dessert into a spectacle.

The scent of vanilla and buttercream filled the air as guests shuffled closer, craning their necks toward the curtained-off display. Kendra and I stepped forward with the others, and her hand brushed against mine, her excitement mirroring the buzz in the air. Dante's grin widened as he dramatically whipped back the curtain.

The gasps came instantly.

Two towering wedding cakes stood on display, each an intricate work of art. The first, an elegant white and gold design, reflected Mara's style—edgy and dramatic. The second, with bright tropical colors and flowers cascading down the tiers, was Sonya's, easy and laid-back.

I barely had time to take it all in before a flash of pink darted past me. Emma.

She hurried toward the front, her eyes wide, her voice carrying over the chatter. "Aunt Sonya? Uncle Max?"

The room stilled as Max and Sonya stepped forward, their faces full of warmth.

"Do you like it?" Sonya's voice held a tremor of emotion.

It wasn't until I followed her gaze to the second cake that my breath caught.

The bride and groom figurines at the top weren't alone. A third figure stood with them—a miniature version of Emma, woven into the centerpiece of their new life together.

I couldn't move.

Emma's joy was immediate, her small hands flying to her mouth before she launched herself at them, wrapping her arms around Max and Sonya. "I love it!" she said, her voice full of the kind of happiness that made your chest ache.

My throat tightened.

Barry and Hailey should've been here for this. Should've been standing beside me, watching their daughter glow with happiness. Should've been the ones to show her, in this exact moment, how fiercely loved she was.

But they weren't.

And yet, she wasn't alone.

Max whispered something to her, his expression soft, his arms holding her close. Sonya pressed a kiss to the top of Emma's head, and the way they surrounded her—completely, unconditionally— made my chest ache with something between grief and gratitude.

This was a promise.

Kendra's hand squeezed mine gently, pulling me back from the storm in my head. "Emma's lucky to have so many people who love her," she murmured, something wistful in her voice.

I turned toward her, catching something in her expression—an echo of longing. "That's not how it was for you?"

She hesitated, then shrugged, but there was no bitterness in the motion. "It was just me, Essie, and Mom."

"Essie?"

A small smile curved her lips. "S is for Sonya. Essie."

"Cute," I said, filing the detail away. "You two were close."

"Like sisters," she teased, warmth returning to her expression. The gold flecks in her eyes caught the light, and for the first time that night, I let myself really look at her.

The low lighting softened the sharp lines of her features, casting a warm glow against her skin. The way she moved, the confidence in her posture, the curve of her lips when she smiled— it all pulled me in.

"Feel like taking a walk on the beach?"

She hesitated just a beat before nodding. "Sure, why not?"

We left the reception behind, the sound of the waves rhythmic against the shore. The moon cast a silver sheen across the water, the breeze carrying the salty air around us. It should have felt perfect. But it didn't.

Something was off.

Kendra's smile never fully reached her eyes, and she kept just enough space between us to make it clear she was holding something back.

"Sin," she said, her voice careful, like she was still figuring out how to say what she needed to. "I've been thinking about what my life will look like when I get back. I just moved in with Sonya, Max, and Emma. And with you being Emma's uncle, we'll see each other at family stuff." She hesitated, chewing her lip. "Then there's the age gap…"

Her words hit like a low-grade jolt.

"I'm not that much older than you, am I?"

"I'm guessing ten years?"

"Is that too much?" I asked, though I could already see where she was coming from. Add in the family ties, and yeah—this wasn't simple. But I admired her for addressing it instead of pretending it didn't matter.

She exhaled. "It's just… complicated. I don't want to mess anything up with Emma. With our families. Not now that we're —" She gestured vaguely. "In-laws."

I reached for her hand, brushing my thumb lightly over hers. "I understand. But some things are worth the complications."

Her lips curled into a hesitant smile. "Maybe if we take it slow…"

I leaned in, letting a teasing glint enter my voice. "Too slow for a kiss? Older men are known to be good at those."

Her gaze snapped to mine, amusement flickering. "Oh really? I find that hard to believe."

"Want to test that theory?"

She hesitated, just for a second. Then we both leaned in, the space between us vanishing.

The kiss started slow, but the spark was instant. Her lips were soft, warm, molding perfectly with mine. The world around us faded, leaving only the quiet rush of the waves, the taste of salt on her skin, the way her fingers curled instinctively into my shirt.

By the time we pulled apart, we were both breathless.

"That was…" Her voice was barely above a whisper.

Then doubt crept back in.

"A bad idea." She took a step back, shaking her head. "I shouldn't have done that."

I cupped her face gently, searching her expression. "Why not? What are you really afraid of?"

Her eyes flickered away, then back to mine, laced with uncertainty. "Getting hurt. Hurting you. Making things harder than they need to be."

I held her gaze. "Life's already complicated. But that doesn't mean we can't have moments like this—ones that make it all worthwhile."

She swallowed hard, torn. "Even if it feels right, it doesn't mean it's not risky."

Another beat of silence. Then she took another step back. "I should go. Goodnight, Sinan."

I let her go, watching as she disappeared into the night, her silhouette glowing under the moonlight.

That kiss… it was going to be hard to shake.

And despite her doubts, despite the complications, one thing was clear: this wasn't over. Not by a long shot.

7

DIVING INTO TROUBLE

Kendra

My alarm blared, dragging me from the kind of restless sleep that felt more like floating than resting. The sun was already climbing, the room filled with soft golden light, and yet I lingered, my body heavy, my mind still stuck on the night before.

That kiss.

I'd thought about it too much. Too long. Too vividly.

Sinan had been right—he *was* good at it. The kind of kiss that rearranged thoughts and left a hum beneath the skin. A kiss that lingered, not just in memory, but everywhere—in the places his hands had ghosted over my back, in the feel of his lips pressing just firmly enough to leave me breathless.

And not only had I walked away, I'd been proud of myself for it.

Now, in the clarity of morning, I wasn't sure whether that had been a smart move or a spectacular failure.

I exhaled sharply, throwing back the covers. *Nope. Not doing this.*

I had places to be—*fish* to see, for crying out loud—and if I let myself spiral any further into what-ifs, I'd never get out the door.

I yanked on my swimsuit and cutoffs, grabbed my dive bag, and hauled myself out of the room before I could reconsider.

And ran straight into Sinan.

Because *of course*.

He was leaning against the wall by the elevator, the morning sun kissing his jawline in a way that should have been illegal, hands tucked casually in his pockets. Like he'd just walked off the cover of *Neurosurgeon Vacation Chic* and had no idea the wreckage he'd left in my head overnight.

His eyes flicked to my gear bag with the word DIVE emblazoned on the side. Sharp. Amused.

"Heading out for a dive?"

Smirking, I adjusted the strap on my shoulder. "What gave it away?"

His gaze lingered, slow and deliberate, before tipping back up to meet mine. "Just a hunch."

Rather than acknowledge the way his voice curled at the edges —smooth, teasing—I focused on keeping my pulse from tripping over itself.

He added, "I assume I don't have to remind you about flying after diving."

With a narrowed glance and a smirk tugging at my lips, I fired back, "And I assume I don't have to remind *you* that I'm a trained professional."

His laugh was low and knowing, and the way he leaned slightly closer sent a ridiculous spark of anticipation zipping down my spine. "Good," he murmured, "because I'd hate to have to start calling you 'the reckless Gambit sister.'"

I gasped, pressing a hand to my chest in exaggerated offense. "That's bold, coming from the man who nearly scalped me yesterday."

His grin widened. "For the record, you were the one who got tangled up with me."

I scoffed. "Excuse me? Your watch hooked into my hair."

"Semantics." He lifted a brow, his smirk infuriatingly smug. "We were attached. Call it fate."

Fate.

The word curled around something in my chest, unexpected and unwelcome, and I looked away first. "More like a near disaster."

The elevator chimed. Saved by the bell.

We stepped inside, the space too small, the air too charged, and for a few seconds, neither of us spoke. The scent of him—clean, woodsy, unfairly good—wrapped around me, and I knew if I looked up, I'd find him watching me.

I did *not* look up.

The doors slid open in the lobby, and I practically escaped onto the tile floor. I needed distance and ocean water, preferably in that order.

But as I walked away, I could feel it—his gaze still on me.

***

The van rumbled down the narrow island road, flanked by lush greenery and flowers so bright they looked like something out of a postcard. Bougainvillea spilled over fences, the scent of jasmine thick in the warm air. It should have been peaceful. It should have been the kind of morning that washed away the thoughts still tangled in my head.

But it wasn't.

I could still feel Sinan's hands on me, his lips on mine, the way that kiss had left something unsettled inside me. I had walked away. I had told myself it was the smart thing to do.

So why didn't it feel like that now?

I gripped the strap of my dive bag, focusing on the rhythmic bounce of the van's tires against the road. Diving was simple. It was about precision and control—things I could count on.

Unlike a man who could walk away at any time.

I exhaled sharply, shifting in my seat. This was ridiculous. I didn't need complications—especially not ones in the form of Emma's uncle.

I was here for the dive. The escape. The silence of the ocean where nothing, not even the mess in my head, could follow.

Still, Sinan lingered. The way he looked at me. The way he kissed me like he knew I'd never let anyone take care of me and wanted to prove he could.

But care was a luxury. And one I had never been able to afford.

The van hit a bump, jolting me back to reality. Through the trees, the ocean glistened, turquoise and endless. The driver called out, "We're here," as the van slowed near the dock.

I took a deep breath, shaking off the weight of my thoughts.

Diving was what I needed. *Not* a man like Sinan.

The dive boat rocked gently in the water, the salty breeze cool against my heated skin. Laughter bubbled from a small group already aboard—two couples, both clearly in that effortless phase of love that made things look easy.

I envied that.

Not in the "I wish I had it way." Just in the "how does that even happen?" way.

I dropped my gear bag next to the bench, introducing myself.

"Lovely to meet you! I'm Jane, and this is my husband, Paul," said the woman nearest to me, her British accent crisp and warm.

The second woman, an American named Lisa, grinned as she looped an arm through her partner's. "And we're Lisa and Tom. Ready for an adventure?"

"I was born ready," I said, grinning.

They laughed, and the warmth of their easy companionship settled around me. They weren't flashy or dripping with money, but there was a comfort in how they stood close, how they touched without hesitation.

I didn't know what that kind of security felt like—having someone who just… stayed.

Before I could get too lost in the thought, Liam, our dive guide, bounded toward us with the kind of energy usually reserved for golden retrievers.

"Alright, folks, welcome aboard!" he announced, clapping his hands together. The Australian accent rolled off his tongue with effortless charm. "We've got crystal-clear conditions, plenty of wildlife. Maybe we'll even see a turtle or two—if you're lucky."

Jane leaned toward me, lowering her voice with a grin. "Isn't he a bit too charming for his own good?"

I laughed. "I think it's part of the job description."

Liam went through the dive plan, breaking down the safety protocols in a way that was casual, but sharp with experience. As he spoke, the tension in my shoulders started to loosen, replaced by the familiar pull of excitement.

This was my element. The one place I knew exactly who I was.

I suited up, the gear settling on me like an old friend. The weight of the tank, the pull of the straps—everything was measured, precise, predictable.

And when I finally slipped beneath the water, the world above melted away.

The ocean had always been my escape.

Down here, everything slowed. The world was quieter, but never silent. The faint clicking of corals, the distant hum of passing fish, the soft, rhythmic exhale of my own breathing.

This was why I dived.

Because down here, money didn't matter. Social status, family expectations, the pressure of living in a mansion that wasn't mine —none of it existed.

The coral reef stretched before me, alive and swaying. Schools of angelfish flickered like silver ribbons, weaving effortlessly through the currents. A sea turtle drifted past, slow and ancient, the light catching on its shell like something out of a dream.

I hovered near a towering coral formation, watching as a pair of clownfish darted between anemones, the way they moved in sync, completely attuned to one another.

Like Jane and Paul. Like Lisa and Tom.

I swallowed against the strange, unfamiliar pang in my chest.

Maybe there was something about this whole place getting to

me. The wedding, the romance, the effortless way people in Sinan's world existed without fear of falling apart.

Maybe it was just him.

I thought about the way he looked at me. The way he teased me, pushed back, never let me put up walls.

The way he felt when he kissed me.

A deep ache settled under my ribs, something I couldn't quite shake.

Because I wanted more.

Breaking through the surface felt like stepping from a dream into harsh, sunlit reality. The sounds of the crew, the calls of seabirds—everything came back too fast, too loud.

I peeled off my mask, dragging my fingers through my damp hair as I climbed onto the boat.

Liam whooped. "That was a ripper of a dive!"

Jane and Lisa exchanged grins, still breathless from the experience.

"Absolutely incredible," Jane said. "I could stay down there forever."

"I hear that," Lisa agreed, wringing out her hair. "If only my air tank agreed."

Liam laughed, shaking the water from his arms. "Fair dinkum, mate. But don't forget—no flying for twenty-four hours. Let those nitrogen bubbles work themselves out."

The words hit differently this time.

Sinan had told me the exact same thing yesterday. Hell, I'd been annoyed when he'd said it.

But now?

Now it didn't feel like a warning.

It felt caring.

The ride back to the hotel was too short.

I tried to focus on the incredible dive, on the memory of the coral, the turtles, the vast stillness of it all. But my mind kept circling back to Sinan.

To his hands steadying me in the sand at the wedding.

To the way he smiled when I challenged him.

To that kiss, slow and deliberate, like he wanted me to know exactly how much he wanted me.

Maybe I shouldn't be so cautious about him.

Maybe his teasing wasn't just him being overprotective, but a way of looking out for me.

And maybe, just maybe, my sister's marriage wouldn't complicate everything.

Back at the resort, when I spotted Sinan walking up from the beach—sun-kissed, tousled, perfect in ways that should be illegal—I knew I was in real trouble.

He smiled when he saw me. That easy, knowing smile. "How was your dive?"

"Good," I said, ignoring the way my breath caught. "You?"

"Saw some sea turtles while snorkeling. Thought of you."

The casual way he said it wrecked me a little bit.

I smiled, trying to keep things light. "Yeah? The dive leader reminded us about the no-fly rule, too. Seems like you're not the only one who likes to lecture me."

He nodded, then tilted his head slightly. "So… do I get an apology now?"

I blinked. "For…?"

"The 'chip on your shoulder' thing."

Damn it.

I sighed, crossing my arms. "Fine. Maybe I was a little…" I searched for the right word. "Prickly."

His grin was slow and entirely too smug. "A little?"

I rolled my eyes, but couldn't fight the smile tugging at my lips. "Let's not push it."

He chuckled. "Fair enough."

And then, as casually as if he were inviting me to grab coffee, he said, "I arranged a bonfire on the beach tonight. Dinner, drinks, the works. You in?" he asked, his voice soft but confident. "Just thought it'd be a nice way to wrap up the trip. I'm heading out tomorrow morning."

I should have hesitated. I should have weighed the risks.

But all I heard was *"I'm leaving tomorrow."*

And suddenly, that mattered more than it should have.

I licked my lips, feeling the weight of the moment settle between us.

One night. No complications. Just this.

I smiled. "Yeah. I'm in."

8

PINEAPPLE KEBABS

I arrived early to make sure everything was perfect. The bonfire flickered, casting golden light across the sand. The seating —cozy but elegant—was arranged just right, and the air carried the scent of salt and slow-burning wood. As the sun dipped below the horizon, the beach transformed. Torches flickered in the breeze, casting shadows on the sand.

I wanted this night to be something she'd remember.

Kendra hesitated at the edge of the fire's glow, her cutoffs and faded t-shirt a stark contrast to the romantic setting. Her fingers fidgeted with the hem of her shirt, her toes pressing into the sand like she was debating whether to stay.

"It's just a bonfire," I called with a smile, lifting a thermos. "And rum punch. House specialty."

She stepped forward warily, accepting the drink. "Just a bonfire? With a full spread of snacks and what looks like designer seating? Where's the velvet rope? I'm starting to think I should have worn something nicer than cutoffs and a t-shirt."

I chuckled, pouring myself a glass. "No red carpets. No fancy expectations. Just us."

She took a sip, her shoulders relaxing. "This punch is incredible."

"They used a rum like the one my mother brought back from the Caribbean for Christmas."

Her eyebrows lifted. "Your mom gives rum as gifts? Sounds like my kind of mom."

"When it's this good, yes. Family vacations were always a big thing for us. The Maldives, Santorini, the Bahamas. We'd explore, try the food, soak in the culture."

"My mom took us to the Jersey Shore every summer, and I thought that was adventurous."

I smiled. "I bet it was."

She chuckled softly, eyes unfocused like the memory was playing behind them. "We never stayed in hotels or anything. One of Mom's old friends lived out there—she let us crash in her guest room, and Sonya and I thought it was the height of luxury because she had a hot tub."

I leaned in, already picturing kid-Kendra wide-eyed over bubbles and jets.

"She let us use it one night, and we were obsessed," Kendra continued. "When we got home, I filled up our bathtub and made Sonya sit in it with me. I lit a candle from the dollar store and called it our 'spa night.' We even made cucumber slices to put under our eyes."

I laughed, the image too vivid not to. "That sounds like a pretty impressive childhood innovation."

She shrugged, but her voice softened. "Mom worked twice as hard before and after those trips to make them happen, but she wanted us to feel like the world was bigger than just our little corner of it."

I nodded, something tugging at my chest. "Sounds like she succeeded."

We settled into the lounge chairs, the conversation turning lighter—diving stories, snorkeling mishaps, and our most ridiculous ocean encounters.

"So," I asked, leaning back, "what's the most ridiculous thing that's ever happened to you on a dive?"

Kendra grinned. "Oh, once a fish decided my hair looked like a good hiding spot. I spent half the dive shaking it off."

I smirked. "I knew it—you're secretly the Queen of the Fish Kingdom."

She rolled her eyes. "Your turn. Any snorkeling disasters?"

I leaned back, thinking. "Once, in the Bahamas, I swam too close to a school of reef sharks. Harmless, really, but I nearly had a heart attack."

Her eyebrows shot up. "Did you panic?"

"Let's just say my flailing might have embarrassed the entire human species."

She laughed, the sound warm and effortless.

The easy rhythm between us settled deeper, the fire flickering as we ate. She had relaxed now, no longer self-conscious, and I found myself watching her too closely—memorizing the way the firelight danced across her features.

"This grilled fish is amazing," she said, savoring a bite.

"It reminds me of a little taverna in Santorini with the freshest catch of the day. The key to a good meal is fresh seafood and simple seasoning."

Kendra clinked her cup against mine. "To not overcomplicating things."

I smiled. "Not my specialty."

She grinned. "Mine either."

We slipped into an easy rhythm as we ate, and when it was time for dessert, I popped open the airtight container of kebabs. The aroma hit me instantly—a blend of brown sugar, cinnamon, and vanilla.

I placed the pineapple kebabs on the grill, and the scent of caramelized sugar began to fill the air.

Kendra's eyes lit up. "Are we grilling dessert? That's genius."

"Pineapple with brown sugar, cinnamon, and vanilla. Followed by S'mores."

Her moan of anticipation was almost indecent. "This might be your best idea yet."

We worked together, turning the skewers, and as she took her first bite, her eyes closed in bliss.

"This is so good."

I grinned. "Glad you approve."

Then came the S'mores—sticky, messy, absolutely worth it.

Kendra handed me a gooey sandwich. "Try not to make a mess."

I took a bite and immediately got marshmallow on my chin.

She giggled, reaching up without thinking, wiping it away with her thumb.

Her fingers lingered. The teasing flicker in her eyes softened into something deeper.

She licked the marshmallow off her thumb—casual, effortless. But my pulse pounded.

Our eyes met. Held.

Something unspoken passed between us, and before I could stop myself, I said, "No one's looked at me like that in a while."

Kendra blinked, a smile tugging at her lips. "Messy and slightly ridiculous?"

I huffed out a laugh, but the truth sat heavy beneath it. "Like I'm not a walking disaster," I said lightly. Too lightly.

She tilted her head, reading more into that than I meant her to. Or maybe exactly what I meant her to.

"You're not," she said, quiet but firm. "And even if you were, you're still the guy who grills pineapple and makes sure everyone else is okay."

I looked away for a beat, the firelight flickering between us. *That's the problem*, I almost said. Making sure everyone else was okay hadn't saved Miranda. It hadn't even saved me.

But I didn't want to bring that into this moment. Not with Kendra. Not here.

So I said nothing.

And maybe that silence said more than I wanted it to.Every-thing else—the fire, the sand, the waves—faded into nothing.

I leaned in.

She didn't pull away.

Her lips tasted like pineapple and chocolate, warmth and possibility.

For a moment, I forgot everything else. The complications, the logic, the fact that she was Emma's aunt and I was supposed to be rational.

Nothing mattered but her.

She melted into me, her arms looping around my neck, pulling me closer instead of pushing me away.

And then, too soon, she pulled back.

Her chest rose and fell, her lips still parted, eyes wide with something that looked too much like regret.

"That was…" Her voice was breathless.

"Yeah."

She took a step back, wrapping her arms around herself, like she needed a barrier between us.

"Maybe that was a mistake."

A mistake.

The word landed like a slap, and I clenched my jaw, forcing myself to stay still.

"It didn't feel like one." My voice was low, too raw, too honest.

Kendra swallowed, gaze darting away. "But maybe we need to think about this."

I didn't want to think.

I wanted to pull her back in and show her exactly how little I cared about consequences.

But I let her go.

"Yeah," I murmured. "Probably smart."

She hesitated, like she might say something else. Like she wanted to stay.

But then she just turned.

And walked away.

I watched her disappear into the darkness, the taste of her still on my lips, the warmth of her still in my hands.

And just like that, the reality I'd been ignoring slammed into me all at once.

Tomorrow, I was leaving.

Tomorrow, I'd board a plane and fly home, back to the carefully constructed life I'd built.

Tomorrow, I was supposed to forget about this. About her.

But how the hell was I supposed to do that?

How was I supposed to walk into Max and Sonya's house and pretend she meant nothing? How was I supposed to see her, be around her, and act like this kiss—this moment—hadn't changed something in me?

Because it had.

And for the first time in a long time, I didn't know what the hell to do about it.

I should have chased after her.

I should have told her she was wrong to walk away.

But instead, I stayed right where I was, staring at the empty space where she'd been, wondering if—for once in my life—someone else had made the right choice.

Because if she was already getting under my skin this much...

Maybe walking away was the only way to keep myself from falling all the way in.

And if that was the case...

I was already too late.

9

CRACKS IN THE FOUNDATION

KENDRA

Three weeks later, the sun had just risen over Pittsburgh, casting a golden glow on the river as I arrived at the bridge site. Early September mornings were my favorite—a whisper of autumn in the air but still warm enough to feel like summer clung to its last breath. By midday, the heat would creep back, the city's rhythm picking up like it always did.

I pulled my gear from the back of my car, setting it out methodically. Wetsuit, rebreather, fins, tanks, weights, buoyancy compensator, depth gauge, and most importantly, my underwater camera—everything lined up in the same careful order as always.

Routine was grounding. Control, precision—things I could rely on. Unlike, say, an unexpected kiss at a bonfire that still had me losing sleep three weeks later.

Misha was already on the barge, their bright yellow jacket standing out against the muted morning tones.

"Morning, Kendra!" Their voice cut through the quiet.

"Morning! Ready for the dive?"

"Always. You've got this down to a science—one of the most prepared divers I've worked with."

I smirked as I adjusted my gear. "I try. Speaking of being

prepared, you know anywhere I can pick up a side gig? Student loans don't exactly pay themselves."

Misha raised an eyebrow, their eyes lighting up. "Actually, yeah. A diving center's looking for instructors. I'll put in a good word."

"Thanks. I owe you one."

Once suited up, I double-checked my equipment, camera secure on the chest mount. *Focus. Breathe. Work.*

I gave Misha a thumbs-up and slipped into the water, the chill a sharp, welcome jolt back to the present.

Descending, the river's murkiness thickened around me. I moved with controlled precision, scanning each beam with my light as my camera documented everything. The structure loomed massive and silent—seemingly strong. Seemingly solid.

Until I saw the crack.

It wasn't just a small fracture. It was deep. Jagged. Wounded.

Algae clung to the surface, hiding the worst of the damage like a secret no one wanted to acknowledge. But the truth was clear. This wasn't a problem. It was a threat.

The closer I examined, the worse it got.

Hairline fractures splintered outward like a spiderweb. I brushed my gloved fingers over the surface and felt the roughness beneath like rusted barnacles—the decay wasn't new. This beam had been compromised for a while. It was a wonder that the bridge hadn't collapsed.

I shifted my light, the beam piercing through the murky water, and spotted chunks of concrete missing from another beam further down. The jagged edges hinted at something worse—a scour.

I maneuvered myself lower, directing the light toward the base of the beams, and saw it: the river's current had eaten away at the foundation, sediment washed out from under the structure. Like a trap waiting for the right moment to spring.

I thought of the Fern Hollow Bridge collapse in 2022. The

headlines. The chaos. The fact that, for years, inspectors had warned about its condition—and no one had listened.

The weight of the discovery pressed down on me. A slow breath left my regulator. *No way in hell was I letting that happen again.*

Breaking through the water's surface, I ripped off my mask, the cool air a shock to my system. Misha was already there, their face shifting from casual curiosity to something sharper when they saw me.

"How bad?" Their voice was tight.

"Bad." I unhooked my camera, flipping through the images. "Look."

Misha leaned in, their usual easygoing demeanor gone. "Shit. That's..." They trailed off, scrolling through the images. "Worse than I thought."

"Worse than anyone thought." The weight of it pressed down on me, even now, on solid ground. "This needs immediate attention."

At the site office, Ken Burdinger barely glanced up from his computer screen when I entered. The room smelled like cinnamon rolls and bad coffee.

"I found a serious problem," I said, placing the camera on his desk. I didn't bother softening my tone.

Ken finally glanced at me, then at the camera. "You've been here what? Less than a month, Kendra?" He sighed. "No need to try so hard to impress everyone."

The comment was a slap I didn't have time for.

"This isn't about making an impression," I bit out. "I found severe structural issues on the Steeltown Bridge."

Ken leaned back in his chair, arms crossed. "Structural issues, huh? Look, I get it. You're new, and you want to prove yourself. But not everything is an emergency. I'll look at it tomorrow."

I stared at him, my stomach knotting.

"You're not even going to check the photos?"

"Right now, I've got bigger things on my plate, like prepping this data for Mr. Parker's speech tonight," he said, rubbing his temples. "Like I said, I'll deal with it in the morning."

Like it was nothing.

Like it wasn't a ticking bomb.

THAT EVENING, I walked into the networking event feeling like I'd stepped into a world I still didn't belong to.

Everything was polished. Smooth. Perfect. The kind of world Sinan had grown up in.

And me? I was a diver with a half-drunk champagne flute, steel-toed boots still in my car, and a professional-but-budget-friendly suit. Sure, it was fine for a normal workday, but here, with everyone looking like they stepped off the set of a business magazine, I couldn't help but feel... outclassed.

I spotted Ken and Mr. Parker, laughing, relaxed. Like the fate of a city's infrastructure wasn't sitting in my camera.

Like I hadn't told them something that mattered.

Misha appeared at my side. "You good?"

"Oh, yeah," I muttered. "Just... taking it all in."

Misha laughed, oblivious to the tension rolling off me. "You've been networking? The mayor just arrived. Perfect chance to make connections. Relax. You've got this."

But I didn't.

Not when the cracks in the bridge were still in my head.

Not when I kept thinking about how easy it was for people like Ken to brush things off.

And definitely not when Sinan's voice played in my mind—steady, calm, the way he'd said *'We'll figure it out'* the last time we talked.

Each second felt like an hour, the pressure building until I couldn't take it any longer. I had to get out of there—before I did something rash. Like grabbing the microphone and announcing to everyone that the Steeltown Bridge was on the verge of collapse.

I placed my half-empty glass on a nearby table and slipped

out, the weight of my decision pressing on me. As the elevator doors closed, I leaned against the wall, my thoughts spinning. How could they ignore something so serious? The potential disaster played out in my mind—rush hour, the bridge giving out. It was too horrific to imagine, but I couldn't stop picturing it.

I PARKED IN THE DRIVEWAY, gripping the steering wheel a second longer than necessary.

Between Ken's dismissal and that networking event where he pretended everything was fine, my brain was overloaded.

I shoved the car door open and walked inside—only to stop cold at the sound of his voice.

Sinan.

For a second, I just leaned against the door frame and listened. His voice was deep. Even. Familiar.

He sat at the bar with Emma, helping her through an equation, his brow furrowed in concentration.

He was steady. Exactly what I needed but couldn't admit.

I stepped inside, and he looked up, our eyes locking. Too long. Too much.

Emma's brow furrowed, pencil hovering over the workbook. "Wait, Uncle Sin, how did you get that answer again? I thought you said x was four, but that doesn't work here."

Sinan leaned closer, pointing at her book. "Remember to distribute first. See here?" He tapped the page. "Once you do that, the rest falls into place."

Her eyes lit up, that spark of understanding brightening her face. "Oh, got it! Thanks!"

She spotted me then, her grin widening. "Hi, Aunt Kendra. Uncle Sin's pretty good at algebra. He helped me figure this one out."

Sinan smirked. "I'm decent, but I bet your Aunt Kendra's the real expert."

I raised an eyebrow. "Only if you want to ace the next test."

His gaze held mine. For a second, I forgot about the bridge. About everything.

That heaviness I'd been carrying suddenly felt lighter, like when you finally set down a heavy bag after a long day.

Then Emma gathered her books and dashed off, and it was just us.

"You okay?" Sinan asked. "You look like you've had a rough day."

I exhaled, my chest tight. "It's the bridge I inspected today." The words spilled before I could stop them.

And just like that, it was easy.

I told him everything—the cracks, the corrosion, the way Ken dismissed me.

Sinan listened, his focus unshakable. "You're not overreacting," he said firmly. "You need to push harder. If Ken won't act, go over his head."

I let out a breath. God, this was what I needed. Someone to help me look at the problem from a different angle. Someone to make everything seem simple.

"You're doing your job—doing it well, too. We need to make sure this gets handled the right way."

Hearing him say "we" sent a wave of relief through me. No wonder his patients must feel so reassured; his confidence was unshakable. "Thanks, Sinan. It's just... the way he dismissed it, like I was yelling into the void. It's infuriating."

Emma popped back in. "You two look like you're plotting world domination. Ice cream break?"

Sinan grinned. "Rocky Road?"

I smirked. "Fitting, considering the day I've had."

Emma giggled as Sinan scooped the ice cream. "Rocky roads are always better with chocolate and marshmallows."

Sharing dessert brought a moment of calm, a small but welcome comfort.

Emma wolfed down her ice cream. "Marley and I are going bowling after school tomorrow. Her mom's taking us."

"Does Sonya know?" I asked, still feeling responsible.

"Yep, already texted her," Emma said before hopping off her chair. "Goodnight," she said as she bounded out of the room.

"Let's move outside," Sinan suggested. "The fresh air might help clear your head."

I followed him into the backyard. The cool night air settled around us as we made our way to the fire pit. Sinan quickly started the fire, his strong, sure hands moving with an efficiency that was hard not to admire.

As the flames flickered, I thought of that bonfire on the beach. Of the kiss.

Of how stupid I'd been to think I could just walk away from it.

My cheeks heated, and I bit back a smile. Getting too close to him was dangerous, but I couldn't deny how much I enjoyed it.

10

FLICKERS OF CHANGE

Sinan

I poked at the fire, watching the flames flicker and crackle in the cool night air.

"Too bad we don't have any pineapple kebabs," I said, casting a playful glance Kendra's way.

She laughed, the sound slicing through the heaviness that had settled between us. "Yeah, those were pretty amazing. Guess we'll have to settle for the fire and… decent company."

"Decent, huh?" I teased, leaning back on the stone bench. "That last night was more than memorable, though."

Her expression shifted—subtle, but enough for me to catch it. A flicker of hesitation. Something unspoken hovering in the space between us.

"Yeah, it was," she admitted.

Silence stretched, thick with everything we weren't saying. Everything we hadn't figured out yet.

Then, as if snapping herself out of it, Kendra exhaled sharply and shook her head. "I never thought I'd be juggling a potential bridge collapse a few weeks later. I just… I don't know if anyone's going to take me seriously. Ken brushed me off, and it's freaking me out. I'm certain something's going to go wrong."

I watched her for a second, my fingers twitching with the urge to reach out. To touch her hand, to remind her she wasn't alone. Instead, I kept my voice steady. "You found something big. If Ken won't listen, then you'll have to push harder. Like in an emergency, right? Timing is everything. People need to know how urgent this is."

She met my gaze, uncertainty flickering in her eyes. "I guess. It's just hard to feel like I'm not overstepping. Being new doesn't exactly make me feel like they're going to listen."

She glanced away, fidgeting with the zipper of her jacket. "And honestly... I've never been great at asking for help." Her voice dropped a notch, a rare crack in her usual confidence. "Feels like if I don't handle everything myself, I've somehow failed."

That stopped me. She wasn't just frustrated—she was carrying it all, alone. Probably had been for a long time.

"Kendra," I said gently, "asking for help doesn't make you weak. It makes you smart. Especially when the stakes are this high."

She looked back at me, eyes searching. I held her gaze, steady.

"You're not in this alone," I said. "Not tonight, and not tomorrow either."

A slow breath left her lungs, like some of the pressure she carried had finally started to lift.

"Hearing you say that… it helps," she said softly.

**I gave her a slow nod, but something inside me tightened. That need to jump in, to steady her, to fix it all for her—it wasn't new. I'd felt the same pull with Miranda. The difference was, I'd failed her. Missed the signs. Let things spiral. And now here I was again, sitting across from someone who didn't ask for help easily, who carried too much and kept it close to the chest.

But Kendra wasn't Miranda. She wasn't asking me to save her. She was just asking to be heard.

And somehow, that made me want to show up even more.**

The fire crackled in the background, casting a warm glow that mirrored the shift between us—something softer, something deeper.

"You really care about what you do," I said after a beat. "That's rare. It's not just a job—it's who you are. You care, and it shows."

She glanced down, a faint blush coloring her cheeks. "Thank you. It's nice to hear that."

There it was again. That pull. That feeling I'd been trying to ignore.

We'd already crossed a line once. We weren't just two people making polite conversation over a fire. That kiss wasn't just a kiss. And every second I spent with her now made me more sure of it.

Kendra straightened, her eyes sharpening as she flipped the mental switch. "I've got the photos from today," she said, already shifting into work mode. "Start with those. Add my report and dig into the historical data. That'll give me a solid foundation."

"Good. And if you need expert opinions, I know a few people. Structural engineers, architects—people who can validate what you've found."

Her eyes lit up. "That would be amazing. I can already see how to lay this all out. And honestly, the more I think about it, this isn't a company-wide issue. It's a Ken issue. If I can get my report to the right people, they'll take action."

"Then let's make sure you're the one leading the charge."

She nodded, determination sharpening her features. "I'll pull everything together tonight. With the amount of data I'll throw at them, they'll have no choice but to listen."

A slow smile spread across my face. Her drive was magnetic.

"You've got this," I said, meaning it.

And that was the problem.

I wasn't supposed to care this much.

I wasn't supposed to admire the way she fought for what mattered. Or how she got this fire in her eyes when she talked about her work.

I wasn't supposed to notice the way the glow from the fire

danced along her cheekbones, or how the breeze toyed with her hair.

But I did. I noticed everything.

And that meant I was screwed.

Because Kendra wasn't just a casual flirtation.

She wasn't just my sister-in-law's little sister.

If this got complicated—and it would, because when had my life ever been simple?—it wouldn't just affect me.

It would affect Sonya and Max. Emma. Hell, the entire dynamic of my family.

I should have shut this down already. I should have put distance between us.

But instead, I was sitting here, watching her work through a problem, thinking about how fiercely I wanted her to succeed.

Thinking about how fiercely I wanted her, period.

She let out a breath and grinned. "I should get started. The sooner this report is done, the better."

She started to stand, and I knew I should let her go.

But I didn't want to.

I wasn't ready for the night to be over.

Not yet.

My hand twitched at my side. For half a second, I nearly reached for her wrist, nearly pulled her back to sit by the fire for just a little longer.

But I didn't.

Because if she stayed, that would mean something.

And I wasn't sure I was ready for what came next.

"You've got this," I said instead, my voice lower than I intended.

She hesitated, her eyes lingering on mine like she was waiting for me to do something.

But I didn't.

And then she turned and walked inside, disappearing into the house.

I stayed there, watching the fire, knowing damn well this wasn't something I could keep pretending didn't matter.

How the hell was I going to pretend she meant nothing to me the next time I saw her?

11

CONCRETE CONCERNS

.

Kendra

I trudged into the kitchen the next morning, greeted by the familiar clink of Sonya's mug against the granite counter. She glanced up from her breakfast, eyebrows raised in concern.

"You look exhausted," she said, taking a sip of coffee. "Rough night?"

"Yeah, stayed up late working on a report about the bridge inspection I did yesterday," I replied, reaching for my own mug. The dark roast smelled delicious, and I craved its magic touch. "I couldn't stop thinking about the structural issues I found. It's severely compromised."

As I poured my coffee, my thoughts drifted—not to the bridge, but to Sinan. The conversation we'd had by the fire played on a loop in my mind, his steady voice, the way he'd understood more than I expected. I smiled into my cup, remembering how easy it had been to confide in him. How difficult it had been to leave him by the fire.

Sonya broke my reverie. "I'm sure you'll figure it out," she said, her tone as breezy as the morning air. "You always do."

I stared at her for a beat, half wanting to dive into the

complexities of the situation, but what was the point? Sonya was already glancing at the clock, sliding her chair back.

"The bridge is a critical access point," I tried again, hoping for more than casual reassurance. "If the repairs aren't made soon—"

Sonya grabbed her bag, already heading for the door. "Don't stress too much. You're great at your job, Kendra. Just do what you do best."

I set my mug down with a little too much force. "Sonya, this isn't just about doing my job well. If this bridge fails, people could die."

That finally got her attention. She paused, her expression softening as she really looked at me. "I know, Kendra, I do. I just don't want you to carry all of this on your own. You'll fix it. But don't forget to breathe, too."

Her voice was gentle, meant to be comforting. But she didn't understand. This wasn't just another stressful work problem. This was something bigger, something that could unravel into disaster if I didn't push hard enough.

I gave her a tight smile. "I'll breathe when the bridge isn't one bad storm away from making national headlines."

Sonya exhaled, giving my arm a quick squeeze before she left, but the unease lingered long after she was gone.

I stared at my coffee. Maybe I was overthinking things. Maybe my boss would suddenly develop a sense of urgency. And maybe —just maybe—Sinan would turn out to be terrible at something so I could stop finding him so damn attractive.

I wasn't holding my breath on any of those.

As I settled into my cubicle and opened the bridge files, an internal email pinged into my inbox.

Subject: *Urgent – Updated PENNDOT Guidelines & Public Infrastructure Review*

From: Ken Burdinger

Due to recent federal funding and increased scrutiny following several regional bridge collapses—most notably Fern Hollow in '22—the state has notified all engineering firms with municipal contracts that compliance audits may be scheduled in the coming months. Priority will be given to high-traffic routes and aging infrastructure.

My heart pounded as I read it. The Steeltown Bridge checked both boxes. The memo didn't name names, but it might as well have had *Steeltown* in bold across the top.

I dove back into my report, determined to make every line airtight. As I sifted through internal files on previous inspections, something odd stood out. Pittsburgh Steel Solutions had never been assigned to this bridge before. Instead, the job had bounced between firms with questionable reputations. So why us now? Had the city pulled the contract due to negligence—or was this just another casualty of budget cuts and bidding wars?

The question gnawed at me, adding a deeper layer of unease to an already troubling situation.

My fingers flew across the keyboard, notes piling up fast. The more I dug, the more obvious it became—this wasn't just a maintenance issue. It was a catastrophe waiting to happen.

Lost in thought, I didn't hear Josh until he cleared his throat with theatrical volume.

I looked up. Of course. Josh. Office politics personified.

"Morning, Kendra," he said, leaning against my cubicle wall with calculated nonchalance. "Heard you talked to Ken yesterday."

My pulse ticked up. "Yeah. It's urgent. The bridge needs immediate attention."

Josh smirked. "See, if you'd come to me first, we could've polished your work before bothering Ken."

Translation: *If you'd let me slap my name on it, I'd be getting the credit right now.*

He nodded toward my screen. "You saw Ken's memo? The state's sniffing around for weak spots. Someone's going to end up under a microscope. Those numbers you're running better be squeaky clean."

I tightened my grip on my pen. "Good thing I don't fudge them, then."

He raised a brow, his tone turning patronizing. "Just trying to help. You're new. There's a process—channels. Not everyone gets to skip the line just because they want to impress Parker."

Ah. There it was. Not just office politics—resentment.

Josh wasn't here to help. He was bristling at being passed over. I was new, but I'd stepped into something he clearly thought he deserved.

I kept my tone cool. "This isn't about politics. It's about public safety. If you've got a problem, take it up with Ken."

Josh's jaw ticked. "Some of us have been here five years and never got a fast track like this. Must be nice to come in hot and have people listen."

There was a flicker of something vulnerable behind the bravado—bitterness, maybe. Or fear. But then it vanished, tucked neatly behind his usual smug tilt of the head.

"Ken wants you in the conference room at nine. Mr. Parker's joining."

Of course. Delivering the message like he was my boss.

"Thanks for the heads-up," I said, biting back the irritation— and the sympathy—I didn't quite know what to do with.

As he walked away, I turned back to my screen, jaw clenched. Let him play his games. My report would stand on its own.

Office politics weren't going to stop me from doing what was right.

By nine, I was in the conference room, copies of my report stacked in my arms. Ken sat at the head of the table, looking mildly irritated, and beside him was Mr. Parker, his senior supervisor, flipping through some documents with a critical eye. The room felt thick with tension. Josh lounged in his chair, trying too hard to appear laid-back, while Misha offered an encouraging nod from across the table.

"Let's get started," Ken said, his tone brisk. "I understand you're alarmed, but if there were real structural concerns, don't you think the last guys would've flagged them? You're new, Kendra. Maybe double-check your data before we go lighting fires with the city."

I clenched my jaw. "I double- and triple-checked my findings."

Ken sighed like I was being difficult. "Then walk us through what you found."

I took a breath and launched in. "During my inspection of the Steeltown Bridge, I found significant structural issues. The underwater supports are deteriorating, and it's a serious public safety risk." I handed out the copies of my report, watching Mr. Parker study the pages. "What's worse, past inspections were handled by outside companies, and they ignored crucial warning signs."

Mr. Parker frowned as he flipped through my report. "And you're absolutely sure these issues are as urgent as you say? Bridges get wear and tear, but total failure is rare."

"They're critical. I'm sure you'll agree."

He didn't respond right away. Instead, he lingered over one of the photos. The room was silent except for the sound of the pages turning.

I felt the shift happen in real time.

His forehead creased, his frown deepening as he flipped back to an earlier section. He studied it again. When he finally spoke, his voice was sharper. "Ken, what's the protocol for escalating matters like this?"

Ken shifted in his seat. "We—uh—we pass it up the chain."

Josh, sensing things weren't going Ken's way, crossed his arms. "Are you sure you're not overreacting? It's a big claim for someone who's only been here a few weeks."

Suppressing a surge of frustration, I kept my voice even. "I'm confident in my findings. The photos speak for themselves. This isn't about my experience level—it's about the safety of thousands of people who use that bridge every day."

Mr. Parker exhaled sharply. "Ken, this situation should have been escalated immediately."

Ken cleared his throat. "Understood, Mr. Parker. It won't happen again."

Mr. Parker's gaze landed on me. "Kendra, you've done a thorough job here. How did you manage to pull this together so quickly?"

"I discovered the problems during my dive yesterday morning," I explained. "I told Ken right away, and he told me to put a report together. I worked on it overnight so it would be ready first thing today."

He nodded, his face grim but approving. "This is critical. We'll need to get this in front of the city engineer immediately. Ken, make sure Kendra stays involved in this. She needs to see it through."

Ken's jaw tightened, but he nodded. "Of course, Mr. Parker."

Without missing a beat, Mr. Parker turned to Ken. "Ken, it's your responsibility to make sure issues like this are escalated immediately. Your team depends on you to act swiftly and communicate effectively. This situation should've been addressed yesterday."

Ken nodded stiffly, looking as uncomfortable as I'd ever seen him.

Relief swept through me. Mr. Parker had acknowledged the seriousness of the problem and was keeping me in the loop. It was more than I'd hoped for—a chance to make a real impact.

As the meeting wrapped up, Mr. Parker gave me a brief nod. "Well done, Kendra. We need more people as diligent as you. Keep it up."

Pride swelled inside me. "Thank you, Mr. Parker. I won't let you down."

The exhilaration of the moment followed me out of the conference room. I had done it—I'd made them listen. As I made my way back to my cubicle, Misha caught up with me.

"Kendra, you were incredible in there!" Their eyes sparkled with excitement. "That report—you nailed it."

I smiled, feeling their enthusiasm wrap around me like a warm hug. "Thanks, Misha. I couldn't have done it without your support."

They waved off my modesty with a grin. "Please, don't be humble. You're the rockstar here. I'm really glad you're on the team."

I watched them head back to their desk, my heart still racing from the rush of success. Sitting down at my computer, I felt the buzz of success humming through me. My first instinct was to call Sinan, to share the victory with him.

I pulled out my phone, my thumb hovering over his name. Last night's conversation by the fire replayed in my mind—his steady voice grounding me, his quiet confidence reinforcing my own, the way he'd helped me shape my argument so I'd be heard. The memory tugged a smile from me, warmth curling in my chest. But then I hesitated. Was I relying on him too much? Was this shifting into something I wasn't ready to name?

I set the phone down with a sigh. As much as I wanted to share the news with him, I needed to keep my focus on work. There'd be other times for celebrations. I just didn't want to blur the lines between personal and professional too soon.

Later that evening, I prepped spaghetti and meatballs for a family dinner, the familiar scents of garlic and herbs filling the kitchen. The day's events replayed in my mind, but through all of it, I kept circling back to one thing.

Sinan.

He's not just someone I like. He's becoming my sounding board. And maybe I'm not used to letting people see that side of me—especially not someone like him.

I hesitated, then pulled out my phone and typed out a message. Stared at it. Erased it and started over.

> Me: Thanks again for your advice last night. It really helped. They're taking the bridge issue seriously, and we're moving forward aggressively.

I hit send, nerves fluttering inside me. Had that been the right mix of casual and work-focused? Minutes passed, each one stretching longer than the last. I paced my room, my thoughts bouncing between the conversation we'd had, the connection we'd shared, and the flutter of hope that maybe, just maybe, this was something more.

When my phone buzzed, I nearly jumped. I opened the message with a rush of excitement.

> Sinan: Knew you'd crush it. I say we celebrate properly. Something strong, something sweet, and something with a view. Thoughts? 😊

I stared at the text. Was that a line, or just *who he is*? Was this just drinks? Dessert? Or was he saying…

Nope. Not over-analyzing.

The flutter in my chest turned into something warmer. Something real.

I smiled, realizing just how much I liked the idea of celebrating with him.

Maybe more than I should.

12

MIDNIGHT DIPS AND MOONLIT MESSAGES

SINAN

After a long, draining day at the hospital, Kendra's text about her success at work hit like a much-needed dose of relief. The day had been brutal—a life lost in a tragic accident still lingered in my mind, the kind that weighed down my entire team. Her message was a welcome distraction, proof that somewhere, good things were still happening.

Despite the late hour, I flipped on the pool lights and dove in. The cool water jolted my system, a reset button for my brain. But as I powered through lap after lap, my thoughts kept drifting.

Kendra.

Our conversation by the fire stuck with me more than I expected. The way she'd talked about her work—so passionate, so determined—was refreshing. And the attraction? It wasn't just lingering; it was growing.

That was the problem.

She wasn't just anyone. She was Max's sister-in-law. Emma's new aunt. Someone I'd see over and over, no matter what happened between us.

And then there was Miranda. Her addiction. The downward spiral. The drug theft. I hadn't seen it coming, and I couldn't

shake the guilt, misplaced or not. I'd missed the warning signs—
what if I missed them in someone else? What if I got too caught
up in something that blinded me again? The fallout from Miranda
still clung to me, especially at work. People had opinions. People
talked.

Even though I hadn't been responsible for her choices, my name
had been tangled in the mess. Some colleagues still whispered
about it, like I should have known, like I should have fixed it. And
if I started something with Kendra? They'd talk again. Not just
about the timing, but about the age difference. She was younger,
still carving out her career, still figuring out who she wanted to be.
Would people see me as the guy who couldn't handle someone his
own age? Someone his equal? Would they assume I was looking for
a rebound—someone uncomplicated, someone less likely to come
with as much baggage as Miranda had?

And if they did... was that something I could ignore?

I pushed through another lap, but none of it stopped my brain
from looping back to her. Scoffing at me with her dive bag slung
over her shoulder. Scolding me for almost ruining her carefully
arranged hair at the wedding. Her eyes glowing with desire next
to the bonfire. The taste of cinnamon and pineapple on her lips.

After a few more laps, I finally pulled myself from the water,
droplets trailing down my skin as I reached for a towel. The
underwater lights flicked off with a click, and the pool vanished
into darkness, leaving only the faint shimmer of water settling in
the night. Pittsburgh stretched out below, its lights glinting
against the hills, a reminder of why I loved this city. But the
peaceful view didn't quiet my mind.

Inside, I climbed the floating staircase to the master suite,
rubbing a towel over my hair as I went. I couldn't shake how
impressed I was by Kendra. She had that rare quality—a calm,
unwavering determination that made you take notice. She didn't
back down. She didn't flinch. And that made everything more
complicated.

The family ties. The ghost of Miranda. The age gap.

I tossed the towel aside, caught my reflection in the mirror. Damp, curling hair, lingering exhaustion in my eyes, a face that looked as drained as I felt. The weight of the day still clung to me, but underneath it, there was something else. A flicker of something I hadn't felt in a long time.

Hope.

That was Kendra. She made things feel... possible.

Stepping into the shower, I let the warm water wash away the tension in my muscles, but my mind kept circling back to her. As much as I tried to rationalize it, I couldn't deny that the thought of seeing her again made me want to move forward instead of staying stuck.

Drying off, I grabbed my phone. She deserved to know just how proud I was of her for standing her ground today. That grit, that fire—it wasn't just impressive. It was something I wanted more of in my life.

I hesitated for only a second before typing.

> Me: Wanted to say I'm really impressed. You handled everything like a pro. I hope you're giving yourself a chance to celebrate tonight— you've earned it.

I hit send, realizing it was already after ten. Too late? Maybe. Anticipation and doubt swirled as I set the phone down.

The buzz came almost immediately—

> Kendra:

A pang of disappointment hit. *That was underwhelming.* Before I could overthink it, another message appeared.

> Kendra: Lol. I have to admit, it felt great! A shining moment.

Relief washed over me.

> Me: You totally deserve it. And whenever you're ready to celebrate, let me know. No pressure— just whenever it feels right.

I dropped onto the bed, more at ease. If she needed space, fine. My phone buzzed again almost instantly.

> Kendra: Sounds like fun! Does Monday after work sound good? I have a meeting to attend... so after it's over?

> Me: Perfect. Looking forward to it.

My thumbs hovered before I hit the call button.

"Hey, Sin." Her warm voice carried a hint of laughter despite the late hour.

"Hey, Kendra." I sank back into the pillows, smiling. "Monday sounds great. But I called because I want to hear more details about your victory. Lay it on me."

A soft chuckle. "You should've been there. I felt like a super-hero swooping in to save the day. That report? Totally nailed it. I'm pretty sure it's what convinced Mr. Parker to put me on the team overseeing the repairs."

"You're running with the big dogs now? Knew you could do it."

"I love challenges, but sometimes I worry I push too hard. What if I blow the opportunity Mr. Parker's giving me?"

"You push because you care," I said, keeping my tone light but firm. "It's okay to stumble. Everyone does. That's how we learn. Believe me, I've faced plenty."

Today's loss flickered in the back of my mind—a patient we couldn't save. It was always hard, knowing I'd done everything and still couldn't change the outcome. But this wasn't about me, not tonight.

"I almost left neurosurgery once," I admitted. "And it wasn't just the long hours or burnout. It was the aftermath of something personal. Someone I'd been seeing... things went sideways. Badly. And I didn't see it coming." I tightened my grip on the phone.

There was a beat of silence on the other end, just the sound of her breath. I hated that my ex was invading even this moment, but I had an sudden and deep intense need to be understood. To be seen. By Kendra.

"I doubted myself," I said quietly. "Not just as a doctor, but as someone who's supposed to recognize when something's broken. I thought I should've seen the warning signs. Should've done more. Should've fixed it. But I didn't. And it made me question everything."

"You?" She sounded surprised. "Doubting yourself? You always seem so... confident."

"I try to be," I said with a shrug she couldn't see. "That's why I'm always looking for better ways to tackle things. Like the technique I've been developing for brain hemorrhages—less invasive. I've even submitted my findings to a medical journal. Those breakthroughs? That's what keeps me going."

I paused, then added more quietly, "That, and having a solid support system. My parents, Max, Ford... you too now, actually."

Another pause, then her voice, softer this time. "Thank you. It means a lot to hear you say that. I'm not used to having many people in my corner. With my mom gone, it's been just me and Sonya for a long time."

"Well, you can count on me now. And the whole Ross family, for that matter." The second I said it, I wondered if I'd just planted myself squarely in the *family* zone.

Her voice was thoughtful. "So, where are you right now? Have you gone to bed?"

Not a family-zone question. "Maybe," I grinned. "Why do you ask?"

"Just picturing you... probably all serious and doctor-like, even in bed."

I chuckled, rolling onto my back. "And you? How do you look right now?"

"Relaxed," she said, her voice dipping slightly. "In my teddy and shorts."

I smiled at the ceiling. "Sounds cozy."

A hum from her end. "It is. But no more details—you'll have to use your imagination."

The tease was light, playful, and totally disarming. I let it linger between us.

"You know," she added after a beat, "it's nice talking to someone who doesn't expect me to have it all figured out."

Before I could respond, she yawned and added, "But it's late, and we both need sleep. Night, Sinan."

I exhaled slowly. "Night, Kendra."

As I set the phone down, I lay there staring at the ceiling, her voice still echoing in my ears. The tension from the day had eased, but the pull she had on me hadn't.

Two steps forward, one step back.

The conversation left me clearer. Calmer.

But mostly? It left me wanting more.

13

WHERE THE BRIDGE LEADS

KENDRA

A few days later, I sat at my desk in my third-floor suite, sunlight streaming through the tall panes as I worked. My morning had started with a familiar Saturday ritual: pen, paper, and some math. I ran the numbers again, calculating how soon I could pay off my student loans.

If I stayed strict with my budget, I could knock them out in four years—tight, but doable. The alternative was more tempting: allowing myself a bit more breathing room, maybe travel a little, splurge on things I'd long denied myself, and still be debt-free in five. Five years didn't sound so bad, especially with the extra income from my dive school gig.

The only reason I could even aim for four years was because Max and Sonya refused to accept rent. I'd fought them on it, but Sonya had shut me down with one pointed look and an offhand comment about how I should save for something more important. I wasn't sure if she meant my future or a really impressive espresso machine, but either way, I was grateful.

I allowed myself a small smile before heading downstairs, the scent of coffee pulling me toward the kitchen.

Sonya sat at the island, buried in a pile of fifth-grade papers, while Max flipped banana pancakes like a pro.

"Morning! Want pancakes?" Max grinned, catching one mid-air.

I slid onto the stool beside Sonya. "Obviously."

It was a far cry from the grab-and-go mornings of our childhood—cold cereal, an empty kitchen, and a mother already gone to her first cleaning job. Sonya had taken care of me back then, just like she always had. And now, years later, we were still looking out for each other—just in a much fancier kitchen.

"Uncle Max, am I still going with you to Grandpa Don's today?" Emma's voice cut through my thoughts.

Max set a plate in front of her. "You bet. And guess what? Margot Robbie's having lunch with Grandpa Don."

Emma's eyes widened. "I get to meet Barbie? That's awesome!"

Max chuckled. "Yep, but first—eat up."

I laughed at the sight of them, the easy banter, the warmth. This was the kind of morning Sonya and I never had growing up.

Emma finished her pancakes and slid off her stool, joining Max by the door.

"Have fun today," Sonya said. "And, Emma? Don't talk Margot's ear off."

"Mom, I'm not that bad," Emma groaned.

My breath caught. Mom.

It hit me harder than I expected. Emma had never called Sonya that before, at least not in front of me. The word carried a weight that made my throat tighten. It felt real. Permanent. The adoption must have been finalized.

Max ruffled Emma's hair on their way out. "Alright, superstar. Let's not keep Margot waiting."

As Max and Emma headed toward the door, I whispered, "So, it's official?"

Sonya nodded, her eyes shimmering. "As of yesterday. Emma didn't want a big fuss, but… yeah. It's official."

I squeezed her hand. "That's amazing."

She smiled, a quiet kind of pride lighting her face. "It really is."

Max and Emma's voices trailed off, leaving the house in a soft, comfortable quiet. Sonya took a sip of her coffee and gave me a knowing look.

"You've been here a while now," she mused. "And I've noticed you still hold on to some of those old habits."

I arched an eyebrow, unsure where she was going with this. "Like what?"

"Like treating your budget like a religion," she said, lips quirking. "I bet you were working on it again this morning. Listen, I know you want to knock out those loans—I get it. But you don't have to keep yourself on such a tight leash. Give yourself a little breathing room. It's okay to enjoy life a bit more."

I hesitated, thinking about my morning calculations. "You're right. I ran the numbers today. If I stay strict, I could be done in four years. But... maybe five wouldn't be the worst thing. It'd give me a little more room to breathe."

She nodded, satisfied. "Exactly. You've worked so hard, Kendra. It's okay to give yourself some grace. You've earned it."

I exhaled, feeling a weight lift. "Thanks, Essie. I needed that."

THE WEEKEND FLEW BY, and suddenly, it was Monday. Arriving at the office early, I settled into my cubicle, preparing for the meeting with city officials about the bridge repairs. The atmosphere felt charged, like everyone was aware of the urgency now. My report had set things in motion.

As I scrolled through my notes, Brianna, a colleague from another department, breezed over with a bright smile.

"Kendra! Everyone's talking about the report you pulled together overnight. That was impressive."

I blinked. "They are?"

"Oh yeah. Josh has been grumbling about it all morning," she said with a smirk. "But don't let that get to you. Word is, Mr. Parker's been singing your praises."

Warmth flickered through me. "Thanks. It's been a whirlwind."

"Whirlwind or not, you're owning it," she said. "Just remember to breathe. You've earned it."

"I'll try," I said, rolling my shoulders, the tension still tucked deep between my shoulder blades.

She winked. "Keep it up, and you'll be Employee of the Quarter in no time." Then she glanced around before leaning in. "Did you hear the buzz? Rumor is the state's moving up their inspection schedules."

"Because of Fern Hollow?" I asked, already half-bracing for the answer.

"Yeah, and because half the bridges around here are way past due for repairs. They want to show voters they're putting safety first."

My stomach twisted. If they were watching… and we missed something big...

She disappeared down the hall, leaving her words trailing behind like smoke. I sat frozen for a beat, her praise echoing louder than I expected. Mr. Parker singing my praises? Employee of the Quarter? It didn't feel real. It felt like someone else's highlight reel—someone with a stronger résumé and fewer moments of doubt.

I ran my palm down the front of my blazer—the one Sonya had nudged me into buying yesterday. Navy, tailored, clean lines, professional. I looked like I belonged here. But inside, a small, unwelcome voice whispered, *For now.*

Because what if I'd missed something? What if my report wasn't as airtight as I thought? The stakes weren't just career-level anymore—they were life-and-death. And if the state showed up tomorrow, digging through our files with a magnifying glass, I'd be front and center. The girl who raised the alarm. Or the girl who didn't catch it all in time.

I exhaled, forcing my focus back to the spreadsheet on my screen. No time for spiraling. Engineers had been working nonstop since my report dropped. Proposals were already taking shape. I wasn't just the one who noticed the problem—I was helping to fix it.

And now, I had a seat at the table.

This public meeting would be the first official step in implementing a solution.

When I arrived, Mr. Parker greeted me with a nod. "Glad you're here, Kendra. Ready?"

"Absolutely."

As I handed out the latest updates to the city officials and local representatives, the door opened, and my breath hitched.

Sinan walked in, effortlessly polished in a tailored suit.

What was he doing here? Then I spotted his name tag—he was representing Pittsburgh Hospital. Of course. The bridge was vital to their emergency services.

Still, seeing him here changed everything.

He introduced himself to the room. "Dr. Sinan Bachar, representing Pittsburgh Hospital. This bridge is critical for patient transport. I'm here to ensure the city takes our needs into consideration when planning the repairs."

Mr. Parker's face lit up. "Dr. Bachar! An honor. You operated on my friend Randy Brown last fall—he's doing great thanks to you."

Sinan shook his hand. "Glad to hear it."

The meeting unfolded, and I fought to stay focused, but every time our eyes met, my pulse quickened. We were working toward the same goal, and somehow, that made me feel closer to him.

When Mr. Parker opened the floor for comments, Sinan's voice cut through the room. "If this bridge fails—like Fern Hollow did in 2022—the consequences will be devastating. Delays could cost lives. We need action now."

Mr. Parker turned and gestured to me. I distributed the latest findings. "Our team has been working all weekend," I said. "We're ready to implement the emergency repairs plan as soon as we get the green light, and then we can move on to the more extensive repairs."

Deputy City Manager Allen Bishop flipped through the documents, nodding. "This issue is now at the top of the mayor's agenda. We'll be moving quickly."

The meeting wrapped up, and as the room emptied, Sinan approached. "You were incredible in there."

His words sent warmth through me. "Thanks. Your comments were crucial. You really drove home the stakes."

He grinned. "Public safety is serious business. You conveyed that perfectly. I knew you'd be great—tenacious and smart."

I smirked. "Flattery will get you everywhere."

"Good to know," he teased. Then, glancing at his watch, he added, "It's getting late, and I'm starving. How about we skip the drinks and go straight to dinner?"

My stomach growled in response. I laughed. "Dinner sounds perfect. Lead the way."

It didn't take us long to walk to Pittsburgh's Market Square, where the glow of string lights and the hum of the crowd made everything feel alive. At the restaurant, we were led to a small outdoor table under the warmth of patio heaters. The night air was crisp, but the quiet energy between us made the chill easy to ignore.

Once our drinks arrived, I filled Sinan in on my Sunday morning spent crunching numbers, working through my plan to pay off my student loans. At first, I hesitated—my financial struggles felt so different from his world. But he listened, genuinely interested, as if my rambling wasn't just background noise. His attention reframed it all, making me feel less like I was scraping by and more like I was making progress.

Until now, my focus had always been on survival—one step ahead of falling behind. But as I sat across from Sinan, I realized something had shifted. My work, the dive gig, the stability of this house—it wasn't just about getting by anymore. I was building something, and the realization brought a mix of excitement and unease. Did I belong in the same world as him? Could I talk about my struggles without sounding... small?

The low hum of Market Square faded into the background as Sinan leaned back, curiosity lighting his eyes. "You've got a solid plan for your loans, but it makes me wonder—if you woke up tomorrow with no debt, no financial pressure, what would your dream life look like?"

I swirled the wine in my glass, considering. "No limits? I'd still be diving. Somewhere warmer, though. Australia, the Galápagos... maybe even Antarctica."

His brow lifted, amused. "Antarctica? That's a choice. I can see it—bundled up, diving with penguins."

Laughing, I shook my head. "Freezing, but worth it."

His smile softened. "The way you talk about diving—it's freeing. Like the rest of the world disappears."

I paused, caught off guard by how well he understood. "That's exactly it. It's the one place where I can just... *be*." I hesitated before asking, "What about you?"

He leaned forward, his voice quieter. "I've been building toward it for years. I work with Doctors Without Borders, going to places where healthcare is a luxury. I'm working to start up some clinics in medical deserts—bring medicine to people who need it most."

I blinked, impressed. "Wow. I had no idea."

He shrugged. "It's what I've always wanted to do. Medicine is powerful, but only if people can access it."

I leaned forward, meeting his eyes. "I admire that about you. You have so much, but you still push yourself to make a difference. I'd like to think I'd do the same."

A small smile flickered across his lips. "Miranda and I didn't see eye to eye on that. She loved traveling, but it was about luxury, shutting the world out. I wanted purpose. We didn't fit."

I nodded. "That's hard. Love isn't always enough if your values don't align."

"Exactly." He exhaled. "For a while, I thought we'd compromise, but the more I bent to make it work, the more I lost sight of what I actually wanted. And once she was gone... I didn't miss *us*. I missed who I was before I started changing for her."

The weight of his words settled between us. He wasn't bitter, just clear-eyed.

"Do you ever wonder if things could've gone differently?" I asked carefully.

He shook his head. "No. I used to think I'd failed her, that maybe if I'd paid closer attention, I could've stopped what happened. But those were her choices. And I've made mine." His voice softened. "I don't talk about her much, but with you... it doesn't feel like looking back."

A quiet warmth spread through me. "That's probably because we're both moving forward."

His lips curved slightly, something shifting between us. Then, as if lightening the moment, he leaned back with a teasing glint in his eyes. "So, about my backup career as a chef... my soufflé technique is coming along."

I laughed. "A soufflé? Is that when you'll know you've made it?"

"Absolutely." He tilted his head with mock seriousness. "And you'll be the first to try it—assuming you don't laugh when it collapses."

The easy banter lifted the heaviness from the conversation. We talked about travel, places he'd been, places I wanted to go. It felt like more than just a date—like we were finding places where our paths lined up.

By the time we left the restaurant, Market Square had quieted. The night air curled around us, but the warmth of our conversation lingered.

Sinan glanced up at the sky. "You should visit Istanbul one day."

Something electric passed between us. "Maybe," I said, the thought sparking quiet excitement. His words planted a seed—not just about Istanbul, but about all the paths I hadn't let myself consider before.

"Walk you to your car?" he asked.

I nodded, and we started toward the lot. Our hands brushed occasionally, each touch sending a small thrill through me. The chemistry between us had shifted—he wasn't just someone I found attractive. He was becoming something more.

At the crosswalk, the city noise faded into a distant hum of headlights and footsteps. In the glow of the streetlights, everything beyond the two of us blurred.

My pulse beat faster as I caught the way he was looking at me —like I was something unexpected, something worth figuring out.

He moved closer.

"This isn't a great idea, is it?" I murmured, though I didn't step back.

Sinan's gaze flicked to my lips before locking onto my eyes. "Maybe not." His voice was lower now, rougher. "But tell me you don't want this, and I'll back off."

I didn't say it. Because I *did* want this. More than I probably should.

Instead, I did the exact opposite—I kissed him.

It wasn't hesitant this time. The moment our lips met, heat spread through me, and I was drowning out the crisp night air. His hand cupped my face, anchoring me in something steady and sure, like a promise neither of us had spoken yet.

When we finally pulled apart, breathless, my fingers still curled into the fabric of his jacket, I let out a soft laugh. "We are *terrible* at keeping this platonic."

"Yeah," he admitted, amusement glinting in his eyes. "Completely failing."

I shook my head, trying to will my thoughts into something coherent. "What are we doing, Sinan?"

A car passed by, sending a gust of cool air between us. He let out a breath, his expression turning more serious. "I don't know yet. But I don't want to pretend this isn't happening."

That was the moment. The one where I could back away, tell him we were in too deep, that it wasn't worth the risk.

Instead, I found myself nodding.

"We don't have to figure it all out tonight," I said, my voice softer now. "But maybe… we stop pretending we're just friends."

His lips quirked. "I like that plan."

The tension between us shifted—still charged, still unspoken—but something had settled. A decision, even if it wasn't defined yet.

He reached for my hand, fingers lacing through mine like it was the most natural thing in the world. "Come on, I'll walk you to your car."

And just like that, we weren't pretending anymore.

14

TEXTS, TICKETS, AND TWISTS

Sinan

As I drove home after dinner with Kendra, I felt lighter, happier than I had in ages. The memory of our kiss lingered, warm and electric, replaying in my mind—the way her lips had fit against mine, the way her eyes sparkled with excitement and just a hint of shyness. It had been a long time since a night had left me feeling this exhilarated, like I was stepping into something real.

Kendra was different. Grounded, straightforward, refreshingly unconcerned with pretense. She wasn't trying to impress anyone —she just was. That quiet confidence, the way she approached life with equal parts determination and humor, pulled me in more than I wanted to admit. With her, I didn't feel like I had to prove myself, like I had to be anything other than who I was.

I navigated the familiar city streets, my thoughts circling back to our conversation at dinner. The way she talked about money— practical, focused on security rather than status—made me respect her even more. She had goals, a plan, and no illusions about how hard she'd have to work to get there. She wasn't waiting for someone to rescue her; she was building a future on her own terms.

That kind of independence was rare, and damn if it didn't make me admire her even more.

By the time I pulled into my garage, I was still thinking about her. I wasn't just attracted to Kendra—I *liked* her. And that realization hit deeper than I expected.

Before heading inside, I stopped by the pool, letting my gaze sweep over the city skyline. The quiet hum of Pittsburgh at night settled something in me. I wanted to be the kind of partner Kendra could count on, someone who supported her the way she supported herself. The more time I spent with her, the clearer it became—our lives complemented each other in ways I hadn't anticipated.

But the moment I stepped into my house, a chill crept in, like reality pulling me back from the warmth of the evening. I grabbed a glass of water and flipped open my laptop, scanning through emails, expecting the usual mix of work updates and junk.

A reminder about my Duquesne Light bill. A last-minute offer for sold-out Taylor Swift concert tickets.

And then, one name pulled me out of my contented haze: Miranda.

My stomach tightened. I hesitated, then clicked.

Sinan,

I hope you're doing well. First, I want to thank you for helping me with my legal bills. I truly appreciate it.

I hate to ask again, but I'm in a really difficult spot. My upcoming court hearings are crucial, and I'm becoming desperate. The lawyers have already burned through the money you sent. If you could help me out just once more, I'd be eternally grateful. This could determine my fate, and I have no one else to turn to.

Thank you,
Miranda

A familiar mix of frustration and guilt settled in my chest.

Miranda always sounded desperate. Always just one more favor, one more thing she needed.

I exhaled, rubbing a hand over my face. We hadn't been together in over a year, but every time she reached out, it was like reopening an old wound. I'd spent too long believing I could have saved her. That maybe if I'd caught the warning signs sooner, things would have turned out differently.

But I knew better now. Miranda's choices weren't mine to fix.

I stared at the email for another second before closing it without responding. The relief was immediate, like cutting a weight loose. I didn't owe her anything. I wasn't responsible for her.

And more than that—I didn't *want* to be.

Reaching for my phone, I typed out a message, instinct pulling me toward the one person who made me feel lighter.

> Me: Had fun tonight. Especially the kiss.

A few seconds later, my phone buzzed.

> Kendra: Me too. The kiss was definitely a highlight.

A grin tugged at my lips. I wasn't ready to lose this momentum.

> Me: How about Friday night? Would love to see you again.

Her reply was quick, teasing.

> Kendra: Wow, moving pretty fast, aren't we?

The idea hit me like lightning, and I didn't hesitate before typing my next message.

> Me: Feels more like we're crawling. After waiting this long, I need to impress you. How about Taylor Swift tickets?

A pause. Then my phone rang. Kendra's name flashed across the screen. I answered, her voice filled with a mix of amusement and disbelief.

"Taylor Swift? You're pulling out the big guns. Are we really doing this? Starting something…more?"

The question hung between us, heavier than I expected. This wasn't just casual flirting anymore. It was real, and we both felt it.

"Don't you want to?" My voice softened, steadying hers.

A pause. I could picture her biting her lip, thinking. "I do, Sinan. But what if things don't work out? We're connected through Sonya, Max, Emma… I don't want to mess things up for everyone if we don't last."

It was a valid concern. The ties between us weren't ones we could easily untangle.

"We don't have to tell anyone yet," I said. "No pressure. No big announcements. Let's just see where this goes."

A beat of silence. Then a soft sigh—acceptance.

"Okay. That sounds like a good idea."

Relief washed over me. We had a plan. A way to figure this out without complicating everything too soon.

"Great. So… does that mean you're coming to the concert with me?"

She laughed, the sound light and warm. "Yes, Sinan. I'll go to the concert with you."

I hung up, unable to wipe the smile off my face. The night had started with a kiss and ended with the promise of something real.

Then, reality hit.

The concert was sold out. *Completely.*

Panic gripped me as I rushed downstairs, laptop in hand. Frantically, I scoured every resale site, but every page had the same message: **SOLD OUT.**

I scrubbed a hand down my face. *Brilliant plan, Sinan.*

Then, I remembered that email and immediately clicked the link. I managed to score two tickets. The price was ridiculous. I hesitated for half a second—then clicked *purchase.*

The confirmation email hit my inbox, and relief flooded me. It was worth it. *She* was worth it.

I shut my laptop, exhaustion catching up to me, but the excitement refused to fade. Crawling into bed, I chuckled to myself.

I'd better start brushing up on my Taylor Swift lyrics. No way was I blowing this date.

With that, I fell asleep, dreaming of *Blank Space* and the possibilities ahead.

15

―――――

SWIFTLY FALLING

KENDRA

When I got home on Friday, the kitchen was alive with activity. Emma sat at the table, deep in her homework, while the aroma of garlic and rosemary filled the air.

"Aunt Kendra!" She perked up, grinning. "We talked about Career Day at school, and if I visit a relative's workplace, I get the day off!"

"Oh, really?" I leaned against the island, dropping my bag. "Any idea whose job you want to check out?"

She shrugged. "Nothing sounds all that interesting."

Sonya glanced over from the stove. "I thought you'd jump at visiting Ross Film Productions. Or maybe Kendra's engineering firm?"

Emma wrinkled her nose. "Maybe..."

"There's always the dive shop. Scuba diving?"

That elicited a brief flicker of interest.

Sonya shot me a look, then added casually, "Or we could ask Uncle Sinan to take you to the hospital. They put on a huge Career Day every year."

Emma practically bounced in her seat. "Really? You think he would?"

Sonya chuckled. "I'm sure he'd love it. You might even get to see a surgery."

Emma's enthusiasm was instant. "That sounds *awesome*! Can we ask him?"

I ruffled her hair, smiling. "Next time we see him."

Sonya arched a brow at me. "You sure you don't want dinner before you head out?"

"Thanks, but I'm good," I said, already making my way upstairs.

Standing in front of my mirror, I adjusted my sparkly headband, smoothing my pink and silver blouse. *Taylor Swift level sparkle? Check.* Tonight was big—our first *real* date. Butterflies and all.

I had just enough sense to grab a hoodie and pull it over my glittery hair before heading back downstairs. With the hood up and sunglasses on, I quietly slipped through the house.

Almost made it.

"Where are you off to?" Max called from the next room.

"Out with friends!" I shot back, already at the door.

"Have fun!" he chuckled.

Relieved, I slid into my car and typed Sinan's address into the GPS.

When I pulled up, I took in the sight of his house—modern lines, massive glass windows, lit up against the evening sky. A huge patio with a swimming pool taking up one side of the lot. The kind of place you saw in movies. It made me half-expect Chris Pitt to walk by, sipping espresso.

Sinan opened the door just as I reached the steps, his smile warm. "Hey, Kendra. Come on in."

Inside, the sleek interior was softened by warm lighting and the unmistakable comfort of a space that wasn't just staged—it was lived in. Beyond the windows, the city stretched for miles, twinkling like a field of scattered stars.

"This place is incredible," I murmured.

He grinned, a hint of pride in his expression. "Thanks. I wanted it to feel like a home, not just a fancy house."

"Well, mission accomplished. Now I need the grand tour."

Sinan's grin turned playful. "Welcome to the guided experience. First stop, the shoe rack—an engineering marvel of rows and symmetry conveniently located near the front door. Next, the coffee table books, carefully curated to make me look more intellectual than I actually am."

I laughed, eyeing the architecture and medical journals stacked neatly. "You're already a neurosurgeon. How much smarter do you need to look?"

"Excellent question." He gestured dramatically. "Shall we continue?"

His playful ease melted my nerves, grounding me.

When we reached his bedroom, I took in the contrast—sleek design, personal touches. A photo of Emma and a man who looked just like Sinan caught my attention.

"This is Barry?"

Sinan picked up the frame, his expression softening. "Yeah. Hailey took it a few weeks before..." He trailed off.

"I can see how much it means to you," I said quietly.

He nodded, lingering on the picture before setting it down.

I took in the rest of the room, trying not to stare at the bed. My heart thudded as I pictured what it would be like to stay here with him, to tear those pristine sheets apart in the heat of the moment, to wake up to that breathtaking view of the city. The thought made me a little dizzy, excitement swirling in my chest.

"Kendra? You okay?"

I blinked, realizing I'd missed something he'd said. "Sorry, what?"

He smiled, a little bemused. "I said we should probably head back downstairs."

As we settled in the living room, I shifted the conversation to Emma's Career Day hopes. "She was thrilled when Sonya suggested she visit the hospital with you. You totally upstaged my offer to take her diving."

He chuckled. "That's a relief. The idea of her diving under a bridge stresses me out. But yeah, I'd love to show her around. She seems really curious about everything."

The way he said it—*curious, not just excited*—made my heart warm. He wasn't just indulging Emma; he *saw* her. He wanted to be part of her life.

"Thank you," I said sincerely. "That'll mean a lot to her."

He smiled. "It'll be fun for me too."

Something about the moment hit deeper than expected. Maybe it was the way he said *for me too*, like he already knew how much it mattered.

He checked his watch. "We should head out if we don't want to miss the opening act."

We headed into his garage, where his sleek Jaguar gleamed in the dim light. The ride to the stadium was effortless—easy conversation, the kind that made me forget to feel nervous.

And then we were there.

The stadium pulsed with anticipation. Taylor opened with *Welcome to New York*, and the bass vibrated through my entire body. The crowd became one electric wave, everyone singing at the top of their lungs.

Sinan surprised me. He wasn't just standing there, humoring me—he *got into it*. During *Shake It Off*, he attempted one of the dance moves, and I nearly doubled over laughing.

"This is amazing!" I shouted over the music.

He pulled me close, his grin wide. "Glad you're having fun."

The sound system sent the music thundering through the air, the vibrations running up through the floor, and I felt every beat pulse through my body. The light-up bracelets everyone wore blinked in sync with the music, creating a sea of twinkling colors that only added to the magic of the night.

We danced. We sang. We *lived* in it.

By the time Taylor closed with *Love Story* and confetti rained down, I was completely caught up in the moment. It had been perfect.

Afterward, he led me to a quiet, tucked-away restaurant. The warmth of the place was a perfect contrast to the high-energy concert. Over tapas and wine, the conversation flowed easily, laughter threading between serious moments.

"So," Sinan said, a playful glint in his eyes, "what was your favorite part?"

I grinned. "Dancing with you during *Shake It Off* was definitely a highlight."

He chuckled, reaching for my hand. "I was hoping you'd say that. We make a good team on the dance floor."

"Yeah, maybe Taylor will call us for backup next time," I teased.

The easy rhythm of the night made everything feel weightless.

As we left the restaurant, the crisp night air wrapped around us, but the warmth of the evening lingered.

Sinan glanced at me as he drove. "Thanks for tonight. I didn't realize how much I needed this."

I smiled. "Me either."

As we pulled into Sinan's driveway, the low hum of the engine was the only sound between us. The night had been perfect—electric, effortless—but now, with the air thick between us, something else took over.

He turned toward me, his gaze heavy-lidded, voice low. "Come inside?"

It wasn't just an invitation. It was a challenge. A promise.

Every nerve in my body hummed in response. The heat in his eyes sent a slow pulse of anticipation through me, a thrill curling low in my stomach. My heart pounded, caught between the *yes* my body wanted to whisper and the practical voice in my head reminding me how exhausted I was.

I swallowed, my pulse skittering as I glanced toward the house. It would be so easy to say yes, to follow him inside, let whatever was crackling between us finally explode into something unstoppable.

Sinan reached out, brushing his knuckles down my arm, the softest touch, but it set fire to my skin. "Kendra…" His voice was husky, edged with restraint, as if he was giving me a choice but barely holding himself back from making it for me.

My breath hitched. The ache to close the space between us was almost unbearable. The entire night had been building to this—every shared glance, every accidental brush of fingers, every teasing comment that had edged us closer to the inevitable.

And yet…

I exhaled, shakily. "I want to," I admitted, my voice barely above a whisper. "But if I walk inside with you, I won't want to leave."

A slow, wicked smile curved his lips. "That's not a problem for me."

I huffed a quiet laugh, pressing my hands against my thighs to keep from reaching for him. "I *know*. That's the problem."

His eyes darkened, a low rumble of amusement in his chest. "So what are you saying?"

I bit my lip, shifting in my seat as his gaze dropped to my mouth. My entire body tingled, drawn to him like gravity. I wanted to lean in. To press myself against him. To see what it felt like to unravel in his hands.

Instead, I inhaled sharply and whispered, "Rain check?"

Sinan exhaled slowly, as if grounding himself. His fingers skimmed my wrist, tracing the inside where my pulse thrummed like a drumbeat. He leaned in, close enough that his breath ghosted over my lips, making my stomach tighten.

His voice was pure sin. "You *will* collect on that, right?"

Heat coiled low in my belly. "Oh, definitely."

A satisfied smirk played at the edges of his mouth. "Good."

And then he kissed me.

Not a soft goodnight. Not a casual *see you later*.

It was deep, unhurried, and devastatingly thorough. His hand slid to the nape of my neck, fingers threading into my hair, tilting my head just enough to take exactly what he wanted. The heat between us surged, winding tight, making my knees weak even though I was sitting.

I whimpered against his lips, gripping the front of his jacket, anchoring myself as his tongue teased against mine. He made a sound—low, satisfied—before pulling back just enough to murmur, "Go before I start trying to change your mind."

I was breathless, aching, caught between frustration and exhilaration. "Pretty sure *I'm* the one trying to keep this from escalating."

His smirk deepened, his fingers still tangled in my hair. "You sure? Because I think we're both failing spectacularly."

I let out a shaky laugh and forced myself to pull away, already regretting it.

His gaze followed me as I opened the door and stepped out into the cool night air. I turned back, leaning on the car for just a second longer.

"Goodnight, Sinan."

His eyes swept over me one last time, like he was memorizing me, before he exhaled heavily. "Goodnight, Kendra."

The moment stretched, neither of us wanting to break it.

Then, finally—*reluctantly*—I stepped away, my body still buzzing with everything that almost happened.

As I drove home, my lips tingled, my skin flushed. I'd barely left, and already, I was counting down to that rain check.

I slipped into the house quietly, thinking I'd made it—until Sonya's voice cut through the dark.

"Late night?"

I turned to find her watching me, arms crossed, smirk in place.

"Taylor Swift," I blurted, grinning.

Her eyes widened. "Now *I'm* jealous."

Before I could bask in the win, her expression shifted.

"There's something else," she said, voice careful. "Dad tried to contact me."

The words slammed into me.

"What?"

Sonya's gaze darkened. "He left a voicemail. No details. Just that he wanted to talk."

A mix of anger and unease settled deep. "Why now?"

She shook her head. "I don't know. But I wanted to give you a heads-up. He might try reaching out to you too."

I clenched my jaw, pushing down old hurt. *He doesn't get to walk back into our lives.*

"Thanks for the warning," I said, my voice steady.

Sonya nodded. "Get some sleep. We'll figure it out."

I climbed the stairs, the night's joy still flickering inside me—strong enough to hold back the shadows.

In by bedroom, I stripped off my clothes and cleaned off all that glitter. As soon as I dropped into bed, my fingers found my clit, imagining his hand there. I imagined our kiss as I touched myself, licking my lips as I imagined the taste of him.

It didn't take long before I called, "Sin," softly into the night.

My body relaxed, and I quickly fell asleep, dreaming about Sinan.

16

BALANCING ACT

SINAN

Getting ready for my regular cooking class at Not a Yacht Club was usually a mindless routine—swap work clothes for something casual, grab my favorite knives (yes, knives; I'm a surgeon, not a murderer), and head out. But tonight, my head wasn't in the kitchen. It was still wrapped around Kendra and our night at the Taylor Swift concert.

Catching my reflection in the mirror, I barely recognized the grin on my face. I had it bad. That kiss? The kind of thing people write ballads about. And the way her eyes sparkled when she laughed? Yeah, I was done for.

As I threw on a shirt and jeans, a lightness settled in my chest, something I hadn't felt in years. Losing Barry and Hailey, dealing with Miranda's endless drama—it had left me numb. But Kendra had changed that. She'd woken me up again.

A flicker of unease crept in as I grabbed my keys. We'd agreed to keep things quiet for now, but sneaking around wasn't exactly my strength. Subtlety? Not my best quality. And with my friends? Forget it. They'd sniff something out the second I walked through the door.

The drive to Not a Yacht Club gave me time to collect myself.

As I navigated through evening traffic, I practiced looking normal, rehearsing casual responses to inevitable questions about my week. By the time I pulled into the parking lot, the sunset painting the Ohio River in amber and gold, I'd convinced myself I could keep my composure. But the smile that kept threatening to break through? That might be harder to explain away.

Inside the restaurant, the guys were in full swing. Max and Ford were chatting, while Reed passed by with a tray of drinks, shooting me a grin.

Grayson, the newest addition to our group, waved when he spotted me. He'd fit in fast, which made sense—his surprise dance routine with his sisters at the wedding had already cemented him as part of the crew.

"Sinan! About time," Ford called, smirking.

I slid into my usual spot. "Blame traffic. Or maybe I'm just fashionably late."

Max clapped me on the shoulder. "As long as you're ready to show us all up in the kitchen."

I smirked. "I'll try not to embarrass you too badly."

Grayson grinned sheepishly. "Since I'm the rookie, I'm the most likely to set something on fire. No promises."

Laughter rippled through the group as Dante, our host and master chef, clapped his hands for attention. "Alright, tonight's menu—Turkish kebabs, hummus, and fresh pita bread. A nod to Sinan's roots."

I chuckled. "Easing us in, huh? Maybe next time we can tackle baklava from scratch—the way my mother makes it. See if you guys can handle phyllo without turning it into a disaster."

Ford smirked. "If anyone can, it's Dante. The guy made *two* wedding cakes in the hotel's kitchen. Man, they were so good people were sneaking extra slices."

Max nodded. "And don't forget those cake toppers. That was next-level."

Dante grinned, waving off the praise. "Baking under pressure is nothing compared to dealing with you guys in my kitchen."

Ford shot me a look. "Still, precision, patience, attention to detail... sounds a lot like surgery, doesn't it, Dr. Precision?"

I laughed, shaking my head. "I'll stick to fixing brains. Less chance of a powdered sugar explosion."

Dante went on to explain the marinade first, then shifted to prepping hummus. "While the meat marinates, you'll start on the hummus. Chickpeas, tahini, lemon juice, garlic, olive oil—blend until creamy. It'll give us something to nosh on while we wait for the kebabs. It's simple, but incredibly tasty."

Ford and I were partners today and quickly got to work, chopping, marinating, and debating the best ratios for seasoning. The easy rhythm of the group settled me, at least until he started eyeing me a little too closely.

"You seem distracted tonight," he said finally, pausing mid-chop. "Work stress, or is Miranda causing trouble again?"

Given I was trying to keep my mouth shut in order to avoid lying, the question hit too close, but I forced a casual shrug. "Actually, neither. I went on a date last week." I snapped my mouth shut too late. Why had I brought *that* up? I added, "It's new, so we're keeping it low-key."

Ford's eyebrows shot up. "New, huh? Dating a nurse and trying to keep it quiet?"

"Something like that," I hedged. "We just don't want to complicate things."

His grin widened. "Yeah, good luck keeping it a secret. You're not exactly subtle, Sinan."

I huffed a laugh, but his words left me uneasy. Keeping this quiet? Probably not going to last long.

The conversation shifted back to food, and I reached for an avocado from the open shelf, catching Dante's eye for permission.

"Avocado in hummus?" Ford asked skeptically. "Is that a thing?"

I smirked. "Trust me, it adds a creamy texture."

"Avocado makes everything better," he said.

As we worked, the easy rhythm of the night returned—until a sudden flare of flames caught my eye.

Grayson, looking entirely too panicked, waved a skewer of kebabs now *engulfed in fire.*

"Uh, guys?" His voice wavered. "Is it supposed to do this?"

"Only if you're trying out for the fire department," I said, keeping my voice steady. But the sight of those flames climbing closer to the sprinkler system had my pulse kicking up. "Grayson, put it down. *Now.*"

He panicked and waved it harder—sending flames dangerously close to the ceiling.

Dante sprinted over with a towel. "Stop *waving it around!* You're about to torch my restaurant."

Grayson dropped the skewer onto the counter, and Dante quickly smothered the flames. The room filled with the smell of charred wood and burned meat.

Silence.

Then Reed, barely containing his laughter, muttered, "Well, that's one way to add some sizzle to the evening—but you might have gone a bit too far."

A ripple of relieved chuckles broke out.

Dante rubbed his temples. "Grayson, you *weren't* even supposed to be cooking them yet. They need to marinate."

Grayson groaned. "I *may* have gotten ahead of myself."

Ford clapped him on the back. "Next time, maybe just stick to chopping."

We took a break while the meat continued to marinate, settling in with some hummus and drinks. But as we relaxed, Max slid into the seat beside me, swirling his gin and tonic.

"Ford tells me you've got someone new in your life."

I froze for half a second before forcing my expression neutral. "It's still early. We're keeping it quiet for now."

Max watched me carefully. "Secrets don't stay that way for long. Especially when they're close to home."

My pulse kicked up. *Did he know?*

I kept my face neutral, giving a half-laugh. "We're just figuring things out. No need to complicate it."

Max's gaze held steady. "Fair enough. Just be careful. Secrets have a funny way of turning into bigger problems."

Dante chimed in. "Max is right. But hey, when the time's right, you'll know."

As everyone cleaned up from the hummus break and returned to cooking, Max's warning echoed in my head. He was right—secrets had consequences, especially in a group as close as ours. I couldn't shake the feeling that I was balancing on a tightrope, and sooner or later, I'd have to choose which side to land on. The question was: when that moment came, would Kendra be there to catch me?

Taking things slow with Kendra was one thing. But keeping it quiet? That was another story entirely.

17

CAREER DAY

Sonya groaned as she ended a call, rubbing her forehead like it physically pained her. "You have *got* to be kidding me."

Emma and I both turned toward her as she tossed her phone onto the counter, her chai tea sitting untouched beside a stack of papers.

"What now?" I asked, already bracing myself.

"The sub I lined up for today just bailed," she said, dragging a hand through her hair. "Which means I can't take Emma to Career Day."

Emma's spoon clattered into her cereal bowl. "Wait—so I *can't* go?"

The devastation in her voice was palpable. While I might not have been all that excited about spending a day at a hospital, Emma had been counting on this.

I sighed. "I'll take her."

Emma gasped in excitement. Sonya spun toward me, her eyes wide with gratitude. "Really?"

"Yeah, my schedule's light today." I pulled out my phone and texted Ken.

Me: I need to take a personal day. Family emergency..

A few seconds later, his less-than-thrilled response came through.

Ken: Fine. But you'll be catching up tomorrow. No one's going to hold your hand.

Me: Understood.

I pocketed my phone. "It's handled."

Sonya nearly collapsed in relief. "You're a *lifesaver.*"

"I'm *Emma's* lifesaver," I corrected. "She's the one giving me the big, sad eyes."

Emma, fully aware of her persuasive powers, grinned.

I grabbed a piece of toast and shot a quick text to Sinan.

Me: Surprise! Guess who's bringing Emma to Career Day? Brace yourself for some serious auntie points.

Sinan: Can't wait! I'll make sure your tour is VIP level.

Me: I expect nothing less than surgical magic. Maybe a crown. Emma too, I suppose.

By the time Emma and I arrived at the hospital, the place buzzed with Career Day energy—clusters of kids in wide-eyed awe, parents herding them through hallways, doctors and nurses offering patient smiles. Emma practically vibrated with excitement.

Then Sinan appeared, effortlessly professional in scrubs and his white coat, his presence commanding the space in a way I found increasingly hard to ignore.

"Kendra. Emma." His smile—warm, confident—sent a subtle thrill through me. "Ready for your private tour?"

Emma beamed. "Absolutely!"

Sinan led us through the hospital, pausing to explain different departments with an easy authority that had Emma hanging on his every word. When we reached neurosurgery, he took us up to an observation deck overlooking an ongoing procedure.

Emma's excitement wavered. "It feels weird, watching someone's brain like this. Won't he mind?"

"This is a teaching hospital," Sinan explained. "Patients sign waivers. If they don't want observers, we respect that."

She peered through the glass, her expression a mix of fascination and queasiness. The patient's head was held in place by a metal frame, the surgeon bent over with a magnifying headset.

"Is he going to be okay?" she asked.

"He's in the best hands," Sinan reassured her. "But if it's too much, we can move on."

She hesitated, then nodded. "Yeah. I think I've seen enough."

As we left, Emma picked up her pace, clearly relieved. I lingered, trailing just behind, taking in the way Sinan moved through the hospital—confident, in his element. Completely irresistible.

We rounded a corner, slipping back into the rhythm of the hospital when a young man nearly toppled over with a stack of charts.

"Riley! Perfect timing," Sinan called.

The guy adjusted his grip, grinning sheepishly. "Hey, Dr. Bachar. Trying to get through these before rounds."

Sinan smirked. "Kendra, Emma—meet Riley Norwich. My top intern and part-time house sitter."

At that, Riley puffed up, clearly pleased. "Nice to meet you both. Though, I think the house-sitting gig is my real claim to fame."

Clearly, another one of Sinan's devotees. I could practically see Riley basking in his glow.

I arched a brow. "If Sinan trusts you with his house, that's high praise."

Riley shot a smug glance at Sinan. "He trusts me with his espresso machine, if that tells you anything."

Sinan rolled his eyes. "Before this turns into a testimonial, let's keep moving."

The tour continued, Emma testing out the Heimlich maneuver in a training session, Sinan guiding her with that signature patience that made my chest feel uncomfortably warm. I was trying—really trying—to focus on her experience, but every time he brushed close, the memory of that last kiss pulsed between us.

We stopped at an office where an older doctor with white-flecked blond hair sat reviewing brain scans. Sinan knocked lightly.

"Kendra, Emma, this is Dr. Val Sigurdsson. Val, meet my niece, Emma, and her aunt, Kendra."

Dr. Sigurdsson looked up, smiling warmly. "Ah, so this is Emma. And Kendra, nice to finally meet you."

My stomach clenched. Finally? My pulse kicked up a notch, scanning Val's expression for any hint of recognition beyond professional courtesy.

Sinan hesitated for the barest fraction of a second—so slight most people wouldn't catch it. But I did. Then, smooth as ever, he said, "Ah, yes, from the bridge project I'm consulting on."

Emma's curiosity flickered. "Uncle Sinan talks about you at work?"

Sinan smiled easily. "I talk about the bridge project. Kendra's just an important part of it."

Emma seemed satisfied. I was decidedly not. My skin felt too tight, my breath too shallow. Val's gaze held no suspicion, but for a split second, I'd felt exposed—like a tightrope walker realizing too late they'd stepped without a net.

Sinan, unfazed, grinned. "Let's go visit some of my patients."

I forced my feet to move, but the unease lingered. Had Sinan really covered that slip, or had Val just chosen not to push?

We made our way to the pediatric wing, passing brightly painted hallways adorned with colorful murals. Nurses smiled warmly at Sinan as we walked by—a clear sign of the respect he commanded.

In a private room, Sinan introduced us to Melanie, a young Hispanic girl recovering from surgery. Her head was wrapped in bandages, but her smile was bright.

Sinan crouched beside her. "How are you feeling today?" His voice was softer now, all warmth and reassurance.

Melanie shrugged. "Okay, I guess. My head still hurts."

"That's normal, but you're healing fast. You're a warrior."

Her eyes lit up at that, and my chest squeezed.

Then a nurse rushed in, urgent. "Dr. Bachar, Ethan's hallucinating again. His mom is frantic. We need you."

Sinan was on his feet instantly, a shift in his entire demeanor—sharpened focus, quiet authority. "I'll be right there." He turned to me and Emma. "Stay with Melanie. I'll be back soon."

We nodded, and he hurried off, leaving me with the two girls who quickly became engrossed in a discussion about video games.

I found myself listening, straining to hear his voice, and caught it from the room next door.

"Ethan, it's okay. You're safe here," he said, steady and sure, grounding the boy in reality with a presence that could anchor anyone.

Being here today was something else. He wasn't just brilliant, but compassionate. Unshakable.

Emma continued chatting with Melanie, her thoughtfulness making me proud, but my focus kept drifting—to the way Sinan commanded a room, to the way he'd looked at me when he said my name, like he was already picturing what came next.

Eventually, Sinan returned, looking slightly tired but satisfied. "How are things here?"

"Great," Emma replied, beaming. "I was telling Melanie about a video game called *Stray,* where you play as a stray cat in a world filled with robots."

"I can't wait to try it," Melanie told him.

Sinan chuckled. "Sounds like fun."

We said our goodbyes, and Sinan left to check in on his patients while Emma and I grabbed a quick lunch in the hospital café. Afterward, we joined a small group heading to the helipad. Emma loved the thrill of standing on the rooftop, wind whipping through her hair, but her enthusiasm took a nosedive in pathology. She pushed to the front—only to freeze when she saw what they were actually examining.

A human lung.

She paled and backed up so fast she nearly tripped over her own feet. "I thought pathology meant X-rays."

"That's radiology," I whispered.

She shot me a glare. "Now you tell me."

As we walked away in search of Sinan, she whispered, "Don't tell Uncle Sin, but even though I want to help sick people, I don't think I want to be a surgeon. There are other jobs, right?"

"Absolutely. You could be a dermatologist, a researcher, a physical therapist. There are tons of ways to make a difference."

Her shoulders loosened. "Good. Because I don't ever want to hold someone's lung."

We found Sinan finishing up a conversation with a colleague. When he spotted us, he smiled. "Ready for a break? West Park's all decked out for Halloween—hay bales, pumpkins, the works."

The crisp autumn air carried the scent of burning wood and cinnamon, mingling with the city's ever-present hum. Leaves skittered across the sidewalk as we walked, Emma peppering Sinan with questions about the hospital while I tried—unsuccessfully— not to stare at him.

"Why neurosurgery?" I asked, genuinely curious. "It seems like such a demanding field."

"I've always been fascinated by the brain—it controls everything we do, yet there's still so much we don't understand. But what sealed it for me was a patient early in my career. He'd suffered from debilitating back pain for years, and every doctor deemed surgery too risky. I investigated, found a solution, and took the chance. It worked. Watching him walk without pain for the first time in years made me realize—this was what I was meant to do."

Before I could respond, a fluffy white Westie trotted past us on a bright blue leash, its tiny paws making determined strides across the pavement.

"Oh, I love Westies," I murmured.

The owner overheard and slowed, introducing us to Linus, who promptly rolled onto his back for belly rubs.

Sinan crouched beside me, his voice warm, his presence entirely too close. "I love dogs too, but my schedule makes it hard to have one."

Emma, oblivious to the way my breath had hitched, nodded sagely. "Dogs always know how to make you feel better."

"They do," Sinan agreed, scratching behind Linus's ears. "Maybe one day, when life's a bit less hectic."

Something about the way he said it made my chest tighten. Maybe one day. Maybe if things were different.

Linus gave a happy little bark before his owner led him away, and we continued walking through the park, the moment lingering in my mind longer than it should have.

By the time we made it back to the hospital entrance, the sky had deepened into late afternoon. Emma turned to Sinan with a grin and threw her arms around him. "Thank you, Uncle Sinan! Today was amazing!"

"I'm glad you enjoyed it, Emma. I hope you found it inspiring."

She smirked at me. "Next year for Career Day, can I take you up on that scuba diving offer?"

Sinan gasped, hand over his heart. "Scuba diving? Kendra, how could you! I wanted to be the cool one."

I shot him a wicked grin. "Maybe you both should join me next year. A little underwater adventure wouldn't hurt, right?"

He held up his hands in mock surrender. "No, thanks. I'm more of a land creature."

Emma strode ahead, leaving us alone in the fading light.

Sinan reached for my wrist, his touch sending a jolt through me. His voice dropped, intimate. "I want to see you again. Soon. Just the two of us."

A slow smile spread across my lips, my pulse thrumming. "I'd love that."

"Text me later?" His thumb brushed over my wrist before he let go.

"Count on it," I said, my skin still tingling from his touch.

18

COLD SECRETS AND WARM PROMISES

Sinan

Pittsburgh's city lights blurred past as I navigated the evening traffic, but my mind was elsewhere—wrapped around Kendra. Her laugh, the brush of her hand, the way her eyes lit up. Career Day had been days ago, yet I could still feel the warmth of her presence lingering like an aftershock.

With dinner plans set for Friday, anticipation tugged at me. This was more than attraction—it felt like something falling into place. I'd told myself to keep things casual, but that was a lie. I was in deep.

Pulling into the garage, I checked my phone, already hoping for a message from her. Instead, my stomach twisted as Miranda's name lit up the screen.

I let the call go to voicemail. Seconds later, a text pinged.

Miranda: Check your email.

Sighing, I moved inside. As I set my things down, I glanced toward the pool through the windows. Too many leaves were starting to fall into the water, and the cool breeze was a reminder that it was time to close it for the season.

Reluctantly, I opened my laptop. The unread message sat at the top of my inbox.

Subject: Please Read - Urgent

I clicked on it, bracing myself for the onslaught.

Sinan,

I hope you're doing well. Your mother called me today. She misses me and wanted to know how I'm doing. I lied and said everything is great. Thank you for not telling her about my situation. It's all so embarrassing.

I'm facing another court appearance, and my legal team needs more money. If I don't get the funds, I could be in serious trouble.

Remember everything I did for you during our residencies? The support, the sacrifices? You promised we'd always have each other's backs. I'm asking for your help, just one last time.

I'll be in Pittsburgh next week. Maybe we could meet?

Please, Sinan. I'm desperate.

Miranda

I exhaled, rubbing a hand over my jaw. Same tactics, different day. But something in her words pulled me back—to Chicago, to who we had been before everything unraveled.

I first met Miranda during my surgical residency. She was in anesthesiology, sharp-witted and always three steps ahead. We'd clicked immediately, both drawn to the thrill of medicine, the intensity of the OR.

One night, early in our training, an emergency C-section came through. The mother was in distress, the baby's vitals crashing. The attending wasn't there yet, and I was frozen, running through worst-case scenarios. Then Miranda stepped in.

"We've got this," she'd said, her voice steady.

She adjusted the patient's sedation, talked me through my panic, and by the time the attending arrived, we were already mid-procedure, stabilizing the baby together. Later, over coffee in the on-call room, she'd smirked and said, "If we survive residency, I say we take over the world."

I'd been drawn to that fire, that confidence. Back then, she was the person I trusted most.

But trust had its limits.

I called her, cutting her off before she could start. "I'll help with the lawyer fees this one last time, but that's it. No meeting, no more favors. You need to start handling this on your own."

There was a pause, a beat where I could hear the wheels turning in her head. Then, quietly, "Thank you."

A flicker of guilt niggled at me, accompanied by a new kind of exhaustion, heavier than before. Miranda had been a huge part of my life once, but those days were over. And yet, she still lingered at the edges, a reminder of past mistakes. A reminder of how I'd failed her.

As I hung up, my thoughts shifted to my mother. She loved poking into my life, her curiosity relentless. I'd learned to edit what I shared with her—offering tidbits, never more than necessary, a habit born from necessity. Her interest often felt stifling, and keeping some parts of my life private was the only way I could breathe. Some things were better left unsaid.

Shaking it off, I changed into swim trunks and headed outside. The cool night air hit me as I skimmed leaves from the pool, the rhythmic motion settling my thoughts. This had always been my reset—the silence, the water, the sky stretched out above.

I floated on my back, staring at the stars, the heated water wrapping around me like a cocoon, holding off the October chill. My mind drifted to Kendra, and for the first time in a long while, I let myself relax. She was different. No manipulation, no games. Just warmth. Honesty. She didn't demand anything from me—she just was, and somehow, that was enough to make me want to give her everything.

The contrast hit me hard. Miranda had always been a storm,

pulling me in, tossing me around, leaving me disoriented. Kendra was the opposite—steady, effortless, real.

Climbing out, the cold air bit at my skin, sharp and bracing. The last remnants of Miranda's hold evaporated, carried away with the rising steam.

Inside, bourbon in hand, I did what I *actually* wanted to do. I called Kendra.

"Hey, you," she answered, voice light, teasing.

"Hey yourself." I settled against the couch, closing my eyes. "I wish I could see you tonight."

"I wish you could too," she admitted. "But I'm at home with Sonya and the fam. It's chaos central."

I grinned, picturing it. "Do you think they'd mind if I just showed up? I could bring cookies. Everyone loves cookies."

She laughed, and warmth spread through my chest. "Tempting, but Sonya might lose her mind if you walked in right now. Let's not push our luck."

"Fair," I conceded. "Still, it's tempting. Just to see you."

A pause. Just long enough to make my pulse quicken.

"Soon," she promised, softer this time.

I exhaled, dragging a hand through my hair. "I have an early surgery tomorrow. Five A.M. start."

"Wow. That's brutal. You should get some rest."

"I should," I agreed, not moving an inch. "But I couldn't go to bed without hearing your voice."

She hesitated, just enough to let me know she felt it too.

"You know," I mused, shifting to a lighter tone, "I haven't had to sneak around like this since high school. Feels like I'm breaking curfew."

Kendra snorted. "Let me guess. Your mom always caught you."

"Every time. Sixth sense." I chuckled. "What's next? Climbing through your window?"

She laughed, the sound warm, teasing. "You sure you've got the balance for that?"

"My ninja skills are questionable," I admitted. "But I'd risk it."

The laughter faded, and something heavier settled between us. Not uncomfortable—just... present.

"This sneaking around is getting to me," I admitted. "I feel like we're lying to our families."

She sighed. "I know. I'd hate for them to find out through gossip."

"Right? I feel like a terrible spy. Less James Bond, more... I don't know, someone bad at espionage."

Kendra chuckled. "We'd be the worst secret agents."

A pause.

"When do you think we should tell them?" she asked, quieter now.

I hesitated. "I don't know. I want to be sure we're solid first. But hiding this is getting old."

"Same," she admitted. "I really like you, but I want us to have staying power. Until then... I guess we keep sneaking around."

A thought hit me, one I wasn't sure I should voice. But I did anyway.

"Maybe we should wait on... you know, getting physical. Just until we're ready to go public."

Silence.

Then, soft but teasing, "You're probably right."

The tension between us hummed.

I exhaled. "Alright then. We'll wait. But just so you know, I really like you, and I'm counting the days until we don't have to sneak around like a couple of teenagers."

"Same," she murmured.

A playful smirk tugged at my lips. "I mean, sneaking around *is* a little romantic."

"Like Romeo and Juliet?"

"Without the tragic deaths."

"Good call," she laughed. "We should avoid poison and daggers."

"Noted."

Another pause, but this one felt... nice.

"Well," she sighed, "at least we have cell phones. Romeo and Juliet didn't have that."

I grinned. "True. Though sneaking into your window *would* be dramatic."

She laughed again, soft and warm. "Maybe let's hold off on the balcony climbing."

"Fair enough." I let my head rest against the couch, closing my eyes. "We'll get there. And when we do... no more hiding."

She sighed, but it was a happy one. "I can't wait."

19

A CHILLY REUNION

Kendra

"Big plans for Halloween?" Misha leaned against the edge of my desk, arms crossed, watching as I shut down my computer.

I stretched, rolling my shoulders. "Yep, a wild night of handing out candy and hanging with Emma. She changed her costume again—now she's going as a pathology doctor with fake body parts."

Misha snorted. "That kid's going places. Hope she doesn't scare off the neighborhood kids."

"She might. Which is why I fully support her," I said with a grin, grabbing my coat. "What about you?"

"Costume party. A friend's renting out the upstairs of The Lantern," they said, then gave me a pointed look. "You sure you don't want to come? Could be fun."

I laughed, shaking my head. "Tempting, but I'm sticking with candy duty."

Misha sighed dramatically. "Fine, but don't complain when you see my Instagram and realize you made the wrong choice."

With a final wave, I headed out of the office, stepping into the crisp October evening. The city pulsed with movement—office workers rushing home, last-minute shoppers carrying plastic pumpkins, kids already trick-or-treating in brightly colored costumes. The scent of fallen leaves and street vendor hot dogs mingled in the air, blending with the occasional whiff of something pumpkin-spiced.

I pulled my coat tighter against the wind, my mind already shifting to the comfort of home—hot cider, a warm blanket, and Emma's enthusiastic play-by-play of her trick-or-treating route.

Then, just as I reached the sidewalk, a man near the entrance caught my attention.

There was something about him—a flicker of familiarity I couldn't place. He wasn't dressed in costume, but something about the way he stood, his posture, sent a ripple of unease through me.

His face broke into a smile, and my pulse kicked up, an instinctive surge of adrenaline making my hands colder than the wind.

"Hello, Kendra," he said, stepping toward me. His voice held an odd mix of hesitation and familiarity, like he was testing how I'd react.

I stopped, every sense on high alert. "Do I know you?"

The way his smile barely shifted sent a chill through me—one that had nothing to do with the autumn air.

That's when it clicked. The recognition hit me, not from real-life encounters, but from the countless times I had replayed that horrible YouTube video where he'd publicly humiliated my sister. *Oh God, it's him.*

"I'm your father, Jimmy Harlow."

My blood ran cold. The wind cut sharper now, biting at my cheeks, or maybe that was the sudden flood of emotions tightening my throat. Of all the ways I'd imagined meeting him, this wasn't one of them. Sonya had warned me about him trying to contact her, but I'd never thought I'd run into him like this. Not on the street, not today, and definitely not now, of all times.

Jimmy's practiced smile made my skin crawl. Smooth. Too smooth. Did he really think a little charm would erase everything?

The denial that I was his daughter? The way he'd ignored me my entire life? My fingers twitched as I instinctively pulled back, putting distance between us. "What are you doing here?" My voice barely sounded like my own.

He sighed, shoulders drooping in what looked like well-rehearsed regret. "I know I wasn't there for you, but I want to make things right."

"Now?" I couldn't stop the bitterness from seeping into my voice. "You've had years."

He shrugged awkwardly, managing to look pitiful and desperate all at once. "I've changed. Can we talk, please?"

I stared at him, heart still hammering, trying to push through the fog of emotions. "How did you find me?" I demanded, struggling to keep my voice steady as the noise of my pulse threatened to drown out my thoughts.

Jimmy—no, I wouldn't call him father—offered a small, awkward smile. "A Google search, actually. I saw your profile on your company's website. Congratulations on the new job, by the way."

I crossed my arms, skepticism clear on my face. "And why are you here? What do you want?"

His smile faltered, replaced by a look of regret. "I'm here to apologize, Kendra. I know I've never been there for you. I left your mom before you were even born, and I've regretted it ever since. I want to make amends."

A sharp laugh escaped before I could stop it. "You regretted it?" I repeated, the words tasting bitter in my mouth. "Is that why you refused to claim me? Why I have Mom's maiden name instead of yours?"

Jimmy's lips parted slightly, like he hadn't expected me to know that. His gaze darted away, and the silence that stretched between us said more than any excuse he could come up with.

"I was young," he muttered finally. "And stupid. I made a mistake."

"No, a mistake is leaving your phone in a cab or buying a

stock that tanks," I said coldly. "You walked away from a preg-
nant woman and refused to claim your own child. And now,
suddenly, you care?"

"I know I was wrong. I want to fix that. Make amends."

The bustling crowd of office workers passing by made our
conversation feel surreal. "Not here," I said, my voice tight. "We
can talk, but let's walk."

We walked toward Market Square, his voice filling the chilly
air with stories about his time in rehab, the jobs he'd tried and
failed at, and the people who'd given him second chances. He
talked about missed opportunities, the friends he'd let down, and
how he was finally on the path to recovery. It all sounded
rehearsed, the words too polished, too carefully crafted to
convince me to see him as a changed man. But all I could feel was
skepticism. His words were like the wind—blowing past me,
leaving only a faint chill.

"You look a lot like my sister," Jimmy offered. "Lorraine
passed away recently."

"Oh, so I had an aunt," I said, deadpan. "Interesting. Any
cousins you've also forgotten about?"

He flinched, clearly not expecting that. "I, uh, lost touch with
her years ago."

"You don't say." My sarcasm was thick, but honestly, how
could I not be angry? This man hadn't just abandoned us—he'd
erased us. And now, he wanted back in?

"Lorraine left behind a nice house in Squirrel Hill," he said,
almost wistful. "I wonder what'll happen to it now."

It hit me with a sharpness that nearly stole away my breath—
she'd lived right here in Pittsburgh and I'd never even known
about her.

As we walked, I stayed a step ahead, letting the cold air
sharpen my senses. He was too smooth, too practiced. The way he
smiled, the way he seemed so eager to please—it made my skin
crawl. Was this how he got away with so much for so long? By
being too charming?

We arrived in Market Square, its lively atmosphere contrasting sharply with my inner turmoil. I spotted people in costumes sitting at outdoor tables next to heaters, enjoying their dinners. It reminded me of my date here with Sinan. What would he think of my father? Would knowing about my family's dysfunction change how he saw me? The thought made me angry.

"You know," I began, my voice trembling with emotion, "it's hard to believe you're sincere. You left us, abandoned us for years. Then you showed up six years ago and slandered Sonya. You made our lives miserable."

Jimmy's face fell, and he sighed heavily. "I know. I've done terrible things. But I've changed, Kendra. I'm sober now, and I've repented. I want to make things right."

My throat tightened. "Right. And I suppose it's just a coincidence that you decided to reach out now—when Sonya and Max are successful, when I'm finally on my feet. What is it, Jimmy? You think you can squeeze some money out of us now that we don't look like struggling kids anymore?"

His expression flickered, just for a second. A flash of something—not quite anger, but not quite denial either. Then it was gone, replaced by something more neutral. "That's not why I'm here."

Before this, I'd only ever seen Mom's old photos of him and that horrible YouTube video. Now, he stood in front of me, flesh and blood, real in a way I wasn't sure I was ready for.

I took him in—the lines on his face, the hesitant way he carried himself, as if expecting rejection at any moment. But I couldn't see past the man who had caused so much pain. Did I own him anything? Even just a moment of my time?

"I need time to think about this," I said finally, my voice softer but still guarded. "I'm not saying I forgive you. But Sonya and I are doing okay now. We've both worked hard. I just don't want any more chaos."

Jimmy nodded and reached into his pocket, pulling out a

folded piece of paper. "Here's my phone number. Call me when you're ready to talk."

I stared at it before finally taking it, the weight of it heavier than the thin slip should have been. A strange mix of emotions churned inside me—anger, sadness, and a tiny, infuriating spark of hope I wanted to crush beneath my heel.

"I'll think about it," I said, my voice steady even as my insides roiled.

He gave me a small, hopeful smile. "Thank you, Kendra. I really appreciate it."

I watched him walk away, the world tilting under my feet. Part of me wanted to rip up the number. The other part wanted to believe people could change. That he could change.

But I wasn't a little girl anymore, and I knew better than to trust blindly.

I exhaled shakily, the crisp October air doing nothing to settle the storm inside me. I should go home, be with Emma. It was Halloween, and I'd promised to spend the evening with her. But the thought of walking through that door, pretending everything was normal, felt impossible.

I wasn't ready to wear a mask of indifference. Not tonight.

My fingers tightened around my phone before I even registered pulling it from my pocket. I needed something solid, something steady to hold onto while my world spun.

I dialed before I could overthink it.

Sinan picked up on the second ring, his voice instantly soothing. "Kendra? I didn't expect to hear from you tonight. Is anything wrong?"

"I need to see you. Can I come over?" My voice wavered, betraying the emotions I was barely holding together.

"Of course. Just be warned—I'm drowning in trick-or-treaters tonight."

The corner of my mouth twitched, but it wasn't quite a smile. "I don't mind."

By the time I reached Sinan's house, the streets were alive with costumed kids darting from porch to porch, their laughter ringing through the crisp night air. The normalcy of it felt surreal, like I was watching from behind a glass pane.

Guilt gnawed at me—I should be home, celebrating with Emma. Instead, I was here, trying to find a way to quiet the noise in my head. I sent her a quick text, letting her know I wouldn't make it, my stomach twisting as I hit send.

Sinan opened the door before I could knock, standing there in a doctor's coat splattered with fake blood.

I blinked, then let out a surprised laugh, the sound breaking through the heavy fog around me. "Nice costume."

"Just wait until you see the reactions," he grinned, holding out a bowl of candy.

The moment felt so absurdly normal that I almost couldn't process it. My world had just been flipped upside down, and here he was, handing out candy like the universe hadn't just played a cruel joke on me.

But maybe that was what I needed. A little normal.

As we passed out candy, I told him everything. The moment Jimmy showed up, the tangled mess of emotions he'd left in his wake, the war inside me over whether to believe he'd changed. Sinan listened, never interrupting, his brow furrowed in concentration. I half-expected him to judge me for even entertaining the conversation, but instead, he handed out candy to a little vampire, then turned back to me with nothing but compassion in his eyes.

"The whole situation sounds complicated," he said finally. "But Kendra, be careful. Sometimes, people have hidden motives when they show up out of the blue like this."

I bit my bottom lip. The same thought had crossed my mind. "You think he might be after something?"

Sinan hesitated, then nodded. "People don't just reappear because they've had a change of heart. Usually, they want something—money, forgiveness, a rewrite of history. Trust isn't a gift you hand over. It's something they have to earn, slowly, one step at a time."

Something in his tone caught me off guard. Not the words, exactly—but the weight behind them.

I studied him. "You're speaking from experience."

He didn't deny it. Just gave me a small, quiet smile. "Yeah. But we don't have to unpack that right now. Tonight's about you."

I wanted to ask more, but the look in his eyes—steady, open, but guarded—told me he wasn't ready. And maybe that was okay. We had time.

"Thank you," I said softly.

His hand found mine under the table, warm and solid. "Anytime."

For a while, the sheer number of trick-or-treaters nearly over-whelmed us. At one point, Sinan nudged me toward the house. "Backup candy's inside. Hurry, or I'll have to start handing out protein bars."

By the time I returned, we were both drowning in a sea of kids demanding candy. I focused on the moment, losing myself in the simplicity of it—the laughter, the delighted shrieks, the feel of Sinan's arm brushing against mine as we worked together.

Eventually, the rush died down, and the quiet settled in, the soft crackling of jack-o'-lantern candles the only sound. Sinan let out a deep breath and wrapped an arm around me, his warmth anchoring me in a way I hadn't realized I needed.

"Thanks for the help tonight," he murmured. "That got intense."

"Glad I came. You were nearly overrun." But the moment of levity faded as my thoughts drifted back to Emma. I'd missed tonight with her. At her age, there was no guarantee she'd go trick-or-treating again.

Sinan must have sensed my shift because he pressed a soft kiss to my forehead. "You'll make it up to her."

I let out a slow breath, nodding. "I will."

The night air was crisp, the sky a deep indigo, and for the first time since Jimmy had appeared, I felt like I could breathe again.

Sinan tightened his hold on me, his voice quieter now. "I think you're incredibly brave for even talking to Jimmy."

I swallowed hard. "I don't know if I should even talk to him." The thought of opening myself up to more disappointment felt like walking into a storm without an umbrella.

"Take your time. You don't owe him anything."

His words settled over me, comforting but not erasing the guilt.

I'd make it right with Emma. I'd find a way to show her that missing tonight didn't mean she wasn't my priority.

But for now, this was where I needed to be.

BRIDGES, BOUNDARIES, AND BONDING

Sinan

I sat in my office at Pittsburgh Hospital, the hum of activity in the hallways a familiar soundtrack. My office was a modern, bright space with big windows showcasing the city's skyline. From my desk, I could see the iconic bridges that connected Pittsburgh's neighborhoods—structures that, until recently, had been just another part of the cityscape. But now, thanks to Kendra and her work, those bridges felt more personal, like they carried a piece of my heart along with all that steel and concrete.

My office was a mess of medical journals, reports, and a half-empty coffee mug. Standard issue for a doctor. But my thoughts kept drifting to tonight's date with Kendra, a much more appealing prospect than the mountain of paperwork in front of me.

I flipped open a planning document for the Steeltown Bridge repairs. What was supposed to be a routine task had turned into something more significant. I had volunteered to be part of the bridge impact team, partly to spend more time with Kendra. But now, it felt like a way to prove to myself—and maybe to her—that I was serious about this.

As I skimmed through the document, something caught my

eye. The proposed changes to ambulance routes were, to put it mildly, a disaster waiting to happen. The idea of ambulances stuck in traffic while patients waited for care made my stomach twist. This wasn't just a minor inconvenience; it could turn into a real crisis.

I scribbled down notes, my handwriting growing more impatient with each concern. This needed to be fixed, and fast. The bridge repairs were important, but not at the cost of patient care. With Kendra involved in this project, it felt even more urgent to get it right.

Taking a quick break, I turned to my email. The usual flood of messages awaited, but one subject line made my heart skip a beat: "Coming to Town - Urgent." It was from Miranda.

I hesitated before clicking on it, bracing myself for whatever drama she was about to bring. Just seeing her name was enough to stir up a mix of emotions. With a deep breath, I opened the email and began to read.

Sinan,

I hope you're doing well. I wanted to let you know that I'll be in Pittsburgh soon. We should meet up—there's a lot we need to discuss.

By the way, your mother, Aylin, called me again. She seemed really concerned about our breakup, but I reassured her that we parted ways because we were just too different. I didn't mention anything about the drug charges, of course. I still can't believe how stupid I was to take such risks.

It's clear your mother still cares a lot about me, and I can't help but wonder if I should finally tell her everything. She might be willing to help with my legal issues, especially since I'm going through such a difficult time.

Looking forward to seeing you.

— Miranda

I stared at the screen, frustration bubbling up. My mother had contacted Miranda again? Just when I thought things couldn't get more complicated. The mention of the drug charges was like a jab in the ribs—Miranda knew exactly how to push my buttons. I could almost hear her voice, dripping with faux concern, as she laid the groundwork for more manipulation.

Why couldn't my mother just respect my boundaries? I had made it clear I didn't want her involved, yet here she was, stirring the pot. Guilt gnawed at me—I hadn't been completely honest with her about the breakup, but Miranda's legal issues were a disaster I refused to let spill over onto my family. Still, I couldn't shake the worry that my mother might feel sorry for Miranda and offer to help.

I glanced at the clock—2:20 P.M. here and 9:20 P.M. in Istanbul. I needed to nip this in the bud. Grabbing my phone, I dialed my *anne*, pacing the office as the phone rang. Each ring ratcheted up my frustration until, finally, she picked up.

"Sinan, my dear, how are you?" My mother's voice was warm, but there was an undercurrent of concern I knew all too well.

"We need to talk, Mother," I said, struggling to keep my voice even.

"Don't use that English word. I'm your *anne*."

"Sorry, *Anne*," I corrected, pinching the bridge of my nose. "But this is important. I asked you not to contact Miranda."

There was a brief pause before she responded. "I know, but you never said why. Sinan, I just wanted to understand what happened. She was part of our lives, then she was gone. You never explained. Besides," her tone sharpened, "I want grandchildren, and you're not getting any younger."

I clenched my jaw. "*Anne*, it is *not* your place to contact my ex-fiancée," I snapped, frustration bubbling over. "You need to stay out of my personal affairs."

"Do not raise your voice at me, Sinan," she replied, a quiet reprimand laced with hurt. "You shut me out. You're the only son I have left now, and I can't help but worry about you."

The reminder of Barry hit like a gut punch, but I forced myself to stay on track. "Communicate? *Anne*, I've told you everything you need to know. Miranda and I broke up. It was difficult, and I asked you to respect that."

"I just want what's best for you," she insisted. "And I want to see you settled, with a family of your own."

A bitter laugh nearly escaped me. "That's exactly what I wanted too. But I chose wrong."

I raked a hand through my hair, the old embarrassment creeping in. How naive had I been? I'd spent years believing Miranda was my partner, someone I could trust. We'd been interns together in Chicago, both running on caffeine and adrenaline, pushing through endless shifts. I could still remember the moment I'd fallen for her—when she'd sat with an elderly patient after a rough surgery, holding his hand long after visiting hours ended, making sure he wasn't alone. That was the woman I thought I was going to marry.

But that version of Miranda had disappeared somewhere along the way. Or maybe she'd never really existed at all. Maybe I'd been blind to the signs—to the way she thrived in chaos, how she always managed to shift blame, how she had a knack for making me feel guilty even when she was the one at fault.

I'd been played. And worse, I'd let myself be played.

The thought made my stomach turn. I refused to let my mother pull me back into that mess.

Taking a deep breath, I shifted gears. "If you want to focus on family, think about Emma. She could use more support, and she hasn't seen you since the funeral. But please, *Anne*, stay out of my relationships. Trust me to handle my life."

A long pause. Then, finally, her voice softened. "Alright, Sinan. I'll try to stay out of it. But remember, I only want the best for you."

I sighed, the exhaustion settling deep. "I know, *Anne*," I said, my anger giving way to something more tired, more resigned. "But I need space to figure things out on my own."

"Of course," she murmured. "Take care, Sinan."

"You too. Goodbye."

I hung up and let my head fall back against the chair, the tension in my shoulders refusing to ease. Had I made the right call, not telling her the full truth about Miranda? Maybe. Maybe not.

I could have told her about the legal issues, about Miranda's recklessness, about how deep the mess really went. But then my mother would *have* to fix it. She'd reach out, get involved, try to help Miranda in some misguided attempt to make things right—for me, for the life she thought I should have had.

No. That door needed to stay closed.

I exhaled sharply, rubbing my temples before opening my laptop again. Miranda's email sat there, a weight I wasn't ready to deal with. But I clicked on it anyway, reading her plea for money, for another favor.

The guilt gnawed at me, but I shut it down. I wasn't responsible for her anymore. She needed to clean up her own mistakes.

And I was done being played.

I began typing my response, keeping it short:

Subject: Boundaries

Miranda,

Thanks for letting me know about my mother contacting you. However, I need to be very clear: we should not meet while you're in town. It's important for both of us to move on and focus on our own lives.

Additionally, please do not attempt to involve my parents in your legal or personal matters. They are not a resource for you, and I will not tolerate any attempts to manipulate their kindness.

I hope you can understand the importance of respecting these boundaries.

Best,

Sinan

As I hit send, a sense of relief washed over me, though a hint of tension still lingered. Miranda was in my past, but her shadow loomed. I needed to be honest with Kendra, but without dragging her into this mess.

Sitting back, I reflected on the secrets I was keeping—the complexities with my mother, Miranda's manipulations, and the challenges of keeping my relationship with Kendra under wraps. It was all starting to feel like too much. I realized I needed to simplify, to focus on what truly mattered.

Kendra was one of those things. She brought light and warmth into my life, a refreshing contrast to the chaos. Unlike Miranda, who had always been obsessed with status and wealth, Kendra valued family and genuine connections. She was selfless, caring, and everything I admired.

Despite my concerns, I couldn't wait to see her tonight. Amid the chaos, she was my beacon of calm. The upcoming Thanksgiving celebration at Don Ross's place loomed large, with its own set of complications. But for now, I wanted to focus on the peace and happiness she brought into my life.

2 1

TURKEY TROUBLES

Kendra

Sonya steered the car up Don Ross's long driveway, Mara in the back seat, as we took in the extravagant holiday display. A gardener arranged silk poinsettias among the ornamental cabbages in massive urns, while another man strung lights around a towering spruce, prepping it to be the lawn's star attraction. Candy cane lights lined the driveway, adding a whimsical touch to the stately residence.

Don, Max and Ford's father—and Mara and Sonya's *very* well-to-do father-in-law—never did anything halfway, and the house ahead of us proved it.

When we reached the house—a *literal* estate—I couldn't help but gape. Wreaths with red ribbons adorned every window, and a massive golden-bowed wreath dominated the front door. As we got out, an animatronic Santa near the steps boomed, *"Ho, ho, ho!"* making me yelp.

"Well, if the North Pole ever needs a backup location, I think Don just applied," Mara deadpanned, giving robotic Santa a sarcastic salute.

"He really went all out," Sonya said, her voice warm with

134

amusement. "It's festive, though. My fifth-grade class would love this."

Don swung the door open, grinning. "Like the Santa? Works better than a doorbell." He took a bag from Sonya, pecking her on the cheek. "This is perfect. I provide the house, and you three do all the work."

"If we left it to you, we'd be eating something with a brand logo stamped on the foil," Mara quipped. "Sponsored by Stark Industries."

Inside, the warmth and scent of pine and cinnamon wrapped around us. The grand foyer's twinkling lights and garland-draped staircase looked straight out of a Hallmark movie.

Sonya led us straight to the kitchen, which was *ridiculously* well-equipped—marble counters, gleaming appliances, more cabinet space than I'd ever seen, and a butler's pantry. We got to work: Mara tackled pies, Sonya handled stuffing, and I took on the turkey.

Just as I was about to place it in the roasting pan, my hand slipped. The turkey *thudded* to the floor and skidded across the sleek tile.

"Oh no!" I gasped.

Mara sprang into action. "That turkey just tried to speedrun Thanksgiving. Five-second rule. Achievement unlocked."

Sonya knelt beside her, spritzing cleaner like a seasoned veteran. "Don't worry. Bacteria don't stand a chance against 325 degrees and a teacher's stubborn determination."

Once the turkey was safely roasting, I focused on *not* causing any more kitchen disasters. The scent of baking pies and spices filled the air, making it feel even more festive.

Santa's "Ho, ho, ho!" echoed from outside, signaling the arrival of the rest of the family. Then the front door opened, and voices spilled in—Max, Ford, Emma, Don. And then *his* voice. Sinan.

A thrill ran through me. Game on.

The excited bark of a small dog followed, and moments later, Mara's little dog, Zephyr, burst into the kitchen, his nose twitching as he tried to soak in all the delicious smells.

"Who's my good boy?" Mara cooed, dropping a cube of cheese for him. Zephyr devoured it in a flash before darting back to Emma, who scooped him up, much to his delight, because that gave him access to her ears, his favorite body part.

Sonya and Mara greeted their husbands with kisses, while Sinan and I exchanged a quick glance, both striving for casual. The challenge? Pretending we were just acquaintances, especially in this warm, family-filled setting.

Emma bounced over, eyes bright. "Aunt Kendra, did you help with the pies? I *can't wait* to try them!"

I ruffled her hair. "We've got pecan, pumpkin, and apple. Which is your favorite?"

"Pumpkin, obviously," she replied, smoothing her hair and slipping into that newly adopted teenage tone I wished she'd never picked up. Then, catching herself, softened. "I mean, they all sound great."

Maybe the hair-ruffling was too much—*note to self, middle schooler, tread carefully.*

Sonya gave Emma a gentle nudge. "Would you mind checking the dining room, kiddo? Make sure everything's set for dinner."

Emma rolled her eyes, but the smile betrayed her fondness. "On it."

We were just settling back into kitchen prep when Santa's *"Ho, ho, ho!"* rang again, followed by Don's voice. "Surprise, everyone! You won't believe who's here!"

A tall, devastatingly handsome man strolled in. My heart stuttered.

Bradley Hunter. *THE* British movie star.

"Bradley, welcome to our humble Thanksgiving," Don declared, grinning. "Everyone, this is Bradley Hunter. He's in town filming and graciously accepted my invitation."

Bradley flashed a devastatingly smooth smile. "Hello, everyone. Thanks for having me. This sure beats dinner at a restaurant."

Max and Ford, clearly already acquainted, introduced their wives before Don turned to me.

Bradley's gaze lingered. "And who might this lovely lady be?"

Heat crept up my neck. "I'm Kendra, Sonya's sister."

His grin widened. "A pleasure, Kendra. Looking forward to my first real Thanksgiving with such delightful company."

Out of the corner of my eye, I caught Sinan's jaw tighten ever so slightly.

Mara, Sonya, and I turned back to finish dinner. When we finally carried the food to the dining room, we shuffled around choosing seats. By some miracle, I landed directly across from Sinan.

Our gazes locked, something unspoken humming between us.

Then Bradley slid into the seat beside me, leaning in with an easy grin. "So, Kendra, what do you do when you're not dazzling Thanksgiving guests?"

I hesitated for half a second. Civil engineer. I always said it like it meant something—which it did—but sitting across from a movie star at a mansion owned by a film mogul, with two sisters married into Hollywood royalty and my secret boyfriend basically dripping in generational wealth, it suddenly felt... small. Like I was the kid who wandered into the wrong room at a grown-up party and decided to wing it.

I forced a smile and went with my standard response. "I'm a civil engineer. Right now, I'm overseeing bridge repairs."

His eyes lit up. "Impressive. You'll have to tell me more. I'm still getting the hang of Thanksgiving—seems like an excuse to overeat."

Under the table, I felt a foot nudge mine. Assuming it was Sinan, I nudged back playfully.

But when I glanced at him with a grin, he looked... confused.

My stomach dropped. If that wasn't Sinan's foot, then—

I turned *just* as Bradley smirked.

"Oh, Kendra," he murmured, clearly entertained, "are you flirting with me?"

My face burned. "I—uh—I thought you were…the dog."

Bradley chuckled, eyes twinkling. "Best mix-up I've ever experienced."

Sinan's grip on his fork tightened.

To salvage my dignity, I forced a grin. "Well, Bradley, I usually *charge* for footsie, but for you? It's on the house."

Laughter rippled around the table. Bradley leaned in, clearly enjoying himself.

"So, Kendra," he mused, "tell me more about these bridges. Sounds fascinating."

I glanced at Sinan, who looked like he wanted to *storm the gates of Troy*. I needed to shift the focus.

"It's mostly technical," I said breezily, trying to play it cool. "Definitely not Hollywood material."

I could already hear my inner critic whispering, *Or dinner party material either.*

"Nonsense." Bradley winked. "A movie about bridge engineers could be a hit. Especially with someone as captivating as you in the lead."

Before Sinan could respond, Ford suddenly spoke up, amusement dancing in his eyes.

"So, Kendra," he called from across the table, "Max tells me he thinks you're seeing someone. What's with all the secrecy?"

I shot Max a look, but he just smirked.

"I *cannot* imagine why I'd want to keep my personal life… personal," I said sweetly.

Ford wasn't about to let it slide. "Come on, Kendra. We're family. You can tell us. Who's the lucky guy?"

Mara jumped in, trying to help. "Ford, give her a break. Maybe she just wants some privacy."

Max, enjoying the chaos, decided to stir the pot further. "Why's everyone focused on Kendra? What about Sinan? *He* admitted to sneaking around with some nurse."

Sinan's gaze flicked to me before he forced a casual smile. "It's nothing serious yet. Just… getting to know her."

Ford wasn't about to let up. "Come on, Sinan. What's she like?"

Before he could answer, Don leaned in with curiosity, his gaze shifting between me and Sinan.

Abort mission.

"I've got a better idea," I cut in. "How about a Hollywood story, Don? I bet you have a million."

Don grinned. "Alright, alright. I'll save you this time, Sinan. Let me tell you about the time I almost got thrown out of a premiere…"

Laughter spread through the room, tension fading as Don launched into a lively story about a famous director, a wardrobe malfunction, and an irate security guard.

Later, as laughter rippled around the table and Emma launched into an enthusiastic retelling of how Zephyr had "almost" caught a squirrel last week, I found myself leaning back in my chair, a little stunned by how… okay everything felt. This house, this family, this chaos—I wasn't born into any of it. I didn't come with the right pedigree or a last name that meant anything outside of Sewickley. But no one seemed to care.

Sonya nudged the pie plate toward me, her smile soft and familiar. "Last slice is yours. Mom's rule still stands—even if we're in a mansion."

Mara leaned over and muttered, "If this was a Marvel crossover, Bradley would be the charming villain in disguise."

I snorted into my napkin. Sinan caught my eye across the table and mouthed, *You okay?* And I was. Maybe I didn't always feel like I belonged in a room like this. But tonight, no one was questioning whether I did—except maybe me.

Bradley leaned closer. "You know, Kendra," he murmured, "I'd love to hear more about your bridges. Maybe over dinner? I'll be in town filming for a few more weeks."

Sinan's expression darkened slightly, but I smiled, keeping my tone light. "That's kind of you, Bradley, but I'm more of a *dinner with friends* kind of girl."

Bradley chuckled, undeterred. "Well, if you change your mind…"

I shot Sinan a reassuring glance.

This was *definitely* going to be an interesting evening.

2 2

JEALOUSY AND JITTERS

SINAN

Watching Bradley Hunter flirt with Kendra was like slow torture. Every lingering glance, every too-charming laugh, every ridiculous line—my jaw clenched tighter each time. The man needed a scriptwriter because his attempts at charm were as subtle as a sledgehammer.

Kendra wasn't encouraging him, but she also wasn't shutting him down outright. Not that Bradley seemed to care. Some men mistook politeness for interest, and he was one of them.

Dinner became an exercise in restraint. I kept stealing glances at Kendra, hoping to catch her eye, to share a moment of mutual understanding. But she kept her expression neutral, calmly navigating the increasingly absurd situation like she was defusing a bomb made of napkins and charm. I admired that control, even if it made me want to drag Bradley outside for a conversation about boundaries.

As the meal wrapped up, Sonya shifted the conversation. "Should we have pie now or let things settle?"

"Let's wait," Don said, leaning back in his chair. "Have another glass of champagne. Relax. Take a nap. It's Thanksgiving. No rush."

"Except dishes," Mara pointed out. "They won't wash themselves."

We started clearing the table, and I was relieved when Bradley got distracted by his own ego.

"I've been perfecting this dance move for my next film," he announced. "Took me ages, but I nailed it. Want a preview?"

Mara and Sonya exchanged grins. "Absolutely," Mara called.

I leaned back, half-hoping he'd embarrass himself.

"Prepare to be dazzled!" Bradley declared, striking a pose and steadying himself with theatrical flair. One foot lifted, a spin initiated—then his toe snagged the edge of the tablecloth. Time slowed as glasses tipped, silverware clattered, and champagne arced through the air. Plates slid off the table like falling dominos, crashing to the floor in a chorus of chaos.

Silence.

Then laughter erupted. Bradley, sprawled in the wreckage, grinned sheepishly. "Guess I need more practice. Please tell me no one was filming that."

Kendra and I exchanged a look, a private moment of shared amusement. At least the guy had humility.

As the cleanup began, Sonya handed me a broom. "Sinan, sweep up the broken bits. Bradley, sop up the liquids. Kendra, can you help with the kitchen?"

"Sure thing," she replied, carefully picking up the intact dishes and following me into the kitchen, which was already a whirlwind of activity with everyone trying to clean up and pack away leftovers.

I was reaching for a towel when I brushed too close to the gas burner. Within seconds, flames shot up from the fabric.

"Whoa!" I yelped, yanking my hand back.

Kendra reacted instantly, grabbing my wrist and shoving the towel under the sink. Water hissed as the flames died. "Hey, hot stuff, be careful there," she teased, eyes sparkling.

"Didn't mean to add to the show," I muttered, drying my hands with a fresh towel.

"At least it wasn't the turkey," she quipped.

Zephyr, Mara's ever-enthusiastic Papillon, darted between our legs, searching for handouts. I maneuvered around him, but he jumped up at precisely the wrong moment. My elbow jolted, and the container of gravy I'd been holding splashed down my shirt.

Mara rushed over, scooping up the guilty party. "Zephyr! I'm so sorry, Sinan."

I laughed, shaking my head. "Thanksgiving charm at its finest."

Kendra handed me another towel. "Let's get you cleaned up."

As she dabbed at the stain, warmth sparked between us. Her fingers brushed against my stomach, lingering a second too long before she caught herself. Our eyes met—too much, too obvious. I forced a chuckle, stepping back, suddenly aware that Don was watching from the doorway.

He tilted his head. "You planning to wear gravy the rest of the night, Sinan?"

"Considering making it my signature look," I deadpanned.

Don chuckled, then waved me toward the hall. "Come on. I've got a fresh shirt upstairs. Max left one here that should fit you."

A few minutes later, I returned in a crisp navy button-down, the faint smell of cedar clinging to the fabric. Slightly too snug in the shoulders, but worlds better than walking around like a walking leftovers platter.

When I reentered the kitchen, Kendra gave me an amused once-over. "Much better. You wear 'not covered in gravy' well."

"I try," I said, tugging at the collar, but Don's curious gaze was still on us.

Hoping for an escape from scrutiny, I drifted toward Don's grand living room but he followed. So much for avoiding scrutiny.

"So, Sinan," he began, settling against the fireplace mantel in a practiced power move. "You haven't brought anyone special around since Miranda. What's the story?"

I chuckled, attempting nonchalance. "Busy. Not much time for dating."

Don lifted a skeptical brow. "What about that nurse?"

Before I could formulate an escape, Emma strolled in, innocent curiosity on her face. "Uncle Sin, why haven't you had a girlfriend since Miranda?"

One by one, the others followed. Great. Now I was an after-dinner interrogation subject.

I hesitated. "Well, Emma, I've been seeing someone. It's just… not serious yet."

Her eyes widened. "Who is she?"

Ford and Max exchanged knowing looks. Don's smirk deepened. Kendra, off to the side, sipped her drink like she was contemplating running for the door.

"It's, um, someone I'm getting to know. We're taking things slow," I hedged, hoping Emma wouldn't push.

Sonya, ever the hero, stepped in. "Alright, everyone, let's give Sinan a break. This is why people dread Thanksgiving—prying questions from nosy relatives. That and politics can clear a room faster than dry turkey."

That got some laughs, and the conversation shifted, much to my relief. I shot Sonya a grateful look. At least someone had my back.

As the evening wound down, we moved on to dessert. The apple pie was a masterpiece—flaky, spiced to perfection.

Don raised his glass. "To family, friends, and unexpected surprises." His gaze flickered between me and Kendra. "And to the new relationships that make life interesting."

I worked hard to keep my expression neutral, but I felt Kendra tense beside me. We clinked glasses, sharing a quick glance, neither of us willing to give anything away.

Bradley, finally sensing the night was over, grinned at Kendra. "If you ever need an escort to another family dinner, you know where to find me."

I resisted the urge to groan.

"Thanks," Kendra replied, voice laced with equal parts amusement and exhaustion. "I'll keep that in mind."

As we gathered our coats and said our goodbyes, Max clapped me on the back. "Great having you here, Sinan. Next time, maybe bring that mystery woman of yours."

I chuckled, keeping my answer vague. "We'll see, Max. We'll see."

I glanced at Kendra one last time, catching the private smile we shared. This wasn't just sneaking around anymore. Sooner or later, we'd have to tell them. But for tonight, our secret was still ours.

23

FAMILY TIES AND FRAYED EDGES

Kendra

December should've been crisp and frosty, the kind of morning where my breath curled in the air and the ground crunched underfoot as I took my Saturday morning walk. Instead, the world felt out of sync—warm, damp, and thick with the scent of rain-soaked leaves. If it weren't for the twinkling lights in shop windows and the holiday displays popping up around town, I could've sworn it was early autumn, not three weeks before Christmas.

Jimmy's name flashed on my phone again—just a single message: "Still hoping we can meet up soon. No pressure." I didn't reply. I really didn't want to think about him right now. His messages weren't frantic or aggressive. Not yet. Just persistent. But something in the timing felt off. Why now? Why after a lifetime of ignoring us?

By the time I got back, the rich scent of coffee greeted me—courtesy of Sonya and Max, already deep in conversation at the kitchen island.

I barely made it to the coffee pot before Emma barreled into the room, eyes bright. "Aunt Kendra, guess what? Grandma Aylin and Grandpa Cem finally got their visas! They're coming to visit in the spring!"

"That's fantastic, Emma!" I matched her excitement, even as a knot formed in my stomach. Meeting Sinan's parents—who still had no idea I existed—was no longer just a vague possibility. It was officially on the horizon. No pressure or anything.

Breakfast flew by in a blur of Emma's enthusiastic itinerary planning. Then Max kissed Sonya goodbye, grabbed his keys, and called out, "Ready, kiddo?"

Emma snatched up her backpack. "Bye, Aunt Kendra! See you later!"

With them gone, the kitchen settled into a brief lull until Sonya gave me *the look*. The one all teachers perfected.

"So," she said, too casually, "where exactly have you been sneaking off to in the evenings?"

"Scuba training," I said automatically.

Her eyebrow arched. "Scuba diving? In *December*?"

"Heated pool at the university," I shot back, pouring my coffee.

She sipped hers, unimpressed. "You do realize I'm your sister, not an auditor. If something's up, you can tell me."

I hesitated. Dodging Sonya's questions was exhausting, and maybe it was time to be honest—at least about one thing.

"Actually, I need to tell you about Jimmy," I admitted. "He tracked me down at work."

Her eyes widened. "What? When? And why didn't you tell me?"

"Halloween," I said with a wince. "That's why I bailed that night. I came home, saw you guys all happy, and… I just couldn't bring it up."

Sonya's face darkened. "Did he want money?"

"Surprisingly, no. Just… to reconnect. But the whole thing felt off. I haven't been in touch with him since."

Her jaw tightened. "We don't need him in our lives, Kendra. He humiliated me, and he doesn't get a second chance."

I nodded, the weight in my chest easing slightly. Still, a part of me wanted to get to know him. Learn something about the man who'd contributed half my genetic material.

She squeezed my hand. "If he shows up again, you tell me. We're in this together."

I hesitated, then nodded. "Will do."

Her expression softened, but only slightly. "Now, if you'll excuse me, I have a classroom of fifth-graders to wrangle. They might be easier than this conversation."

At my noontime yoga class, I tried to focus on my breathing, but Misha caught me slipping. We were supposed to be in *Child's Pose*, but I'd somehow ended up in what could only be described as *Existential Crisis Pose*.

"Hey, you okay?" they whispered, balancing effortlessly in Warrior II. "You've been out of it all class."

I grimaced. "It's Sinan… all my self-doubt about him is spinning around up here," I said, tapping my temple.

"When you talk about him, you normally get this goofy smile," Misha whispered back. "But right now, you look like you just realized you hit 'reply all' on a rant about your boss."

I sighed. "We come from such different worlds. He's got this fancy apartment with a skyline view and a wine fridge. I used to think Olive Garden was high-end dining."

Misha smirked. "You *are* a sucker for unlimited breadsticks."

"I'm serious," I muttered. "I keep wondering if I actually belong in his world or if I'm just waiting for someone to notice I don't."

Misha held a plank like it was nothing. "I used to think that about my ex—the lawyer with an actual *butler*?"

I blinked. "I forgot about Butler Guy."

"Right? I stressed over everything—like, do I know which fork to use? Am I pronouncing '*charcuterie*' right?" They snorted. "But none of it mattered. What mattered was whether we *worked* together. And we didn't, but not because of my background. I spent too much time worrying about *fitting in* instead of asking if I even liked his world."

That hit me square in the gut.

Misha nudged my foot. "So maybe ask yourself: do you actually *want* his world, or are you too busy worrying whether it wants you?"

***

Jimmy: "I'll keep trying. We're family. That has to mean something."

A shiver ran down my spine. I didn't like being the focus of Jimmy's attention. Especially after so many years of complete and total silence. He had to want something. But what? He'd ignored me for most of my life. Why now? A single line like that—*We're family*—shouldn't make my stomach twist, but it did. He wasn't reaching out. He was circling.

When I arrived at Sinan's, he greeted me with a warm smile, his home a welcoming cocoon—firelight flickering, the scent of chai lingering in the air.

I plopped onto the sofa beside him, resting my head on his shoulder. "So," I said, tracing circles on his sleeve, "now that we've survived my family, I think it's time to tackle yours." I conveniently left out Jimmy. The man wasn't *family*.

He chuckled. "You think you're ready for Aylin and Cem? My mom will probably skip dessert and go straight to the interrogation."

I smirked. "Should I prepare a PowerPoint? Maybe a family tree?"

He kissed my temple. "You joke, but my dad's family tree is practically a national archive."

That got my attention. "Oh?"

Sinan leaned back, amusement flickering in his gaze. "His ancestors can be traced back to *Mimar Sinan*."

I blinked. "As in… *the architect*?"

"*The architect*," he confirmed. "My dad's family is full of engineers and architects. It's basically a dynasty. He'll love that you're a civil engineer."

I let out a low whistle. "And here I thought *you* were the impressive one."

"Oh, I still am," he teased. "But yeah, even my mom was a little intimidated at first. My father's family had big expectations. She doubled down on tradition to prove she belonged."

The weight of his words settled over me. "Should *I* be worried?"

Sinan squeezed my hand. "They'll have concerns. My mom values tradition. When Miranda made it clear she wouldn't quit her job as a doctor, my mom started emailing her links to nanny agencies."

I cringed. "Yikes."

"She plans *ahead*," he said wryly. "But as much as she's rigid, she's got a soft spot too. It just takes time to get there. My dad? He'll love you immediately."

I exhaled. "That's something, at least."

Sinan brushed his fingers down my back. "Hey. We'll figure this out. Together."

"So," I said slowly, "I think it's time for us to stop sneaking around. No more lying about scuba lessons or pretend work emergencies."

He grinned. "I'm with you. No more hiding. Thanksgiving was unbearable."

We shared a smile, and I felt my confidence grow.

Then his fingers trailed lower, and his voice dropped. "So, now that we're officially done hiding... does that mean I can kiss you properly?"

I tilted my head, teasing. "You mean you *haven't* been?"

Our lips met, slow at first, then hungry. The world outside shrank, leaving only the warmth of his hands, the press of his body against mine. I laid back on the Turkish rug, pulling him with me.

Just as I reached for his belt buckle, a faint buzzing broke through the moment.

I stilled. "What's that?"

We turned toward the window—and my jaw dropped.

A drone, camera aimed *directly* at us, hovered outside.

"Are you *kidding* me?" I groaned, scrambling to my feet. "I'm ready to go public, but this isn't what I meant!"

Sinan yanked me up with him, half-laughing. "Well. That's a first."

"Quick," I hissed. "Get out of sight!"

We darted to the kitchen and crouched behind the counter, breathless, equal parts stunned and amused.

"Next time," I muttered, "we *close the blinds.*"

Sinan peeked over the counter. "Good idea. But at least we've got a story for our kids about 'the surveillance drone that ruined the mood.'"

I rolled my eyes. "Not a PG story. So… close the blinds?"

He smirked. "How about upstairs?"

A thrill ran through me. "I *like* the way you think, Dr. Bachar. And this time? We *definitely* close the blinds."

As we crossed the room, he hit a switch, and the blinds hummed shut, wrapping us in soft, private darkness.

He took my hand, his gaze warm. "No more hiding, right?"

I nodded, the intimacy of our own little world settling around us. "No more hiding—except from drones."

Our lips met again, this time unhurried. As he led me toward the stairs, the weight of our secret romance lifted, leaving behind nothing but anticipation.

We stumbled upstairs, our movements urgent. I'd gotten glimpses of his bedroom over the past few months—first during my brief tour, where I'd witnessed its sleek, modern elegance firsthand, and later through video calls that had given me a more intimate view of the space. Now, those crisp white sheets I'd fantasized about peeked from beneath the gray coverlet, teasing like a courtesan revealing a hint of décolletage. But I barely had time to take them in before Sin swept me into his arms, and we fell onto the bed together.

"Wait one minute," I protested, gesturing toward the curtain-less windows.

"Reflecting coating. No one can see in."

Relieved, I rolled to face him. When our eyes locked, his gaze was full of scorching heat. And I was kindling bursting into flame.

We came together, our lips crashing into each other as we tasted and plunged, desperate for each other. Yes, we'd kissed before this, but there'd always been that mental stop sign that had kept us from going too far. I'd been so attracted to him that I hadn't trusted myself to come close to that barrier.

Not anymore. Now I pulled Sin in, sliding my hand, lowering it far enough to cup that gorgeous ass I'd been coveting for months, then gliding up again to feel the ripple of his firm muscles as he explored my body as well. This was my new amusement park, and I was thrilled with every inch of it.

Moonlight spilled across us on the bed, and his brown eyes seemed to glow as he looked into my eyes. He pulled away for a moment and ran his gaze up and down my body. "I've been imag-ining this moment for so long. I want to do so much with you. Have you under me, over me, riding me."

I let out a shuddering sigh. "All of that sounds perfect. All tonight?"

He gave a wicked grin. "All tonight."

His eyes were lasered in on mine. I reached to unzip his pants, but he was faster, climbing to his feet, snatching off my shoes, and making my jeans disappear with one smooth tug. When he had me stripped down to just my black lace bra and panties, he stopped to savor the view. "Do you always wear matching sets?"

I gave a slow smile, pleased to have pleased him. "Whenever I know I'll see you, I do."

He let out a moan. "I love that. I love that even though we agreed to wait, you still wanted me so much that you dressed for me."

"I've been dreaming about this moment." I glanced down at my panties. "I want you to finish undressing me."

With a delighted smile, he pulled down on the sides of my panties, slowly dragging them down my legs until he finally dropped them on the floor. He pulled me upright and then undid my bra. It joined its mate on the floor, and I loved seeing those bits of satin and lace lying together in this masculine room.

He spread my knees apart to step between them, but I pulled them shut. "No fair. I get to see the goods too." I waved my hand imperiously. "Go on. Strip, Dr. Bachar."

With a smoldering gaze that raked down my naked body, he stripped away that crisp cotton shirt and jeans revealing the boxer briefs I'd somehow known he'd be wearing. Black, snug, and hugging him perfectly, even down to the tented bulge that left little to my imagination I didn't get to admire the look for long though, because an instant later, his briefs were gone as well, his cock springing free.

He moved to his nightstand and quickly sheathed himself in a condom before returning to me. I was so ready for him now. Waiting had been the right choice for us, but that hadn't made the wait any easier.

I fully expected him to settle in between my thighs, but he surprised me by lying down next to me. He began kissing me. Caressing me. He kissed me everywhere but where I needed him most. When I reached for him, he pushed my hands away, teasing me with a murmured, "Wait."

After another minute, he finally zeroed in on that part. I thought my head might explode when I felt his fingers graze my mound. I was so sensitive and wet that his soft touch nearly had me bucking off the bed. "I like that," he said with the low rumble of a laugh. "I like how sensitive you are."

"I like it too," was all I could manage to say.

That low, rumbling laugh came again as he propped himself on one elbow and then shifted a bit so he could lower his mouth to my clit. He flicked his tongue over it, tasting me and making my back arch once again. He pressed a flat palm to my belly, his tongue working me into a frenzy, bringing me to the edge. But then he hesitated, lifting his head. "Want me to keep going, or should we change things up?"

I blinked, then blurted, "I want to feel you inside me."

"Are you okay starting on top?" he asked.

I didn't answer, I simply flew upright, pressed him down onto his back, straddled him, and positioned myself above him. I waited there a moment with my hands braced on his shoulders, staring down into his gorgeous blue eyes. I watched his reaction as I sank down, wet and ready. The joy and bliss on his face was perfection. Everything I could have hoped for. And the feel of him inside me—everything I'd hoped for.

I rode him. Rode his fantastic cock. And oh, my, did it ever fit me to perfection, as if custom created, just for me.

His grip tightened on my hips. "You look so incredibly sexy. Your head tossed back, riding me just the way you like it."

"So do you," I whispered back, breathlessly.

He grabbed my hips even tighter, his grip firm, pleasure welling inside me. When his fingers found my clit, I shattered. Every cell exploding in an instant. I could barely think, but even through that fog, I sensed he was right there with me, pressing his hips up high to fill me—so high that he lifted me off the bed. I had to grip his shoulders to keep from falling off that wild, driven man. I held tight, riding him, riding our orgasm.

His thrusting slowed, but pleasure still pulsed through me. I collapsed onto his chest, his warmth grounding me.

Sin wrapped his arms around me, holding me close, then he rolled us to one side and pulled me to him. We curled up together, my back to his front, both breathing hard as we recovered.

He pressed his lips to my neck. "That was phenomenal."

"Agreed," I managed to say, although my throat was dry.

"Water?" he asked, reaching for a cup on his nightstand.

I drank greedily, and then we curled up with one another. His hand began roaming over my hips, up my side, then cupping my breasts. Even though my body still thrummed with satisfaction, his touch sent shivers of aching need to my core and made me crave him once again. I rolled onto my back and reached for him.

"Your list included under you, over you, and riding you," I said, my voice husky with desire. "We've checked off two of those. Care to tackle the third?"

"As you wish. But I've decided to add a few more to that list."

"Oh? Such as?"

"Standing behind you. Kneeling in front of you. Reverse cowgirl. Against the wall. On top of the table. In the shower."

A slow grin spread across my face. "I like the way you think, Dr. Bachar. We should get started on that list. I have to teach a dive lesson at the university pool early tomorrow morning though, so I'm not sure how many we'll be able to check off the list this evening."

"In that case," he said, his eyes gleaming at the challenge, "we'd better get started." With that, he spread my knees wide and moved between them.

24

LOVE, LAUGHTER, AND LOGISTICS

SINAN

I awoke in the middle of the night to find Kendra nestled against my side, her breath soft and rhythmic, her arm draped over me. After that last round, we'd both drifted off, thoroughly spent and entirely content. A grin tugged at my lips as I watched her, feeling the warmth of her presence seep into me. Gently, I brushed a strand of hair away from her face, marveling at how this initial spark between us had ignited into something real.

Her eyes fluttered open, and when she saw me watching her, a slow smile crept across her face. "Hi there."

"Hi there," I murmured, brushing my lips against hers. "Did I wear you out? You were sleeping pretty hard."

She laughed softly, stretching. "Did I talk in my sleep? Because if so, I probably muttered something embarrassing like, 'Sinan, Sinan,' over and over."

I chuckled. "Actually, you were pretty quiet. I think I wore you out in the *best* way."

She sat up, the blanket falling away to reveal her naked body as she ran a hand through her hair. "I hate to say it, but I should probably head back. I have to teach that dive class in just a few hours."

I couldn't help the pang of disappointment. "Can't you just stay? I'll make sure you're up on time."

She let out a sigh while leaning into my shoulder. "As tempting as that is, I left all my gear at home, and besides, I'd like to keep the details of my private life private, and showing up in yesterday's clothes would be a dead giveaway."

I traced my fingers along her arm, reluctant to let her go. "That'll get easier once we're officially out as a couple."

"Here's hoping it doesn't get harder first," she replied, flashing a half-smile as she stood, gathering her clothes.

I got up, slipping on my sleep pants so I could see her to the door. As she dressed, I admired the way she moved so comfortably and naturally. I knew I was going to miss her the second she left. "We need to do this again soon."

She grinned, winking as she tugged on her blouse. "I have a feeling you'll see me sooner than you think."

We walked downstairs, the house quiet in the early morning stillness. At the door, she took my hand, her gaze soft and serious. "I'm glad we're going public with this," she said. "Feels like a big step, but a good one."

"It does." I gave her hand a squeeze. "This is the start of something amazing."

She leaned up for one last kiss, and with a quick smile, slipped outside into the chilly night. I watched her car pull away, excitement thrumming through me. I knew that what lay ahead would bring challenges, but with Kendra by my side, it felt like the best kind of adventure.

Back inside, I sat on the couch for a moment, letting the warmth of the evening linger, but reality soon crept back in. One more task to tackle before I called it a night. I grabbed my phone. It was early morning in Istanbul—just the right time for a catch-up call with my mother. I dialed, and she picked up on the second ring.

"Sinan! What a surprise!" she said, her voice bright and familiar.

"I know, *Anne*. I wanted to talk to you about your visit this spring."

"We're so excited! It's been far too long," she replied. "Your father and I can't wait."

"Speaking of, is he there?"

"No. He left last night to go to the Uludağ Ski Center with his friends. You know how he loves winter sports."

I smiled. "That sounds about right. Well, I figured I should get ahead of your planning and schedule some things while you're here. Maybe the Andy Warhol Museum… do you plan to stay for a month, as usual?"

"Of course. Maybe a little longer."

"I should have guessed," I said with amusement. "Actually, there's something I wanted to tell you before you both get here." I took a deep breath. "I've met someone—her name is Kendra."

A brief pause. "Oh?"

"She's Sonya's sister. You remember Max and Sonya, right? Emma's guardians?"

"Of course. Max works in film. Sonya is… a teacher?"

I nodded, even though she couldn't see me. "Right. And Kendra's a civil engineer. She moved here recently for work, and we met at their wedding."

Silence stretched between us for a beat too long.

"How serious is this, Sinan? You haven't mentioned her before. Is she the reason you and Miranda didn't work out?"

Her bluntness caught me off guard. "No, Anne. I'd never cheat on someone. Miranda and I ended things over a year ago. This is something new."

"Sonya's sister…" Her voice carried a weight of contemplation. "Older or younger?"

"Younger," I admitted. "There's about a ten-year gap."

Another pause. I could practically hear the calculations happening in her mind.

"I see," she finally said, her tone carefully neutral. "And you believe this will last?"

"I do." I softened my voice, trying to ease her concerns. "I wouldn't be telling you otherwise."

She exhaled, and I could tell she was still processing. "Your father will be interested in her profession, at least. He admires engineers."

That was as close to encouragement as I was going to get.

"She's been open to learning about our culture," I added. "She's even started picking up some Turkish."

"Really?" A flicker of interest broke through.

"She's committed, *Anne*. I need you to trust me on this."

A pause. Then, finally, "We'll meet her in the spring. I'm reserving judgment, but I'll keep an open mind."

It wasn't an enthusiastic blessing, but it was enough for now.

"Thank you," I said, relieved. "That means a lot."

"As long as you're happy, that's what matters," she said, though I could hear the subtle caution in her voice. "I just want the best for you."

"I know. And you'll see—she's special."

As I ended the call, I let out a slow breath. One hurdle cleared. There were more to come, but for now, I'd take the win.

25

JIMMY, LAWYERS, AND ONE VERY SMART KID

Kendra

"Morning," I said later that same day, pouring myself a cup of coffee with trembling hands. Sonya and Max were sitting at the kitchen island. This was the perfect time to talk to them.

"Morning," Sonya replied, her eyes bright with curiosity. "You got in late last night from that *private dive lesson.*"

I didn't miss the emphasis she put on those words, but apparently, Max did.

Max glanced up from his phone, barely paying attention. "Got a busy day?"

I took a deep breath and faced them across the kitchen island. "Actually, I wanted to talk to you both before Emma comes down."

Sonya raised an eyebrow, half-smiling as though anticipating what I'd say. "What's up?"

"You already know I've been seeing someone. It's time to tell you—" I hesitated, feeling the weight of the moment, "it's Sinan."

There was a brief pause as my words sank in. Sonya's eyes widened in surprise before a slow smile spread across her face. "So, scuba diving, huh?" she teased.

I blushed, shaking my head. "Yeah. Not every time. Sorry for lying."

Max's reaction was more measured. He set down his phone, serious. "And how long has this been going on?"

"A few months. Since not long after the wedding. We tried to avoid each other, but it didn't work. We wanted to make sure whatever this is between us had legs before we went public."

Max leaned back, arms folded. "I'm happy for you, Kendra, but if things don't work out, family gatherings could get awkward. I don't want Emma caught in the middle and have to choose sides."

I appreciated his concern. Emma was at the heart of everything. "We've thought about that, and it's why we waited until we were sure."

Sonya placed a reassuring hand on Max's arm. "Remember when we started dating? It was delicate with me being Emma's teacher. It wasn't easy, but we managed."

Max exhaled, nodding. "I get it. But Emma's been through a lot. I don't want her to be hurt if things go south between you and Sinan."

"We're not announcing a breakup," I reminded him gently. "We're announcing a relationship. We both want to make this work."

Max sighed, rubbing his jaw. "As long as you're sure."

"We are."

Sonya smiled, reaching across the island to squeeze my hand. "I'm happy for you. And I'm sure Emma will be thrilled."

Relief washed over me. One hurdle cleared. Emma was next— I could already hear her feet pounding down the stairs.

Emma burst into the kitchen, her face lighting up at the sight of the banana pancakes stacked high on the counter. "Morning," she said, hopping onto a barstool.

We all settled in, the room filling with the sounds of breakfast —forks clattering, syrup glugging, orange juice being poured.

As we ate, I glanced at Sonya, who gave me an encouraging

nod. I took a deep breath. "Emma, there's something I want to tell you."

She looked up from her pancakes. "What's up?"

I reached for my coffee, taking a sip to steady myself. "Your uncle Sinan and I have started seeing each other."

Emma rolled her eyes and smirked. "About time. I figured that out ages ago. Honestly," she said, sparing a glance for Max and Sonya, "how did you two *not* see it?" She gave a dramatic sigh, the quintessential pre-teen attitude on full display.

Sonya raised an eyebrow. "You knew?"

"Duh, obviously. You two were *so* busted at Thanksgiving. It was hilarious. Marley and I totally called it. So… does this mean you're, like, officially a thing now?"

I blinked. "Yes, you three are the first to know."

Emma grinned. "Duh, you two were terrible at sneaking around." She grabbed her phone and dashed off. "I need to call Marley."

"I guess she showed us." Max shook his head, rising to his feet. "Maybe she should become a detective or an FBI investigator."

His phone beeped. "That's my alarm. I've got a call with Julian Torres. I hate leaving you with the kitchen mess—"

Sonya waved him off. "Go ahead. It's about the film in Indonesia, right?"

"That's the one. Filming starts in a couple of months. Lots of details to hammer out."

Once we were alone, Sonya turned to me. "I'm happy for you. But can I offer some big-sister wisdom?"

I shrugged and nodded. I'd half-expected something like this. Sonya had been looking out for me since the day I was born. "Always."

"Sinan's already well-established—his career, his house, his everything. You're just getting started. That kind of imbalance can sneak up on you if you're not paying attention. Mutual respect and equality matter. How you start sets the tone."

I huffed out a laugh. "We've already talked about it. A lot, actually. We're doing our best to keep things on even ground."

Sonya's smile softened. "Good. Just keep being honest with each other. That's what matters most."

"I will. And thanks for the advice, Essie."

She chuckled, nudging me lightly. "You're lucky I'm here to dish it out. Otherwise, you'd be stuck waiting for Mom's posthumous wisdom to kick in."

I blinked. "The letters?"

Sonya nodded. "Yeah. We're three and a half years in. Only a year and a half to go before we're allowed to open them."

I groaned. "Mine's probably a list of everything I've done wrong already. Good thing you're the one holding onto them. I would've peeked years ago."

Her grin turned sly. "I know. That's why I didn't tell you where they're hidden."

I took a quick walk around the neighborhood. On the way inside, I checked the mail and found two identical letters addressed to me and Sonya Gambit...my sister's maiden name.

Curious, I tore mine open. The contents had me starting over from the beginning to make sense of it. A moment later, I tracked down my sister in the living room. She had her laptop balanced on her knees, but she closed the screen when she saw my face.

"Got a minute?" I asked, hesitating in the doorway.

She frowned at my tone. "Sure. What's up?"

I handed her the letter. "You and I got matching letters. They're from a lawyer. Apparently, we had an aunt."

Sonya blinked. "We *had* an aunt? What does that mean?"

"Aunt Lorraine. Jimmy's sister. She died a few months ago."

The confusion on Sonya's face shifted into wariness as she glanced at the letter like it had just transformed into a snake. "And why is a lawyer writing us about it?"

"Because Lorraine left behind an estate, and we're listed as next of kin. But here's the catch—they're also trying to find Jimmy."

Sonya let out a breath and leaned back. "You've got to be kidding me."

"I wish I were," I admitted. "The lawyer says Jimmy was listed as a potential beneficiary, but no one's been able to track him down."

Sonya's lips pressed into a thin line. "So what does this mean for us?"

I shrugged. "I'm not sure yet. It depends on what's in the estate. If there's money or property involved, it could get complicated. The lawyer wants to meet and go over details, but… I don't know, Sonya. Do you think—should we at least try to get ahead of this?"

Sonya scoffed. "By reaching out to *him*? No way. He doesn't deserve anything."

"I agree," I said. "But this isn't our decision to make—it was Aunt Lorraine's. Whether we like it or not, someone will find him eventually, and if we don't get ahead of it, it'll only drag out the estate process. And if he hears it from a lawyer instead of us, you *know* he'll show up, claiming we froze him out and playing the victim. At least if I reach out first, we control the conversation and the timing."

Sonya exhaled sharply. "Kendra… I don't like this. I don't trust him. And I *don't* want to let him back into our lives, even for something like this."

"I don't either," I admitted. "But I also don't want him blind-siding us. If I reach out first, I can set the boundaries."

She stared at me for a long moment, then sighed. "Fine. But only texts, Kendra. No calls. No meetings. And if he starts with his usual manipulations, you cut him off."

"Deal."

I headed upstairs, needing a few minutes to compose a text. I was nervous about letting him get a foothold in our lives. Was Aunt Lorraine's estate good news for him? Likely not, considering her executor was contacting all three of us. Clearly she'd included me and Sonya in her will, and that might tick Jimmy off. I needed to proceed carefully.

Jimmy's number still sat in my contacts, untouched since Halloween. My fingers hovered over the screen before I finally typed.

> Me: Hi. It's Kendra. I'm open to talking. But let's start slow. Just texts for now.

I hit send, my heart pounding. Seconds later, my phone buzzed.

> Jimmy: Great! Let's grab coffee tomorrow afternoon.

My stomach twisted.

> Me: Not what I said. Can't we just text first?

> Jimmy: You kids and your texting. In person is better for me.

> Me: Not for me.

A pause. Then another text.

> Jimmy: I'd like to reconnect with Sonya too. Can you set up a meeting?

I exhaled slowly.

> Me: I'll think about it.

I wouldn't. Sonya had made her feelings clear. I wouldn't push her into something she didn't want. Why didn't I just tell him?

Maybe because for now, I had enough on my plate, and saying

no to him was one step too far. Short-sighted? Likely. Cowardly? Definitely. But I was at capacity.

The rest of the afternoon passed in a blur of chores. As I folded laundry, did a deep clean in the kitchen, and tidied up around my suite, my phone buzzed incessantly with messages from my father. Each one seemed more desperate than the last, pleading for my help in reconciling with Sonya. I wasn't sure how to respond, so I didn't, but my silence didn't deter him. Sonya, busy with her own day, didn't cross my path at all—giving me too much time alone with my thoughts and my phone's relentless buzzing.

> Jimmy: What did she say? Did she agree to meet?

> Jimmy: Kendra, please, I need your help. I want to make things right with Sonya.

> Jimmy: I know I messed up, but I want to make amends. Please convince her to meet with me.

> Jimmy: Just one meeting, that's all I'm asking for. Please, Kendra.

The relentlessness of his texts began to wear on me. I had been so sure that contacting him was the right step, but now, doubt started to creep in. Was I making a mistake? Was I opening old wounds that were better left closed? Sure, I'd always wished for a dad. A real dad who'd take me ice skating or for a ride in his jeep…but I'd never had that, and it was pretty obvious that wasn't the sort of dad Jimmy would be.

I stared at his last message, my thumb hovering. If he wanted something to focus on so badly, I had just the thing.

> Me: A lawyer contacted me and Sonya. Aunt Lorraine left behind an estate, and they're trying to find you. If you want to reconnect, maybe start there.

I hit send before I could second-guess myself.

For once, Jimmy didn't respond immediately. The silence was almost eerie. But also… blessedly welcome.

As evening approached, I dug through my closet for my ice skates, finally pulling them down from the top shelf. I sat on my bed, running my fingers over the worn leather. Mom had taught us to skate, gliding effortlessly across the ice while Sonya and I clung to her hands. Most people dreaded cold snaps, but for me, the freezing temperatures meant perfect skating weather.

Except this year, it wasn't freezing. The unseasonably warm weather had left the sidewalks clear, the usual December chill replaced with a crisp, mild breeze. Even so, PPG's rink was open, and I was looking forward to seeing if Sinan could actually skate or if he'd exaggerated his skills. Most likely, he was amazing at it.

I should've been buzzing with excitement, but Jimmy's messages gnawed at the edges of my good mood. He left me wondering if I was making a mistake letting myself fall for Sinan. Lately, he was the first person I turned to for comfort—was that healthy, or was I just looking for the stability my father had never provided?

I shoved the thoughts aside and grabbed my skates. Tonight wasn't about Jimmy. It was about me and Sinan.

The drive to his house was a blur of half-formed worries and ignored text notifications. By the time I pulled up, my nerves were a tangled mess, but the second Sinan opened the door, his warm smile softened the edges of my anxiety.

"Hey, you okay?" he asked, his gaze searching mine.

I forced a smile. "Just a lot on my mind. Hoping tonight will take care of that."

His brow furrowed, but he let it go. "Ready to skate?" He grabbed his own skates from the floor.

"Absolutely."

We headed out wearing lightweight jackets, a weird but welcome change for December. The drive downtown was beautiful—city lights reflecting off the rivers, bridges glowing against the night sky.

As we crossed into downtown, I exhaled. "Telling my family about us went so well today that I decided to tackle another issue." I hesitated, then admitted, "I got a letter from an executor handling an estate. Turns out Jimmy's sister passed away a few months ago. She left something behind, and Sonya and I are next of kin. But they're also trying to track down Jimmy."

Sinan glanced at me. "And?"

"I texted him. Told him about the lawyer after he started pestering me. I figured it might distract him from obsessing over reconnecting with us."

His jaw ticked slightly, but he kept his focus on the road. "How did that go?"

I exhaled. "It started with me setting boundaries—texting only —but he immediately pushed to meet in person. Then he started in about reconnecting with Sonya, message after message, like I was his personal scheduler." I paused. "But then I told him about the lawyer trying to find him—about Aunt Lorraine's estate—and he just… stopped. Not a single text since."

Sinan glanced at me, brows lifting slightly. "That quiet must've been a relief."

"It was," I admitted. "But it also freaked me out a little. Like, did he get what he wanted? Is he plotting something? Or maybe he's just finally gone quiet because he has a new target now."

Sinan reached for my hand. "You don't have to do anything you're not comfortable with."

I squeezed his fingers, trying to ground myself. "I know. I just —I don't trust his motives. And now I'm not sure if silence is better or worse."

"Then trust your instincts," he said gently. "Just because you reached out doesn't mean you have to give him control."

His words settled over me like a balm, easing some of the tension.

PPG Place shimmered ahead of us, the towering Christmas

tree glowing at the rink's center. Even with the warm weather, the ice remained solid, skaters gliding under the lights. We laced up, stepping onto the ice, and I immediately found my balance, the familiar glide soothing me.

I caught Sinan watching me, amusement dancing in his eyes. "Okay, show-off," he teased.

I grinned. "Let's see what you've got, Dr. Bachar."

He pushed off smoothly, matching my pace with surprising ease. I skated backward, expecting him to wobble or flail a little. Instead, he followed me without missing a beat, moving with practiced control like he'd been born on blades.

I narrowed my eyes, slowing down. "Wait. You actually *can* skate?"

He shrugged like it was no big deal, but there was definite smugness in his smile. "I told you I wasn't exaggerating."

I spun around and picked up speed, hoping to catch him off guard—but he kept up effortlessly, even pulling ahead on the turns.

I was both annoyed and completely charmed.

"I don't know whether to be impressed or personally offended," I called over my shoulder.

"Why not both?" he said, breezing past me with a grin that should've been illegal.

I caught up to him, breathless from the cold and the sudden shift in emotional terrain. Somewhere between my doubts and his unexpected skating prowess, I realized something unsettling: I'd underestimated him.

Not just on the ice—but in all the little ways that mattered.

Here he was, gliding through this unexpected night like he'd been waiting for a moment to prove he belonged in my world too —not just as a surgeon or Emma's uncle or the man with the very opinionated Turkish mother—but as my person. And that realization hit me harder than the chill in the air.

"You've been holding out on me," I muttered, trying to sound annoyed but failing to hide the smile creeping in.

"I have a few tricks left," he said, slowing down beside me.

"Next time, I'm bringing cones," I said. "You're going to have to earn your bragging rights."

He leaned in slightly, his breath warm against my cheek. "Challenge accepted."

We spent the next hour racing, spinning, and trying to outdo each other, laughter echoing against the mirrored glass buildings. For the first time all day, I wasn't thinking about Jimmy.

After a final lap, we skated off, swapping our skates for sneakers. "Hot chocolate?" Sinan asked, already steering me toward the kiosk.

Sitting on a bench, we sipped from steaming cups, watching families twirl around the rink. "This was exactly what I needed," I admitted.

Sinan nudged my shoulder. "Glad to hear it. Want to check out the gingerbread houses?"

"Absolutely."

Inside PPG Place, the scent of pine and gingerbread filled the air as we wandered through the elaborate displays. I told Sinan about the massive gingerbread house at the Ritz-Carlton in Philly Mom had taken us to see, and he laughed.

"Did kids sneak bites?"

"I wouldn't have dared. That's where Santa sat. Besides, by mom had rules."

Sinan smirked. "So what you're saying is, I should challenge you to build one?"

I narrowed my eyes. "Are you saying I can't?"

"I'm saying we should make one together."

I pretended to consider it, then grinned. "Fine. But only if we go all out—architecture plans, structural integrity, the works."

Sinan leaned in. "You're on."

The idea of building something together—creating a new tradition—warmed me in a way I hadn't expected. Maybe I didn't have to worry so much about fitting into Sinan's world. Maybe we were making our own.

After exploring the displays, we headed back to Sinan's, the city twinkling in our rearview. For once, my mind was quiet.

Inside, we curled up on the couch, the house filled with the cozy scent of cinnamon tea. My phone vibrated again—Jimmy.

I sighed. Instead of blocking him, I silenced the phone completely. I would deal with him later.

Right now, I just wanted to focus on Sinan.

I smirked, glancing at him. "I brought an overnight bag. It's in the trunk of my car."

Sinan's eyes darkened with mischief. "Did you now?"

He grabbed my keys and disappeared for less than a minute before returning with my bag in hand.

"Now, where were we?" he murmured, leaning in.

Then—a low, mechanical buzzing.

We both froze. My gaze snapped to the window.

A drone. Hovering. Watching.

Sinan groaned. "Not this again."

I rolled my eyes. "We need a plan for this."

Sinan's lips quirked. "What? Make signs?"

I snapped my fingers. "Exactly! 'Go away, drone!' Or, 'Privacy, please!'"

He laughed. "How about, 'Do this again and we call the cops'?"

I smirked. "We'll work on our messaging."

But not tonight.

Grabbing his hand, I pulled him toward the stairs, my earlier tension finally, blissfully gone.

2 6

GINGERBREAD DREAMS

I slipped out of bed the next morning and headed for the shower, intent on surprising Kendra with breakfast in bed and then giving her another orgasm, or three.

As soon as the water began steaming up the room, I opened the shower door, only to hear the bathroom door open behind me.

Kendra.

Our eyes met, and she moved closer, giving me a long lingering kiss. Her hand found my morning hard-on, and I immediately forgot I'd planned to cook her breakfast. What can I say? The woman had a talent for distracting me. We stepped into the shower, after I lathered up that gorgeous body of hers, I began kissing her entire body, my lips sliding over her skin.

Kendra tightened her grip around my swollen cock until I could barely see straight.

I braced my feet, lifting her up so she could wrap her legs around my waist. I pressed her back against the tile wall as I thrust into her, the warm water cascading over us. She let out a lusty moan and bit my shoulder, hard enough for me to feel the pinch, but not hard enough to really hurt. I thrust into her harder as her fingers dug into my back. As her orgasm approached, she let out a deep-throated moan, completely lost in the moment—in the sensations.

As my orgasm hit, I dropped my head back, a deep moan of surrender escaping me.

This woman. This perfect, amazing woman. I was so relieved I could call her mine now. Publicly claim her.

I couldn't just leave her hanging, so I pulled her close, nibbling on her neck as the water cascaded around us. When I slid my hand between her legs and cupped her pussy, she let out a moan. She was wet, both inside and out, making it easy to slide my fingers inside of her. The water tried to wash away her natural lubrication, so I moved to one side, shielding her.

As my fingers moved in and out of her, she held onto me, leaning her shoulders against the tile wall, breathing hard and fast. She lifted one foot up onto the bench in the shower, granting me greater access to her.

"Is this good?" I murmured.

"Best way to wake up," she panted. "Just a little more."

I kissed her again, harder this time. She took everything I had to offer, drinking me in like a woman emerging from a desert. She began grinding into my hand, and I couldn't have been happier.

I dipped my head and sucked one of her nipples into my mouth, eliciting another moan from her.

That's when she came. She fisted her hands into my damp hair and held on for dear life as her body trembled. I rubbed and sucked and pleasured this woman until she was begging me to stop. I slowed, drawing out her pleasure, easing her to the end of that orgasm.

When she was done, she let go of my hair and slid her hands to my shoulders.

"That was…"

I cocked one eyebrow. "Adequate?"

She giggled. "That hardly begins to describe the mind-blowing orgasm you just gave me."

I couldn't help it. I grinned.

"You look mighty pleased with yourself."

"What can I say? I like pleasing my woman."

Her eyes softened at that. "And I like it when you call me your woman."

We lingered in that bliss a little longer, savoring the quiet intimacy of the moment. But when the water finally started to cool, we rinsed off the last of the soap and dried off.

By the time we made it to the kitchen, my stomach reminded me how long it had been since last night's dinner. I got started on the bacon while Kendra brewed coffee, and mixed pancake batter. The rich aromas of breakfast soon filled the air, blending with the golden sunlight streaming through the windows.

I stole a glance at her as she whisked the batter. Even in her oversized hoodie and sleep-mussed hair, she was effortlessly beautiful. *My woman.* That thought settled something deep in my chest.

Then her phone vibrated.

Kendra glanced at it and sighed, rubbing her forehead.

"Jimmy again?" I guessed.

"Yeah." She pulled a face, "Three more texts. I think he must've finally passed out because he hasn't sent anything since two in the morning. Good thing he's on mute."

I frowned. "What's he saying now?"

"The usual—pushing for a meeting, wanting me to get Sonya involved." She shook her head and flipped a pancake. "I told him I'd think about it, but I'm not setting up a meeting. Sonya's made it clear where she stands."

I leaned against the counter, watching her carefully. "You sure you want to keep engaging with him at all?"

She hesitated, stirring absentmindedly. "I don't know. Part of me thinks cutting him off is the best option, but then there's the legal side of this. If he's listed in the will, he's going to find out about the inheritance one way or another."

I set down the coffee mug I'd just picked up. "I get that, but you don't owe him that courtesy. Especially if he's already trying to manipulate you."

She sighed. "I know. I'll talk it over with Sonya again before deciding on my next move."

I didn't like the idea of her dealing with Jimmy at all—but I knew better than to push. "Just say the word if you need backup."

She smiled, and I caught a flicker of gratitude in her eyes. "Will do."

I let it drop, shifting the conversation to lighter things. "So, any plans today?"

"Max and Sonya have a Christmas party, so I'm hanging with Emma," she said, flipping a perfect golden pancake. "Want to join us?"

"Absolutely. How about we build a gingerbread house together?"

Her face lit up. "Yes! We'll need gumdrops, candy canes, M&Ms—oh, and licorice for the roof!"

"Send me a list. I'll take care of the shopping." I poured us each a cup of coffee and handed hers over with a grin.

A few minutes later, we sat down to breakfast, our laughter and light conversation blending with the clatter of forks on plates. It felt easy. Right.

As Kendra gathered her things to leave, she flashed a warm smile. "See you tonight."

We shared a lingering kiss before she finally slipped out the door, leaving me with a full stomach and a heart that felt a little fuller too.

I lingered by the sink, enjoying the quiet hum of the morning as I cleaned up. But when my phone buzzed, and *Miranda's* name flashed across the screen, the easy warmth of the morning drained away.

With a sigh, I picked up.

"Hello?"

"Sinan, I hate to ask, but I need more money," she said, her voice trembling with desperation. "Legal fees are piling up, and I have court dates coming up. Please, I don't know who else to ask."

My hand tightened around the phone. "Miranda, I told you before—I can't keep helping you. This is something you need to handle on your own."

"If we'd gotten married, I'd be entitled to so much more. You owe me, Sinan. You can't just abandon me like this."

I swallowed, reminding myself to stay calm. "Miranda, you have to take responsibility for yourself. Find a job. Support yourself."

"I just got out of rehab! I lost my medical license! What am I supposed to do? Flip burgers? That won't bring in the kind of money I need."

"I'm sorry, Miranda, but this isn't something I can fix for you," I said, knowing I had to draw a line. "Don't call me about this again." With that, I ended the call, a mix of guilt and relief washing over me.

As I cleaned up the kitchen, my thoughts drifted to Kendra, and a knot tightened in my chest. Miranda wouldn't stop pushing, wouldn't take no for an answer. And Jimmy was doing the same to Kendra—relentless messages, demands for her time, pressing at the edges of her patience. It wasn't the same situation, but the feeling was eerily familiar. That pressure. That expectation. The way both of them acted like their needs should take priority over everything else. I hated seeing Kendra caught in that, just like I hated how Miranda always found a way to pull me back into her mess. I sighed, shaking off the thought. It was different. It *had* to be.

For now, I had better things to focus on.

That afternoon, my phone buzzed with a text from Kendra.

Kendra: I checked Sonya's baking tools. Can you pick up a piping bag and tips?

> Me: Say what? What is this black magic you speak of?

> Kendra: Lol. You use them to make frosting decorations, like roses. Check the baking aisle for a kit.

> Me: I'm on it. Roses will look great on a gingerbread house. 😬

> Kendra: 😊 Leave the supplies in the car when you get here. Emma wants the gingerbread house to be a surprise for Max and Sonya. I'll send you that list of candy we need.

I headed to the store, navigating the holiday crowds. The candy aisle was a colorful blur of gumdrops, candy canes, and licorice, and I tossed everything on the list into my cart. In the baking aisle, I finally located the piping bag and tips, double-checking the label to make sure they were the right ones.

As I drove to Kendra's, I thought about whether I should tell her about the call from Miranda. I decided against it—Emma would be around, plus there really wasn't any point in rehashing it tonight. I'd handled it, and that was that.

When I arrived, the house was lit up with holiday lights, a wreath hanging on the door. Leaving the bags in the car, I walked inside to find Max and Sonya finishing up their preparations. Sonya, radiant in a sparkly green dress, greeted me with a smile and a quick hug.

"Kendra told us everything. I had no idea you were seeing each other, but I'm really happy for you both."

Max, adjusting his tie, gave me a nod. "So, you and Kendra?"

"She's pretty amazing." I'm pretty sure I wore a goofy grin.

Max folded his arms, his expression serious. "Treat her right. I didn't realize that's who you were talking about in cooking class when you said you were seeing someone."

I raised my hands in surrender. "Sorry for hiding things. We weren't ready to tell everyone."

"Just know we're watching you." Max pointed two fingers at his eyes and then at me, making us all laugh, breaking the tension.

Sonya shook her head, amused. "Alright, boys, we'd better go, or we'll be late."

The moment they walked out the door, Kendra appeared at the top of the stairs, smiling as she came down. "Did they give you a hard time?"

I grinned. "Nothing I couldn't handle."

She laughed and took my hand. "Come on, Emma's been dying to start on that gingerbread house."

"I'll grab the supplies," I said, heading out into the cool night air. I returned with my arms full, and as soon as I stepped inside, Emma rushed me.

"We've been planning the gingerbread house all day, Uncle Sinan! We need to start now if we're going to finish before Mom and Dad get home."

Kendra and I exchanged amused glances. Emma's excitement was infectious, and as we unpacked the groceries, holiday music played softly in the background.

Emma inspected each bag with the focus of a master architect. "Did you get everything on the list?"

"Of course. Even the all-important piping bags and tips."

"Perfect!" Emma grinned, already scheming. "And by the way, I knew you two were a couple way before Thanksgiving."

Kendra nudged me playfully. "Looks like we weren't as sneaky as we thought." We both laughed, sharing in Emma's fun.

We mixed the dough, rolled it out, and soon the sweet scent of gingerbread filled the kitchen. Once the pieces cooled, we carefully laid them out on the counter, each one cut with precision to match the exact dimensions of Max and Sonya's house.

"We even measured, Uncle Sinan," Emma informed me proudly. "It's *to scale*."

"Of course it is," I muttered under my breath, smirking at Kendra.

She simply winked and handed me a frosting bag.

Construction was a three-person effort. Kendra oversaw the build, double-checking that the walls lined up just right. Emma placed candies with near-professional precision, making sure every gumdrop shrub and M&M window matched their real-life counterparts. I handled the frosting, piping straight, careful lines to hold everything together.

"A little more to the left, Sinan," Kendra instructed, grinning. "We want that roofline perfect."

I smirked, shifting the frosting bag. "Yes, ma'am."

Every detail came together—the gumdrop walkway leading up to a pretzel-stick front porch, a perfectly iced bay window that matched the one overlooking the backyard, and even a tiny candy-cane swing set in the yard, an homage to Emma's favorite spot. Frosting icicles dripped from the roof's edges, mimicking the ones that always formed outside their real house.

When Max and Sonya returned, Max's eyes widened. "Whoa! That's *our house*! You guys nailed it."

Sonya beamed. "It's perfect!"

"Complete with the four of us in the windows," Emma told them proudly, pointing to the gumdrop-sized candy figures we'd made. "There's Kendra, waving from her bedroom. You and Dad are here in the front window, and I'm up in my bedroom."

I wiped my hands on a towel, smiling. "Kendra designed it, Emma did the decorating, and I kept it from falling apart."

Kendra nudged me. "You were the glue—literally."

Laughter filled the room, but Kendra's phone buzzed. I caught Jimmy's name on her screen, and she quickly silenced it.

"Everything okay?" I asked.

"Yeah," she said, forcing a smile. "Same old. Nothing you need to worry about."

DECK THE HALLS AND SETTLE THE SCORES

KENDRA

The following Saturday night, just a few days before Christmas, I curled up on Sinan's sofa, mesmerized by the view through his floor-to-ceiling windows. The city below twinkled like a miniature model, each light shimmering against the wintry backdrop. I loved this view in every season. Pittsburgh's older homes, mostly from the 1800s, provided a timeless charm, but the modern lines of Sinan's house stood out against the city's glow.

String lights twinkled along the windows, their muted glow warming the space. Wreaths with pinecones and berries hung on the walls, while pine centerpieces filled the tables. Star lanterns added an elegant touch, their soft light creating a cozy, festive atmosphere.

We had an entire evening together, but since he was on call, we stayed in, debating movies while sipping hot cocoa. The fireplace crackled, adding a cozy warmth to the night.

Sinan leaned back, his arm draped over the back of the couch. "I can't tell you how many restaurant dinners I've had to walk out on over the years."

I smirked. "So you're saying I should never order the expensive meal when you're on call?"

"Exactly," he said, eyes gleaming. "Though, if I ever bail, you're welcome to order the whole menu out of spite."

I laughed, about to reply when his phone buzzed. The shift in his posture told me everything.

"Emergency?"

He nodded, already reaching for his keys. "I'm sorry."

Disappointment prickled, but I understood. "Go. Save lives."

He pressed a lingering kiss to my lips before heading out. I sighed, folding the blanket on the couch, then shrugged into my coat. My phone chimed with a text. When I saw who it was from, my stomach twisted.

Jimmy.

Jimmy: Why aren't you messaging me? Is it because you think you'll get a payout from my sister? Think again. I'm getting angry. Contact me, or I'm pulling out the big guns. You won't like me when I'm angry.

A chill ran down my spine. Did he actually think he could intimidate me?

I fired back.

Me: Try any more intimidation tactics, and I'll block you.

No reply.

At first, I felt a small victory—but silence from a man like Jimmy didn't feel like surrender. It felt like a pause before the next move. I *needed* to tell Sonya.

But when I got home, the house was filled with holiday warmth—Sonya and Max snuggled up on the couch watching *Elf*, Emma in the kitchen popping popcorn with Marley. I opened my mouth to tell her, but stopped.

It could wait.

"Goodnight, you two," I called instead.

Sonya waved. "Don't forget, book club's on Monday instead of Tuesday."

Max gave me a thumbs-up.

Upstairs, I opened *The Women* by Kristin Hannah and let it pull me under, needing the escape. It had me hooked, and I found myself reading straight through to the last page.

By Monday morning, when I arrived at my office in the sleek downtown high-rise that always made me feel like a real adult, I'd managed to convince myself Jimmy wasn't a real threat.

The pre-holiday buzz filled the office, festive lights strung along the windows, but my inbox told a different story.

> Josh: You have a problem with the load distribution calculations. Fix it. I'm telling Ken.

My stomach dropped. I yanked open the project file. It *was* my miscalculation. Not catastrophic. But bad enough that if we didn't adjust, it would cause delays—and I'd hand Josh the ammunition he needed to undermine me.

I grabbed my notes and headed straight for Misha, finding them alone in a conference room. "I messed up the stress calculations on the bridge reinforcement."

Misha scanned the file, their sharp gaze flicking over the numbers. "Yeah, I see it. You didn't factor in the additional lateral load distribution from the recent modifications. Fixable, but Ken's not going to love it."

"Josh is already making sure he knows," I muttered, frustration creeping in.

Misha rolled their eyes. "Classic Josh. If he spent half as much time actually engineering as he does trying to trip people up, he might be halfway decent at his job." They tapped the page. "Okay, let's rerun this with adjusted tolerances. You catch it before construction, it's a correction. You catch it too late, it's a disaster. You're handling it the right way."

Their words steadied me, and we worked through the correction. The tension in my chest eased as the numbers finally aligned properly.

Then Josh appeared in the doorway, arms crossed, a smirk playing at his lips. "Wow. You had to run to Misha?"

I exhaled slowly, keeping my voice even. "I double-check my work when I find an issue. That's what responsible engineers do."

Josh leaned against the doorframe. "Right, but here's the thing, Kendra. This keeps happening. Maybe you're not ready for this role. Maybe Ken should reconsider who's involved in this phase of the project."

My pulse spiked. "Are you seriously suggesting that making a correction—before it became a real problem—is a sign of incompetence?"

His smirk widened, but before he could open his mouth, Misha stood. "Josh, let me break it down for you. Kendra corrected the mistake before it impacted anything. That's competence. You, on the other hand, just sent a snarky email instead of fixing it yourself. What exactly are *you* contributing here?"

Josh's jaw tightened. "Just making sure Ken knows where things stand."

"You mean making sure *you* look good," Misha said smoothly, unfazed.

Before Josh could fire back, a familiar voice cut through the tension. "What's all the commotion?"

"Allison," Misha murmured under their breath.

We all turned as she walked in, her presence instantly shifting the energy in the room. She glanced between us, then held out a hand. "Show me the file."

I passed her the revised calculations, my heart hammering. She flipped through them, her expression unreadable.

For a moment, she said nothing. Then: "You caught it before it impacted the project?"

"Yes," I said, keeping my voice steady.

She handed the papers back. "Good. That's the job."

A breath I hadn't realized I was holding escaped.

Allison turned to Josh. "Why are you standing around? Shouldn't you be working?"

His expression hardened, but he muttered something about needing to check on another phase and stalked off.

Allison looked at me. "You'll see these kinds of guys your whole career—the ones who don't actually build anything but spend all their energy trying to tear other people down."

I nodded, the truth of it settling in.

Her voice softened—just a fraction. "Fixing a mistake before it becomes a real problem? That's what separates the good engineers from the ones who just act like they know everything."

I swallowed the lump in my throat. "I won't let it happen again."

She gave a small nod, her gaze steady, assessing. "See that you don't." With that, she turned sharply on her heel and strode out as briskly as she'd entered.

Misha let out a low whistle. "Well, that's about as close to a compliment as Allison gets."

I exhaled, finally allowing myself a small smile. "I'll take it."

Josh might've been trying to knock me down, but I wasn't falling. Not today.

That evening at book club, nestled in Gertrude's warm, cinnamon-scented living room, I finally said it out loud.

"I regret ever texting Jimmy."

Mara arched an eyebrow, curled into an armchair under a throw blanket that read Just One More Chapter. "You sure it's not a viral marketing stunt for a new horror movie? Because that text had serious creepy uncle in a ski mask energy."

Sonya sat cross-legged on the sofa beside me, her mug of peppermint tea clasped in both hands. "What did he say this time?" Her voice was quiet, but there was steel underneath.

I exhaled and pulled out my phone. "You're not going to love it."

I showed her the latest text.

> Jimmy: Why aren't you messaging me? Is it because you think you'll get a payout from my sister? Think again. I'm getting angry. Contact me, or I'm pulling out the big guns. You won't like me when I'm angry.

Sonya's jaw tensed. "That's a threat. Block him. Now."

We locked eyes, and I nodded.

"We're not in second grade, Kendra. He doesn't get another warning," Mara said, already halfway to opening her own phone. "Do you want me to dig up his old Myspace profile and roast him into obscurity? Because I will."

I opened the message thread one last time. My hands didn't even shake as I tapped the screen and blocked his number. It felt final. And right.

Gertrude, reclined in her favorite wingback chair with a scarf tied artfully around her neck, patted my hand. "That's how you tell the difference between enemies and rivals, dear. A rival wants you to *rise*. An enemy wants you to *fall*."

She paused, then added, "Also, if any man ever tells you 'you won't like me when I'm angry,' you tell him you already don't like him when he's sober."

Sonya blinked, then laughed, the tension breaking slightly. "Gertrude!"

"What? I'm old, not dead. I've dated enough jackasses to know one when I see him. Or hear about him via a threatening text message."

I smiled—genuinely. The edge of panic I'd been carrying all weekend loosened a bit.

"I already blocked him," I said. "I just needed to say it out loud. To hear myself admit that I'm done giving him chances."

Mara raised her glass of mulled wine. "To being done. With trolls, with threats, with men who use 'big guns' as metaphors."

Sonya tapped her glass to Mara's, then turned to me, her voice softening. "I'm proud of you. You've done more than I think you realize."

And for the first time in weeks, I believed her.

Later, at Sinan's, we sat outside by his fire pit, the city lights stretching below us. From this high up, Pittsburgh looked like something out of a snow globe—twinkling bridges crisscrossing the rivers, their reflections shimmering on the dark water.

Sinan handed me a blanket before lacing his fingers through mine. "How was book club?" he asked, his voice warm.

I hesitated, then said, "Honestly? Talking with my friends helped me realize how much I overthink things. At work. With my family. Even… with us."

Sinan's head tilted. "With us?"

I shrugged. "I just worry sometimes. That I don't fit into your world."

He took my hand, squeezing gently. "Then let's build a world that fits both of us."

My heart clenched. This man was steady. Safe. Everything Jimmy wasn't.

Before I could respond, he smirked. "Want to roast marshmallows?"

I laughed. "You totally planned this."

"Guilty."

Minutes later, our playful teasing turned into something slower, deeper. The night melted away in soft kisses, sticky fingers, and whispered promises.

But in the back of my mind, Jimmy's words lingered.

"You won't like me when I'm angry."

And for the first time, I believed him.

2 8

─────

KNEADING REASSURANCE

Sinan

The Christmas decorations were gone, leaving the hospital feeling colder, emptier. Some patients, like Steve, probably felt the same way—stuck in the in-between, waiting for life to feel normal again.

Spotting Nurse Alvarez in the hallway pulled me from my thoughts. "How's our patient in Room 552?" I asked quietly, keeping my tone low so as not to alarm nearby visitors.

Her face mirrored the weariness I felt. "He's stabilized, but those seizures took a toll. We're keeping a close eye on him."

I nodded, feeling the familiar weight of responsibility pressing down. "Keep me posted on any changes," I replied before continuing down the hall.

As I neared Steve Thompson's room, I mentally prepared myself. Steve had been one of my more complicated cases—his car accident had caused severe brain trauma, broken bones, and damage to his organs. His physical injuries had healed remarkably well, but the lingering effects of the head trauma were a different story. His confusion and frustration had become an increasing source of tension.

187

I found Steve sitting on the edge of his bed, his fingers gripping the bedspread tightly, his brow furrowed in frustration.

"Morning, Steve," I greeted him, pulling up a chair beside him. "How are you doing today?"

He blinked up at me, as if pulling himself back to the present. "I don't know… I don't—" He trailed off, rubbing his temples. "I was gonna say something. It's right there… but I lost it again."

"You were telling me how you're feeling," I said, giving him space to collect his thoughts.

His gaze shifted to the window, then back to me, his voice low and raw. "I don't feel good. My head… I can't think. And I don't know what's wrong with me anymore."

"You've been through a lot," I said gently. "Your broken bones, your injuries—they've healed faster than we expected. But your brain? That's different. It needs more time."

He shook his head, his fingers tapping restlessly on the bedspread. "It's been months, right? Months, and I still can't hold a conversation. My brain just… stops. I get lost halfway through talking. And I can't even remember what I was trying to say." His voice rose with each word, the frustration spilling out.

"That's because your brain is still healing," I said, trying to calm him. "The fact that you're even sitting here, talking to me, is a huge step forward. We're moving you to a rehabilitation facility where they can help you take the next steps in your recovery."

His eyes widened in surprise. "A rehab facility? Am I… am I ready for that?"

"You are, Steve. Physically, you've come a long way. You're strong enough for rehab, and there, you'll have specialized support. You'll be working with therapists who can help retrain your brain and rebuild your cognitive function."

He stared at me, his hands still fidgeting with the blanket. "But what if I don't get better? What if I'm just stuck like this?"

I leaned in, meeting his gaze. "You will get better. It's not going to happen overnight, but you're not stuck. Every day you're healing, even if it doesn't feel like it. The rehab facility will help you with the mental part of your recovery, just like we helped with the physical."

His shoulders slumped, the tension slowly easing out of him. "I guess. It's just hard… being like this. I want to get back to… I don't even know."

"I know it's hard, but you're not alone," I said, resting a hand on his shoulder. "You've made it this far, and you'll keep moving forward. We're here to help you *every* step of the way."

He nodded, though I could still see the doubt flickering in his eyes. "I hope so," he muttered, looking down at his hands. "I just… I don't feel like me anymore."

I paused, watching Steve struggle with his words. "You'll find yourself again," I promised. But as I walked out, the doubt in Steve's eyes stayed with me, heavier than the hospital air.

I needed a reset, something to pull me out of the fog. The thought of seeing Kendra after my cooking class gave me something to look forward to. There was warmth waiting for me outside these sterile walls.

That evening, I headed to the cooking class at *Not a Yacht Club*, a venue as welcoming as its name was ironic. The scent of simmering garlic, onions, and herbs filled the air, instantly grounding me. Laughter and conversation hummed around me as we gathered around Dante, ready for the night's lesson.

Dante Bastione clapped his hands together, a grin splitting his face. "Alright, folks! Tonight, we're making homemade pasta with my grandmother's famous sauce. Trust me, after this, you'll never look at boxed pasta the same way again."

Ingredients were laid out before us—flour, eggs, tomatoes, fresh herbs—like an artist's palette. Dante showed us how to work the dough, his hands moving with practiced ease. "Now, *yinz* can pair up and get rolling," he added, slipping in Pittsburghese with his usual flair.

I teamed up with Max, who eyed the flour like it might explode. "Ready to make some magic?" I nudged him.

He let out a laugh. "If by magic, you mean a complete gooey mess, then sure."

We got to work, forming a well in the flour and cracking eggs into the center.

"Slow and steady," Dante advised. "Patience is key."

Around us, familiar voices filled the kitchen. Ford and his other brother Sean worked at the next station, their banter punctuated by laughter. Sean, ever the daredevil, cranked the pasta machine like he was revving an engine. "Piece of cake," he quipped. "Or, you know, pasta."

Ford adjusted the setting and ran their dough through again. "This thing's weirdly satisfying."

Max and I took our turn, feeding our dough through. I was too focused on not botching it to notice Ford approaching until he grabbed a spoon and gave our sauce a stir.

"Mind if I join you guys?" he asked.

"Of course not," I said, though something about his tone had me bracing.

Ford hesitated, then lowered his voice. "Look, Sinan... I've been meaning to talk to you about Kendra."

I set down the spoon. "What about her?"

He exchanged a look with Max, who gave a subtle nod. "You know we're happy for you. But this isn't just about you two—it affects all of us. Emma, Sonya... our family."

Max folded his arms, his voice measured. "We just want to make sure you're serious. Kendra's been through enough. If this doesn't work out, it's not like breaking up with someone you met at a bar."

I met their gazes. "I know what's at stake. Kendra and I aren't rushing into anything. We're building something real."

Ford exhaled. "That's what I need to hear. Because, man, you got serious with Miranda fast. And that ended bad."

I clenched my jaw, the weight of my past pressing in. "Kendra's nothing like Miranda. This is completely different."

Something in my voice must have convinced them because Ford gave a slow nod. The tension between us eased, and the conversation drifted back to lighter things.

After the last of the pasta had been devoured and the kitchen began emptying, I lingered, watching Dante wipe down the counters.

Noticing me hovering, he arched a brow. "Something on your mind, Sin?"

I hesitated, then pulled up a stool. "Mind if we talk?"

He tossed the towel over his shoulder and leaned in. "Hit me."

I let it spill—Ford's concerns, my lingering doubts about Kendra fitting into my world, the weight of everyone's expectations. Dante listened, patient and unruffled.

Then he smirked. "Classic surgeon move, you're overthinking. Love isn't an operation, Sinan. It's not about precision, just trust. Do you trust her?"

I exhaled. "Yeah."

"Then stop trying to control the outcome." He shook his head. "You let pressure get in your head, and you'll end up breaking something good before it even has a chance to grow."

His words settled over me, grounding. I nodded. "Ford's just looking out for her."

"Of course he is. That's what family does. But from where I'm standing? You and Kendra have something real. Don't let other people's doubts turn into your own."

I left the kitchen with a lighter step, Dante's words trailing after me.

Outside, the cold air bit at my skin, but I barely noticed. My phone buzzed.

Kendra: Heading to your place. See you soon?

Me: On my way.

As I drove through the snow-covered streets, streetlights casting golden reflections on the wet pavement, I felt something close to certainty.

Whatever came next, Kendra and I could handle it.

And I couldn't wait to see her tonight.

SNOWFLAKES AND SHOWDOWNS

KENDRA

The coffee machine gurgled as I stood in the kitchen, waiting for my first cup. A sliver of winter sun peeked through the window, offering no real warmth against the January chill. I reached for my phone, expecting nothing but emails.

And then I saw it.

A text. Time stamped at 3:12 A.M.

> Unknown: You think you can steal from me and get away with it? That money was MINE. Lorraine would never have done this if she was in her right mind. You and Sonya conned her. You owe me what's MINE. I'm not settling for a measly ten grand. Meet me tomorrow or I swear, you'll regret it. You won't like me when I'm angry.

My stomach twisted.

So, he must've spoken to the lawyer

I barely registered Sonya walking in until she nudged my arm. "You're up early for a Sunday." She caught my expression and frowned. "What's wrong?"

Wordlessly, I handed her my phone. I watched her face tighten as she read.

"That bastard," she muttered. "Lorraine left us that money because she knew exactly what kind of person he was." She handed the phone back, jaw clenched. "And for the record? I talked to the lawyer on Friday. The will's official now. You and I split the estate. Jimmy gets ten grand, just like Lorraine specified."

I exhaled, trying to push down the frustration bubbling up inside me. "He's going to make this ugly, isn't he?"

Sonya's grip on her mug tightened. "Jimmy doesn't know how to do anything else."

I hesitated. "Do we even bother meeting him?"

She sighed, considering it. "If we don't, he's just going to escalate. Better to shut him down in person before he starts making a real mess."

I nodded. "Let's do it tomorrow."

No more fear. No more waiting. Jimmy didn't get to control us anymore.

The next day was dreary, the snow melting into dirty slush that clung to my boots as I trudged toward the pizza place. Sonya, having taken the afternoon off, walked beside me, steady and sure. The gray sky suited my mood.

Outside the entrance, the scent of garlic and spices wafted through the door, making my stomach grumble despite my nerves. Sonya elbowed me, her eyes glinting. "If this were a movie, the ominous music would kick in right about now."

I smirked. "And Jimmy would be twirling his mustache."

"Complete with a villain monologue about how he was the true heir all along."

I chuckled, tension easing. "Worst case, we throw pizza at him."

She grinned. "And I hit him with the teacher glare."

The restaurant's warmth dulled the edge of my anxiety, but Jimmy's presence in the corner booth snapped it right back. He was slouched in his seat, arms crossed, tapping his fingers impatiently against the table. His gaze locked onto us the second we walked in.

Jimmy's eyes narrowed as we slid into the seats across from him. "About time," he muttered.

Sonya didn't waste a second. "You're not getting a cent beyond what Lorraine left you."

Jimmy's eyes darkened. "She wouldn't have done this if you two hadn't poisoned her against me."

I let out a sharp laugh. "*Poisoned* her? Jimmy, Lorraine knew you. She watched you waste every opportunity you ever had. She made her choice, and it had nothing to do with us. We never even met her."

His mouth twisted. "Oh, *please*. You think you deserve that money more than her own brother?"

Sonya met his glare head-on. "Apparently, *she* thought so. Lorraine knew exactly what she was doing."

Jimmy leaned forward, voice dropping to a low hiss. "You don't think I can fight this? I *will*. I'll drag this through the courts. I'll make your lives miserable."

I exhaled sharply, meeting his glare head-on. "You don't have a case. The will is airtight. But you *do* have ten grand. That's more than you ever gave *us* growing up, so consider it repayment."

His mouth curled in a sneer. "Oh, *that's* how you wanna play it? I bet that rich boyfriend of yours—that sugar daddy—what's his name? *Sinan*? I bet has no idea about all the dirty little secrets you and your mom covered up. All that debt you have."

My stomach clenched, but I didn't flinch. "There are no secrets, Jimmy. And what debt are you talking about? Mom's medical bills? My tuition?" The second the words left my mouth, I regretted giving him even that much. The less he knew, the better.

"Oh, please." He leaned back, smirking. "You think you're better than me? You think you deserve that money? You're just like your mother and sister—always begging for a handout."

Sonya's hand curled into a fist. "That's *enough*."

Jimmy smirked. "No, I don't think it is." He leaned in, eyes gleaming. "I can make trouble for you, Kendra. You *owe* me."

A sharp, ice-cold anger settled in my chest. "No, Jimmy. I don't owe you a damn thing."

The restaurant noise hummed around us, but in our corner, everything had gone deadly quiet.

I stood, my pulse steady. "This is your last warning. You take the ten grand Lorraine left you and walk away. Or you get nothing, just like her will says. But either way, we are done with you."

Sonya rose beside me, her voice firm. "Try harassing us again, and we go to the police."

Jimmy's sneer faltered just slightly before he recovered. "You think this is over?"

I met his gaze, unshaken. "I know it is."

Then, without another word, we turned and walked out.

The cold air outside hit my lungs like a jolt, but instead of weighing me down, it cleared my head.

Sonya smirked. "Well, that went better than I expected."

I let out a breath. "Yeah. I half-expected a pizza fight."

She laughed. "If that had happened, we'd have a great story for book club."

I smiled, warmth filling the space where anxiety had been. "Thanks for being there. I couldn't have done it without you."

"Anytime, sis." She pulled me into a quick hug.

As we walked on, I realized I'd gained more than closure today. I'd gained an ally in standing up to Jimmy.

And that made all the difference.

I headed back to the office, bolstered by Sonya's support, but Jimmy's threats replayed in my mind like a bad song stuck on repeat. I stepped into the elevator, exhaling slowly. Time to shove it aside and focus on work.

The doors slid open to reveal Josh, standing square in the exit like he owned the place. Basic elevator etiquette was clearly beyond him.

"Hey, Kendra," he said casually, pushing past me instead of

letting me exit first. "Bridge planning meeting's been moved to three."

I nodded, suppressing a sigh. "Got it. Thanks."

At my desk, I buried myself in project reports, forcing my focus away from the gnawing tension in my chest. I ignored my phone as it buzzed with notifications. No distractions. Not today. Not after this morning.

At 2:55, I grabbed my notes and headed to the conference room—only to find it empty, save for abandoned coffee cups and a few scattered handouts. My stomach twisted as I checked the calendar on my tablet.

The meeting had never been rescheduled.

Heat crawled up my spine. Josh had set me up. The smug bastard had deliberately misled me, making sure I'd walk in too late to contribute.

I clenched my fists, forcing myself to breathe. I should have taken Sinan's advice seriously—I needed to start watching my back. This was going on record. Every petty stunt Josh pulled would be documented from now on.

Before I could even sit down, Mr. Parker's assistant appeared at my cubicle. "Mr. Parker wants to see you."

Great.

Tension coiled in my gut as I made my way to his office. The moment I stepped inside, I could tell this wasn't a casual chat.

"Kendra, take a seat," he said, his expression unreadable. "Why weren't you at the meeting?"

I kept my voice even. "Josh told me it was moved to three. By the time I got there, it was over."

Mr. Parker's jaw tightened as he dialed his phone. Seconds later, Josh strolled in, all fake concern.

"Kendra says you told her the meeting was rescheduled," Mr. Parker said, his gaze locked on Josh.

Josh's face was a masterpiece of practiced innocence. "Oh—there must've been a mix-up. I mentioned tomorrow's reschedule. Today's meeting was always at two."

Liar.

I forced my expression to stay neutral as frustration simmered beneath the surface.

Mr. Parker exhaled sharply. "I won't tolerate office politics or sabotage. Consider this a warning—to both of you."

A warning? *For me?* Fury and disbelief twisted together in my chest. I gritted my teeth. "Understood."

Josh shot me a smug glance as he walked out, but as soon as the door shut behind him, Mr. Parker's posture shifted. He leaned back in his chair, eyes assessing.

"Kendra, you're doing exceptional work," he said, his voice softer now. "Don't let office drama distract you. The lesson here is simple—trust but verify. Next time, confirm details before assuming changes."

I nodded, though his reassurance felt hollow.

Just as I turned to leave, he added, "Actually, I wanted to discuss something else. Despite today's… hiccup, your contributions to the bridge project have been outstanding. You've earned Employee of the Quarter."

I blinked. "Seriously?"

A small smile tugged at his lips. "And with it, a full week of paid vacation. Consider it a thank-you for your hard work."

A week. A whole week.

Shock stole my words, and I finally managed, "I—I don't know what to say. Thank you."

He waved it off. "Just keep doing what you're doing."

I left his office in a daze. Five minutes ago, I was contemplating murder-by-paperweight, and now I had a free vacation? The emotional whiplash was unreal.

Back at my desk, I barely had time to process it before Allison leaned against the cubicle partition. "Employee of the Quarter, huh?" she mused, a rare grin crossing her face. "Congrats. First vacation I had in years when I won that one. Just a heads-up— they'll expect even bigger things from you now."

"Thanks," I said, still a little stunned.

She gave me a nod, something almost like approval in her gaze. "Enjoy the time off. You earned it."

Of all people, Allison—the Iron Lady of Bridge Repair—had just given me a compliment.

Maybe I was finally earning my place here.

I exhaled, letting my shoulders relax as I stared at my phone. The day had been a mess—a rollercoaster of sabotage, warnings, and unexpected victories. But one thing was clear.

I needed to tell Sinan.

I thought of our quiet walks, the way he always said, You're not in this alone, you know. His steady presence had been my anchor more times than I could count.

But dumping all my baggage on him at once? That felt... heavy.

I'd tell him about Josh. The vacation. The Jimmy situation? That could wait. One battle at a time.

For the first time all day, I felt in control. I could handle this.

I'd already won today's fight.

Tomorrow? That was another story.

30

ISLAND ESCAPE TURNS INWARD

Sinan

The hum of the hospital faded as my mind zeroed in on one thing: my paper. It had gone live yesterday, and today I'd finally see the reactions. My rounds were a blur, anticipation thrumming beneath my skin. By the time I reached my office, my pulse raced.

I dropped into my chair and opened my inbox.

"Congratulations on Your Publication!"

I clicked, barely breathing. High download rates, positive reviews, early citations—it was a resounding success.

I switched to social media. My paper was trending in medical circles, debated, shared, even picked up by major news sites.

Validation. Finally. Maybe this called for a parade. Or, at least a cupcake.

Grinning, I thought of Kendra. She'd been sitting next to me on the flight to Turks and Caicos when I'd finalized the manuscript. She'd be thrilled.

A knock at the door snapped me out of my thoughts. Val Sigurdsson leaned in, his Nordic features split into a grin.

"Sin, congratulations! Your paper's making waves."

I smiled. "Thanks, Val. It's surreal."

"Believe it. You've set a new standard." He clapped me on the shoulder. "You should do something to celebrate."

As Val left, I considered the idea. My patient load was light, just a couple of surgeries I could reschedule. Maybe this was the perfect time for a break. Clear blue waters, warm sand, Kendra by my side…

Yeah. I knew exactly how to celebrate.

When I arrived home, still buzzing from the day's excitement, Kendra was already there. I'd given her my entry code weeks ago, and she often stopped by after work. Tonight, I found her in the kitchen, humming softly as she sautéed chicken.

She glanced up. "You look like you're bursting with good news."

I grinned. "Remember that paper I was working on during our flight? It just got published—huge success, even trending."

Her face lit up. "That's amazing, Sin! Congratulations!" She set down the tongs and wrapped her arms around me.

I laughed, holding her close. "Feels like everything's finally falling into place."

"We should celebrate."

"Exactly what I was thinking. How about somewhere sunnier than Pittsburgh?"

She tilted her head. "Like…?"

"The Maldives. Just the two of us."

Her grin faltered. "That's… far. You think we're ready for that step?"

For a brief moment, my mind flickered to the past. Miranda, with her perfect facade that eventually cracked. Lillian, my college girlfriend who'd broken up with me the day *after* our trip —because she hadn't wanted to miss Paris. I wasn't about to repeat those mistakes. But this wasn't about rushing things. It was about *us*. About celebrating with someone special.

"It's time we took a real trip together," I said, watching her carefully. "Besides, my parents are arriving soon, and since they'll be staying with me for a month, it'll be hard to find time for just us. I want something special before that. You deserve a break… from Jimmy, from the bridge project, from all of it."

Kendra hesitated, then a slow smile spread across her face. "It sounds perfect. When do we leave?"

"As soon as you can arrange time off—a few days?"

She blinked, then laughed. "You move fast. But I've got vacation time to burn, and no looming deadlines."

"You're in?"

She nodded, but when I added, "And just so we're clear, I'm paying for everything," her smile wavered. A small frown formed, but I held up a hand.

"No arguments. This is my way of celebrating our wins—my paper, your Employee of the Quarter award, and us."

Her expression softened. "Okay, but next trip is on me—as long as we keep it in the U.S."

"Deal." I kissed her and stepped back. "Now, how about I open some wine while you finish up that chicken?"

Over dinner, excitement built as we planned. The next few days flew by in a blur of preparations. I rescheduled my surgeries, took myself off rotation, and by the end of the week, our bags were packed.

We were off on our adventure.

As the plane descended, I held Kendra's hand, our gazes locked on the crystal-clear waters below. The Maldives unfolded beneath us—turquoise shallows fading into the deep blue of the Indian Ocean.

A familiar pang tightened my chest. I'd done trips like this before. I'd watched Miranda light up over lavish resorts, seen her admiration twist into entitlement. The luxury had mattered more than the moment itself.

But Kendra? She wasn't clinging to my arm like I was her ticket to paradise. She was simply watching, taking it all in with quiet awe.

The knot in my gut loosened.

We grabbed a taxi, the vibrant colors of the island flashing past. As we checked into the resort, Kendra's eyes widened.

"This place is incredible," she murmured, her voice filled with pure wonder.

I braced for the complaint that always followed with Miranda —too humid, too small, too anything. But nothing came. There was just Kendra, fully present, her smile making the moment feel bigger.

Relief settled deep in my bones. "I'm glad you like it. I wanted this to be special."

Our private villa sat on a pier stretching over the water, rustic on the outside but sleek and modern within. Floor-to-ceiling windows framed the endless ocean, and just beyond the bedroom doors, a private infinity pool blurred into the sea.

Kendra stepped onto the deck, peering over the water's edge. I smirked. "Careful not to fall in."

She spun to face me, laughing. "If I do, at least I'll go out with a great view."

No hidden barbs. No unmet expectations. Just joy.

I walked up behind her, sliding an arm around her waist. "We need to toast to our arrival. Let's grab cocktails and plan the next few days."

She leaned into me. "As long as we don't stray too far. This villa is too perfect."

We didn't rush. We strolled to the beachside bar, the waves lapping gently against the shore. The bartender greeted us with easy warmth. I ordered a *Fini Raa*, Kendra a *Rani Foni*.

She took a sip of mine, rolling the taste on her tongue. "This Fee-nee Ree is amazing."

I grinned. "Fee-nee Ree, Fini Raa… close enough. Guess you'll have to order another round to get it right."

Her laughter was light, easy, threading through the moment like it belonged there.

Miranda's voice flickered in my mind—her sharp critiques, her calculated charm. But Kendra? She wasn't working this moment for an angle. She was simply in it.

God, it felt good.

We wandered the resort, soft sand underfoot, the infinity pool glimmering beneath the sun. The spa, with its open-air treatment rooms tucked into lush greenery, promised real relaxation. Kendra chatted with the staff, asking about treatments and activities—not to push for special treatment, but because she genuinely cared.

I hadn't realized how much I'd been waiting for the other shoe to drop, for the first real sign that this was another doomed trip, another illusion.

But it never came.

That night, we dined in the hotel's underwater restaurant, surrounded by schools of fish floating past the glass walls. A sea turtle glided by as if inspecting the diners, and Kendra pressed her hands to the window, eyes wide with pure, unfiltered wonder.

"This place is incredible," she whispered.

I smirked. "If I'd known this was all it took to impress you, we could've skipped the Maldives and gotten you an aquarium."

She laughed, turning to me. "A plastic tank and some turtle food? Sold." She shook her head. "But... this does have its charm."

She reached across the table, fingers brushing mine. I laced them together.

For the first time in a long while, I felt at ease.

After dinner, we walked back to the villa under a sky painted in pinks and golds. Kendra settled into a lounge chair, pulling me down beside her.

"This place is even more magical than I imagined," she murmured.

"I wanted it to be special."

"It already is."

I watched her as the sunset reflected in her eyes. The weight in my chest—of past mistakes, of wondering if I was repeating them—began to loosen.

"This is the kind of sunset they write songs about," I mused.

She laughed. "Pretty sure we're living the lyrics right now."

I rested my forehead against hers, heart pounding. Three words hovered on my tongue. Did I love her? Was that why I felt like I was freefalling?

Or was it just the Maldives, the magic of the moment?

I kissed her, long and deep, letting the rush of it drown out the doubts.

This wasn't about the past.

This was ours.

And I didn't want to let her go.

31

PARADISE PARADOX

Kendra

Soft dawn light filtered through the sheer curtains, painting the room in a golden glow. The rhythmic lap of waves beneath the villa stirred me awake, the scent of salt and jasmine floating in on the breeze.

For a moment, I just lay there, absorbing it all. The endless ocean stretching beyond the floor-to-ceiling windows, the gentle sway of the villa's stilts over the water. The stark difference between this and my usual mornings—alarm clocks, steel-gray Pittsburgh skies, and half-cold coffee on my way to work.

A soft splash broke the stillness.

I turned my head just in time to see Sinan step out of the pool, water gliding over the sculpted lines of his back, catching the early sunlight like scattered diamonds. He reached for a towel, rolling his shoulders in a slow, deliberate stretch.

And *damn*, he was gorgeous..

Since we'd arrived, there had been moments—*flickers*—where he seemed distracted. But last night, the space between us had closed again.

The sheets pooled at my waist as I sat up, trailing my fingers over the cool, crisp linen. This place—it was like something from a dream. Sleek wooden beams, airy white drapes shifting in the breeze, the quiet hum of the ocean filling every corner. The way the villa blended into the world around it—natural yet impossibly refined.

Yet, as breathtaking as it was, a part of me felt like an intruder here. Like I was borrowing someone else's life for the week.

Sinan caught my gaze, his lips curling into a slow, knowing smile. "Morning, beautiful."

His voice was still muzzy with sleep, sending a pleasant shiver down my spine.

I slipped out of bed, padding barefoot onto the deck. The teak was still cool enough to make me second-guess skipping slippers, but the view made it worth the chill—the horizon awash in soft pinks and deep blues. Breakfast waited on the table: golden pastries, ripe tropical fruit, and plates arranged with the kind of effortless elegance I'd only ever seen in glossy travel magazines.

"This place is so…" I hesitated, plucking a piece of pineapple from the tray. "Extravagant."

Sinan smirked, tilting his head. "That a bad thing?"

"No." I bit into the fruit, the sweet burst of flavor lingering on my tongue. "Just—surreal. Like I stepped into someone else's first-class ticket."

His expression softened. "You belong here, Kendra. And you deserve to be spoiled."

I exhaled, pushing past the familiar pull of guilt. Middle-class reflexes—the quiet discomfort of *too much*. But Sinan had worked for this. He'd earned this moment, this break, just as much as I had. I wouldn't let my own hang-ups ruin it.

"You're right," I admitted. "I'll try to just… enjoy it."

His fingers brushed over mine in silent approval.

After breakfast, we wandered to the spa, the sun warm on our backs as the wooden walkway creaked beneath our steps. Inside, the air was thick with eucalyptus and lavender, instantly soothing.

A quick steam session loosened every last bit of tension I

hadn't realized I was still carrying. A cold plunge jolted me awake, every nerve ending sparking. And by the time I lay on the massage table, staring through the floor's glass panels at fish drifting lazily below, I felt... weightless.

Sinan was beside me, eyes closed, a rare, genuine smile playing on his lips.

Seeing him like this—at ease and unguarded—was a better balm than any massage.

By the time we returned to the villa, lunch was already set: sushi, fresh salads, delicate desserts arranged like edible art.

"This is a lot," I said, taking in the sheer volume of food.

Sinan chuckled, pouring two glasses of white wine. "We'll eat what we can and save the leftovers for future lunches."

"I can live with that," I teased, picking up a perfect roll of sushi.

We spent the afternoon snorkeling, slipping into another world beneath the waves. Coral reefs bloomed in brilliant colors, tropical fish darting like quicksilver around us. Sinan swam beside me, fluid and effortless.

When we surfaced, he grinned. "You're like a mermaid."

I laughed, breathless. "You're not too bad yourself, Dr. Bachar."

Back at the villa, I checked my phone. A text from Sonya popped up.

> Sonya: Jimmy violated his probation. Bar fight.
> He won't be bothering us for thirty days.

Relief rushed through me.

"Yes!"

Sinan looked over, brows lifting. "Good news?"

I exhaled, tension I hadn't realized I was holding melting away. "Jimmy's back in jail."

A flicker of something darker crossed his face. "I didn't realize he was still bothering you."

"He's pissed about his sister's will, but it's over now," I said, locking my phone. "At least, for a while."

And for once, I didn't feel the weight of it pressing down on me.

The next few days passed in a blissful haze—the kind of perfect, sun-soaked days and steamy nights that you never wanted to end.

We rode motorbikes along winding island paths, the warm wind lifting my hair as Sinan led us toward hidden beaches. We picnicked on the sand, the ocean breeze cooling the heat of the afternoon. We ended every night in each other's arms, tasting, touching, and giving all we had.

Our last night there, stretched out on a secluded beach beneath a sky heavy with stars, Sinan reached for my hand.

"This trip has been incredible," I whispered.

"Not as incredible as you," he said, his voice low and steady.

Back at the villa, we left the lights off, letting the soft glow of the pool guide us inside.

And as we stepped into the quiet warmth of the room, I finally let go of the last, lingering doubts.

This wasn't borrowed.

This was ours.

And I wasn't going to waste a second of it.

3 2

LOVE, LIES, AND TURKISH DELIGHTS

SINAN

Two weeks later, I stood at Pittsburgh International's arrivals terminal, scanning the crowd for my parents. Cem and Aylin were easy to spot among the crowd. My *baba*, ever composed, pushed a luggage cart with quiet efficiency while my *anne's* sharp eyes swept the sea of faces. The second she spotted me, her whole face lit up.

"Sinan!" she called, switching seamlessly to Turkish as she pulled me into a tight embrace. The familiar scent of her perfume —jasmine and something warm that reminded me of home— wrapped around me.

I held her a moment longer than usual. Too many missed calls. Too many excuses. Too much time lost.

Baba's smile was warm but tired. "Long flight," he said in Turkish, clapping my shoulder.

"I bet. Let's get you home."

The March air hit us as we stepped outside, crisp and damp with the last traces of winter. As I loaded their luggage into my Mercedes sedan, Aylin launched into a familiar complaint.

"Sinan, you wouldn't believe the visa process. They asked for

210

everything except our blood type! I was waiting for them to demand a lie detector test."

Baba sighed. "It wasn't that bad."

I caught *Anne's* smirk in the rearview mirror. "If it weren't for your father, we'd still be filling out forms."

At my house on Mount Washington, *Baba* paused to admire the sweeping view of Pittsburgh, but *Anne* zeroed in on a sweater hanging in the front closet.

Her brows lifted. "Whose is this?"

"Kendra's."

The slight purse of her lips was all the reaction I needed.

"When will I meet her?" she asked, her tone measured.

"Soon," I said. "She's staying with Sonya and Max, so you'll meet her when we visit Emma."

Aylin exhaled slowly. "Good."

She didn't elaborate, but I caught the undertone of judgment. The sweater alone had been enough to make her wary.

As we drove to Sonya and Max's house, I cleared my throat, choosing my words carefully.

"Before we get there," I said in Turkish, glancing at them in the rearview mirror, "I want to make sure you're both prepared for something."

Anne arched an eyebrow. "Prepared for what?"

"Emma calls Sonya and Max 'Mom' and 'Dad' now."

The weight of my words settled over them. *Baba's* expression was unreadable, but *Anne's* lips pressed into a thin line.

"Barry and Hailey are her *real* parents," she said carefully.

"But Max and Sonya adopted her," I said evenly. "She's been with them for over a year now and feels safe with them. *They* are her parents now."

A beat of silence.

Baba sighed, his voice softer. "She must love them very much."

"She does. And they love her."

Anne said nothing, her gaze fixed on the passing streets.

As we walked up to Sonya and Max's house, Emma burst through the front door before I even had a chance to knock.

"*Babaanne! Dede!*" she squealed, flinging herself into their arms.

Anne's face softened instantly as she held Emma close. "My beautiful *torunu*," she murmured. "I've missed you."

Once inside, *Baba* handed Emma a small box, his eyes kind. "For you."

Emma's eyes widened. "Turkish Delight! Like in *The Lion, the Witch, and the Wardrobe!*"

Max chuckled. "She's been obsessed with that book lately. Perfect gift."

Sonya stepped forward, extending a warm hand to my parents. "Welcome. It's so nice to have you here." Then she turned. "And this is my sister, Kendra."

Kendra descended the stairs, wearing leggings and a sweater, casual but effortlessly beautiful.

Aylin's gaze skimmed her like an appraisal, her posture stiffening. The warmth she'd shown Emma cooled in an instant.

She leaned toward me and muttered in Turkish, "Miranda was always so polished. You could take her anywhere."

The jab landed like a slap.

Kendra's expression barely flickered, but I saw the slight tension in her jaw. She'd caught Miranda's name.

Emma's eyes took on a devilish gleam. "Would you like me to translate? *Babaanne* said—"

"Emma!" Sonya jumped in. "The cookies. Oven timer."

Emma smirked, then left for the kitchen.

Aylin stayed beside me, lowering her voice. "Sinan, is this woman serious?"

I kept my tone firm as I replied quietly in Turkish. "Of course she is. She's kind, smart, and I'd be proud to take her anywhere, *Anne*. Please, show her some respect."

She didn't answer.

Baba, sensing the tension, stepped forward, extending a hand to Kendra. "Sinan tells me you're a civil engineer. I've always found that field fascinating."

Kendra brightened. "It's a challenging but rewarding career."

Aylin offered Sonya a tight smile. "Your home is lovely. I love the fresh scent of lemon oil. It's so… tidy."

Sonya's expression didn't waver, but I caught the slight shift in her shoulders. "Thank you. Our mother cleaned houses for a living. We grew up keeping things neat."

Aylin pressed her lips together. "I see."

I knew that tone.

She wasn't just disapproving—she was marking the divide between *us* and *them*.

After the cookies were safely out of the oven, Emma returned to the living room with a plate of them and flopped down beside Sonya.

"Mom, can I have one now, or do I have to wait?" she asked, already reaching for one.

I didn't miss the way *Anne's* shoulders stiffened at the word 'Mom'. It was subtle—just a momentary hesitation—but her fingers curled slightly at her sides, like she was gripping an invisible thread.

Sonya, not noticing, smiled warmly. "Just one for now. Let's make sure everyone gets some."

Emma immediately snatched one up.

Baba watched the exchange thoughtfully, but *Anne* kept her gaze on the plate of cookies, her jaw tight.

I exhaled quietly. At least she hadn't been blindsided. But maybe combining this with meeting Kendra was becoming too much for her.

Emma switched back to Turkish, chatting about her latest school project.

Anne, still rattled, found something to critique. "Your pronunciation needs work."

Emma faltered, her smile dimming slightly.

Baba chuckled, ruffling Emma's hair. "Don't listen to your *babaanne, torunum*. Your Turkish is improving."

Emma brightened. "In that case, can you help me convince Mom and Dad to let me get a pet? I want a cat."

But she said *kredi* instead of *kedi*.

Baba let out a hearty laugh, his whole face lighting up.

I couldn't help but chuckle, too. "Emma, you meant *kedi*, not *kredi*. Unless you're trying to get a credit card instead of a cat."

Emma only looked slightly chagrined. "Oops! Though a credit card might be useful."

Max shook his head and grinned. "Nice try, kid. A credit card is definitely not happening. You have a better shot at getting a pet llama."

A round of genuine laughter rippled through the room, easing the tension for a brief moment. As the laughter faded, Aylin turned to Kendra with polite curiosity. "Kendra, do you speak any other languages?"

I tensed. This wasn't just a question. It was a test.

Kendra met her gaze evenly. "Some Spanish. Enough to get by, not enough to impress."

I knew that tone in her voice—carefully measured, almost breezy. But beneath it, I saw the tightness in her posture, the way her shoulders squared just a bit too much. Kendra could hold her own in any room, but moments like this reminded me she still carried that old fear of not belonging. That someone might decide she wasn't enough—because of where she came from, or what she didn't have.

Aylin hummed. "And no Turkish?"

Kendra smiled. "Not yet, but Emma's been teaching me."

Emma perked up. "She knows *merhaba* and *teşekkür ederim*! And I bet she knows *kredi* and *kedi* now."

Aylin's lips pressed together into a thin smile. "How nice."

I stepped in. "Kendra doesn't need to speak Turkish."

Aylin sipped her tea. "Of course. But culture matters."

Kendra didn't flinch. "I agree."

Aylin exhaled. "Well, I suppose not everyone is good with languages." She turned to Sonya. "Did you use real vanilla or that imitation nonsense?"

Kendra's face stayed perfectly neutral, but I knew better. That kind of comment didn't glance off her—it lodged somewhere deeper. She'd spent her whole life proving herself, carrying the unspoken fear that someone might eventually look at her too closely and find her lacking. It wasn't just the language or the background or the money. It was the constant, low hum of wondering if she'd ever be seen as enough.

The moment passed, but I gave Kendra's hand a reassuring squeeze. She squeezed back.

She wasn't backing down.

That made me so proud of her.

Max appeared from the kitchen, a container of cookies in hand. "To take home with you," he said with a grin.

Anne stifled a yawn, and I saw the opening. "It's been a long day. Let's get you home."

The car ride was quiet—until we stepped inside my house.

Then the dam broke.

Aylin turned to me, her expression sharp as glass. "I don't understand why you're wasting your time with Kendra."

Exhaustion settled deep in my bones. "*Anne…*"

"There are so many other women—ones who actually fit your life. Miranda, for instance."

That was it. *No more.*

I squared my shoulders, my patience finally gone. "There's a reason I'm not with Miranda anymore, and you need to hear it." My voice was steel. "She's a drug addict. She stole medication from the hospital, and she's facing felony charges. That's the woman you think is perfect for me?"

Aylin stared at me, visibly shaken. "That can't be true. Miranda was raised properly. She went to the best schools. She's a doctor."

I let out a bitter laugh. "And yet, she's the one begging me for money, which is why I didn't tell you sooner. At first, I thought I could fix it. That if I gave her time, helped her through it, she'd turn things around. And then, when she didn't... when it kept getting worse and she kept asking me for more money—I didn't want to deal with your judgment on top of everything else." My voice was quieter now, but still firm. "I wasn't going to defend someone who wasn't worth defending. So I just... let it go."

Aylin shook her head, as if she could make it untrue.

"Kendra?" I continued. "She's never asked me for a damn thing. She works hard. She's kind. And she doesn't pretend to be something she's not."

But the worst part? She still wonders if that's enough. I see it in quiet moments—in the hesitation before she introduces herself at a work event, or the way she shrinks back when people start listing their Ivy League credentials. She doesn't need their approval, but she's still learning how to believe that. And when my mother tears her down with polite smiles and veiled barbs, it only sharpens that old wound.

Anne's mouth pressed into a thin line. "She's from nowhere, Sinan. Nothing. You barely know her."

Baba finally spoke up, his voice calm but firm. "Aylin, we married young. We barely knew what we wanted out of life, yet you still chose me."

"That was different."

"Why?" I demanded.

"Our parents were in favor of the match," she said, her voice quiet but unwavering.

"And you've already decided you're against Kendra?"

Anne sighed, rubbing her temples. "We'll talk about this later."

I knew we would.

The rift wasn't mended.

But tonight, it was enough that I'd finally said the words out loud.

33

DRAMA ON THE DOORSTEP

KENDRA

The early April drizzle outside matched my mood as I drove to work. Heavy clouds pressed low over the city, the rhythmic patter of rain offering a strange comfort. The Ohio River flowed beside me, its surface rippling like the waters of the Maldives. I let my mind drift back to those carefree days—just me and Sinan, free of expectations.

Traffic crawled, my thoughts trailing back to how easy everything had felt then. I missed that simplicity. Since Sinan's parents' arrival two weeks ago, our time together had become scarce, and our relationship felt—suspended. His mother's constant judgment hovered over me, an invisible wall I couldn't break through. I knew avoiding her wasn't the answer, but Aylin's scrutiny left me feeling suffocated.

Just three more weeks. I can manage that.

Refocusing, I shifted gears—mentally and literally. Work had been going well, and last weekend's dive class left me feeling proud. At least in that space, I had control.

But today was different. My six-month review with Mr. Parker was scheduled, and despite earning *Employee of the Quarter* in

January, my stomach still tightened at the thought. I'd put in the effort, built strong relationships, and even been recognized for my contributions—but a small voice in the back of my mind warned me not to get too comfortable. Praise didn't guarantee security. I needed to keep proving myself.

Twenty minutes later, I entered the small, windowless conference room, my heart skipping a beat. It wasn't just Mr. Parker waiting for me. Ken Burdinger sat beside him. My pulse quickened. Ken was the project supervisor, and I hadn't expected him to be here.

"Good morning, Kendra. Please, have a seat," Mr. Parker greeted me with a warm smile.

Ken gave a curt nod, and I sat, trying to keep my nerves in check.

Mr. Parker flipped through his notes. "I've been reviewing your work over the past six months, and I have to say, I'm impressed. Your project management skills, your teamwork, and the quality of your work have been excellent."

Relief washed over me, and I couldn't help but smile. "Thank you. I've really enjoyed working here."

Ken spoke up, his tone surprisingly approving. "You've shown a lot of growth. You're diligent and good at catching errors. I know I was tough on you, but it was to set the bar high. You've proven to be a valuable asset."

Surprised, I nodded. "I appreciate that."

Mr. Parker leaned forward. "That's why we're making some changes. Effective immediately, you'll be reporting directly to me. We're giving you more responsibility, starting with leading the team when the state inspection committee arrives. No date set for that yet, but you'll need to start preparing. Misha and Josh will still be your teammates, but you'll be taking on a leadership role within the department."

It took me a second to absorb what he was saying. A promotion. A leadership role.

"We're not changing your title drastically," Ken added. "But you'll be stepping into a *Project Lead* role. With that comes a three percent salary bump, effective immediately."

My heart soared. *Project Lead.* Not senior, but still a step up. "Thank you so much! This means a lot."

"You've earned it, Kendra," Mr. Parker said. "We need someone who can handle pressure, especially with the inspection coming up. I have no doubt you'll do well."

As I rose to leave, I caught a glimpse of Josh through the glass wall of the conference room, head down, typing with unusual focus. A few months ago, his snide comments would've gotten under my skin. Now, I just saw someone who had spent five years climbing a ladder only to watch me get a boost past a few rungs. I didn't excuse how he acted, but I understood it better now. Insecurity wore a lot of faces—Josh's just happened to smirk when it showed up.

I walked out of the room on air. Misha caught up with me as I made my way back to my desk.

"How'd it go?" they asked, their blue eyes twinkling.

"I got a raise! And a promotion! I'm going to be leading the team for the state inspection."

Misha let out an excited gasp. "That's fantastic! You totally deserve it. Not that I'm surprised—*Employee of the Quarter* and now this? You're on a roll!"

I grinned, still in a daze. As we approached Misha's workspace, I glanced at Josh, who had kept his distance lately. "Hey, Mish, have you noticed Josh has been... less of a jerk lately?"

Misha smirked. "Oh, I had a little chat with him."

My eyebrows shot up. "What did you say?"

"I told him if he didn't knock off trying to undermine you, I'd have a nice conversation with HR about his behavior. I've dealt with bullies my whole life. Josh is just another troll."

I blinked in surprise. "Wow, Misha. I didn't realize you had it in you."

They laughed. "Someone's gotta be the office superhero, right?"

I laughed too. "Thank you, Mish. Really."

"All in a day's work," they said, waving it off. "Now go bask in your well-earned promotion."

The unexpected support from Misha—and even Ken's praise—left me feeling more grounded. I blocked out thoughts of Sinan's mother and turned my attention to what I *could* control. Jimmy's presence, for one, was no longer a problem—between blocking his number and his stint in jail, my peace of mind was solid where he was concerned.

When I arrived home, I found Sonya in her room, holding up two nearly identical earrings with a look of deep concentration.

"Sonya, I got a promotion today!"

She spun so fast she nearly dropped the earrings. "No way! That's *amazing*!" She grabbed my hands, then narrowed her eyes. "Wait… was this even in question? I mean, you *were* Employee of the Quarter. They basically *had* to promote you."

I laughed. "I appreciate your confidence in corporate logic."

Sonya grinned. "We *have* to celebrate at book club tonight."

A warmth spread through me. Work had changed. My role had changed. And maybe—just maybe—I was changing, too.

But as we pulled up to Mara's house, my good mood vanished. I spotted a familiar profile sitting in a car parked out front, and dread sank deep into my gut.

"That's Jimmy," I muttered.

Sonya's grip tightened on the steering wheel. "What the hell is *he* doing here?"

Before we could even process what was happening, the driver's side window rolled down, revealing Jimmy's smirk.

"Ladies," he drawled, "miss me?"

Sonya's voice was ice. "Why aren't you in jail?"

"Thirty days goes by fast," he said, stretching as if he had all the time in the world. "Figured I'd drop by. Check in."

I folded my arms. "How did you even know we'd be here?"

He chuckled. "Your little book club isn't exactly private. Maybe don't broadcast your plans all over the internet."

The idea of him lurking on social media made my skin crawl.

"What do you want, Jimmy?" I asked, keeping my voice steady.

He leaned back, the smug grin never faltering. "Oh, I think you already know. My lawyer said contesting the will wasn't worth it. No-contest clause, ironclad paperwork, blah blah blah. But you know what I don't need a lawyer for? Talking to my daughters. The two women who—let's not forget—stole what's rightfully mine."

Sonya scoffed. "Lorraine didn't 'forget' you, Jimmy. She knew exactly what she was doing. And what you deserved."

His expression darkened, the smirk slipping for the first time. "She left me ten grand. Ten measly thousand dollars. While you two walked away with over half a million. You don't think that's a little unfair?"

I crossed my arms. "No. Lorraine made her choice. She didn't owe you anything."

He exhaled sharply, his frustration barely concealed. "Look, I get it. You've got your pride. But let's be real here—ten grand is a joke. We both know you can afford to make this right. You're sitting on a pile of money that should've been mine."

Sonya didn't hesitate. "Not a chance."

Jimmy's eyes flickered with anger, but then his smirk returned. "Fine. If you won't be reasonable, I'll have to get creative."

A chill ran down my spine. "What's that supposed to mean?"

He turned to Sonya, his tone suddenly light, casual. "Let's just say I know stories about your husband's business dealings that would make for some interesting headlines. Real interesting. Hollywood loves scandals."

Sonya went rigid. "You're bluffing."

Jimmy's smirk widened, his eyes glinting with malice. "Maybe. You wanna take that chance?"

Sonya didn't flinch. "You pull this crap again, I'll call your probation officer and make sure you're back behind bars."

For a moment, something flickered in his expression—panic?—but he recovered fast. "You don't scare me."

"Don't I?" Sonya shot back. "You already violated your parole with that bar fight. You're lucky you're out now."

His jaw tightened. He knew she was right.

Then his gaze flicked to me, and a slow, knowing smile crept across his face.

"And you, Kendra? Still got that rich doctor footing the bill? What's the arrangement, exactly? You playing house with him, letting him think you're some sweet little thing who isn't in it for the money?"

My stomach clenched, hands instinctively curling into fists. "You don't know anything about my relationship."

He let out a low chuckle. "Oh, I know plenty. Guys like him? They don't marry girls like you. They *rent* you."

Rage surged through me, hot and blinding.

Sonya took a step forward. "That's enough."

But Jimmy wasn't finished. He leaned closer, voice dripping with mock sympathy. "You think he's gonna stick around when he figures out you're just like Mom? Always needing something? Always looking for a sugar daddy to pick up the slack?"

It took everything in me not to react, not to give him the satisfaction of seeing that his words had landed. But deep inside, a tiny voice whispered—*is he right?*

I clenched my fists. "Get out of here, Jimmy."

He held my gaze for another long second, like he was daring me to crack. Then, with a muttered curse, he started the engine and peeled away.

Sonya exhaled sharply, running a hand through her hair. "God, I hate that man."

I nodded, but Jimmy's words clung to me like a stain I couldn't scrub off.

Guys like him don't marry girls like you.

I shook it off. He wanted to get inside my head. That's what he did.

Sonya squeezed my arm. "You okay?"

I forced a breath. "Yeah."

But I wasn't sure. Because Jimmy had always known exactly where to poke to make me doubt myself. And tonight, he'd found a crack.

34

ROMANCE IN THE LIMELIGHT

Even after a couple of weeks, I still hadn't adjusted to the relentless push and pull of trying to be everywhere at once. Work, family, Kendra—each demanded more of me than I had to give, and no matter how hard I tried, I was falling short. Cem and Aylin usually split their month-long visits between me and Barry, but now, I was the only son they had left. Their expectations, their grief, their need to make up for lost time—it all landed squarely on my shoulders.

I spoke to Kendra every day, but it wasn't enough. Especially not after that confrontation with Jimmy.

The night she called, her voice tight with frustration, telling me he'd ambushed her, I'd wanted to drop everything and drive to her place. But she wouldn't let me.

"I handled it, Sinan."

Yeah, she'd handled it. But that didn't mean I liked it. The way she brushed it off—like it was just another thing to deal with, like she was already getting used to putting out his fires—made me uneasy.

And I hated that I wasn't there to back her up.

But I couldn't just disappear on my family, either. I hadn't seen my parents in over a year, and Emma needed me. She was tough —resilient, even—but she felt her father's absence more acutely with her grandparents around. *Baba* had taken her under his wing, but I could see how she now looked to me as a buffer in these family gatherings.

So I split my time as best I could. Checking in on Kendra as much as she'd let me. Being present for my parents, even when my mother's scrutiny made me want to escape. Stealing moments with Emma, making sure she knew she wasn't alone.

I was doing my best.

But my best still didn't feel like enough.

At least my parents would be leaving on the first of the month. Then things could go back to normal.

That illusion lasted until Val burst into the scrub room, eyes crinkling behind his mask like he was announcing a lottery win.

"Sinan! Huge news, man!"

I shot him a skeptical glance as I rinsed my hands. "Let me guess, we're getting that new coffee you've been lobbying for in the break room?"

"No, better! The hospital board is throwing you a gala. You're the man of the hour."

I groaned internally. Of course they were. Another fundraiser for the donors—only now with my face on the invitations.

"Great," I said flatly, but Val wasn't deterred.

"This is big. The Omni Penn Ballroom, tuxedos, fancy hors d'oeuvres you can't pronounce, people fawning over your brilliance."

Before I could respond, Riley, my surfer-dude, house-sitting intern, bounded in, forever looking out of place in scrubs.

"Dude, I heard about the gala! That's legendary! You're like… the Michael Jordan of neurosurgery now."

I stifled a grin. Riley had a talent for turning everything into the ultimate compliment. "Thanks, Riley, but let's not get carried away. It's just a hospital fundraiser."

"Fundraiser, schmundraiser," Riley said, undeterred. "You're gonna be in a tux! That's James Bond-level coolness, but with scalpels."

Val chuckled. "Oh, and by the way—it's in just under two weeks. First Friday in May."

I blinked. "Two weeks?" That was... soon. "What, did their original guest of honor drop out?"

Val scratched his chin. "Actually... yeah. The keynote speaker —some medical ethics professor from Carnegie Mellon—got caught up in a controversy. The board didn't want the bad press."

I let out a dry laugh. "Ah. So I'm the understudy. Good to know my brilliance is only worth a gala when they're desperate."

"Hey," Riley said, undeterred, "Michael Jordan probably warmed the bench once too, man. Now you're stepping in for the big game."

I exhaled, rubbing the back of my neck. Two weeks. No way my parents would leave as planned next Friday—not when a gala in my honor was happening that night. They'd extend their stay, adding another layer of chaos to an already packed schedule.

And the tux and speech were the easy part.

The real challenge? Kendra walking into a high-society event with my mother watching her every move.

That meant tonight would be the warm-up. She was coming over for dinner—her first time spending any real time with my parents again since that tense, uncomfortable meeting the day they'd arrived. Sure, they'd seen each other in passing, but Aylin always managed to disappear whenever Kendra visited me. My mother planned to be in the kitchen all afternoon today, preparing an elaborate meal, which could mean one of two things: either she was extending an olive branch or she was preparing for battle. With her, it was impossible to tell.

"Dude, you don't look too happy about the whole thing. Bummed about the monkey suit?"

Val clapped Riley on the back. "Hey, you'll be there too, Riley. And not in some high school prom rental."

Riley blinked, looking momentarily bewildered. "A tux? I mean, I have a suit somewhere…"

Val shook his head, smirking. "Kid, it's gotta be a tux. And they aren't surf gear. You need one that fits properly. Maybe Sinan can give you some pointers. The guy's practically a style icon around here."

I shrugged, suppressing a smile. "Riley, I'll send you a few recommendations. Just… maybe leave the board shorts at home."

Riley grinned sheepishly. "No board shorts, got it, Dr. B."

With that, I turned toward the operating room. "Let's focus on the surgery before we start tux fittings."

The moment I stepped into the OR, everything else fell away. The pale blue of the surgical drapes, the steady rhythm of the monitors, the precise movements of my team—this was where I thrived.

The surgery progressed smoothly, each step as precise as a symphony. The tension in the room eased as the hematoma was removed without complications. It was moments like this that kept me anchored—the kind where the weight of responsibility lifted, even if only for a breath.

As I stepped back to let my intern close under my eagle eye, one of the nurses, Claire, glanced up, the smile lines around her eyes deepening. "Congratulations on the gala, Dr. Bachar. Do you plan to give a speech?"

I nodded absently. "I suppose I'll need to start working on it."

Back in my office, the post-surgery exhaustion hit, but there was no time to unwind. I skimmed my emails and spotted the hospital's official notice about the gala.

A speech. Of course, they'd expect one. Something heartfelt, acknowledging the team, inspiring enough to loosen a few wallets. I leaned back, the weight of the day settling over me.

I started jotting down ideas, but my mind kept drifting.

Kendra.

I pulled out my phone, meaning to text her about the gala, but I found a message from her waiting for me.

> Kendra: Heads-up, some chatter at work about the state launching a bridge safety crackdown. Nothing confirmed yet, but if it happens, it's going to be huge. Might get slammed at work.

I frowned, my fingers hovering over the screen.

> Me: Sounds stressful. You think Steeltown Bridge will be on their radar?

Her response came fast.

> Kendra: 100%. If this happens, that bridge is going to be front and center.

> Kendra: I'm going to be buried under prep and inspections.

I exhaled, rubbing my temple. So much for hoping things would settle down.

> Me: Sounds like a lot. Keep me posted?

> Kendra: Will do.

I stared at the screen for a second, thinking about the gala. The timing wasn't great—not when she was about to be overwhelmed with work. But not inviting her? That would send the wrong message.

Of course, she was coming with me. That wasn't a question. The only question was when to bring it up.

I'd set up that first meeting with my parents to fail before we'd even stepped through the door. The drive over, I'd casually mentioned how Max and Sonya were "Mom and Dad" to Emma now—like that wasn't something that could hit a nerve. I'd been so focused on managing expectations that I hadn't realized I was making things worse.

I wouldn't make that mistake again.

Dinner tonight was low stakes. No big event, no pressure. Just a meal, a conversation, a chance to move forward.

And the moment I saw Kendra tonight, I'd invite her to the gala properly. Not over text. Not as an afterthought. But as someone I wanted—because I did.

I turned back to my speech notes, my fingers hovering over the keyboard. Before I could type, another email notification popped up.

From Miranda.

I hesitated, already dreading the contents.

Sinan,

I really need your help. I'm about to lose my apartment, and if I can't pay my lawyers to fight for me, I'll end up in jail. I know we've had our differences, but you're the only person I can turn to. My job situation hasn't improved, and I'm drowning in debt. Please, you're the only one who can help me. I don't have anyone else. Can't you find it in your heart to help an old friend in desperate need? Just this once, I promise. You know I wouldn't ask if I wasn't out of options.

Please, Sinan, I'm begging you.

M.

A dull ache settled between my shoulders.

At one point, I might have entertained the idea of helping her. This was classic Miranda—reaching out, desperate, manipulative, trying to pull me back into the chaos she thrived on. Exactly the kind of plea I would have given in to once.

But not anymore.

I wouldn't let her jeopardize what I had with Kendra. She was my focus now, my future. Miranda's never-ending spiral of self-destruction was my past.

I hovered over my keyboard, my first instinct to delete and block. But then I hesitated.

Should I tell Kendra?

It wasn't that I wanted to keep things from her, but... what good would it do? She was already stressed about work. Bringing this up would only add more to her plate. And honestly, there was nothing to tell. I wasn't responding. I wasn't letting Miranda back in.

No need to worry Kendra over something that was already handled.

Decision made, I clicked. **Block sender.**

I leaned back, rubbing my jaw.

One thing was clear—I wanted Kendra by my side at that gala. But I had a strong feeling she was about to be completely overwhelmed. And I wasn't about to add to her stress.

For now, I'd keep this to myself.

I muttered under my breath, "Goodbye, Miranda. You're the past."

Then I picked up my phone again, typing a new message to Kendra.

> Me: Will you still be able to make it to dinner tonight? No pressure, but my mom plans to cook all day and she'll probably judge every bite you take and every word you speak. Fair warning.

I hovered for a second, then hit send.

I wasn't sure if she'd still be able to come, but I wanted to give her the chance.

And more than that—I wanted this to be different.

I wanted my parents to *see* Kendra, not just as someone I was dating, but as the person who meant everything to me.

I leaned back, rubbing my jaw, waiting for her response.

3 5

HOW TO IMPRESS HIS MOM (HINT: NOT LIKE THIS)

KENDRA

I checked the clock for the third time in five minutes. 6:27 P.M.

Sinan would be here any minute to pick me up.

I smoothed my palms over my jeans, but it did nothing to loosen the knot of tension coiled in my stomach. Dinner with his parents. Just me, Sinan, his *baba*, and his *anne*—the woman who had looked at me like a questionable engineering decision when we'd first met.

Sonya lounged across from me, flipping through a home décor magazine, as if this were just a normal Tuesday evening and not the prelude to my potential social demolition. Max was in the kitchen, chatting with Emma as she debated which dessert to claim for herself out of the three options Sonya had available.

I swallowed and glanced at my sister. "This dinner is a terrible idea."

Sonya didn't look up. "Nope."

I scowled. "She's going to scrutinize everything I say."

"She just needs time." Sonya's tone was maddeningly even. "First meetings are always awkward."

"She didn't find Max awkward."

Sonya shrugged. "Max is an adorable golden retriever of a

human. He's mom-approved from a mile away. Besides, they already knew him since he was Barry's brother-in-law."

I groaned. "So, I need to be... what? More Max-like?"

"Absolutely not." She put the magazine down and gave me one of those big-sister looks. "You just need to be you. She'll come around. Give her time."

Before I could argue, headlights flashed through the window.

I bolted upright as a car pulled into the driveway.

Emma, ever the human alarm system, popped into the living room. "Uncle Sin's here!"

Max chuckled. "You say that like the pizza guy just arrived."

Emma grinned. "Sin actually brings pizza sometimes. He's a top-tier uncle in my book."

I barely had time to grab my jacket before the front door opened. I spotted Sinan stepping inside, holding his phone to his ear.

He looked ridiculously good for someone coming off a hospital shift—tired but relaxed, his navy button-down just barely wrinkled. Some of the tension in my chest eased. I stepped toward him but paused when I caught the tail end of a low phone conversation.

"No, I'm not sending you more money," he said, voice hushed but clipped. A pause. Then, sharper, "That was the last time."

The hairs on the back of my neck prickled. I lingered, just out of sight, suddenly feeling like an intruder in my own home.

Miranda.

It had to be her.

Who else would be asking him for money? And why hadn't he told me if she was still reaching out?

Before I could decide whether to ask, Sinan turned, catching sight of me. His expression softened instantly, and he shoved his phone into his pocket like nothing had happened.

"Big news," he said as he took my hand and drew me into the living room. "They're throwing a gala in my honor." He shot me a dryly amused look. "It's... a thing."

Wait. What?

I blinked. "A gala? For you?"

Sonya straightened, suddenly paying attention. Max stepped out of the kitchen.

Sinan shrugged. "It's a hospital fundraiser in disguise. My name just happens to be on it."

Max shook his head. "Or maybe they actually want to celebrate you."

I smiled at Sinan, pride rising despite his downplaying. "When is it?"

"It's next Friday." He met my gaze. "Be my date?"

"That's fast" I said, a bit stunned. With those bridge inspections looming, would I even have time?

Emma pounced. "Ooh, can we come too? Who doesn't want to see Uncle Sinan all dressed up and giving a speech?"

Sonya smirked. "Watch out, Sin. Emma's probably already drafting a critique."

Emma nodded sagely. "Maybe I'll even give you some pointers. And by the way, you better be ready to dance."

Sinan raised a dubious eyebrow. "Dance?"

Emma's grin turned shark-like. "Oh yeah. You'll need to keep up."

Before he could protest, she leaped into a TikTok routine, sharp, fast, and entirely unnecessary.

Sinan groaned. "Emma, I'm running on three hours of sleep. No way I'm learning that."

Emma turned to me, poking my arm. "Come on, Aunt Kendra, join me!"

I sighed dramatically but fell into step beside her. We'd done this one before. I grinned at Sinan mid-dance. "We're going to put you through your paces, Doctor."

He exhaled in mock surrender. "Alright, Emma. I'll bring my best dance moves. But be warned—my waltz might just steal the show."

Emma huffed. "We'll see about that."

Laughter rippled through the room, and suddenly, the gala felt like more than just some fancy event.

It was a moment we'd all be in together.

Then my phone buzzed.

I pulled it out, expecting something casual—maybe a "good luck" message from Misha and a reminder to use coasters. Instead, my stomach plummeted at the text:

> Harlan Parker: URGENT: Emergency state inspections. 48 hours. Immediate Compliance Required.

My pulse kicked up, and a second text came through.

> Harlan Parker: Steeltown Bridge is top of the list. I expect my entire team back in the office within the next hour.

I swore under my breath.

Max frowned. "Kendra?"

I looked up, pulse hammering. "I have to go to the office. Now."

Sinan's expression sharpened. "What's wrong?"

"The state's forcing emergency inspections." My voice came out clipped, tight. "We have two days to prepare." I shot to my feet, already running through all the documents I'd need to prepare in my head.

Sonya's brow furrowed. "Wait, what does this mean?"

"It means if we don't get this right, they'll shut down any bridge that doesn't pass muster." I grabbed my bag. "And given Steeltown's issues? That's the one they'll come for first."

Sinan stood. "I'll drive you—"

"No, I'll be fine—I'd rather have my car." I exhaled, forcing my brain to shift into work mode. "But I have to cancel dinner with your parents. I hate doing that, but—"

His hand brushed my arm, grounding me. "It's okay," he said, voice steady. "This is important. I get it. I'll pass along your regrets."

I searched his face for disappointment, irritation—something. But all I saw was understanding.

I swallowed. "Thanks. And please apologize to your mother for me."

Then I bolted for the door.

The moment I stepped into the office, the tension was thick enough to cut with an oxyacetylene torch. A cluster of engineers stood around a conference table, faces tense, phones buzzing nonstop.

Josh, my least favorite coworker and full-time pain in my ass, gave me a slow once-over in my *impress-Mrs.-Bachar* outfit— pressed slacks, a crisp button-down, and the kind of blazer that screamed I swear I'm respectable—before smirking. "Look who finally decided to show up."

I ignored him, dropping my bag and pulling up a summary report on my tablet. "What's our status?"

Ken Burdinger turned from the window, his face unreadable. "The governor's office wants preliminary reports by noon tomorrow. Full assessments by Friday. If we blow this, we'll get crucified in the media."

His gaze locked on me. "And make no mistake—Steeltown Bridge is the one they're watching."

I tightened my grip on my tablet. No pressure or anything.

Josh leaned back in his chair, arms crossed. "Maybe if we'd started prepping sooner, we wouldn't be scrambling now."

I clenched my jaw. "We *did* start prepping. But I don't control state bureaucracy."

He smirked. "No, but you sure like pretending you do."

I inhaled sharply, shoving down my irritation. *Not the time. Not the place.*

Ken clapped his hands. "Enough! We have 48 hours. Let's move."

The room erupted into motion, but as I got to work, one thought stayed lodged in my mind—

Sinan had been right about one thing.

I wanted to *build a bridge*—not just literally, but with his family. With his mother, who still wasn't convinced I was the right person for her son.

And now, once again, work was forcing me to put that on hold.

AYLIN BACHAR'S GUIDE TO RELATIONSHIP RED FLAGS

Sɪɴᴀɴ

By the time I walked through the front door forty-five minutes, exhaustion had started settling deep in my bones. Twenty hours awake, three surgeries, and now this—coming home without Kendra.

The moment I stepped inside, my mother's sharp gaze flicked behind me, immediately noticing I was alone.

Her lips pressed together. "Where is Kendra?"

I sighed, setting down my bag. "She got called into work."

Anne's brows lifted. "Work? Who ever heard of an engineering emergency?" Her words came out cool, edged with displeasure.

Baba, ever the diplomat, leaned forward. "Is there a problem?"

I nodded, bracing for impact. "The state is forcing immediate bridge inspections, and Kendra is overseeing one of the first. It's a massive undertaking—she didn't have a choice."

My mother's fingers tightened around her teacup. "I cooked all day."

Here we go.

"I know, *Anne*," I said evenly. "It smells delicious. She asked me to tell you she's sorry."

"Sorry." She placed her teacup down with an overly delicate clink, the tension radiating off her. "I'm sure she is."

I could already feel this entire conversation spiraling, so I did what any smart man would do—I changed the subject.

"I have some big news to share. The hospital is throwing a gala in my honor. Next Friday."

Baba brightened instantly. "Ah! That's wonderful, *oğlum*. We're so proud of you."

My mother's irritation vanished in an instant. "Oh, Sinan! That's marvelous news." She clasped her hands together, her voice lifting with excitement. "Of course, we must attend. We'll extend our stay another week."

I exhaled, relieved by the shift. Maybe this could be a win after all.

"I imagine it's a formal dinner?" she continued, already moving into planning mode. "I'm sure you'll be seated at the head table. I'll sit next to you, of course."

I hesitated. "Actually, I'll be bringing a date."

My mother's smile barely faltered. "Oh?"

I met her gaze. "I'm bringing Kendra."

And just like that, the tension snapped back into place.

My mother's expression didn't shift immediately—she was too composed for that—but I saw it. The slight downturn of her lips, the flicker of something behind her eyes.

A pause, too long to be casual.

"Kendra." She set her teacup down again, slower this time. "Are you sure she's... the right choice for such a prestigious event?"

"Of course she is. She's my girlfriend."

Baba, ever the peacemaker, smiled. "We'll get to know her better at the gala, then."

My mother nodded, but the warmth from a moment ago was gone. "If she's truly serious about this family, she should have made more of an effort."

I frowned. "What does that mean?"

"She canceled dinner at the last minute." Her tone was mild, but the underlying message was razor-sharp. "That's not the behavior of someone committed to you, Sinan."

I exhaled slowly, forcing down my frustration. "She didn't cancel because she didn't care—she was called into work."

Aylin took a careful sip of tea. "So you've said."

"She didn't have a choice."

"Everyone has a choice."

I clenched my jaw.

"She didn't even call me herself," my mother continued, tapping a fingernail lightly against the porcelain rim of her cup. "A message through you doesn't count."

"She was rushing to the office."

Aylin's expression remained unreadable. "It doesn't take long to make a phone call, Sinan."

My patience snapped.

"*Anne*, she didn't cancel because she was careless." I kept my voice steady, but I felt the edge creeping in. "She's overseeing a major state inspection that could shut down bridges if things aren't up to code. This is her career—her responsibility."

She arched a delicate brow. "And you don't think a woman should prioritize her relationship as well?"

I exhaled sharply, rubbing my temple. "I don't want someone who sits at home and waits for me. Kendra is passionate about her work, just like I am about mine."

My mother sighed, shaking her head. "Passion is good. Obsession is not."

I clenched my jaw, forcing myself to stay calm. This wasn't just about dinner—this was about her belief that Kendra wasn't the *right girl.*

Baba sighed, ever the peacemaker. "Aylin, I'm sure Kendra feels terrible about missing dinner."

"I don't want apologies." She waved a hand dismissively. "I want to know what kind of life you think you're building with a woman who can't prioritize you or your family."

I pinched the bridge of my nose, pushing down my frustration.

There was no winning. If Kendra wasn't at the gala, *Anne* would be furious. But if she didn't behave perfectly, my mother would use it as proof that she didn't belong. Maybe there was something I could do to shift the odds in her favor. To make sure when Kendra walked into that ballroom, no one—*not even my mother*—could deny that she belonged.

I needed Kendra there. And what's more, I needed her to *own* it. She needed a dress that would make her shine.

Aylin sighed, shaking her head as she reached for her tea again. "I don't dislike her, Sinan."

I nearly laughed. She said that the same way someone might say, *I don't hate lima beans.*

"She's a lovely girl, but you and I both know she won't fit in our world. You can already see it."

My grip tightened on the back of the chair. "She'll be at the gala, Anne. And you'll see why she's the one I choose."

My mother simply took another sip of tea. "I suppose we will."

And I was going to make damn sure Kendra left no doubt.

THE NEXT MORNING, I checked my phone before heading into surgery. No messages from Kendra.

Not surprising—she was knee-deep in the bridge crisis.

I shot her a quick text anyway.

> Me: You've got this. I believe in you.

Fifteen minutes later, her response came in.

> Kendra: I appreciate that. Tell that to the hundred emails waiting for me.

Me: Want me to fight them? I'm good with a
scalpel.

Kendra: Very tempting.

I grinned, shaking my head. But as I pocketed my phone, an idea hit me.

I'd come up with the brilliant idea to get her a dress, but with the bridge snafu, I knew she'd be too swamped to go shopping.

Fine. No problem. I'd bring the dresses to her.

It took me all day to make it happen, but I managed the scheduling win of a lifetime. Ever try convincing a dress shop to let you take a bunch of their gowns to "try on?" Not an easy sell. But nothing a credit card couldn't fix.

By the time I walked into Kendra's office building that evening and tracked her down in the break room, she looked like she was one email away from setting something on fire.

Her wavy, brown hair was a little more frazzled than usual, her blouse slightly wrinkled, and her expression screamed: *I have not slept in twenty-four hours.*

"Sinan?" she blinked, looking up from the coffee machine. "What are you—"

I set the four garment bags onto the break room table.

She stared. "Did you... bring an entire dress boutique to my office?"

I shrugged. "You're too busy to shop, so I improvised."

"This couldn't have waited until I was out of crisis mode?"

"Not if we want the perfect dress. What if you end up working until the last moment and never find time? What if your dress needs to be altered? What if you hate all the dresses I brought and we have to start over?"

She dragged a hand down her face. "I don't know whether to kiss you or ask if you're insane."

"Both are acceptable options," I said lightly, unzipping the first bag. "Now, try these on before your coworkers think I moonlight as Pittsburgh's most aggressive personal shopper."

Kendra groaned but grabbed the first gown. "You, skedaddle and keep guard on this door. I don't need my coworkers seeing me my underwear."

Ten minutes later, she stepped out of the break room, wearing a sleek black dress with an open back—and I momentarily forgot how to breathe.

She did a slow turn, watching my face. "Well?"

I cleared my throat. "You look…" *Like you belong in a magazine. Like you just knocked the air out of my lungs.*

"Not a fan?" she teased, stepping back. "Maybe I should try the next one."

"I—" My brain short-circuited as she disappeared again.

The second dress was deep emerald green, hugging her in all the right places. The third was a dark sapphire blue, strapless, the kind of gown that looked like it belonged on a red carpet.

By the time she stepped out in the fourth one—a champagne-colored dress that shimmered under the office lights—I was completely undone.

I swallowed hard as she turned toward the mirror, her fingers smoothing the fabric along her hips.

"This one," she murmured, more to herself than to me.

"Yeah," I said, my voice gruffer than I expected. "That one."

She caught my reflection in the mirror, her gaze lingering on mine.

For a second, everything else—bridges, my mother, the gala, the stress—disappeared.

It was just her.

And that was the moment I knew.

I love Kendra.

It hit me with the force of a falling steel beam. Or rusted bridge.

I wasn't ready to say it, not yet. But God, I felt it.

She turned to me, the usual humor in her eyes softening into something deeper. "Thanks for this, Sinan. You didn't have to."

"*Yes, I did.*"

She held my gaze for a beat longer before smirking. "Okay, but one question… why did you bring four dresses?"

I shrugged. "Because I know you. And I knew you'd reject at least three."

She laughed, the tension in her shoulders finally easing. "Unbelievable. You actually do pay attention."

I smirked, picking up the other dresses. "Just a little."

INSPECTORS, DINNER, AND A DIPLOMATIC BREAKDOWN

KENDRA

By the time Friday morning arrived, I was running on fumes, but we'd done it. We'd pulled it off.

Forty-eight hours of scrambling, double-checking reports, coordinating engineers, and fielding a barrage of emails had left me physically and mentally wrecked. Preparing for the inspection had been grueling, but worth every exhausting moment. Our team had performed under pressure, and despite all odds, we'd met the impossible deadline.

We had a bit of a breather over the weekend, but I still went into the office both days. How could I not when the Steeltown Bridge inspection was first up on the agenda for Monday? I made sure I could lay electronic hands on stress test data and water intrusion reports, as well as everything we'd done so far to address the issues. The emergency repairs had stabilized the structure, and we had a solid plan in place for the permanent fixes. I should have felt relief as we finally approached the finish line. Instead, my head pounded, my body ached, and the exhaustion clung to me like wet cement.

The morning wind bit at my skin as I stood at the base of the bridge, tablet in hand, pulse sluggish with exhaustion. My fingers ached from double-checking data and typing reports through the night. My head throbbed from too much caffeine and too little sleep.

Josh handed me the inspection packet without meeting my eyes. "If you'd let me, I would have *double-checked* everything."

There was nothing wrong with the offer on the surface—but the emphasis he put on double-check lingered like a challenge.

I smiled politely, ignoring the jab. "Thanks, Josh. I've already reviewed it twice, but I appreciate the offer."

He gave a tight nod and turned back to his tablet, muttering something under his breath that sounded a lot like, "Must be nice to have direct access to Parker."

And then, as the state inspection team arrived, my stomach dropped.

Standing just beyond the cluster of inspectors, arms crossed, smug as hell, was *Jimmy*.

What the hell was he doing here?

Mr. Parker muttered beside me, "Do you know that guy? You look like you've seen a ghost."

One I never escaped.

"Let's just get through this," I said through gritted teeth, even as my heart hammered against my ribs.

The lead inspector, Meredith Cho, a woman with a sharp gaze and a no-nonsense stance, stepped forward. She flipped open a tablet and scanned the screen before lifting her eyes to me.

"Hello, Mr. Parker, Ms. Gambit," she said, her tone cool but professional, "before we begin the physical assessment, I need to address something."

I forced my face into neutral, unshakable professionalism. "Of course."

Meredith tilted her screen toward me. "We received a tip from a 'concerned citizen' this morning about possible hush money being paid to cover up structural deficiencies on this bridge. Would you like to comment?"

The ground tilted beneath me.

For a split second, my brain blanked and my jaw dropped.

A hush fell over the team. Even Mr. Parker, who was usually the first to dismiss anything ridiculous, went rigid beside me.

And then I heard it.

A low chuckle.

Jimmy.

I didn't have to look at him to know he was relishing this moment.

I inhaled slowly, preparing to answer, when I realized Meredith Cho was looking at Mr. Parker.

He wasn't rattled. He was furious. "That's a serious accusation."

Meredith's expression didn't shift as she examined him. "Which is why we're asking you directly."

I tightened my grip on my tablet. *Think, Kendra. Think.*

"Every safety measure on this bridge has been reviewed, double-checked, and logged," Mr. Parker said evenly. "All structural reports are available for review, and no corners have been cut."

Meredith didn't flinch. "And what about the financial aspect? Any external incentives offered to encourage a 'positive' outcome?"

He met her gaze, head-on. "*Bribes*? Absolutely not."

She studied him for a beat. "Would you be willing to provide financial transparency for the project's expenditures? Our auditors will need to take a look."

"Of course," he said smoothly. "You'll find nothing unusual. I'll personally ensure you get every relevant document."

Another flick of her eyes over Mr. Parker's face, then mine. Calculating.

And then, finally, a small nod. "Noted. Let's proceed."

I exhaled carefully, keeping my expression calm and unreadable.

The inspectors turned their attention to the bridge itself, and

Mr. Parker immediately leaned toward me, his voice a low growl. "What the hell was that?"

"Bullshit." I shot a glance at Jimmy, who looked like the cat that ate the canary.

Mr. Parker followed my gaze and swore under his breath. "You *do* know him, don't you? You think he had something to do with this?"

"Yeah."

He muttered something that might have been a prayer or a curse. "Tell me about this after we're done with Ms. Cho. We need to get ahead of this. If the media catches wind—"

"I know," I snapped.

And I did.

Because that was Jimmy's real play.

He hadn't sent that tip expecting them to find anything. He just wanted the accusation out there. Something for reporters to sink their teeth into. A scandal to make Steel City Structural Solutions and *my* name pop up in search results next to words like bribery and corruption.

And if I didn't pay him?

He'd spread more rumors.

As the inspectors moved along the bridge, I risked a glance at Jimmy.

He lifted his phone and mimed typing, grinning wickedly.

My stomach twisted as if he'd reached inside me and clenched a fist around my gut. Another email, I realized. Another false tip, another grenade he'd toss just to watch me scramble.

I inhaled deeply, grounding myself.

Not today, Jimmy. Not ever.

I straightened, rolling my shoulders back, and marched after the state team.

Tuesday Morning

> Sinan (7:54 A.M.): Survived the night? Let me know if you need a food drop.

> Me (8:06 A.M.): Could use ten coffees and a miracle. The inspectors keep coming back with more questions.

> Sinan (8:07 A.M.): Sending moral support. Dinner Thursday with Mom still okay?

> Me (8:25 A.M.): Hard to say. I hope so.

Wednesday Late

> Sinan (11:12 P.M.): Don't forget to sleep. Mom keeps asking if you're still coming tomorrow night.

> Me (11:13 P.M.): Don't want to miss it again. Just want to finish these charts. I'll be there.

By the time I pulled up to Sinan's house after work on Thursday, exhaustion clung to me like a second skin. The past week had been brutal. Finalizing reports, answering last-minute questions from inspectors, dodging concerned glances from my team—every second had been stretched too thin.

And now I had to sit through dinner with Aylin, who probably saw my absence last time as a personal insult.

I sighed, letting my head fall back against the car seat. I just needed to get through tonight.

My phone buzzed, and I reached for it automatically.

> Jimmy: Just a heads-up. Sinan's been lying to you.

I froze. What the hell was he talking about? And why hadn't I blocked his new number yet? Oh, yeah, because I wanted to know what he had planned.

But how could he possibly know anything about Sinan?

Before I could even begin to process, another text came through.

> Jimmy: 24 hours left before I let PSS know you've been stealing from them, sweetheart. I bet they'll be curious about that huge cash deposit you just got. Tick tock.

The nausea curled low in my stomach.

> Me: Stop with the lies and threats. I'm not giving you any money.

> Jimmy: Not threats. Promises.

I gripped the steering wheel, breathing hard.

I wasn't just fighting for Sinan's mother's approval—I was actively trying to keep my father from ruining my career.

But there wasn't time to deal with Jimmy now. I shoved my phone back into my purse and forced my hands to unclench.

One battle at a time.

I exhaled slowly, squared my shoulders, and stepped out of the car.

The moment I stepped inside Sinan's house and saw Aylin's face, I knew it.

I shouldn't have come.

She smiled politely, but her sharp eyes flicked over me, lingering a little too long on my wrinkled blouse and dark under-eye circles. I caught the briefest purse of her lips before she masked it with warmth and a forced smile.

"You look tired," she said smoothly. "Long day?"

I forced a smile of my own. "Long week. But I wouldn't have missed dinner."

Before Aylin could respond, *Baba* stepped forward, his smile genuine.

"Kendra! It is good to see you," he said warmly, his voice carrying the ease Aylin's lacked. "Come, sit. You work too hard."

Relief flickered through me. At least one person in this house wasn't scrutinizing me like I was under a microscope.

"Thank you, Mr. Bachar," I said, my shoulders easing slightly.

"Cem," he corrected, waving a hand. "No need for formalities. We are all family here."

Aylin's lips pursed just slightly at that.

As I stepped past Sinan, my gaze flicked to his phone sitting on the counter. The screen lit up with a single letter—M.

Sinan moved fast, swiping it away before I could see more. His expression stayed neutral, but the motion was quick. Instinctive.

"Work?" I asked, trying to keep my voice light.

He slipped the phone into his pocket, shaking his head. "Nothing important."

I nodded, but unease curled in my stomach. He'd told me he blocked Miranda. That he was done dealing with her mess.

Had that changed?

Aylin called us to the table, and I pushed the thought aside. I had bigger problems to deal with tonight. But that flicker of doubt lodged in the back of my mind.

I followed them into the dining room, gripping my phone tighter than necessary. Jimmy's threats still hovered in my mind like a dark cloud.

Still, I forced myself to engage—to smile. I needed this dinner to go well.

I took my seat, flashing Aylin my most polite expression. "Dinner smells amazing. Did you make everything yourself?"

Aylin perked up slightly. "I did. I always believe a well-prepared meal brings family together."

I smiled. "That's a lovely sentiment."

Aylin's eyes gleamed just a little. "Yes. Though, of course, making time for family can be… challenging, depending on one's obligations."

I should've let it go. But I was so, so tired.

"I agree," I said lightly, spearing a piece of lamb. "It's been a rough week, but I'm glad I could be here tonight."

Aylin hummed. "Yes, Sinan mentioned the emergency inspections. Very… demanding."

I nodded, bracing for her next move.

Aylin smiled over her wine glass. "I suppose you wouldn't know, but I actually received an interesting email this afternoon."

Ice slid down my spine.

I kept my expression neutral. "Oh?"

"Yes." She set her glass down. "I learned that someone is spreading rumors about the bridge inspection process. Quite scandalous, really."

My stomach twisted.

Jimmy. But how could Aylin know about the rumors? Had *he* sent her the email?

She watched me too closely, like a cat toying with a mouse. "It's unfortunate, isn't it? A project's reputation can be destroyed so easily."

My pulse pounded in my ears.

Sinan frowned. "*Anne*, let's not discuss work rumors at dinner."

But Aylin's gaze never left mine. "I just hope no one involved will bring embarrassment to those around them."

And there it was.

I set my fork down, carefully. My fingers were shaking.

"I assure you, *Mrs. Bachar*, my work is solid, and my company is reputable. Any rumors you've heard to the contrary are nonsense."

She smiled sweetly. "Oh, I wasn't suggesting anything like that, dear."

I clenched my jaw, chest tight with frustration.

Sinan exhaled sharply, rubbing his temple. "Let's just eat,

alright? And avoid sensitive topics? I'd like us all to get along so tomorrow's gala can go smoothly."

Aylin tilted her head. "Yes, of course. Though naturally, how we all present ourselves is important. The gala will have many influential people."

Cem, who'd been quiet until now, cleared his throat. "It is an important event, yes, but it should be a celebration. Not a test."

I glanced at him in surprise. His tone was light, but the words felt like a subtle rebuke toward his wife.

Aylin merely smiled. "You're right, I'm sure. But I do believe it's wise to consider all aspects of one's reputation."

She turned to me, her voice honeyed but her meaning unmistakable. "Your father's criminal record does cast a shadow, doesn't it? We must be cautious."

I went still.

Jimmy.

He *had* emailed her. There was no other way Aylin could have known.

And he hadn't just gone after my job—he'd gone after me. My relationships.

My heart pounded as I turned to Sinan, my voice tight with realization. "It was him."

His brows furrowed. "What?"

"My father," I bit out, my pulse roaring in my ears. "He's the one who contacted your mother."

I saw the moment it clicked for him—his shoulders stiffening, his jaw tightening.

Aylin arched a brow. "He didn't seem particularly *fond* of you when he reached out."

Sinan's voice was low, sharp. "You spoke to him?"

"Not directly," she said smoothly. "Just the email. But he did provide quite a bit of insight."

The nausea churned in my stomach. *Of course he had.*

This wasn't about me personally—it was about money. My money. Sonya's money. The inheritance Jimmy thought he was entitled to. He'd already realized his legal options were worthless, so now he was coming at us sideways, trying to manipulate people around me into thinking I owed him something.

For a fleeting second, I considered it. Just giving him what he wanted. Writing him a check, getting him out of my life once and for all. Would it be worth it? Would that buy peace?

No.

Who was he to dictate where Aunt Lorraine's money went? Who was he to think he could steal from her—even in death? What made him believe he was owed anything more than what she'd already given him?

She'd made her decision. She'd known exactly what she was doing when she left the bulk of her estate to me and Sonya. And Jimmy? He'd been lucky to get a dime.

Bile rose in my throat. He wasn't just harassing me—he was trying to chip away at everything I had. My credibility. My job. My relationship.

Sinan turned to me, his concern unmistakable. "Kendra—"

I stood abruptly, pushing my chair back. The walls felt too close, the air too thick. "I can't do this tonight. I need to cool down and get some sleep, not sit here and be grilled."

Aylin exhaled sharply, but I ignored her.

Cem sighed but didn't argue. "Let her go, Sinan," he murmured.

But Sinan didn't just let me go.

He pushed back his own chair, standing as I stepped away. "Kendra, wait—" He reached for my arm, not to stop me, but to anchor me. "You don't have to go alone."

My throat tightened. That was the problem.

"I do." My voice was quieter now, but no less certain.

His grip loosened, but he didn't look away. "Then at least let me take you home."

A war raged inside me—I wanted that. Him. His presence, his steadiness. But right now, I needed to withdraw.

I swallowed hard. "I need to be by myself for a bit. Just tonight."

His jaw tensed, but he nodded. Not happy, but understanding. "Will you call me when you're home?"

I hesitated, then gave a small nod. "Yeah."

He exhaled, running a hand through his hair. "I'll see you at the gala."

I forced a smile that didn't quite reach my eyes. "Yeah. You will."

Then I turned and walked out the door.

3 8

MIRANDA'S LAST STAND

SINAN

The hospital buzzed with its usual energy the following after-noon, but my mind kept drifting—not to the long morning of surgeries I'd performed or tonight's gala speech Emma had made me rehearse with her last weekend, but to Kendra.

I hadn't spoken to her since just after she'd made it home last night.

I hated how we'd left things—how *she'd* left things. She'd called me, letting me know she'd made it home safely, but she hadn't wanted to talk. She'd wanted some space.

Still, it was a day later and I needed to check in.

I pulled out my phone.

> Me: Hey, how are you holding up?

She didn't answer right away, but I hadn't expected her to. She'd been so slammed at work this past week that I was used to delays. I exhaled, running a hand through my hair.

A sharp knock on the door yanked me back to reality. Val stepped in, his face tight with concern. "Got a minute?"

I straightened, bracing myself. "What's up?"

"Miranda's been seen around the hospital." He shut the door behind him.

I stiffened. "What?"

"She's been telling people you two are still together... and that she's coming to the gala tonight."

Heat flared behind my ribs. *Miranda, showing up here, spreading lies?*

"That's ridiculous," I said flatly. "We broke things off over a year ago."

Val nodded. "I know. But she's convincing enough. Figured you'd want to handle it before it spirals."

Anger simmered beneath the surface. "Thanks for the heads-up. Can you help shut that down?"

"Already working on it," Val said, giving my shoulder a firm pat before slipping out.

I barely had time to process that before another knock came. A heavier one.

And then my mother stepped inside, dressed for the gala in heavy makeup and an elegant black gown, but looking worried.

My pulse jumped. My mother wouldn't have shown up at the hospital right now unless something was wrong.

I shot up from my chair. "*Anne*? What's going on? Is *Baba* okay?"

She stepped inside, closing the door softly. "He's fine," she said, but her tone was heavy. "This is about Kendra."

I exhaled, panic subsiding but unease settling in its place. "If this is about last night, we all know who sent you that email. Jimmy's trying to cause problems, and you're letting him manipulate you."

She hesitated for a beat, then shook her head. "This is worse."

I clenched my jaw. "What now?"

Her lips pressed together, hesitation flickering in her expression before she finally spoke. "He called me a little while ago."

My stomach dropped. "Jimmy?"

She sighed. "He said he wanted to warn me about Kendra's 'dishonesty.'"

My fists clenched at my sides. "*Anne*—"

"He claims she's been stealing money to pay off her mother's medical bills."

I swore under my breath.

"And now," she continued, her voice heavy, "he's saying she's been misusing funds from the bridge project to pay off her student loans."

I jerked my gaze to her. "You actually believe that?"

My mother's chin lifted. "I'm not saying I do. But this isn't nothing, Sinan. You might trust her, but you can't dismiss it entirely. Either *she's* lying or *he* is. And if she is—"

"She's not." My voice came out sharper than I intended. "Jimmy's a manipulative liar, and you're letting him set the terms of this conversation. He's doing exactly what Miranda did—trying to twist reality just enough to make the victim look like the problem."

That landed.

Her breath caught. Arms slowly crossed over her chest, but not like before—not to argue, to brace. "You think they're the same," she said quietly.

I nodded. "I *know* they are."

She looked away, blinking, like she'd just spotted something she should've seen a long time ago. "Miranda… she nearly ruined you."

"And Jimmy is trying to ruin Kendra," I said. "That's why I won't back down."

For a moment, she said nothing. Then her arms dropped, and her voice lost its edge. "I just don't want to see you hurt again."

"I know." I stepped closer. "But I trust Kendra. And I need you to trust me."

She met my eyes. After a long beat, she nodded. "Alright. But if anything changes—"

"I'll handle it."

She sighed, smoothing out her jacket. "I'll see you at the gala."

As the door clicked shut behind her, I finally let out a slow, measured breath.

Jimmy wasn't backing down.

I needed to warn Kendra. *Now.*

I grabbed my phone.

No response to my earlier text.

I hesitated, then typed.

> Me: Let me know when you're free. I need to talk to you. It's important.

Another knock interrupted me. The door creaked open, and there she was—Miranda. Speak of the devil.

Her smile, broad and familiar, felt all wrong. Too bright. Too forced.

Frustration flared again, but I kept my voice even. "What are you doing here?"

"Sin, please. We need to talk."

I exhaled slowly, trying to hold on to my patience. "You shouldn't be here."

She shifted on her feet, her bravado slipping for just a second. "I just need a favor."

"No."

Her eyes flickered with something—hurt, maybe. Or just irritation at being shut down so fast. "Sin, I'm out of options. My lawyer says I can get house arrest instead of prison, but I need to pay him first. Her voice wavered, just slightly. "They're saying I'll be transferred to county next week if I don't come up with the money. It's disgusting there, Sinan. You've seen what that does to people."

She tugged at her sleeve, avoiding my eyes. "I know I messed up. I know I don't deserve anything from you. But I don't have anyone else."

I folded my arms, standing firm. "Not my problem. Ask your parents."

Her jaw tightened. "They won't help me. They think I deserve to rot." She let out a short, humorless laugh. "Maybe they're right."

For a brief moment, I saw it—how scared she really was. But it didn't change the facts.

"You made your choices, Miranda," I said, my voice firm but not unkind. "You stole drugs, you got caught, and you ran. You created this mess, not me."

Her shoulders lifted like she was bracing for a blow. Then her expression turned brittle. "If you'd cared enough, you would've seen the signs."

A flicker of something old and painful stirred in me, but I shut it down. "Don't do that. You worked hard to hide it from me. And your thefts? I'm just lucky you didn't drag me down with you."

She swallowed hard, her gaze darting away. But whatever moment of vulnerability had surfaced vanished as she scoffed, shaking her head. "You think Kendra's any different? She's only with you for your money, Sin. Just like everyone else."

I felt the weight of her words, but I refused to let them in. "She's nothing like you."

Miranda let out a bitter chuckle, her voice quieter now. "That's what you think. But one day, she'll realize she doesn't belong in your world. You'll come home to an empty house and wonder why you were stupid enough to believe this time would be different."

Something flickered across her face—regret, maybe, or just exhaustion. But then she straightened, her mask of arrogance slipping back into place.

"You'll regret this," she muttered, turning away.

I didn't answer.

And then she was gone.

I sat heavily in my chair, rubbing my temples. I needed to see Kendra.

Not just to warn her about Jimmy, but because... I needed to make sure she was okay. That *we* were okay.

She'd been so drained last night, so raw from my mother's interrogation. And now Jimmy was pulling this stunt? I should have been there for her sooner.

I glanced at my phone.

Still no reply.

Frowning, I typed again.

> Me: I know things have been overwhelming. Just wanted to check in. Let me know if you're still coming.

We needed to talk. I couldn't let Kendra hear any of this from someone else—especially not from Jimmy or Miranda. That would only fuel the doubt I knew was already gnawing at her.

> Kendra: Sorry—work had me slammed, then was rushing to get ready. Good news is, we're nearly at the gala. See you there.

I checked the time and let out a low curse. It was later than I'd realized.

> Me: Held up at work. Might be a few minutes late.

The excuse felt like a half-truth, but I couldn't just unload everything in a text message.

Grabbing my tux, I headed to the staff lounge. After showering and dressing, I straightened my tie in the mirror, trying to ignore the unease curling in my chest.

Tonight was supposed to be a celebration.

But it felt more like a reckoning.

39

HEARTBREAK IN THE SPOTLIGHT

KENDRA

The grandeur of the Omni William Penn Hotel's ballroom was breathtaking—ornate gilded moldings framing the soaring ceiling, crystal chandeliers casting a warm, golden glow over elegantly dressed guests. Rich mahogany paneling and towering arched windows gave the space an old-money sophistication, the kind of place where generations of Pittsburgh's elite had gathered for decades.

Laughter and conversation buzzed around me, a soft hum of wealth and influence, but I felt worlds away from where I belonged. In this stunning dress Sinan had bought for me, I felt like I was wearing someone else's skin—like he'd made a mistake inviting me and at any moment, someone might tap me on the shoulder and ask if I was lost. I'd fought hard to get here, professionally and personally, but moments like this still made me feel like the girl patching together secondhand formalwear and student loan payments, hoping no one noticed the cracks.

By the time we arrived, exhaustion had settled deep into my bones. The past few days had been relentless—the endless demands of the Steeltown Bridge inspection, last night's tense dinner with Aylin, and Jimmy's threats circling like vultures.

I glanced at his last text message again.

> Jimmy: 24 hours left before I let PSS know you've been stealing from them, sweetheart. I bet they'll be curious about that huge cash deposit you just got. Tick tock.

The twenty-four hours were up. What would he do next? It was like waiting for that second shoe to drop.

"Where's Uncle Sin?" Emma asked.

"He texted me he was running late."

"Ooh, let's check out that ice sculpture!" Emma grabbed Max by the arm and took off.

Where was Sinan?

I checked my phone again. Nothing.

> Me: We're here. Where's our guest of honor?

I stared at the phone for a moment, but got no reply.

The lack of communication gnawed at me. It wasn't like him to be late, especially not tonight. Maybe I was overthinking it. Maybe I was just too drained to think clearly. But the seed of worry had already taken root. Something was wrong. Jimmy wouldn't go after Sinan, would he?

"We should celebrate your release from servitude," Sonya teased. "The inspectors left today, right?"

I blinked at her, focusing on her words. "Thank God that's behind me. Steeltown's repair plan is greenlit."

She grabbed two champagne flutes off the tray of a passing server. "Congratulations! That's huge. You did it."

I tried to let the relief sink in, but I couldn't shake the uneasy weight pressing on my chest.

A familiar voice cut through the room.

"Kendra! Great to see you again."

I turned to find Riley—Sinan's perpetually enthusiastic intern —grinning at me. He looked out of place in his tux, like he wasn't sure whether to stand still or rollerblade through the crowd.

"Big night," he said, eyes scanning the crowd. "Weird seeing Miranda around the hospital today. Thought that was over?"

My stomach twisted.

Miranda?

I forced a neutral expression, hoping he couldn't hear my pulse spiking. "She was at the hospital?"

"Yeah, first saw her around noon, but she kept popping up all afternoon. Thought it was weird since—" Riley must've caught something in my expression, because he backtracked. "Uh, I mean, I'm sure it was nothing. Just… surprised to see her, y'know?"

I nodded, forcing a smile. "Right. No big deal."

But it was in my head now, swirling alongside everything else. She was at the hospital. And Sinan never mentioned it. And now he was way more than "a few minutes late." Plus, there'd been that phone call I'd overheard the night I was supposed to have dinner with his parents last week. What had he said? "I'm not sending you more money?" So, clearly he'd been supporting her.

I exhaled sharply, shaking off my swirling thoughts. I was exhausted. This was the perfect mindset for jumping to conclusions. Time to slow down and think clearly. All I needed to do was talk to him, and we'd straighten this out.

Then as Sonya and I moved deeper into the ballroom, a nearby conversation stopped me in my tracks.

"Did you hear about Sinan meeting with his *ex* today?" a woman's voice said, loud enough to cut through the din.

My breath hitched, and I caught Sonya's eye. She'd obviously overheard it too.

"I heard the hospital board is worried about her showing up tonight. She claims Sinan promised to help keep her out of jail."

"She said he gave her a check last month—enough to cover her rehab bills—she's got proof. I wonder if they're still engaged after all."

The blood drained from my face.

Sinan gave her money?

"He's been paying her legal bills, too," another voice added, casual but barbed, each word hitting like a knife. "I bet they're still together."

My pulse quickened. Still together? That wasn't possible.

"She's supposed to be here tonight," the woman continued. "Sinan and Miranda, back on display."

I couldn't breathe.

Jimmy's words echoed in my head. *Sinan's been lying to you.*

I turned to Sonya, panic tightening my throat. "Did you know about this?"

Sonya's horrified expression was all the answer I needed. "Kendra, no—I thought he was done with her."

I needed air. I needed to think.

Sonya, sensing my rising panic, grabbed my hand. "Let's go to the ladies room, okay? We'll figure this out."

Inside the restroom, I gripped the edge of the sink, the cool marble grounding me as my heart raced.

Was Jimmy right?

My father's warning, Miranda's presence, the whispers—it was all too much.

"Kendra." Sonya's voice was steady beside me, but I barely heard her. "What are you thinking?"

Tears stung my eyes as the betrayal settled in, deep and sharp. "Did you know about Miranda?" My voice wavered. "Did you know she was still in his life?"

Sonya shook her head, clearly distraught. "No, I swear I didn't. Sinan told me it was over. I thought... I thought it was behind him."

The shock was like a physical weight, making it hard to breathe. "He's been paying for rebab? All her legal bills?" I whispered. "Why didn't he tell me?"

Sonya's phone was already in her hand, texting Max. "You and I should go. I don't want this to get any worse tonight. I'll tell Max to stay with Emma and take an Uber home."

I nodded numbly, grateful for her calm, though everything inside me felt shattered.

She led the way through the crowd toward the exit, holding on to my hand as if worried she might lose me. I stumbled in her wake, barely able to avoid bumping into people.

Then, a sudden wave of applause made me drop Sonya's hand and stop in my tracks.

Sinan stood near the entrance, looking effortlessly polished in his tuxedo, the very picture of composure. The crowd surged toward him, hands clapping, voices overlapping with congratulations. His parents stood nearby, beaming with pride, their smiles wide and approving.

For a split second, I wanted to believe in him. I *needed* to believe in him—to tell myself that there was some logical explanation, that this wasn't what it looked like.

But the hurt twisted inside me, sharp and unforgiving.

There I was, unraveling from the inside out, while he stood there, completely at ease. The contrast made my stomach turn.

Then his gaze found mine.

For a fleeting moment, relief flickered across his face. But then he saw me—*really* saw me. My stiff posture, my too-tight grip on my clutch, the betrayal burning behind my eyes. His expression shifted in an instant, relief giving way to concern, then alarm.

He excused himself from the crowd, his stride quick and urgent. But it was too late.

I was already breaking.

"Were you with Miranda?" The words left my mouth before I could stop them, brittle and shaking with betrayal.

Sinan paled. "Kendra, I can explain—"

"Is it true?" My voice rose, raw and unsteady. "Are you paying her legal bills?"

For half a second, he hesitated. Just half a second.

But it was enough.

"Yes, but it's not—"

I didn't hear the rest.

A cold rush of blood pounded through my ears as Jimmy's voice whispered in my head. *Rich people don't change. They lie. They cheat. They only care about themselves.*

I took a step back, everything around me warping. "You never told me she was still texting you. You wouldn't explain that weird call last week. You brushed off that message from her last night. Then Riley mentioned Miranda was at the hospital today. And now people are whispering that you're paying for her rehab and paying her lawyer?"

Sinan's jaw tightened. "Kendra, please—I'm not paying any more, I swear."

But all I could hear was the lie.

All the doubts, all the suspicions, all the ways I had fought to believe in him—cracked, then shattered.

I shoved past him, my breath coming in shallow bursts. I needed out.

The whispers around me sharpened into a suffocating hum, the weight of a dozen eyes pressing down.

Then, just as I reached the edge of the crowd—

Miranda walked in.

Sinan stiffened, his shoulders going rigid as she approached, her stride slow and deliberate.

Her eyes flicked toward me, but her smirk was for him. "Sorry I'm late." Her voice was all syrupy sweetness. "Were you worried? I told you I'd be here."

Sinan turned toward her, his jaw clenched, his mouth already forming sharp words. I saw the tension in his body, the anger tightening his features.

But it didn't matter.

To everyone watching—to the eager onlookers whispering behind their champagne flutes—it looked like something else entirely.

And I could feel it—those whispers slicing through me like

glass. In their eyes, I wasn't the accomplished engineer or the woman Sinan had chosen. I was the charity case, the interloper who didn't belong. The impostor playing dress-up in a ballroom of trust funds and legacy admissions. I'd spent the whole night fighting to hold my head up, but now? Now I just wanted to disappear.

To them, this looked like a lover's spat—where Sinan and *Miranda* were the lovers, and I was the interloper.

The scandal. The betrayal. *The other woman.*

I couldn't do this. I couldn't stand here and let them make me the fool.

I turned and fled before I could hear another word.

40

A TUX, A TWIST, AND A TORN HEART

SINAN

Kendra's final words still echoed in my head as she pushed past me, her eyes filled with hurt—I stood frozen, my tuxedo suddenly too tight, watching her hurry away through the press of donors and elegantly dressed guests.

She was gone.

And I'd barely managed any sort of explanation.

A ripple of applause reminded me where I was—at the gala they'd thrown in my honor. The crowd's expectant hum felt distant, drowned out by the rush of panic in my chest.

I had to go after her.

I took a step forward—

—and Miranda slipped in front of me, cutting off my path.

Not now.

My jaw clenched. This was the last thing I needed. "Miranda," I snapped, voice low. "I don't have time for this. You need to leave."

She let out a soft laugh, her voice just loud enough for a few nearby guests to hear. "Oh, Sinan, always so dramatic. I'm here to support you—like old times."

My stomach twisted.

She knew exactly what she was doing—playing the part of the scorned yet lingering ex, letting the audience around us fill in the blanks. No wonder Kendra thought I was hiding something. I had been—even if it wasn't what she thought.

"Stop it," I hissed, stepping closer so only she could hear. "This isn't about us. We ended over a year ago. I'm with Kendra."

Miranda's lips curled, her gaze flicking toward the ballroom doors where Kendra had just disappeared. "Maybe she's realizing that doesn't matter. Especially since you've still been paying my bills. Did she catch wind of that?"

My pulse hammered.

"You think this is a game?" I exhaled sharply, anger seething. "I don't owe you anything, Miranda. Leave. Now."

A presence appeared beside me—Val, tension written all over his posture. "Need backup?"

Riley was right behind him, brows furrowed as he glanced between us. "Security's on standby."

Miranda turned, that plastic smile still in place, addressing a handful of donors who had paused to watch. "Guess I'm not wanted. But I told Sinan I'd show up. Promises are important, wouldn't you say?"

My hands curled into fists. She was twisting the knife, dragging this out long enough to keep the gossip circulating.

"So is integrity," I shot back. "And you lost yours a long time ago."

Miranda stiffened as Val signaled the security guard, who stepped forward. Her expression flashed with annoyance, but she raised her hands in mock surrender.

"Fine," she murmured. "But you'll regret this, Sinan. One day, Kendra will see you're the same selfish, tight-fisted, controlling man you were with me."

She hesitated at the threshold, the smugness cracking just slightly. "You think I enjoy being this person?" she whispered. "Do you think I planned to end up like this?"

Then, as quickly as it appeared, the vulnerability vanished

behind another sharp look. "But fine. You want me gone? I'll give the crowd a show."

Then she turned on her heel, tossing one last withering glance over her shoulder as security escorted her out.

I forced myself to breathe, though my gut churned.

"You good?" Val asked quietly. "What about Kendra?"

I shook my head, a knot forming in my throat. "She left. And she was furious. She overheard… everything. God, Val, she thinks I've been hiding a relationship with Miranda."

Val's grip clamped onto my shoulder, solid and grounding. "Then go find her. As soon as you can."

I swallowed hard, glancing at the stage. Chris Lawrence was waving me over—time for the speech.

Worst possible timing.

"I can't yet," I muttered, the words tasting like acid. "They need me on stage."

Val's jaw tightened in understanding. "Make it quick. We'll keep an eye out for Miranda in case she tries to come back."

"Thanks." My voice came out rough.

Then, as if this night weren't already spiraling, my mother appeared.

Her clutch was gripped tightly in her hands, her usual smugness replaced by something troubled.

"I always liked Miranda," she admitted, her voice measured. "But I had no idea she could… create such a scene."

I exhaled, running a hand through my hair. "Neither did I."

Aylin's gaze dropped for a moment, something unreadable in her expression. Finally, she sighed, her voice tight with regret. "The way she spoke to you—like she had a right to your life." Her lips pressed together. "She's shameless. I see that now."

I blinked. That was… unexpected.

Aylin hesitated, then smoothed a hand over her clutch. "And Kendra," she continued carefully, "I might have judged her too harshly."

That got my attention.

She exhaled sharply. "That young woman is nothing like... her." A trace of disgust colored her tone as she nodded toward the doors where Miranda had disappeared. "No matter our differences, at least Kendra never stooped to such cruelty."

A flicker of reluctant admiration.

That faint bit of praise almost managed to make me smile.

Anne caught my expression and arched a wry brow. "I'm not saying I think she's the perfect woman for you," she added quickly, "but... she's kind. She supports you in her own way. Maybe that's the kind of woman you really need."

I searched her face, but she seemed sincere.

"Thanks, *Anne*." My voice was quieter now. "If she ever speaks to me again, I'll let her know she finally has your support."

My mother's eyes widened in alarm. "No. I wouldn't go that far." She pursed her lips. "You wouldn't, *really*, would you? Please don't."

Chris Lawrence appeared next to me, cutting off the conversation. "You're up, champ. Go knock 'em dead with your speech. The room's full of doctors—someone can revive 'em if needed."

The next ten minutes felt surreal.

Chris introduced me as "the man of the hour," the applause ringing hollow in my ears. I delivered the speech Emma had made me rehearse, forcing a smile, throwing in the corny joke she'd insisted on.

But all I could see was Kendra's stricken face.

As soon as the applause died down and Chris congratulated me, I slipped offstage, ignoring the donors who wanted to shake my hand.

I needed to find her.

My mother called my name, but I couldn't stop.

Not when Kendra might already be halfway across the city, and completely out of my life.

I grabbed my keys from the valet, heart pounding.

I'd messed this up. And Miranda had poured gasoline on the flames.

Now it was time to fix it—if Kendra would even let me try.

Determination churned through the anxiety as I pushed through the hotel's main doors.

I refused to lose her.

4 1

FEAR TRUMPS LOVE

KENDRA

After I rushed out of the hotel, I found myself on autopilot as I drove home. I'd been running on fumes for days, and tonight's debacle had pushed me beyond my breaking point. I drove home on autopilot, trying not to crumble.

Sonya was silent, but it wasn't that comfortable silence that we often shared. It was uneasy and charged. I kept running through the past week's events in my mind, frustrated I'd ignored so many clues, thoughts swirling and coming back to the same conclusion —Sinan had lied to me.

Somewhere in those circling thoughts, my exhaustion managed to take over and I nearly veered into another lane.

Sonya put a hand on my shoulder. "Should I drive?"

"No," I said, cracking the window for some fresh air. "Sorry about that. Won't happen again." I couldn't just sit and be a passenger right now. I needed to drive—to be in control.

I glanced at my phone sitting in the console, not sure whether or not I wanted it to ring. Too many things were coming to a head tonight. Between discovering Sinan had been lying to me for months, Miranda's sudden appearance, and Jimmy's lingering threats, I didn't think I could handle one thing more.

Jimmy's twenty-four-hour deadline was up; I half-expected my phone to explode with new false allegations. I dreaded the idea of a Monday morning call from Mr. Parker about some embezzlement rumor.

"You're doing that thing where you grind your teeth and pretend you're not about to have a breakdown."

I tightened my grip on the wheel. "I can't stop thinking about Sinan's lies… about everything I overheard tonight." My voice cracked. "Maybe Jimmy's right. Maybe I can't trust anyone. I thought I could trust Sinan, and I was wrong. Maybe I'll never fit into his world."

Minutes ago I'd been standing in the Omni William Penn's ballroom, seeing men in bespoke suits, overhearing talk of second homes in Martha's Vineyard. I'm just an engineer with student loans, a father who's extorting me, and a desk job that keeps me working round the clock—I'd never fit into a world like that.

Sonya let out a soft sigh. "People hurt each other, even when they don't mean to. It doesn't always mean you can't trust them. Remember when you discovered the crack in the Steeltown Bridge? Everyone at work doubted you, but Sinan was the one who believed in you. That wasn't a lie. He believes in you."

Her words got lost in the gossip still echoing in my mind, each word carving deeper into the wound. Sinan had secrets—things I should've known. Seeing him with Miranda, the rumors they were together, the money he never mentioned... How could I trust him after this?

I pulled into the driveway, headlights sweeping across the house that had once seemed grand but now just felt like a hiding place. Sonya climbed out first, stretching as she stepped into the cool night air.

And then I saw it.

A big brown box sat squarely on the welcome mat, blocking the door like it had been dropped by a particularly aggressive delivery driver.

I eyed it warily. "Fantastic. Another mystery sitting at my doorstep."

Sonya peered over my shoulder. "Huh. That's a big one."

I sighed, dragging myself up the steps. When I spotted my name on the label, my stomach twisted. "Did I order something and forget about it?"

Sonya gasped. "Maybe it's from a secret admirer! Ooh, or Jimmy, sending you a heartfelt apology gift. Something sentimental, like—" she paused for dramatic effect, "—a coffee mug that says *World's Most Gullible Daughter*."

I snorted a laugh. "Knowing him, it'll be a live snake. Or a glitter bomb. Or a glittery snake."

"Does that mean we should open it out here?"

I nudged the box with my foot. It was light. "Let's take it inside where we can see."

Once inside, I set it on the kitchen counter and ripped the tape off, flipping open the box.

Inside, nestled in crumpled newspaper, was a taxidermied raccoon.

Not a cute, charmingly posed raccoon. Not one of those ironic, hipster-style mounts that looked like they were playing poker or wearing sunglasses. No.

This one was standing upright, its arms outstretched in some bizarre, eternal embrace—its dead glassy eyes locked onto mine. A tiny, handwritten note dangled from its stiff paw.

Kendra - Raccoons are survivors. They always find a way to get at what they want. No matter how many times you shut the door, they get what they're after. I will too. You owe me.

My stomach dropped. "Oh my God."

Sonya clapped a hand over her mouth. Then she let out an unhinged laugh. "*What?*"

I shoved the box away to distance myself from whatever cosmic horror I'd just witnessed. "What. The. Hell."

Sonya, still laughing, wiped at her eyes. "What if this is the first in a series? Next week, we get a squirrel in a tiny top hat."

"A—what?" My brain couldn't even process. "Why would anyone—" I pointed at the box like it was an active crime scene. "Why is this in our house?"

Sonya snorted. "Maybe he thinks you need a low-maintenance pet?"

I glared at her. "Not helping."

She took a deep breath, composing herself. "Okay. But, like… do we throw it away? Donate it? Set it free?"

I gave her a look.

"Right," she said, nodding sagely. "Probably too late for that."

I exhaled sharply, bracing my palms against the counter. "It's not just the raccoon."

Sonya's humor faded. "It's Jimmy. The note."

I nodded, my throat tight.

This wasn't just some bizarre joke. It was a message. A reminder that no matter how many times I shut him out, he would keep coming back. That he wasn't just lurking—he was planning.

And worse?

For just a second—one brief, terrible second—I'd started considering giving him what he wanted.

I could pay him off. Make him disappear. Buy my own peace of mind.

But the thought made my stomach churn.

Who was he to try and overturn Aunt Lorraine's last will? Who was he to decide that he deserved anything more than she had given him?

Jimmy had never earned a damn thing in his life. Why should this be any different?

He hadn't cared about Lorraine. He hadn't kept in touch. He hadn't even known whether or not she'd ever had kids.

If she had wanted him to have more, she would have given it to him.

This money wasn't stolen from him. It had never belonged to him in the first place.

I clenched my jaw, feeling something solidify inside me.

No.

I wouldn't cave.

Sonya nudged the box with her foot. "Sooo… do we name it?"

I let out a choked laugh. "No. We burn it."

She wrinkled her nose. "Sounds stinky. Maybe we just dump it in the garbage."

And somehow, despite everything—the exhaustion, the betrayal, the storm of emotions swirling inside me—I let out a chuckle.

Not a big, cathartic, everything's-fine laugh. But real. Small. Something that cut through the tension, even for just a second.

"I'll deal with this before Emma gets home and starts asking questions." Sonya scooped up the box and marched outside toward the garbage cans.

I let out a long breath as I headed for the living room, shrugging off my coat and plopping onto the sofa where my brain had started spiraling again.

I had believed those whispers so easily. A handful of careless comments, some perfectly timed gossip, and suddenly, I'd been ready to torch my entire relationship.

Had I overreacted?

I wanted to say no. But my gut wavered.

Because the truth was, I *had* overheard that phone call Sinan took last week—the one where he said, *I'm not sending you **more** money.* And he *had* avoided talking about Miranda every time I brought her up. And his mother… God, the way Aylin had looked at me across the ballroom, like I was some embarrassing charity case she wanted to hide behind a fern.

Every time I tried to convince myself I'd jumped to conclusions, another piece of evidence smacked me in the face.

Sonya came in, quiet, watchful.

I looked up at her. "I overreacted, didn't I?"

She perched on the armrest beside me. "Maybe. Maybe not. Your brain's a tornado of worst-case scenarios right now, and Miranda is the human equivalent of a red flag on fire."

I huffed out something between a laugh and a groan. "That's not helping."

She nudged my leg. "Then let's talk it out. Because if you're about to self-destruct, I'd rather it be over something real."

I slumped deeper into the couch. "What if it *is* real?" My voice cracked. "What if Sinan was just killing time with me until Miranda got her act together? What if I was just a placeholder?"

Sonya's expression turned stormy. "First of all, Sinan isn't that kind of man. Second, Miranda *never* had her act together. She was just good at faking it."

I pressed the heels of my palms against my eyes. "It's not just her. It's Jimmy, Aylin, the fact that I've felt out of place since the second I met Sinan's family. I don't belong in that world."

Sonya exhaled. "Kendra. You can't let Aylin's judgment dictate how you see yourself. And as for Jimmy… you have to let me and Max help. You don't have to fight him alone."

Her offer was tempting, but I shook my head. "I'll handle him. He's *my* mistake to clean up."

Even as I said it, Jimmy's voice slithered through my thoughts: *People always leave. No one's honest. You can't trust anyone.*

But wasn't he proof of his own poison? He'd left. He'd lied. He was the one person I could never trust. And yet, somehow, I'd let him back in—let his voice take up space in my head, like he had any right to be there.

But the worst part? The rumors at the gala had only reinforced everything he'd ever said.

Tears welled up, but I forced them down. "I trusted Sinan. And he didn't trust me enough to be honest." My voice came out small. "Maybe I'm not enough for him."

Sonya moved closer, warm and steady beside me. "You know that's not true."

I swallowed hard. "Then why didn't he tell me about the money? If everything was so innocent, why keep it a secret?"

Sonya hesitated, then sighed. "People do dumb things for all kinds of reasons. Fear, pride, wanting to protect someone. Maybe he thought it wasn't worth bringing up. Maybe he was afraid of exactly *this* happening."

I wanted to believe that. I really did.

But the doubt wouldn't let go.

I let out a shaky breath. "What if I've already ruined it? What if he can't forgive me for making a scene at the gala and then running away?"

Sonya studied me, then said softly, "If he loves you, he'll understand."

I flinched.

Because *that* was the real fear, wasn't it?

Not whether he'd forgive me.

But whether he *did* love me.

And whether *I* was capable of loving him back the right way.

I'd spent so much time building walls, assuming everyone other than Mom and Sonya would let me down, that I hadn't even realized how deep my trust issues ran. I wasn't just mad at Sinan —I was terrified that I was becoming Jimmy. That I'd push Sinan away before he had the chance to leave first. And maybe that fear was part of why I let Jimmy keep getting under my skin. The lies, the threats, the constant weight of knowing Monday morning could bring some new disaster.

I swallowed against the tightness in my throat. "I don't want to be like Jimmy."

Sonya's face softened. "You're *not*."

"But I can't stop hearing his voice." My hands clenched. "Like he's whispering in my ear, telling me I'm going to mess this up. That I'll push Sinan away just like he pushed you, and me, and

Mama, and everyone else away. What if I'm already doing that now? What if it's too late?"

Sonya squeezed my shoulder, grounding me. "It's not too late. But you have to decide what you *really* want. Are you done with Sinan? Or are you just scared?"

I closed my eyes.

Scared.

I was so damn scared.

I wanted to be the kind of person who *fought* for love. But right now, I wasn't sure if I knew how.

I swallowed hard. "I need to fix myself first. Before I hurt him."

Sonya nodded like she'd been waiting for me to say that. "That's a good start."

The words settled over me, heavy but right.

I wasn't going to let Jimmy's voice dictate my life.

But I also wasn't ready to fix things with Sinan—not yet.

I pushed to my feet, the exhaustion pressing down harder than ever. "I'm going to bed."

Sonya let me go, but as I reached the stairs, she called out, "Don't let one bad night define everything, Kendra. You're stronger than you think."

I forced a small smile. "Thanks."

Upstairs, I collapsed onto my bed, burrowing under the covers.

Memories of Sinan kept playing in my head—his smile, the way he made me feel seen, the warmth of his touch. But even those moments were shadowed by the nagging doubt Jimmy had planted.

I had to deal with this. I had to get my head on straight before I burned everything down.

With a heavy heart, I turned off my phone, not ready to face the world.

Sleep came slow, and when it did, it was restless.

Tomorrow, I'd face my choices. Whether I liked them or not.

And I wasn't sure if I'd even have a career left by the time I did.

LOVE IN LIMBO

SINAN

I pulled up to Kendra's house, my hands tightening around the steering wheel. The drive over had done nothing to calm me. My thoughts were still spiraling, the memory of her face—hurt, betrayed, shutting down—replaying like a loop I couldn't escape. I'd tried calling. No answer. I'd texted. Nothing.

The porch light was on, glowing against the dark night, but the curtains were drawn, the house sealed off, which was unusual. I took a steadying breath, forcing my pulse to slow as I stepped out and headed to the front door. My heart hammered as I rang the doorbell.

Footsteps. Then the door cracked open, and Sonya stood there, her expression unreadable.

"Kendra's not ready to talk to you."

I tensed. "I need to explain—"

"She doesn't need an explanation right now," Sonya said, voice firm but not unkind. "She needs time."

Frustration built in my chest. I wanted to push past, to tell her that time was the last thing we had. But that wasn't true, was it? Time wasn't the enemy here. My own mistakes were. The secrets I hadn't shared, the way I'd tried to handle things on my own instead of trusting Kendra with the truth.

"She thinks I've been lying to her," I said, my voice rough. "I haven't—"

"Haven't you?" Sonya's eyes softened, but she didn't back down. "Not about Miranda, maybe, but you kept things from her. And after what she's been through with Jimmy, that's a hard thing to overlook."

I ran a hand through my hair, exhaling sharply. "I never meant to hurt her."

"I know," Sonya said. "And deep down, I think she does too. But this isn't something you can fix tonight." She leaned against the doorframe, arms crossed. "You might not have meant to manipulate her, but keeping things from her? That's exactly how it felt. 'Protecting' someone," she lifted her hands in finger quotes, "by keeping them in the dark never ends well. If you want to prove you're not like Jimmy, then respect what she needs—honesty and time."

My jaw tightened, but I nodded. Sonya wasn't shutting me out forever. She was telling me how to get back in.

"Just... let her know I came by?"

Sonya's expression softened further. "I will."

With that, she eased the door shut, leaving me standing under the porch light, surrounded by darkness, my chest aching with everything I wanted to say but couldn't.

I had no choice. I had to wait.

When I walked into my house, the silence pressed in on me, too heavy, too thick. I tossed my keys in a bowl near the door and let out a long breath, trying to shake the weight of the night.

I wasn't alone for long.

My mother was waiting in the dimly lit living room, her hands folded neatly in her lap. She looked up as I entered, and for once, there was no judgment in her gaze. No sharp reprimands. Just quiet observation.

"I assume she didn't forgive you," she said.

I sank onto the armchair across from her, rubbing my temples. "Her sister wouldn't let me past the front door."

My *anne* nodded, as if that made sense. "Good."

I blinked at her. "Excuse me?"

She sighed, smoothing a hand over her knee. "You're used to fixing things quickly. But this… this is something you can't just fix overnight." She hesitated, then said, "I was wrong about Kendra."

I lifted my head, wary. "What?"

She exhaled, looking uncharacteristically tired. "I pushed you toward Miranda because I thought she was the safer choice. Someone from our world, someone who wouldn't challenge you. I thought… that's what love should be. Easy. Convenient."

I let out a short, humorless laugh. "That was never Miranda."

"No," *Anne* admitted, lips pressing together. "And tonight proved it."

I leaned forward, elbows on my knees. "Why did you think Kendra wasn't good enough?"

She hesitated, then looked away. "Because I was afraid."

That threw me. My mother was never afraid of anything.

She inhaled deeply. "I've never told you the full story of how your father and I met."

I frowned. "You were arranged. That's all you ever said."

Her smile was brittle. "Yes, but that doesn't mean there weren't… complications. I loved someone before him. Someone who wasn't part of our world. And I made the mistake of believing love alone was enough."

I straightened, shocked. "You were in love with someone else?"

"I thought I was." *Anne* looked at me then, eyes sharp with old pain. "But he didn't fight for me. When my family said no, he walked away. And so, I married your father."

A long silence stretched between us.

"Why are you telling me this?" I asked, my voice quieter now.

She folded her hands. "Because I see it now. Kendra isn't the kind of person who would easily walk away, Sinan. You are. If you don't fight for her, if you let your fear and your pride get in the way… you'll lose her."

I let out a slow breath, my mother's words settling deep inside me.

"I thought I was protecting you," she continued, softer now. "But I see now… love isn't about avoiding risk. It's about knowing who's *worth* the risk."

I swallowed hard. "And you think Kendra is?"

Aylin's gaze held mine, steady and unyielding. "I think that's for you to prove."

Upstairs, I sat on the edge of my bed, my phone in my hands. I stared at Kendra's contact, my thumb hovering over the call button. I wanted to hear her voice, to explain, to fix this. But Sonya was right—this wasn't something I could force.

So I did the only thing I could.

I used a voice text and started talking.

"I don't care if we're different. I don't care that we don't fit into each other's worlds perfectly. What I care about is you. And if I have to spend the rest of my life proving I'm not like Jimmy— proving I won't walk away—I will."

I paused, swallowing against the lump in my throat.

"But there's more… Jimmy called my mom today, accusing you of embezzlement. I'm worried he'll go after your job. I'm telling you this because I don't want to make the same mistake again by keeping things from you. You need to be ready for what happens at work on Monday morning. But whatever it is, just know—you don't have to face it alone. I'm here. No matter what."

I exhaled slowly. "I'll wait for you, Kendra. However long it takes."

I hit send.

Then, instead of drowning in regret, I grabbed a notebook from my nightstand, flipped it open, and started writing.

Ways to Fix This:
  • Prove she's not second choice.

• Figure out how to protect her from Jimmy.

• Don't just say I love her. Show it.

The pen moved, one line after another. I couldn't control everything, but I could control this.

No more overthinking. No more waiting for answers.

This time, I was writing my own ending.

43

STANDING ACCUSED

Kendra

The cold morning air stung my cheeks as I stepped outside the next morning, coffee mug in hand, my body still heavy with exhaustion. I hadn't slept well.

Between our breakup at the gala and last night's *gift* from Jimmy, every sound had kept me on edge, my brain spinning through possibilities of what Jimmy's next move would be, because I had no doubt that this would escalate.

When I reached the mailbox, a shiver ran down my spine before I even touched it.

I yanked it open.

Nestled between a pile of junk mail and bills was a hand-delivered envelope.

No stamp. No return address.

My hands shook as I pulled it out, flipping it over to open it.

Inside was a photo.

Me. Sonya. Mom.

A family picture I'd forgotten about. It had been taken on the boardwalk in New Jersey when we'd visited the beach the year I graduated from high school.

I turned it over, my breath catching.

On the back, scrawled in my mother's handwriting, was the date.

And below it, a note:

- For Jimmy, so he never forgets his family.

My stomach twisted violently.

Mom must have sent this to him.

My heart pounded as I unfolded the second slip of paper inside.

Jimmy's writing. Bold. Slanted. Pressed too hard, like he'd carved the words into the page.

Family doesn't turn their back on each other. I want what you owe me. Last warning.

I sucked in a breath, the world tilting for a second.

The raccoon was a warning.

This was a threat.

I wasn't just dealing with a bitter, washed-up conman grasping for money.

Jimmy was obsessed.

With the money.

With us.

With proving we were still connected, still bound to him, even if it meant forcing us to acknowledge it.

I crushed the letter in my fist, my pulse roaring in my ears.

No more hesitation.

No more second-guessing.

Jimmy wasn't just a problem I could ignore.

He was a ticking bomb.

And come Monday, when he made his next move, I'd be ready.

I PULLED into the parking garage, gripping the steering wheel tighter than necessary as I eased into my spot. The low hum of the engine did little to quiet the storm inside me.

The weekend had passed in a fog of raw emotions, each hour stretching into the next as I tried—and failed—to shake the weight of Sinan's lies and Jimmy's threats. But today wasn't the day to fall apart. There was too much at stake.

A speech to give.

A mayor waiting.

And Jimmy's words still burning in the back of my mind like a warning flare.

I exhaled sharply, squared my shoulders, and shut off the engine. The moment I entered the office, the familiar buzz of the workspace wrapped around me, offering a thin, temporary sense of normalcy. Phones rang. Keyboards clattered. Conversations hummed. It was the kind of predictable chaos I could usually slip into without thinking.

But today, my pulse was still too high, my skin still too tight.

I spotted Misha typing furiously, their energy a stark contrast to the emotional wreckage I was trying to keep under wraps.

"Hey, Misha," I called in greeting, surprised at how shaky my voice sounded.

They looked up, concern flashing across their face. "You look awful. What's going on?"

"It's my father." My throat tightened. It was like trying to swallow dust. "Everything's coming to a head. He told Sinan's parents I stole money from the company to pay for Mom's medical bills. He's after the inheritance. I need to talk to HR before his lies can do any real damage."

Misha's eyes narrowed with resolve, always my rock in the storm. "That's low, even for him. Go. Be clear, be calm. You've done nothing wrong."

Easier said than done. If only I could apply that advice to my entire life right now. Sinan's face flashed in my mind, and I shoved it aside. One disaster at a time, Kendra. His betrayal was still fresh, gnawing at the edges of my thoughts, but I had to push it aside. If I didn't tackle one storm at a time, I'd drown.

I nodded, trying to absorb Misha's steady confidence. "Thanks. I'm heading there now."

Just as I turned to leave, two security guards approached. They weren't exactly the welcoming committee I'd hoped for.

"Kendra Gambit?" one of them asked, his tone less-than-friendly.

I swallowed hard, pulse quickening. "Yes, that's me."

"You need to come with us to HR immediately," the guard said, making it clear this wasn't optional.

A rush of frustration surged through me. So, it's already begun. Jimmy had gone straight for the jugular. *Typical.*

As I passed Misha's desk, they shot me a wide-eyed look, fingers still flying across the keyboard like they were working on a secret rescue mission. I couldn't help but hope they were.

The HR office felt colder than usual. Maybe it was the fluorescent lighting or maybe it was just the icy chill of dread creeping up my spine. I sat down across from Ms. Stankowsky and Ms. Ellis, two women who looked like they moonlighted as professional poker players. No tells, just hard stares.

"Kendra, we've received a credible accusation that you've been embezzling company funds," Ms. Ellis said, her voice like a cold wind.

I braced myself. Not that it helped much. This was Jimmy's handiwork, of course. But credible? Jimmy? The man whose hot air and lies could fuel a trip to Mars? The idea was almost funny —almost.

"I understand," I said, trying to stay calm. "I already know about the accusation because it came from my father, Jimmy Harlow. He's been trying to extort money from me and my sister. He's lying, and I can prove it."

Ms. Ellis raised an eyebrow like she'd heard it all before. "You can prove it? How?"

Ms. Stankowsky leaned forward, her silence unnerving. "We'll need more than just your word."

I took a deep breath and pulled up the string of threatening texts Jimmy had sent me. As I scrolled, my eye caught on Sinan's name, a series of unread messages from the weekend. A familiar ache tightened in my chest, but I forced myself to move past them. *One disaster at a time, Kendra.*

"I have messages where he threatens to ruin me if I don't give him the money I inherited from my aunt."

Ms. Ellis didn't respond right away. She pulled up an email on her laptop instead. "We received this from him, claiming you've been funneling money from Steel City Structural Solutions to cover personal expenses."

I clenched my jaw as I read Jimmy's lies. He'd actually gone through with it. *Unreal.*

"As I said, Jimmy Harlow is my father," I repeated, keeping my voice steady despite the storm raging inside me. "He's... well, he's been in and out of legal trouble for most of his life. Let me show you his messages."

I handed over my phone. Ms. Ellis skimmed the texts and Ms. Stankowsky leaned closer to look over her shoulder.

As they scrolled through Jimmy's messages, a familiar voice whispered in my mind. *This is what happens when you pretend to be someone you're not.* I clenched my jaw, forcing the thought down. I wasn't pretending. I'd earned this job. I'd earned everything. Even if half the time I still felt like I was waiting to be exposed.

After a moment, their usually stoic expressions cracked—just slightly.

"This supports your claim," Ms. Stankowsky admitted. "But we'll need more to verify."

"Have you gone to the police?" Ms. Ellis asked.

My jaw tightened. "I filed a report over the weekend. They're investigating, but these things take time. Restraining orders don't stop a man like Jimmy, and pressing charges? That's not as easy as it sounds. I was hoping I could get him to back off without sending him back to prison. But maybe—"

The door swung open before I could finish, and Ken Burdinger strode in with Josh right behind him, his usual grumpy expression firmly in place.

"Kendra's guilty," Josh spat, his tone as sour as his expression. "I never trusted her."

Ken shot him a quelling look, effectively shutting him down. "Enough, Josh. I told you to stay out of this." He turned to HR, his tone softening but still firm. "Kendra's been an exemplary employee since she started last year. She won Employee of the Quarter in January. She's the most promising new hire we've had in years."

"Check the financial records," I urged. "Talk to my coworkers. I've done nothing wrong."

Josh began muttering something unintelligible—probably something about my inherent evil, or maybe he just couldn't think of a snappier insult. Either way, I tuned him out.

The door swung open again, and in walked Allison—the Iron Lady of Bridge Repair—her sharp gaze sweeping the room like a structural assessment, instantly noting the tension hanging thick in the air.

"This situation is ridiculous," she announced, crossing her arms. "Kendra just led one of the best state bridge inspections we've had in years. Our temporary repairs and the proposed permanent ones for the Steeltown Bridge passed with flying colors, thanks to her hard work and detailed preparation. She's the reason our team isn't getting dragged through the mud."

Ms. Stankowsky frowned. "That may be true, but serious accusations such as these normally require a probationary period—"

"You're considering putting her on probation based on an accusation? And from a felon with a history of harassment?" She aimed a frigid glare at Ms. Ellis. "That man's spent more years behind bars than I've spent doing bridge inspections."

Ms. Ellis frowned. "We're simply following protocol, Allison. These are serious allegations—"

Ken interrupted. "I reviewed the state's reports myself. The inspectors specifically noted Kendra's organization and leadership during the process. You can check their feedback if you don't believe me."

"Look," Allison added, "go ahead and do your due diligence. But probation? If you take that step, you're sending a terrible message to the rest of the team here at Steel City Structural Solutions. You'll be telling everyone you don't respect us or trust us. We can't afford to sideline Kendra right now."

Ken nodded in agreement. "Allison's right. Kendra's record speaks for itself. This accusation doesn't add up."

Josh let out a short breath, arms still crossed but his posture less combative now. "Look, I still think she got a fast track," he muttered, eyes avoiding mine, "but... maybe she's held up under more pressure than most would."

It wasn't exactly an apology. But for Josh, it might as well have been engraved on a plaque.

I didn't answer. I didn't have to. Because for the first time, it didn't sound like he was gunning for me—it sounded like he was finally *seeing* me.

Ms. Ellis exchanged a glance with Ms. Stankowsky, then let out a sigh. "We won't proceed with probation at this time," she conceded, though her tone was tight, "but we *will* continue to investigate the allegations."

Allison stood from her chair, unimpressed. "Which is what you should have done in the first place. Now let's all get back to work."

Just as I was finally able to take a deep breath, Misha knocked on the door, poking their head in. "Kendra, you're on in twenty minutes. Mr. Parker called asking for you."

I glanced at the clock and felt a jolt of adrenaline. "Twenty minutes? How did I lose track of—never mind, we've got to go!"

Misha grabbed their tablet, already half out the door. "I'll pull up the notes on the way."

Ken nodded, stepping beside me with the steady presence I'd grown to rely on. "Let's make this a good one."

As I rushed out, my pulse still thundered in my ears. The weight of the morning clung to me, heavier than I wanted to admit. I'd fought back against Jimmy's lies. My work on the Steeltown Bridge had been acknowledged. My team respected me.

That should have felt like a win.

Instead, it felt like I'd just survived round one of a twelve-round match, and my opponent had way more stamina.

HR was still investigating. That meant every move I made was under a microscope. One misstep, one mistake, and suddenly, Jimmy's accusations wouldn't seem so absurd.

And Jimmy… he wasn't done.

A new wave of nausea rolled through me. I'd barely survived the morning, and now I had to give a speech in front of the mayor, city officials, and whoever else had decided to show up and silently judge my existence. Fantastic.

I checked my phone. Three missed calls. Two voicemails. One from an unknown number. Great. Either Jimmy was escalating, or I'd just won a free cruise I'd never signed up for.

No time for that now.

I had to get to the City-County Building. I had to stand in front of the mayor and the press and speak with confidence, like I hadn't spent my morning dodging potential unemployment.

Ken walked beside me, his easy stride a stark contrast to the anxiety churning in my gut, and Josh trailed in our wake. Misha scrolled through their notes, muttering something about statistical analysis. They were both acting like this was any other workday, and I envied them for it.

Josh fell into step a few paces behind us, silent now. No snide remarks. No smug asides. Just… quiet.

I glanced back, half-expecting another jab. Instead, he met my gaze for a moment—quick, unreadable—and then looked away.

Maybe it was guilt. Maybe it was self-preservation. Or maybe —just maybe—it was the barest hint of respect.

Not enough to let my guard down.

But enough to notice.

I squared my shoulders, took a deep breath, and plastered on the best I'm-totally-fine smile I could manage.

If I could survive my ex-boyfriend's mother judging my shoe choices, a taxidermied raccoon, and being escorted to HR by security, I could survive this.

Probably.

But deep down, I couldn't shake the feeling that today wasn't the end of the battle.

It was just the beginning.

44

STEEL AND HEARTSTRINGS

Sinan

The drive from the hospital to the Pittsburgh City-County Building was quick—just enough time for me to replay the disaster I'd triggered at the gala on an endless loop. Kendra still wasn't replying to my texts, which shouldn't have surprised me after how badly I'd screwed up.

Showing up at the bridge event felt like my only option now. If she wanted me gone, she'd tell me. But I couldn't sit back and let her fight every battle alone. Not when she was dealing with Jimmy's lies, threats, and whatever storm he had planned next.

Parking outside, I exhaled, watching my breath cloud in the frigid morning air. I tossed my doctor's coat onto the back seat—because nothing screamed *last-ditch apology* like showing up at your maybe-ex's workplace looking like you were here to perform emergency surgery on a city council member.

The words from my mother echoed in my head—her quiet admission that she'd misjudged Kendra, that she'd been wrong. Then, her warning: *Don't let fear make your choices for you, Sinan.*

Right now, every instinct told me to push forward, to fix things. But this situation wasn't a delicate microsurgery where precision and control could solve the problem. There was no scalpel steady enough to undo the damage I'd caused. This time, the only thing I could do was step back, let Kendra lead, and hope she didn't decide to cut me out for good.

Inside, the grand building had that old-world solemnity that always made me feel like I was about to be scolded for something. I found a spot near the back of the large meeting room, scanning the crowd. City officials, engineers, and local leaders milled around, flipping through notes, shifting in their chairs.

For a moment, I second-guessed myself. What if she didn't come? What if Jimmy had followed through on his threats and she'd been fired?

Then the door swung open, and there she was.

Kendra walked in, flanked by Misha and Ken, looking like she'd battled a hurricane to get here—slightly disheveled but still Kendra. Steady. Focused. Determined.

Something in my chest loosened at the sight of her. Even if she never spoke to me again, I couldn't ignore the overwhelming relief at seeing her here. If Jimmy had caused trouble, it hadn't kept her away.

Her boss, Mr. Parker, beamed and turned to the room. "Everyone, this is Kendra Gambit—the engineer who first identified the critical damage leading to these bridge repairs. We're lucky to have her heading up our state inspection team."

Surprise flickered across her face at the unexpected praise. She adjusted the edge of her blouse, her fingers trembling as she stepped up to the podium. Most people would've missed it, chalked it up to nerves. But I knew the signs. Kendra didn't just want to do well—she needed to prove she belonged in this room. Even now, after everything she'd accomplished, she still seemed afraid someone might call her out as a fraud.

But she recovered quickly, standing taller as she addressed the room. "Thank you all for being here. I'll dive right into our progress on the bridge repairs and next steps."

As she spoke, breaking down temporary repairs, load distribution, underwater inspections, and long-term infrastructure plans, she owned the space.

The mix of pride and regret twisted through my chest. Even if she never let me back in, I'd always admire the hell out of her.

Ken, Misha, and Josh sat in the front row. Ken and Misha nodded approvingly, while Josh wore the same scowling expression he always had—like someone had forced him to attend a mandatory team-building retreat.

But then, as the applause swelled, I caught something unexpected. When Kendra stepped down from the podium and passed their row, Josh gave her the briefest of nods. Nothing showy. No grin or backslapping. Just a flicker of something that might have been… respect?

Kendra didn't look surprised. Just tired. But she gave him a small, almost imperceptible nod back.

Whatever had happened between them, it was different now. I couldn't name it, but I recognized the shift—like two colleagues who'd finally agreed to call a truce after a long, private war.

As the meeting wrapped up and people started chatting, I maneuvered through the crowd toward her. She looked calmer now, but the tension in her shoulders still lingered.

"You were amazing," I said, unable to help myself. It probably sounded too much like a proud parent at a school recital, but I meant every word.

She blinked, clearly surprised to see me there. A small, hesitant smile tugged at her lips. "Thanks, Sinan. It means a lot that you came."

That was something.

For a few fleeting seconds, the warmth lingered between us, the energy of the performance still buzzing in the air. But as the crowd thinned, the applause fading into scattered conversations and rustling coats, reality seemed to settle back over her. Her posture stiffened. The hesitation in her smile hardened into something more guarded.

I watched the shift, felt the moment slipping.

"So," I asked, keeping my voice level, "you seemed rushed when you got here. Everything okay?"

She let out a slow breath. "HR nearly put me on probation for 'embezzlement.' Jimmy's behind it—he emailed false accusations about me. Ken stood up for me, and Allison shut HR down."

My hands clenched. Anger curled hot in my chest. I'd known Jimmy was a problem, but this? He'd gone too far.

I fought back the immediate urge to promise to handle it for her. "I'm sorry you had to deal with that. I won't barge in and try to fix everything, but if you need me—legal advice, a contact, moral support—I'm here."

Her mouth pressed into a thin line. "I appreciate it, but it's my mess. Jimmy's never lifted a damn finger except to try to wreck what I've built." She shrugged, looking away. "You wouldn't understand—your entire family's got your back. The only person I have is Sonya."

Her words landed like a direct hit to my ribs. Not because she was wrong, but because she was so used to dealing with her problems alone.

I swallowed, hating how helpless I felt. "I know I can't change your past, but I'm not your dad, Kendra. I'm here. And I'm not giving up on you."

Something flickered in her eyes—an emotion I couldn't quite name.

For a second, her shoulders eased... until she shot me a considering look and then seemed to reach a decision. "I filed a police report over the weekend."

I frowned. "For what?"

Her jaw tensed. "Jimmy escalated. He sent a... package. A bizarre one." She hesitated, her fingers tightening around the folder she was holding. "A taxidermied raccoon. With a note saying he always finds a way in."

The words were ridiculous, but the intent behind them was anything but. My stomach dropped.

"That's not just some sick joke," I said quietly. "That's a threat."

She nodded. "That's why I went to the police. They're investigating, but it will take some time. And Jimmy knows how to stay just inside the lines. The 'gift' could be explained away as a family joke." She exhaled sharply. "I wanted to believe I could handle him on my own, but I know better now. He's not going to stop."

My chest tightened. I wanted to reach for her, to tell her she wasn't alone, but I knew that wasn't what she wanted. Not here. Not now.

"I'm glad you filed the report," I said instead. "And I meant what I said—if you need anything, you can count on me."

Her gaze flickered, but she didn't say anything.

Then she shook her head, exhaustion settling deeper into her features. "I need time. There's too much going on."

My throat tightened, but I nodded. "Okay. I'll wait. For as long as it takes."

She didn't look at me again as she turned away, leaving me standing there with the full weight of my mistakes, my regrets, and the sheer ache of wanting her back.

Everything in me screamed to go after her. To plead my case. To fix it.

But I stayed rooted in place.

Because right now, she didn't need grand gestures. She didn't need me barging in with promises.

She needed space.

I watched her walk away, my chest tight, knowing one thing for certain.

She was worth every fight—even if it felt like I was stepping into round two of the hardest match of my life.

No quick fixes. No hiding. Just the truth.

And if I wanted any chance of standing beside her again, I had to prove I was strong enough to face it.

45

HOPE IN BLOOM

Kendra

"We have news," Sonya said the moment I walked in the door on Wednesday. She and Max led me to the living room, their expressions way too serious for this to be anything good. The way they both looked at me—concerned but braced for a fight—made my stomach twist.

"Okay, what now?"

Sonya perched on the armrest, hands clasped like she was about to mediate peace talks. Max, standing across from us, had his executive face on—calm, controlled, and utterly immovable.

"If this is about Jimmy, I've already gone to the police," I said before they could start. "I turned over the texts, emails, and everything else—including the raccoon." I gave Sonya a pointed look. "Which, by the way, I *did* pull out of the trash and hand over as evidence."

Sonya grimaced. "Ugh. I bet that thing smelled *so* much worse after sitting in the garbage all night."

"Yeah, well, now it's the police department's problem." I crossed my arms. "They took a report, and they're investigating, but let's just say I don't think they're putting their best detectives on *The Case of the Taxidermied Threat*."

Sonya's hand found my shoulder, her grip warm and steady. "You did the right thing—but we're not stopping there."

Max nodded, voice edged with frustration. "We're filing a lawsuit."

I blinked. "A *lawsuit*?"

"He's escalated," Max said, his jaw tight. "The email to your employer wasn't enough. He sent another one—this time to Sonya —threatening to drag *Ross Film Productions* through the mud unless we pay him off."

My stomach dropped. Of course. Jimmy never did anything halfway. His entire life was a masterclass in doubling down on bad decisions.

I exhaled, rubbing my hands over my face. "So first it was blackmail, then he nearly got me fired, and now he's coming after *you*?"

Sonya nodded grimly. "He's using what he did to you to prove he won't give up unless we give him the inheritance."

I clenched my teeth. "And when that doesn't work, what? He sends another creepy message? Drops a dead fish on my doorstep? Calls the press?"

Max's mouth thinned. "That's why we're not waiting to find out. Our lawyer suggested hiring a private investigator. Jimmy's not as clever as he thinks. He's left a trail. This isn't just defamation—it's *extortion*. And since he's already on parole—"

"This could send him back to prison."

Max nodded. "Once the parole board sees the evidence, absolutely. Extortion is a serious offense, and violating parole isn't something he can talk his way out of."

The weight of it settled over me. Jimmy, actually facing real consequences. It should have felt like relief. Instead, exhaustion pressed down harder.

Sonya's voice softened. "If this goes to court, you'll have to testify. You've already stood up to him once. You can do it again."

My jaw tightened. I wasn't scared. I was *furious*. Jimmy had spent his entire life tearing things down, trying to drag everyone else into his misery. He'd failed Mom. He'd failed Sonya and me. And now, he was coming after *Max*? The nicest guy on the planet?

No.

Not this time.

"Absolutely," I said, my voice steady. "He's not getting away with this."

Max gave a firm nod. "We're in this together. He's not slipping away this time."

I glanced at Sonya, her reassuring smile grounding me. *We were in this fight together.*

But as soon as the anger burned through me, a new fear crept in.

Jimmy wasn't just fixated on *me*—he was using the people I cared about to *manipulate* me.

My stomach clenched.

What if he went after *Sinan* next?

I'd been juggling work deadlines, protecting my reputation, and dealing with my father's threats—so consumed by my own chaos, I never stopped to think Jimmy might target him too.

Sinan had money. Influence. A family name that carried weight. And worse? Jimmy had already started looking into him. If Jimmy thought squeezing Sinan could get him what he wanted, why wouldn't he try?

Ice trickled down my spine.

Would he dig up Sinan's past relationships? Feed lies to the media? Show up at the hospital, *cause a scene*?

The thought of Sinan, calm and composed at work, being blindsided by Jimmy's chaos made me nauseous.

I swallowed hard, my throat dry. "Max, if Jimmy's targeting the people around me… what if he goes after Sinan?"

Max's brows pulled together. "That's possible. But Sinan has resources—lawyers, security. Jimmy won't find him as easy to shake down."

That didn't make me feel better.

I let out a shaky breath. "I should warn him."

Sonya nudged my knee. "You could, but our lawyer can let him know. You don't have to take this all on yourself."

But that was the problem, wasn't it?

I had pushed Sinan away. I'd convinced myself he was better off without me and my chaos. But now, my choices might have put him in Jimmy's crosshairs anyway.

Guilt churned in my gut. I didn't want to drag Sinan into this, but if Jimmy saw him as another angle to exploit…

I met Max's gaze and nodded. "Do it. And if Jimmy tries anything, I need to know."

Max nodded, unwavering. "You will."

I exhaled, tension settling deep in my bones.

Jimmy wasn't just a problem from my past anymore.

He was a storm barreling straight through my present, tearing up everything in his path.

And if I wasn't careful, Sinan could get caught in it too.

But for the first time in a long time, Sonya and I weren't fighting alone.

BY SATURDAY, I was stretched so thin I felt like a rubber band about to snap. Sonya decided yoga would cure me; she all but dragged me to Bloom Yoga Studio in Sewickley. Minimalist décor, sunlight pouring through huge windows—if I hadn't been such a bundle of nerves, it might have felt like a sanctuary.

"You've been quiet," Sonya said, unrolling her mat. "Still thinking about Sinan?"

I gave a short nod. "Yeah, but I'm done twisting myself in knots."

She chuckled. "Maybe yoga's not the right place to take that stand." She exhaled as she settled into Child's Pose. "I think you should talk to him."

Before I could answer, the instructor's soothing voice floated through the room, guiding us into our first pose. Saved by downward dog, I supposed. But as I focused on my breathing, I realized ignoring my problems wasn't working. I didn't want to relive every ugly thought or repeat the same fears. Instead, I needed to figure out what I really wanted—and do something about it.

By the end of class, my arms and legs were shaky, but a fresh sense of clarity buzzed under my skin. Sonya rolled up her mat beside me as we stepped outside into the warm evening air.

"Feel better?" she asked.

"Yeah." I met her gaze. "I'm not saying everything is magically fixed. But I'm sure of one thing now—I don't want to lose Sinan."

"Love isn't easy, but it's worth fighting for," Sonya said, her voice softer. "Don't let fear and secrets steal your happiness. Trust me, I've been there. I let my world fall apart for five years because I ran away when a secret blew up my life. I don't want you to do the same."

I stilled, letting her words sink in. Sonya was right. I was letting fear drive me, just like I always had—whether it was Jimmy's influence, or my own self-doubt, I'd been pushing people away for years, expecting rejection before it could happen.

I tucked my mat under my arm, a hint of determination coursing through me. "I was so freaked out by his secrets that I forgot how much I love him. He didn't do it to hurt me—and I know that now."

She nudged me gently. "Exactly. Don't let fear be louder than your feelings."

I squeezed her hand in gratitude, and as we pulled into our driveway a little while later, I'd already decided. This wasn't about rehashing every misstep or letting my insecurities take center stage again—it was about what came next.

By the time we pulled into the driveway, I felt lighter. Not completely free of doubt, but more certain of one thing: I was done running.

"You look better," Sonya said, glancing at me as we walked toward the kitchen door. "Centered. Was it the yoga class?"

"Actually," I said, walking inside, "it was the sisterly advice."

Sonya grinned. "That's what I like to hear."

I hugged her. "Thanks for always being there, Essie." She felt solid in my arms. Reassuring. Someone I could always count on.

I spent so long thinking I had to prove myself to everyone—HR, the mayor, even Sinan's family—because deep down, I kept waiting for someone to say I didn't belong. That I wasn't enough. But maybe I was the only one still holding onto that fear. Maybe I didn't have to keep earning my place—I already had.

"You've got this, Kendra."

Once inside, I grabbed my phone. My heart pounded, but in a good way, as I tapped out a message I'd been too scared to send before:

> Me: Can we talk? Meet me at Phipps at one?

His reply popped up seconds later.

> Sinan: I'm glad you reached out. See you at one.

I exhaled a breath I didn't realize I'd been holding. Now that I'd decided, the anxiety receded enough to let hope slip in. Maybe we were finally on the same page.

At one, I stood just inside the entrance of Phipps Conservatory, clutching my phone as if it held the last bit of courage I had left. The lush gardens and intricate glasswork were almost too perfect —like the universe was mocking me for needing a do-over in a place so serene. Greenery spilled everywhere, all vibrant and calming, while inside, I contained nothing but chaos.

Light filtered through the leaves, casting dappled patterns on the floor, but the beautiful surroundings only highlighted my tension. I spotted Sinan as soon as he entered. His usual confident stride was a little less sure, and his normally crisp outfit had a hint of rumple. That's when it hit me—this wasn't just awkward for me. He was feeling it, too.

Our greeting was stiff, just a quick brush of cheeks, neither of us sure how much space to give or take. So much for easing into things.

"Thanks for meeting me," I started, my voice faltering as I handed him his ticket. It felt like an olive branch wrapped in awkward tension.

He shrugged, his eyes guarded. "I wasn't sure you'd call."

"Neither was I," I admitted with a small shrug. "But it's time we talk." Our footsteps echoed softly on the polished floors, the warm air and humidity wrapping around us like a slightly suffocating hug.

As we reached the Palm Court, the towering palms created a natural canopy overhead, sunlight flickering through the leaves. I could almost pretend we weren't standing in the middle of the mess I'd made.

"I know I shut you out," I began, the words stumbling over each other. "When I heard people talking about you and Miranda, I panicked. I... I was scared. Of how much I care about you. Of trusting you." I was babbling, but at least it was honest.

Sinan looked down for a moment, then back at me. Regret flickered in his eyes. "I should've told you everything sooner. Miranda's been asking me for money ever since she got out of rehab. I helped her once with legal fees, but that was it. She kept pushing, showing up at the hospital, and then the gala. I thought I could handle it without involving you, but clearly, that was a mistake. She manipulated the situation, and you got caught in the middle. I'm sorry."

"That's a lot," I said, my voice shaky. "But why didn't you tell me?"

He sighed. "I thought I was protecting you. But all I did was make things worse. She twisted everything to make it look like I was still involved with her. That's not what's going on, Kendra, I swear."

I took a breath, the memory of hearing those rumors at the gala still fresh, still stinging. "I didn't know what to believe. It felt like I was being pushed away. Like I wasn't enough for you. And that's my own stuff—I get that. But it still hurt."

"Kendra, no." Sinan stepped closer, his voice soft but insistent. "It's not about you not being enough. It's about me thinking I could fix things without being honest. I didn't want to burden you, but that's exactly what I ended up doing by keeping secrets."

I nodded, the tension loosening a little. "I need to know we can move past this. Can we fix this?"

His sigh was deep, but his words were steady. "I'm not saying it's going to be easy. But I want to try. You mean too much to me to let this go. I need you to trust me, even when it's hard."

"I understand," I said, finding strength in my voice. "But trust is built on honesty, and when you kept things from me, it made everything harder." I met his gaze, a flicker of determination rising within me. "I'm sorry for believing the gossip and letting it shake me, but I don't think I could have reacted any differently after what I overheard. You kept me in the dark, Sinan, and that's a place where fear takes over."

He squeezed my hand, his expression softening. "You're right. I didn't handle it well, and that wasn't fair to you. I should've trusted you enough to be honest from the start." He exhaled, regret weighing on his voice. "No more secrets. We'll figure this out together, but I know I need to earn that trust back."

I met his gaze, feeling lighter, like I could finally breathe again. "One step at a time."

"Together," he agreed.

We walked through the garden in silence, our hands brushing now and then, like hesitant steps toward rebuilding what we'd almost lost. The vibrant bursts of tulips and the soft rustling of leaves felt like a promise—a fragile, hopeful promise that maybe, just maybe, we could find our way back to each other.

After a few moments, Sinan glanced at me. "By the way, I got the message from your lawyer about Jimmy. Thanks for the heads-up."

Relief flickered through me. "So... you're not worried?"

He shook his head. "I've dealt with people like him before. He won't get far."

That steady confidence—it settled something in me. For the first time in days, I felt like maybe, just maybe, I wasn't bracing for impact alone.

The tension wasn't gone, but it was softer now, less brittle. It wasn't a grand resolution, but it was a beginning. And in the midst of all the blooming flowers, that felt like enough—for now.

PETALS AND PROMISES

SINAN

Taking Kendra's hand, I tried to focus on the tulips, not the uneasy thrum in my chest. The surgeon in me wanted clean, precise solutions—identify the problem, remove the damage, and restore function. But life wasn't a controlled operating room. There was no perfect incision to fix what had gone wrong. Not with Miranda, and certainly not with Kendra.

She squeezed my fingers, pulling me from my thoughts. A golden ray of sunlight caught in her hair, calming the whirlwind in my head for just a moment.

"I've been thinking," I said as we maneuvered around a couple taking a selfie. "Miranda... I can't keep letting her mess with my life—or with us. Covering her bills was supposed to help, but it backfired."

Kendra raised an eyebrow but waited quietly, used to my overthinking by now.

"I see now how it looked—like she could still reel me in whenever she wanted," I admitted. "But that's not true."

"Sinan," she said, voice steady, "you don't owe her anymore. Letting go isn't abandoning her—it's just cutting off the lifeline she's abusing."

I sighed. "That's what my head says. But walking away feels... cold."

Kendra stopped and faced me, crossing her arms. "Cold? Or just... necessary?"

I frowned, hesitating.

"She's like Jimmy," she continued. "They both think the world owes them something."

Kendra shook her head, disgusted. "Jimmy thinks he's entitled to my inheritance because of some twisted version of family loyalty, and Miranda thinks she's entitled to your help because of the past. But that's the thing—they're *both* adults, and they're both perfectly capable of standing on their own and facing the consequences of their actions. They just don't want to."

The realization hit me like a gut punch. She was right.

Jimmy had latched onto Kendra's success the same way Miranda had latched onto mine. The tactics were different— Miranda used guilt, Jimmy used threats—but the core was the same. Neither of them wanted to take responsibility for their own lives when they could manipulate someone else into doing it for them.

"Damn," I muttered, rubbing the back of my neck. "I really do have a thing for attracting entitled disasters."

Kendra smirked. "What can I say? You're irresistible to emotional leeches."

I groaned, tilting my head back. "That's *not* the legacy I was hoping for."

She softened. "But here's the thing—you're realizing it now. That's what matters. And you *have* helped Miranda. You're just not doing it on her terms anymore."

I exhaled, nodding slowly. "Yeah. No more playing safety net."

A thought flickered across Kendra's face before she turned to me, her eyes sharper now. "Look at it this way: Instead of just handing her fish, you can teach her to fish."

It took me a second to register the metaphor: *Give a man a fish, and he eats for a day. Teach a man to fish, and he eats for a lifetime.*

"Are you suggesting career counseling for someone I accidentally enabled?" I asked dryly.

"I bet it would work. It's still helping without enabling."

A slow grin spread across my face. "So instead of letting her use me as a financial crutch, I push her toward standing on her own two feet?"

Kendra nodded. "Bingo."

Relief crept in for the first time in ages. "So, I'm not abandoning her, but I'm done with this endless cycle of *Fix Miranda's life*. She can stand on her own."

"Exactly, Mr. Fixit."

I stopped and pulled a folded letter from my pocket, handing it to her. "She sent this a few days later. Said the gala was her rock bottom. She doesn't want anything else—just... to say she's sorry."

Kendra scanned the note, her brow creasing. "That's... unexpected."

"Tell me about it," I said, running a hand through my hair. "But look, it doesn't change what happened. She hurt you, and she hurt us. I'm not giving her a pass."

I hesitated, that paper-thin apology still sitting between us. "I don't even know if she means it, not fully. Could be guilt. Could be damage control. But it read like someone trying—finally—to take a little responsibility. And I thought you deserved to see that."

She scanned it, pausing to read aloud, "'I know I looked petty and cruel. But I was scared, and I lashed out. I'm sorry for dragging you into it. And I'm sorry for hurting her.'" She glanced at me. "You think she meant that?"

I shrugged. "I hope so." I used to think fixing things meant stepping in—paying bills, offering lifelines, keeping the pieces from falling apart. But maybe real help starts with letting someone face the mess they've made.

Maybe that's the only way they figure out how not to break things in the first place.

Kendra handed the letter back. "I appreciate you showing me. It's good she apologized, but it doesn't make everything okay."

"Exactly. I'm done feeling responsible for her." I exhaled, rolling my shoulders. "Sometimes the best way to help is to step back."

Kendra smiled and led me toward the fountain, dipping her hand into the water. A playful spark lit her eyes.

"You've got that look," I teased, sidestepping a potential splash. "Should I be worried?"

Kendra cocked her head, grinning. "Depends. Can you handle a little chaos, Doctor?"

Before I could react, she flicked a handful of water at me, mischief dancing in her eyes.

"Hey!" I laughed, dodging, but the water still caught my sleeve. "You *really* want to start this?"

She shrugged, her grin widening. "I didn't start anything. That was totally an accident."

"Oh, it's on." I splashed back, making her squeal.

We circled the fountain, dodging and laughing. For a moment, it was just us, the tension gone, replaced by something lighter and warmer.

"You needed that," she said softly.

"Yeah," I grinned, shaking water from my sleeve. "I think we both did."

47

A SPLASH OF ROMANCE

KENDRA

"I can't tell which of you is winning, Sinan. You or the wetsuit."

I crossed my arms, biting back a grin as I watched my usually poised, hyper-competent boyfriend wrestle with his wetsuit like it had personally wronged him. One arm was stuck halfway through the sleeve, the other flailing as he tried to tug it over his shoulders.

"This... is... impossible," he grunted, twisting awkwardly before finally freeing one arm—only for the other to get tangled. He shot me a glare. "You do this every weekend?"

"Only for the past five years," I teased. "You're doing great, though. Really."

He narrowed his eyes. "Lies."

The early June sun spilled golden light over the dive location, warming the gravel underfoot and reflecting off the calm blue water. The scent of fresh-cut grass mixed with the sharp tang of neoprene, and the clinking of air tanks blended with the excited chatter of students gearing up. This place—this world—was home. And now, for the first time, Sinan was stepping into it.

I still wasn't sure I believed it.

A little over a month ago, he was standing in a tuxedo at the Omni William Penn, completely in his element among Pittsburgh's elite. Now, he was joining my class, struggling into a wetsuit like the newbie he was, determined to be here.

Our eyes met, and the noise around us faded.

"I thought diving wasn't your thing," I said, raising an eyebrow.

He finally wrangled the wetsuit into place—though the zipper was definitely off-kilter—and shrugged, a half-smile tugging at his lips. "Figured it's time I made it my thing. For us."

Something warm and unexpected curled in my chest.

I handed him his mask and fins, fighting the urge to laugh. "Welcome to the class, newbie. Try not to drown."

"Oh, you're really enjoying this, aren't you?" He chuckled, taking the equipment with a mock look of fear. "Here I thought I signed up for fun, not torture."

"This *is* fun," I teased. "Wait until I make you do the underwater mask-clearing drill."

His expression faltered. "I hate everything about that sentence."

I smirked, suppressing a laugh. Watching Sinan—my impossibly polished, always-in-control neurosurgeon—struggle with something so far outside his comfort zone was unexpectedly endearing. But more than that, it meant something.

He was choosing this. Choosing me.

As the other students finished suiting up, I snuck another glance at him. His usual effortless grace was replaced with a kind of determined awkwardness. He fumbled with his air tank, tugged at his straps like they were actively resisting him, and kept shooting me small, uncertain glances, as if checking that he was doing it right.

"Rule number one," I told the group, raising my voice slightly over the shuffle of movement. "Always check your equipment thoroughly before each dive." I pointed at Sinan. "Especially if you have no idea what you're doing."

He chuckled, fumbling with his air tank. "Oh, I've got an idea —it's just not a very good one."

I watched him struggle to adjust the straps. "Need help, or should I alert the lifeguard now?"

"I've got this... I think." He gave the tank one final, dramatic tug. "I've conquered tougher things. Like... your cooking."

I gasped in mock offense. "That was one time, and I warned you about the spicy sauce!"

He grinned. "Yeah, I'm still recovering from that. At least my mom loved it."

Aylin had finally warmed up to me enough to let me cook for them before they flew back to Turkey. She'd loved my spicy sauce —turns out we shared a love for hot food, the spicier the better. Strange thing to bond over, but I'd take the win.

I couldn't help but notice how good Sinan looked in a wetsuit —broad shoulders, lean muscles, the snug fit doing him way too many favors. My heart gave a little flutter, and I had to remind myself to stay professional. I needed to focus.

The lesson moved forward, and though Sinan wasn't the perfect student, he paid attention, fixed his mistakes, and—even better—kept looking to me for reassurance. Every time his gaze met mine, something inside me settled.

Maybe today wasn't just about diving. Maybe it was about trust. Growth.

And maybe, just maybe, this was Sinan's way of proving he wasn't afraid to take the plunge.

Once the students all left, Sinan and I lingered on the dock, the late afternoon light casting soft ripples across the water. It felt peaceful, like we'd turned a corner. Sinan, still in his wetsuit and looking more at ease in this unfamiliar world than I'd ever expected, walked over to me with a glint in his eyes.

"Hey, Dive Mistress," he teased, flashing a grin as he flopped down beside me.

"I see you've learned your place," I said with a grin, feeling lighter than I had in weeks.

His laughter faded into something softer as he sat back, propping himself up on his arms and gazing out across the water. "You know," he started, "being a surgeon... control is everything. I've built my life around it—steady hands, sharp decisions. But with you..." He turned to me, his expression serious now. "With you, I'm learning to let go. To embrace the unpredictable, to accept a little mess. And today... today was a leap for me."

My heart flipped. "You did great out there. I mean, everyone's afraid of something, right?"

His gaze held mine, something deep and unspoken passing between us. "Exactly. And I don't want to be the guy who tries to control everything anymore. Not with us."

Warmth spread through me, the weight of his words settling in. This wasn't just about scuba diving—this was about trust. Growth. Partnership.

Sinan reached into his bag, pulling out a folded pamphlet. "And that's why I was thinking... maybe we take this new 'let go and embrace the chaos' thing to the next level."

I raised an eyebrow, unfolding the glossy brochure. It was filled with pictures of turquoise waters, coral reefs, and sun-drenched beaches. My eyes widened. "The Virgin Islands?"

He nodded, his grin returning. "Yep. Just us, a catamaran, and the open sea. No dive classes, no schedules. Just the wind, the ocean, and us."

"Wait—you booked a *catamaran*?"

"Forty-five feet of sleek perfection," he said, proud. "I've spent more time around boats than you might guess. Regattas, family trips, that one summer on the Amalfi Coast when my uncle tried to make me learn knots blindfolded."

I blinked. "Okay, that's... unexpectedly impressive."

"It's mostly muscle memory. And trauma. Lots of summer-camp trauma." He grinned. "But I promise to impress you—unless I get distracted by rum punch or rope burn."

"I guess I'll be the judge of that."

"Bring it."

I flipped through the pages, excitement bubbling up. "That sounds perfect. But..." I paused, looking at him skeptically. "There's one small problem: I don't know how to sail."

He chuckled, pulling me closer. "Don't worry. We'll have a captain, a cook, and maybe a first mate. I might choose you as my plus-one if we're ever stranded on a deserted island, but I'm not risking our survival on your navigation skills."

I grinned, nudging him with my elbow. "Good call."

He grew more serious, his voice softening. "I want us to start this new chapter somewhere far from everything—just you and me. I've spent my whole life planning, controlling, fixing... but with you, I don't want to be that guy. I want to learn to roll with the waves, let go, and trust. We'll sail wherever our noses lead us."

I felt a swell of emotion, realizing this trip wasn't just a vacation—it was a leap forward, a deeper commitment to us. "I like the sound of that," I whispered, flipping through the images of reefs, clear blue water, and endless skies.

Sinan's voice dropped lower, more intimate. "It's the beginning of something new. You and me. No more holding back."

I leaned into him, resting my head against his shoulder. "With you by my side, I wouldn't want it any other way."

His lips brushed my hair, and for a moment, everything else faded—until it was just us, wrapped in the quiet promise of all that was to come.

48

AND A PINCH OF PAYBACK

Sinan

"You look like a merman. It's a good look on you."

I turned mid-stroke to see Kendra standing near the pool's edge, arms crossed, a smirk playing on her lips. Dressed in leggings and a tank top, she looked completely at home, like she belonged here. Like she belonged with me.

I pulled myself up onto the pool deck, water streaming down my back as I grabbed my towel. "Don't think I don't catch you ogling me at those dive classes."

Her laugh was immediate, light and teasing. "One of the perks of the job." She dropped her purse onto a nearby chair and rocked back on her heels. "But hey, I've got news—big news."

I raised an eyebrow, rubbing the towel over my hair. "What's up?"

She exhaled sharply, her voice tinged with relief. "Jimmy's going back to prison."

That stopped me. My towel stilled mid-motion.

"Wait—what?"

Kendra nodded, her words tumbling out now that she had my full attention. "Max's lawyer sent the evidence to the parole board

—Jimmy's letters, his threats... it was enough to revoke his parole. He's already in custody."

Three weeks. It had been three weeks since that day I first joined her dive class—three weeks of navigating this new chapter between us, of peeling back old wounds and figuring out where we stood. Three weeks of waiting for the other shoe to drop, for Jimmy to twist the knife just one more time.

And now... it was done.

I tossed the towel aside and moved toward her. "That's... huge. How do you feel?"

Her expression shifted, a flicker of tension in her jaw. "Relieved," she admitted, "but also angry. Angry that he keeps hurting us and forcing us to clean up his mess. And part of me... part of me feels like I don't deserve you because of all this baggage."

I frowned. "Kendra."

She sighed, crossing her arms, her voice quieter now. "I know, I know. Logically, I get it. But it's hard not to feel like he's a shadow I can't shake. Like no matter how much I distance myself, he still finds a way to mess up my life—and now yours, too."

That hit me hard. Because I knew exactly what she meant.

I took her hand, squeezing gently. "You're not responsible for Jimmy's choices any more than I'm responsible for Miranda's. He's his mess. Not yours."

She swallowed, her fingers tightening around mine. "Then why does it feel like he'll never stop making me pay for them?"

I pulled her closer, keeping my voice firm but gentle. "Because he wants you to believe that. But you're not his to ruin, Kendra. You never were. You stood up to him. You fought back. And you won."

Her gaze met mine as something in her shoulders loosened. The weight she carried—the burden of a past she never asked for—eased, even if just a little.

She let out a breath, almost a laugh, shaking her head. "You know what's wild? That inheritance he was so desperate to get his hands on? I used it to pay off all my student loans."

I blinked. "All of them?"

She nodded. "Every last cent. No more minimum payments dragging me down. No more interest creeping up like a slow-moving tidal wave. I didn't realize how much fear I was carrying until it was gone. The fear of not having enough, of living paycheck to paycheck, of always wondering if I'd end up like Mom—drowning in bills no matter how hard I worked."

I squeezed her hand again. "That's not your future, Kendra. It never was."

She let out another breath, this one steadier. "I know. But for the first time, I actually believe it."

I brushed a damp strand of hair from her face, my voice softer. "I'm proud of you. Not just for paying off the loans, but for getting here. For knowing your worth beyond Jimmy's mess."

A slow, genuine smile spread across her lips.

"Thanks," she whispered.

Before I could revel in the moment, I yanked her into my arms, still dripping wet from the pool.

She shrieked, half-laughing, half-protesting. "Sinan! You're soaked!"

"And yet, here you are," I teased, holding her tighter, "still in my arms."

Her laughter bubbled up again—bright, free, like a breath of fresh air. But then—before I had a chance to react—she grabbed my wrist, pivoted, and yanked me straight into the pool with her.

The water rushed around us, swallowing our laughter, pulling us under together. For a split second, I was weightless, suspended in the cool embrace of the pool.

And then I resurfaced, dragging Kendra up with me, blinking water out of my eyes. "That was... not what I expected."

She grinned, slicking her wet hair back. "I told you, merman— you can't always be in control."

I pulled her closer, still laughing. "Well, if we're going under, we're going under together."

Her smile turned mischievous. "That's the spirit. I mean, we've survived way worse. Near-breakups, sabotage, Jimmy's threats, Miranda's nonsense..."

I smirked. "A taxidermied raccoon."

She groaned, tilting her head back. "Ugh, do *not* remind me."

"Too late. That photo you sent me of it is seared into my brain forever."

She nudged me. "Maybe I should've named him before handing him over to the cops."

"Oh, I already did. His name is '*Evidence.*'" I grinned. "The most unsettling evidence in police history."

Her laughter rang out, full and unguarded. "You know, if we can get through that, I think we can survive anything."

I leaned in, brushing my lips against hers. "Agreed."

And this time, I wasn't trying to hold on or keep us steady—I was ready to dive in—chaos, raccoons, and all—with her by my side.

TROPICAL DREAMS OF FOREVER

Kendra

"Sinan, you're supposed to *pull* the line, not wrestle it."

"I *am* pulling it," he grunted, bracing his foot against the deck as he yanked at the mainsail's halyard. "Why does it feel like I'm in a tug-of-war with an entire hurricane?"

"Try again," Captain Jake said. "More finesse, less brute force."

Sinan exhaled, adjusted his grip, and with a practiced tug, the mainsail snapped up cleanly, catching the wind in a perfect arc.

"There you go," Jake nodded, clearly impressed. "Looks like someone's done this before."

Sinan shot me a look, smug and only slightly windblown. "Told you I wasn't just a pretty face."

"You're full of surprises," I admitted. And I meant it."

It had only been two days since we'd arrived in the Virgin Islands, and already life on the catamaran had thrown a few surprises our way. We'd prepared as much as we could over the past two months—YouTube videos, a couple of sailing lessons— but nothing compared to *actually* being here. The constant motion of the boat, the strange but oddly soothing rhythm of life at sea, the way even the simplest tasks took twice as long when you had to factor in shifting decks and wind resistance.

And then there were the mishaps.

Like this morning, when Sinan had lost his balance stepping out of the cabin and smacked his forehead on the doorway. Or yesterday, when I miscalculated the angle of gravity during a turn and ended up dumping half a pitcher of fresh-squeezed juice straight into my lap. Or the ongoing saga of "who forgot to latch the galley drawers" every time we hit an unexpected swell.

Sinan finally solved the problem by re-securing a rattling cabinet with a piece of cord he'd found in the gear locker, tying it off in a neat bowline.

"How do you even know how to do that?" I asked, genuinely impressed.

He shrugged. "Sailing camp. And a bit of yacht-racing with my dad in high school."

"You're casually making me fall for you all over again."

"I accept full responsibility."

The sun burned warm against my skin as I glanced toward the horizon, where scattered islands rose from the turquoise sea like something out of a dream. The salty breeze teased my hair, and beneath my feet the gentle rocking of the boat had already become familiar.

"This still feels unreal," I murmured, watching the wake trail behind us.

Sinan wrapped an arm around my waist, his touch solid and grounding. "Get used to it," he said, pressing a kiss to my temple.

Our catamaran—*Wind Dancer*—was everything I'd imagined and more. A sleek, 45-foot beauty with twin hulls that kept the motion steady, a sprawling deck perfect for watching the sunset, and just enough luxury to make me feel like we'd truly left the world behind.

Captain Jake and First Mate Ashley had welcomed us aboard with easy smiles and island charm. Kelly, our cook, made sure we never went hungry—her coconut French toast had already ruined me for regular breakfasts forever.

The day passed in a sun-drenched blur. We snorkeled near The

Baths, weaving through massive granite boulders that created hidden pools of shimmering blue. We steered the boat ourselves under Jake's patient guidance, Sinan getting the hang of the mainsail while I navigated. We ate fresh mango straight off the cutting board, letting the juice drip down our fingers, and in the late afternoon, we stretched out on the trampoline netting at the bow, letting the sea spray cool our sun-warmed skin.

By the time evening rolled in, we were anchored near Jost Van Dyke, and I was ready to sink into the slow rhythm of the night. The water was so still it mirrored the sky, stars blinking in the deep, endless blue.

Sinan, freshly showered and somehow still looking like he belonged on a yacht ad, plopped down beside me on the deck. "So, I think I've figured out the trick to sailing."

"Oh?" I turned my head, intrigued. "Do tell."

"Step one: Make it look effortless." He gestured vaguely toward Ashley, who was handling the anchor with the ease of someone tying their shoelaces.

"Uh-huh," I said, amused. "And step two?"

He grinned. "Let someone else do all the hard work while you sip rum punch."

I laughed, nudging him with my shoulder. "Ah, so your *true* calling is 'leisure captain.'"

"Exactly." He tilted his head toward me, his expression softening. "And maybe first mate to a certain dive instructor."

Warmth spread through me, curling low in my chest. "Good. Because I happen to need a first mate for the rest of this trip."

When we went ashore, a lively festival greeted us—drums, laughter, bonfires glowing along the beach. "This is amazing," I said, grinning at Sinan.

He pulled me close. "I thought you'd love it."

Ashley and Kelly joined in the fun. "You've got to try this," Kelly called, handing me a neon-green drink with a glowing, battery-powered plastic ice cube.

"What is this?" I raised an eyebrow.

"The 'Island Glow,'" Ashley laughed. "Kelly swears by it."

"Swears by it? For what, powering a small boat?" I took a sip, eyes widening at the sweet-tart taste. "Okay, it's good, but it still looks like a chemistry experiment."

Sinan grinned. "Afraid to embrace the glow?"

"Not afraid." I took another sip. "I just believe in drinks that don't look like nuclear waste. I half-expect to get some super-powers as a side effect."

The music was impossible to resist, and soon, Sinan and I were dancing barefoot in the sand, the warmth of the bonfires and the rhythm of the drums wrapping around us.

"Every part of this trip feels like a wonderland," I said as Sin pulled me close.

"That's what I wanted," he murmured. "A wonderland, just for us." He took my hand. "Come on, let's walk."

We wandered along the shoreline, the waves lapping at our feet. The stars above seemed to glow brighter, and in that moment, everything felt perfect.

"This isn't just a vacation," I said, pausing as the waves rushed over my toes, burying them deeper in the sand. "It's everything."

Sinan turned to face me, wrapping his arms around me. He kissed me then, slow and deep, tasting of coconut and rum. A quiet, electric current hummed between us. His laughter was low as I ran my fingers through his hair, leaving it spiked.

"I'm glad you're still into me," he teased, raking his fingers through his hair with the kind of practiced ease that made his hands so hypnotic to watch, "even if you enjoy making me look like a tropical porcupine."

I grinned, pulling him closer. "Those hands of yours are a great distraction from the porcupine situation."

His fingers skimmed my back beneath my top, his touch light but deliberate. Just as heat curled between us, a couple mean-dered a little too close, completely oblivious to the moment they'd just interrupted.

I sighed, stepping back with a smirk. "Looks like we lost our private beach."

Sinan chuckled, unfazed, and took my hand, his grip warm and steady. "Saved by the tourists. Come on, let's head back before we end up as the background couple in someone's honeymoon montage."

I laced my fingers through his, letting the easy sway of our steps match the gentle rhythm of the tide. The night stretched ahead of us, endless and open, the boat waiting just off the shoreline.

"And after?" I asked softly, squeezing his hand.

The question lingered between us, weightless and full of possibility. Out here, surrounded by nothing but the whisper of waves and the glow of distant lights, there was no rush to find an answer.

Sinan glanced at me, his expression unreadable but certain in all the ways that mattered. "I guess we'll have to see where the wind takes us."

The words settled in my chest, warm and sure.

As we walked toward the boat, the ocean lapping at our feet, I knew one thing—whatever came next, we'd find our way together.

50

ISLAND GLOW AFTERGLOW

Sinan

I woke to the gentle rocking of the catamaran, the rhythmic sway lulling me into a rare, perfect stillness. The sun had barely begun its climb, and was casting a soft golden glow through the cabin windows. Kendra was still wrapped in my arms, her body warm against mine, her breathing slow and steady.

For a long moment, I just lay there, absorbing the quiet, the feel of her against me, the way the sea cradled us like we were adrift in our own world. Out here, there was no hospital, no responsibilities, no complicated surgeries—just the two of us and the ocean stretching endlessly in every direction.

Kendra stirred slightly, her fingers brushing against my chest before she blinked awake, her eyes still heavy with sleep. "Mmm," she murmured, pressing closer. "Can we just stay like this forever?"

I ran a hand down her back, feeling the slow rise and fall of her breath. "I was just thinking the same thing."

She smiled lazily, then frowned as the boat rocked a little more noticeably beneath us. "Okay, maybe not forever. I'm fine with a little rocking, but if we hit full roller coaster mode, I'm out."

I chuckled, brushing a kiss over her hair. "Noted. I'll have Captain Jake tone down the waves for you."

She stretched, pressing a kiss against my jaw before reluctantly pulling away. "I guess we should get up at some point. Big day ahead."

I watched as she sat up, her silhouette framed against the sunlight filtering through the window. Today was big—but she had no idea just how big.

As we sailed closer to Guana Island, its details sharpened with each passing moment. The outline of the island transformed from a distant blur into a green, vibrant expanse against the deep blue sky. Beaches emerged, their pristine, white sands stretching like ribbons along the shore. Palm trees swayed gently in the breeze, and the crystal-clear water shimmered beneath the sun, revealing glimpses of coral reefs. It was paradise, plain and simple, and with every ripple in the water, every flash of sunlight, the island came alive—no longer just a picture-perfect postcard, but an invitation to step into the dream.

Captain Jake had let me take the helm for part of the morning sail, and I'd been surprised by how easily the skills came back. Somewhere between youth sailing camps and watching my father bark orders on Mediterranean cruises, some part of it had stuck. I adjusted the trim and corrected our angle as we neared the cove, earning a satisfied nod from Jake.

"You're smoother than most guests who claim they've done this before," he said.

I flashed him a grin. "What can I say? I had an overachieving childhood."

Kendra appeared beside me, squinting into the horizon. "You really do know what you're doing, huh?"

I shrugged. "It's coming back. And it helps having a good teacher."

She reached for my hand, her smile easy and warm. "I'm impressed."

When we anchored in a secluded cove, we stepped ashore, the

warm sand soft beneath our feet. I tried to focus on the beauty around us—the sunlight dancing on the water, the quiet peace of the beach—but my brain wouldn't calm.

"This island is one of my favorites," Jake said, his face serene. "Perfect for a quiet, romantic getaway. We've got a special dinner planned for you on the beach tonight, complete with the pineapple kebabs you requested. Once we set things up, we'll leave you two to enjoy it."

Kendra's eyes sparkled with amusement. "Pineapple kebabs? I knew you were romantic, but I didn't expect you to recreate our Turks and Caicos beach night."

I flashed her a grin, trying to act cool even as her words sent a flush of warmth through me. "My main goal on this trip is to make you happy and keep you that way."

Kendra let out a ripple of laughter. "Mission accomplished."

The day passed in a blur of tropical bliss. We wandered along the island's trails, the scent of flowers mixing with the salty breeze. It felt like we were the last two people on Earth, marooned in our private paradise. Every step, every moment with her felt like a part of something bigger.

By the time the sun started its slow descent, casting a golden glow over the water, we made our way back to the beach. The soft lapping of the waves, the island's peaceful rhythm—everything clicked into place. My hand tightened around hers, more from instinct than nerves.

"This place is so peaceful," Kendra said, her voice low as she squeezed my hand. She had a faraway look, like she was both in the moment and lost in her thoughts. "Could life really be this perfect?"

I didn't answer right away. I just squeezed her hand tighter. This wasn't just a vacation—it was a new beginning.

"Kendra," I began, trying to keep my voice steady despite the storm raging in my chest. "I've thought about this moment for a long time." My heart pounded. "You've brought so much joy, so much love into my life... I can't imagine a future without you."

This is it, I thought as the sand crunched under my knees. My brain was screaming to stay calm, but my heart? It was hammering like a heart monitor going off in the OR. What if she says no? The thought flashed through my mind, sending a jolt through me, but before I could spiral, Kendra's eyes widened, and everything around us blurred, narrowing to just her.

Please, for the love of all things pineapple-flavored, don't panic.

"Will you marry me?" I asked, my voice shaking slightly. So much for being smooth. The question hung there, heavy and tense, like waiting for a pulse to return on the monitor. I gripped her hand tighter, feeling the weight of everything settle in my chest.

Kendra stared at me, eyes glistening with unshed tears, and for a second, I thought she might back away. But then her laughter rang out, warm and bright, just like that perfect night in Turks and Caicos.

"How could I say no to the man who woos me with pineapple kebabs?" she teased, wiping at her eyes, her voice cracking with emotion. "So, I guess you're stuck with me. Yes, I'll marry you."

Relief hit me like a tidal wave. I slipped the ring onto her finger, my hands finally steady. Marriage. A life together. This incredible woman. Was this actually happening?

Yes. Yes, it was.

I stood and pulled her into my arms, everything that had been weighing me down evaporating. She was with me, and that was all that mattered.

"This is the happiest moment of my life," I whispered, pulling her close. She laughed softly against my neck, and just like that, everything clicked into place.

"Mine too," she whispered back, her voice thick with the kind of emotion that fills every corner of your soul.

As we walked along the beach, Kendra lifted her hand, her eyes catching on the ring. She paused, turning it slightly to study the design. "It's beautiful... but these hexagons—this isn't just a regular ring, is it?" She brushed her thumb over the delicate honeycomb pattern in white and yellow gold. "This pattern is used in structural engineering."

I grinned, watching her curiosity take hold. "The honeycomb pattern is known for its strength and elegance. Just like you... like us. It symbolizes the balance we have, the way we fit together."

Her smile deepened, her eyes glinting with a mix of surprise and affection. "I love that," she whispered, her voice softer now, more intimate. She glanced inside the band, her eyes widening again. "Are these longitudinal coordinates for someplace in particular?"

I nodded, my chest warming at her reaction. "Turks and Caicos. Where it all started."

She blinked back more tears, shaking her head in disbelief. "This is perfect. You thought of everything."

"Of course," I said, pulling her closer, my lips brushing her forehead. "I've been planning this for a long time."

Jake grinned as we approached the bonfire, raising a glass of champagne. "Looks like congratulations are in order!" His grin was as warm as the setting sun. "To a lifetime of happiness."

Kelly was right behind him, gesturing toward the beautifully arranged dinner laid out before us. "Something special for you two tonight. Enjoy every bite."

Ashley waved as she packed the last of the gear into the dinghy. "We'll leave you lovebirds to your evening. Have fun!"

Once the crew had returned to the catamaran, it was just Kendra and me. The night was still, the air filled with warmth and love, and my heart? Full. I sat down beside her, letting the reality of what had just happened settle in. She said yes. *She said yes!*

The meal was incredible—grilled seafood that melted in our mouths, fresh fruit that tasted like it had been plucked straight from paradise. But more than that, every bite was a reminder of how far we'd come, of everything we'd built together.

"You remembered every detail," Kendra said softly.

I grinned, opening the plastic container of pineapple kebabs.

"You think I'd forget the kebabs? Those bad boys sealed the deal in Turks and Caicos."

She shot me a playful look, taking a bite. "Is that so? Should I be worried that you'll start commemorating those neon Island Glow cocktails next?"

I chuckled. "No promises. A ring with a flashing ice cube might be on trend."

She laughed, shaking her head. "Please, let's not turn into that couple."

"Okay, fine. But no complaints if I name our first kid *Island Glow*."

Kendra raised her glass, her eyes twinkling with mischief. "To sticking with kebabs and not naming anyone after questionable beverages."

We made s'mores next, just like that unforgettable night in Turks and Caicos. It was the perfect throwback. The marshmallows melted into a gooey mess, and as I wiped some from the corner of her mouth, I couldn't help laughing at how something so small could feel so significant.

"To our future," I said, raising my glass.

"To our adventure," she replied, her eyes glowing in the firelight as we clinked glasses, the stars twinkling above us like they were celebrating right along with us.

The night was flawless—every laugh, every glance, every quiet moment filled with the kind of joy that makes your heart feel like it could burst. When we were ready to head back, I signaled Captain Jake, who arrived with the dinghy so he and Kelly could pack up the last of our dinner and row us back.

Later, as we crawled onto the bed at the bow, the stars shimmering overhead, I showed her just how much I was looking forward to being her husband.

"You know," she whispered afterward, her head resting on my chest, "we could make kebabs a wedding theme."

I groaned, laughing softly. "Only if s'mores are the main course."

She smiled against my skin. "Deal."

51. EPILOGUE - PAWS, PLANTS, AND PROMISES

Sinan

One-and-a-half years later

Despite my mom's protests, Kendra and I had pulled off the lowest-key wedding in history. No fuss, no drama. Just us, Ollie, a handful of family, and, of course, the pineapple kebabs—they had definitely made the guest list. The honeymoon? That had been an adventure we'd never forget: an African safari, complete with vaccines, cameras, and close encounters with giraffes and lions.

"Are you sure you don't want to look for a different house?" I asked, joining her in our bedroom and wrapping my arms around her from behind. "Something you can really make your own? Maybe add a drawbridge?"

Kendra leaned back against me, her eyes sparkling. "This is already my home, Sin. Our home. Plus, with that view—and the bonus drone surveillance—I'm set."

I laughed, pressing a kiss to her cheek. "The drone! I wonder where we stashed those 'We see you' signs, just in case it makes a comeback."

She grinned, the honeycomb pattern of her wedding ring catching the sunlight as she moved across the room. The ring was always there, a reminder of the life we were building together—

strong, steady, and a little unconventional, just like us. I watched her with the same awe I'd felt the day she said "yes."

The soft patter of paws echoed up the staircase, and moments later, Ollie, our Cavalier King Charles Spaniel, bounded into the room, his ears flopping with every step.

"Here, Ollie!" I crouched down, ready for him to crash into me.

He didn't disappoint, barreling into me like a bowling ball. His tail wagged like it had a mind of its own before he darted toward Kendra, eager to follow her every move.

"You've always been his favorite," I teased, standing up. "Probably because you picked his name and gave him the civil engineering cred."

Kendra chuckled. "Not just any civil engineer. Oliver Byrne was a trailblazer. Ollie's just following in his footsteps—by digging up the garden."

I shook my head. "Most people go with Max or Buddy. But no, you had to pick a 19th-century engineer."

"Well, I'm not most people," she shot back, moving toward the patio door.

Later, we stood outside, the city of Pittsburgh stretched out beneath us, but I was more focused on the garden we'd been slowly bringing to life. The air smelled like fresh soil, with hints of rosemary and basil—things I couldn't wait to cook with.

"Not bad for amateurs," I said, brushing dirt off my hands. "We might even have to name a garden bed after Ollie—if he leaves any of it standing."

Kendra grinned, tucking a strand of hair behind her ear as she crouched to plant another herb. "We'll see how long that lasts."

Ollie, as if on cue, trotted over and nosed at the freshly turned soil before deciding to 'help' by scattering it everywhere.

"Ollie, no digging!" Kendra laughed, gently redirecting him.

I shook my head, chuckling. "Maybe he's planning a second career in excavation."

"He's stubborn," she said, finally managing to guide him away from the plants. "But I like that about him."

I smiled, watching her work, feeling an immense gratitude for this life we were building. A life that wasn't just about us—it was about something bigger.

"You know," I said, stretching out my arms, "next week, maybe we should bring him along to help with the excavation."

Kendra looked up, her expression warming. "To Guatemala?"

I nodded. "The hospital's nearly finished. They've already started training local nurses, and thanks to your redesign, the rainwater collection system will cut their water dependency in half."

She smirked. "And thanks to you, we finally got the funding for better road access so emergency patients won't have to travel through a minefield of potholes."

"You mean thanks to *us*." I reached over, tucking a stray curl behind her ear. "Kendra, I wouldn't have been able to push for those infrastructure upgrades without you. I might know how to fix brains, but you—you're out there making sure the ground they walk on doesn't collapse beneath them."

She leaned into me, her voice softer. "I always wanted to build something that mattered. I just never thought I'd be doing it with you."

"Well, now you're stuck with me," I teased, brushing a kiss against her temple. "Hope you don't mind."

She smiled. "Not even a little." The doorbell rang then, cutting through the moment.

Kendra glanced at me, frowning. "Were you expecting anyone?"

"Nope," I said, wiping my hands on my jeans. "Maybe Ollie's learned how to schedule treat deliveries. I'll go check."

I opened the door to find Sonya standing there dressed in s lightweight summer dress, holding two white envelopes, her expression caught between nervous and nostalgic.

"Hey," I said, stepping aside. "You look way too nice to be here to help us with landscaping."

Kendra appeared behind me, brushing dirt from her hands. "Essie? Everything okay?"

Sonya gave a tight smile and held out the envelopes. "Yeah. I mean, I think so. Do you remember those letters Mom gave us before she passed?"

Kendra blinked. "The ones she said not to open for five years?"

Sonya nodded. "Today's the day."

A beat of silence stretched between them.

Kendra raised a brow. "This isn't going to be another 'Mom's Top Ten Life Lessons,' is it? Because if mine starts with 'Don't forget to floss,' I'm out."

Sonya laughed softly. "She made me swear I wouldn't peek. I haven't read mine yet. Thought we should open them together."

"Let me wash my hands first," Kendra said, her tone gentler now. "I've been elbow-deep in the basil patch."

When she returned, Sonya was already on the couch, letter in hand but unopened. Kendra sat beside her, their knees brushing, the weight of unspoken memory settling in.

"You sure you're ready?" Kendra asked.

Sonya took a breath, then nodded. "I think so."

She unfolded the letter, smoothing the creases before reading.

"Sonya, you've always been the strong one. You protected Kendra like a second mother, even when you were still figuring out how to protect yourself."

"I know life hasn't always been easy—especially after what happened with Raven and her rabid fans—but you faced every challenge head-on. You've risen above the noise with grace. I believe in the life you're building and the person you've become."

"You've always had a caring heart. I know you'll keep looking out for those you love—especially Kendra. You've built a life on your own terms, and I couldn't be prouder. I know you'll be a wonderful mother someday because of the way you've always taken care of others. I love you more than words can say."

By the time she finished, tears tracked silently down her cheeks. She rested a hand on her baby bump and shook her head.

"I really thought… after everything that happened online, that I embarrassed her. That she was disappointed in me."

Kendra reached out. "Essie, Mom always knew how much you carried—for both of us. She just didn't always know how to say it. But she saw you."

Sonya gave a watery smile. "I didn't expect it to hit this hard."

Kendra handed her a tissue. "We waited five years for this moment. Of course it hits hard."

Then it was Kendra's turn. She opened her letter carefully, the paper worn soft at the folds.

"Kendra, you've always had an adventurous spirit, a determination that couldn't be dimmed. I knew it the moment you climbed the backyard tree trying to touch the sky."

"You were born to explore—to ask questions, to dive into the unknown. Whatever life throws at you, I know you'll rise above it. Trust yourself. You are more capable than you realize."

"I hope you never lose that spark. In moments of doubt, remember this: you are not alone. You carry the love of a sister who believes in you, and the strength of a mother who saw the world in your eyes."

"You have the courage to chase your dreams, the heart to care deeply, and the wisdom to know when to fight for what matters. Keep exploring, my darling girl—there's so much beauty still waiting for you."

Kendra's breath caught, her fingers tightening around the paper.

"She knew exactly who we were," she said, voice thick with emotion. "Even when we didn't."

"She always did," Sonya said softly.

Kendra sniffed. "Also explains why she let me build a zip line between the garage and the dogwood tree without calling the fire department."

Sonya chuckled. "She probably figured you'd either become an astronaut or break your arm trying."

"Well, I became a civil engineer. Same risk of injury. Slightly better insurance."

I stepped forward then, unable to hold back.

"Your mom was right," I said. "You're strong, and you're building a life that matters. Both of you are."

Kendra turned to me, eyes still glassy but smiling now. "She was right about Essie, too. She's always been the steady one."

Sonya reached over and bumped her shoulder. "We've always had each other."

"And we always will."

I cleared my throat. "Still... Ollie's making a pretty strong case for favorite civil engineer."

Kendra laughed, wiping her face. "Has he officially bumped me down the ranks?"

"You're still my favorite human," I said, grinning. "But he's more committed to digging than anyone I've ever met."

Later that evening, Kendra and I sat outside under the stars, wrapped in a blanket by the fire pit. Pittsburgh glittered below us, a perfect mix of steel and softness.

She leaned against me, the curve of her body warm and familiar.

I couldn't help but think of that woman I met in Turks and Caicos—the one who didn't think she belonged. Now she was redesigning water systems, mentoring interns, and fighting off drones like a pro.

"This is just the beginning," she whispered, leaning into me.

And with her by my side, I couldn't wait to see what came next.

THE END

CARAMELIZED BROWN SUGAR CINNAMON GRILLED PINEAPPLE KEBABS

Level: Easy

Prep Time: 10 minutes

Cooking Time: 7-10 minutes

Total Time: About 17-20 minutes

Serves: 4

Ingredients

- 1 ripe pineapple cut into spears (Pineapples do not ripen once picked, so look for fruit that's heavy for its size, fragrant)
- Bamboo skewers
- 1/2 cup Brown Sugar
- 1/2 cup Butter
- 1 teaspoon Cinnamon, plus more to sprinkle onto the pineapple
- 1/2 teaspoon grated nutmeg (optional)

Directions:

1. **Prepare the Pineapple Spears:** Slicing off the pineapple leaves or use your hands to twist them off. With a serrated knife, trim 1/2-inch from both ends of the pineapple to make it flat, then stand the fruit on one end. Slice off the skin, taking care to stay as close to the skin as possible. Remove any "eyes" that remain using a melon baller or a paring knife. Halve the pineapple lengthwise through the core, then halve lengthwise again. Remove and discard the center core. Slice each section into spears.
2. **Skewer:** Slide bamboo skewer through the piece of pineapple. Place the spears in a metal pan that will fit onto your grill.
3. **Sauce:** *Lightly* sprinkle the pineapple slices with cinnamon. Melt the butter. Whisk together the melted butter, brown sugar, cinnamon, and optional nutmeg. Brush over pineapple. Let skewers soak for at least 15 minutes.
4. **Grill:** Grill for about 7-10 minutes on medium heat or until it is starting to turn golden brown. Remove from grill. I prefer to cook them in the pan, but you could grill them directly over the fire as well.
5. **Serve:** Brush the sauce that dripped into the pan back onto the pineapple before serving.

AVOCADO HUMMUS DIP

Level: Easy
    Prep Time: 20 minutes
    Total Time: 20 minutes
    Serves: 1 large bowl of hummus

Ingredients

- 1 15 oz. can chickpeas
- 1-1/2 teaspoons baking soda
- 2 tablespoons tahini
- 3 tablespoons lemon juice
- 2 cloves peeled fresh garlic
- 2-3 ice cubes
- 1 avocado
- 1/4 cup cilantro (can be omitted)
- 3/4 teaspoon salt
- fresh parsley
- paprika
- olive oil

Directions:

1. Prepare the chickpeas. Put the canned chickpeas in a bowl of warm water with 1-1/2 teaspoons of baking soda. Soak for five minutes. Put your peeled garlic in your lemon juice and let it soak as well to remove the sharpness from the garlic.
2. Rub them with your fingers to release the skins, which will easily float to the surface of the water. Skim the skins from the water with a slotted spoon and discard. Rinse. Dry the chickpeas with a paper towel.
3. Place washed, drained and dried canned chickpeas in a food processor.
4. Chop the chickpeas until they become ground and powder-like. You may need to scrape down the food processor a couple times. This will take around 15 seconds.
5. Add the remaining ingredients: tahini, lemon or lime juice, garlic and salt, plus two to three ice cubes to make the hummus extra thick and creamy. Blend for 5 minutes to create an extra smooth consistency. Taste and adjust salt and lemon juice as needed.
6. Add the avocado and cilantro once the hummus is smooth. The more of these that you add, the more vibrant the color will be. You can also add spices here like cumin or peppers like jalapeños.
7. Blend for one minute, until you no longer see chunks of avocado or cilantro.
8. Place on a plate or in serving bowl. Swirl it with the back of a spoon to create wells for the olive oil. Sprinkle with parsley and paprika, and drizzle with olive oil.
9. Serve with pita chips or fresh veggies such as carrots, celery sticks, or bell pepper slices.

GRANDMA BASTIANO'S SAUCE

Level: Easy
Prep Time: 20 minutes
Cooking Time: 35 minutes
Total Time: 55 minutes
Serves: 10

Ingredients

- 2 tablespoons olive oil
- 1 onion, chopped
- 1 whole head garlic, peeled and chopped
- 2-3 cups sliced fresh mushrooms
- ½ cup chopped fresh basil leaves, or to taste
- 1 (28 ounce) can whole peeled tomatoes
- 1 (15 ounce) can tomato sauce
- 1 (6 ounce) can tomato paste
- ¾ cup Merlot wine (about a tomato paste can's worth)
- 2 teaspoons salt
- Continued on next page

- 1 teaspoon ground black pepper
- 2 teaspoons dried oregano
- ¼ cup white sugar

Directions:

1. Heat olive oil in a large saucepan over medium-low heat. Cook the onion and garlic, stirring frequently, until translucent but not browned, 6 to 7 minutes.
2. Add mushrooms and basil. Stir frequently until the basil is wilted and the mushrooms are cooked through and have given up their juices, about 10 minutes.
3. Add the whole peeled tomatoes, turn up the heat to medium high and bring the mixture to a boil. Using your wooden spoon, chop/smash the tomatoes into pieces while stirring frequently.
4. Add tomato sauce, stir, and bring to a simmer. *Turn down the heat to medium-low* and let the sauce continue to simmer, stirring occasionally for about 15 minutes, until slightly thickened and bubbling.
5. Add tomato paste. Fill the empty tomato paste can with Merlot and pour into the sauce. Stir well to combine.
6. Return sauce back to a simmer, add salt, pepper, dried oregano, and sugar. Let the sauce simmer until the seasonings are blended and the sauce is heated through, about 3 more minutes.
7. Serve over your meal of choice (pasta, rice, meatballs, chicken, on a sandwich, etc.).

BIBLIOGRAPHY

Contemporary Romances
By Sheri Tyler
The Way to a Woman's Heart series - the **Coming Home** trilogy
Slow Simmer
Here's the Scoop
From Bitter to Sweet

The Way to a Woman's Heart series - the **Destination Wedding** trilogy
One Cup of Chemistry
Say Cheese
Kebabs and Kisses

Historical romances
By Sheridan Jeane
Gambling On a Scoundrel

Secrets and Seduction series:
* *Lady Cecilia Is Cordially Disinvited for Christmas*
*(only available via Sheridan's VIP club)
It Takes a Spy…
Lady Catherine's Secret
Once Upon a Spy
My Lady, My Spy
Along Came a Spy

Duke By Dawn (Novella, part of the anthology *Dukes All Night Long*)
August 2025

The Rose and the Spy - a Victorian-era Romantic Suspense trilogy
2026
Whispers and Spies
The Spy In Disguise
Protect the Prince

ABOUT THE AUTHOR

I'm Sheri Tyler, and I write the **Way to a Woman's Heart** series of romcoms set in Sewickley, a small town near Pittsburgh. These books all feature my favorite things: food, books, family, and friends.

More about me?
My alter-ego in writing is Sheridan Jeane. I publish my Victorian-era historical romance and romantic suspense novels under that name.
I'm the daughter of an artist/art-therapist/professor mother and an opera-loving/computer engineer/do-it-yourself father. Growing up, I assumed parents routinely converted their garages into well-stocked art studios complete with potter's wheels, kilns, and every color of paint under the sun. Didn't every second-grader learn how to weld or nail shingles on the roof of the 2-car garage their dad built? And what about all those after-opera cast parties? Weren't they run-of-the-mill too?
No?
Go figure!
That probably explains my quirky outlook on life.

Visit me at www.SheridanJeane.com
Or
www.SheriTyler.com